CW01648189

THE EDGE OF MADNESS

By

Tony Birtley

1

It marked the onset of the double whammy. The call to prayer resonated with such intensity and proximity that one could easily be misled into believing they were enclosed within the minaret itself. The duration was so extensive that it resembled more of a cinematic experience titled *Call to Prayer*: The Movie. In an attempt to find respite, he reached over, fumbling for an imaginary off switch. However, the Adhan, the initial Muslim call to prayer each day, relentlessly assaulted the senses even before the break of dawn. There was no escape from it, not even under divine authority. It seemed that not even God could halt its echoing presence.

Then came the second part of the dawn deluge, the even louder attack, the unmistakable sound of The Reveille, or, to civilians, the alarm call. It was a full-blast recording of that time-honoured military way of waking soldiers, readying them for training or killing. Grant gave out a long groan, convinced he was the one being killed. The deafening sound blared from his battery-powered radio alarm clock, a gift from his mother, a smart woman who realised there wasn't always electricity in the developing world. No one living could sleep through The Reveille, no matter how drunk they were.

A two-bladed fan stuttered in a slow turn from the ceiling, and the heat was already building to a steamy temperature. If it were human, it would be classified as disabled.

He fumbled in the dark, stretching his arm towards the source of the incessant alarm, desperately hoping to connect with the snooze button and silence the mind-numbing sound. The pulsating headache, a brutal reminder of last night's indulgence, refused to be subdued so effortlessly.

The sunlight pierced through the shattered shutters, casting an eerie glow upon the dim and dusty room, a scene reminiscent of a futuristic movie's menacing laser beam. Squadrons (not swarms) of mosquitoes darted through the gaping holes in the tattered window netting, on the lookout for an unsuspecting victim to dive-bomb in their quest for a blood-filled breakfast. Resistance, though non-existent, would have been futile. Sprawled across two beds were several weary bodies, accompanied by four aching heads. Grant reluctantly opened one eye, his retina recoiling from the fragmented light resembling an intense interrogation beam. His hand frantically swatted at the dive-bombing mosquitoes, but the nimble insects outmanoeuvred his attempts. These mosquitoes, proficient in evading even the most skilled swipes, proved quicker than a left-handed player at Wimbledon and more cunning than a befuddled correspondent. No mosquitoes faced cancellation that morning. They lived on, ready to suck the life out of another day. In their wake, they left behind collateral damage, self-inflicted injuries, and exposed body parts that resembled the aftermath of a misguided attempt at a dot-to-dot art competition.

Mosquitoes, a call to prayer, reveille, and the lingering remnants of a hangover were less than ideal ways to commence the day, especially in what had earned its reputation as the most perilous city on earth. Grant, however, viewed it differently. This, in the eyes of him and his kind, was the gritty reality of the 'shop floor'. He stirred from his slumber, albeit gradually, preparing for a new shift.

As he struggled to sit upright, a figure next to him stirred, arching her back slightly as she searched for a body to nestle with. The lithe figure belonged to Siobhan, an aid worker hailing from Dublin, a woman both strong and brave. Much like many Irish, she possessed a remarkable sense of humour and a capacity to drink that seemed to defy biology itself. Grant had always found himself drawn to unconventional women who thrived in dangerous places, individuals with a profound sense of humanity and a deep disdain for injustice. In a city where most fled, Siobhan stood among the courageous few who remained in Mogadishu despite the inherent danger, the discomfort, and the relentless daily pileup of misery.

As a journalist, Grant was well-acquainted with misery; it was a daily companion in his profession, part of a relentless voyage through desolation and hopelessness along an endless journey. The Somali capital served as a pit stop on this adventure. His night with Siobhan became a brief respite, a fleeting encounter with normalcy before the impending madness. However, he pondered whether facing uncertain places with a raging headache and dull reflexes might not be the most effective approach.

His feet fumbled for a pair of flip-flops, but all he found were empty bottles of vodka scattered on the floor. Ashtrays overflowed with cigarette stubs and remnants of alternative means of escape. In Mogadishu, the preferred brand for getting high was Lebanese Gold. In Somalia, it was not only inexpensive but also readily accessible.

In the corner of the room, a secondary groan emerged, ascending towards the ceiling. It reverberated throughout the space, bouncing off the walls like a ball careening unpredictably in a pinball machine. It belonged to Mo whose connection to the day started with, "What the fuck, stop that noise." Mohammed Farouk Bin Tahed, often referred to as Mo, hailed from Cairo and identified as a Muslim. However, his devotion to the Adhan, the initial call to prayer at 5 a.m., often put his faith to the test. His friend, Grant, humorously labelled him a 'Muslim schizophrenic'. Mo No. 1 consistently carried a Quran, while Mo No. 2 was known for always having a bottle of vodka on hand. Mo No. 2's unique perspective on his faith was evident in his belief that the Quran did not outright prohibit alcohol but merely included it as an appendix. According to him, as long as he could maintain his functionality, indulging in alcohol was acceptable within the religious guidelines. Despite his unconventional approach, Mo No. 2 was a charismatic and endearing character.

In contrast to the correspondent, the diminutive (not Small) cameraman was mosquito bite-free with smooth, untouched skin, something that always confounded Grant. They had been a team for nearly a year. Grant's previous cameraman, a big Kiwi who told a good story but ran a mile at the sound of a banging door, let alone an exploding shell or incoming bullets, had left him in the lurch. He found the Egyptian sheltering in a large shell hole in the centre of Beirut's Martyr Square. They shared a cigarette amidst the mayhem and an appetite for hair-raising situations. They hit it off immediately. Mo left his job working for a Japanese company, stating that the correspondent was a boring teetotaller, and joined the Brit for what he called a challenge. They also shared a love of vodka and Lebanese Gold, which they found calming ingredients in times of mayhem, they said. Mo was not just a great companion; he was also the best cameraman Grant had ever worked with. Talented, compassionate, and light years away from most in the industry, he felt his pictures and brought out what each situation was really about the suffering. Mo gave respect and empathy to the victims, and no one who saw his pictures could escape that. It made writing to his pictures almost straightforward.

Mo sat up and shifted his short, bony legs to locate his flip-flops. Another muted groan emanated from the same pile of crumpled bedclothes. By his side lay Siobhan's friend Mary, another aid worker and a friend of Siobhan, a courageous woman in her own right. Mary's life initially charted a course towards devotion to God, but the allure of partying and alcohol quickly diverted her from becoming a nun. How did it all veer off course? Grant could only speculate about the events that led her to such a drastic change, culminating in her presence in Mo's bed, a Muslim. Such a scenario would undoubtedly prompt moral discomfort in any respectable bishop. Grant found himself echoing the sentiments of his devoutly Catholic grandfather, 'Oh, mother of Jesus'. The previous night had been a grand celebration, but now dawn has arrived. The moment of truth was upon them.

The Rodeo Drive Guest House was one of the few places still operating in Mogadishu. Its owner, Farouk, was a tall man with heavy bags under his eyes. He had always dreamed of visiting the famous LA Street he'd seen in an old American movie. The guest house itself was rundown and poorly furnished, with paint peeling off the walls and doors that didn't close properly. Located on Medina Street in downtown Mogadishu, it was as close as Farouk would ever come to Rodeo Drive. The building had crumbling walls, dirty, cracked tiles, and faded green paint that resembled a failed pea soup recipe. It had a smell that reminded people of a recycling centre mixed with a burial pit. Despite all this, Farouk always wore a smile, showing his few remaining teeth, and he tried to make the best of a bad situation. "But we are alive," he would respond when anyone would venture to complain about no water in the showers or broken toilets. "Think positive, Habibi," he would say.

Embracing a positive mindset in Mogadishu proved to be a transformative experience, an outlook that eluded many. With a resounding thud, he struck the vividly green-painted door, his voice cutting through the air, "Mr Grant, Mr Grant, the commandos are here. They are ready."

In the global landscape, Somalia, and especially Mogadishu, stood out as one of the most lawless regions. It was marred by civil war, rampant kidnapping, widespread robbery, inter-tribal conflicts, and brutal gang warfare, among numerous other challenges. For the TV team, this volatile environment proved to be fertile ground.

The commandos operated as mercenaries, guns for hire, armed to the teeth with RPGs, heavy machine guns, Kalashnikovs, and machetes, all for a mere 40 bucks a day, along with their rugged four-wheel-drive vehicle. Familiarly dubbed as 'technicals', they brought not just firepower but also a brash demeanour, an aversion to discipline, and a perspective seemingly detached from earthly norms. In their moral code, God dictated everything, except for indulgences like women and drinking, which remained exempt from their moral scrutiny. In the chaos of Mogadishu, it wasn't morals but technicals that proved indispensable. Operating without them was a near impossibility, especially for a white foreigner, who attracted attention that extended beyond just mosquitoes.

Grant opened the door and smiled at Farouk. "Thanks," he said and then he and Mo trudged down the corridor to what passed for the showers ("I could piss more," Mo always complained), and they ran around trying to get wet. After spending ten days in this place, their yearning became singular, a longing that surpassed even the desire for a hearty breakfast: the simple pleasure of a prolonged, invigorating shower.

As they rinsed off the remnants of the night and gradually regained sobriety, the weight of the day's reality began to settle on both men. Their scheduled expedition into the Karaama district had been likened to Armageddon, labelled a suicide mission, and dubbed a journey into the Bermuda Triangle. Local anecdotes hinted at the district as an abyss where nothing returned once it entered.

Despite their familiarity with risks from years of venturing into war zones, each journey didn't get any easier. While there was always an element of excitement and anticipation, the 'what-ifs' loomed in their minds. Though experienced journalists, they never truly believed that anything catastrophic would happen to them, a sentiment shared by those seasoned in such perilous pursuits. Such misfortune was reserved for others, the unlucky ones, not for the dedicated frontliners who considered themselves immune to the whims of fate.

At 6:15 a.m., the atmosphere shifted as Grant Singleton and Mohammed Farouk Bin Tahed turned their attention to the crucial matter of breakfast. With a touch of unconventional flair, Mo poured a double shot of vodka into sleek metal cups. Grant, producing two meticulously rolled Lebanese gold joints, sparked them to life. They lit the joints and deeply inhaled, then they chinked their glasses and downed the vodka in one.

"We who are about to die, salute you," they both said, echoing the Gladiator's ceremonial greeting to the emperor in ancient Rome before combat. To them, it bore a resemblance to actors saying to each other, 'Break a leg' before stepping onto the stage for a performance.

The Egyptian vodka, though not the smoothest, seemed oddly apt for the impending journey. They crafted an ambiance like the Red Indians preparing for battle.

Mo pressed play on his cassette, unleashing the thumping beat of Van Halen's *Runnin' With the Devil* at a deafening volume. The two girls, aid workers caught off guard by the day, shielded their heads with pillows. Swinging between sips of water to clear their minds and vodka to fortify their resolve, they gradually shook off the haze. With clearing heads, their preparations commenced.

Mo opened a sizable backpack, its contents spilling out onto the bed. Systematically, he assessed each item, meticulously repacking with precision. Among the essentials were battlefront dressings, gauze, iodine sachets, morphine phials, a suture kit, hypodermic needles, a splint, clotting agent, stethoscope, diarrhoea pills, malaria tablets, and a peg, accompanied by a significant chunk of Lebanese gold. Mo insisted it was the true cornerstone of any well-prepared first aid kit. His philosophy held that even in faith, preparedness remained paramount; after all, a Muslim, too, understood the value of earthly provisions alongside divine trust.

"No bedpan?" joked Grant, "and why the peg?"

"I saw it used once in Beirut," said Mo. "If an artery gets hit, you can use it to stop the blood flow. It saved this Lebanese forces guy's life. Honest. So don't laugh, it might save you one day."

Grant retrieved two khaki-coloured flak jackets from beneath the bed, remnants from the Vietnam War. He examined them thoughtfully. The team couldn't afford the latest Kevlar-armored body protection; those were reserved for bigger networks with deeper pockets, not freelancers on a tight budget. While the jackets didn't offer extensive protection, they were better than nothing and, more importantly, cost-effective. The front bore the word 'Press' in bold white letters, while 'TV' was emblazoned on the back. Mo often joked that these labels were like targets, a way for fighters to identify who they were shooting at. Although the jackets wouldn't withstand heavy machine gun fire or artillery shrapnel, they provided decent defence against the common AK47 7.62mm rounds from a distance, as long as they weren't armour-piercing.

Next to the jackets lay two ageing metal helmets, more remnants of the Vietnam War, each emblazoned with the word 'Press.' As they donned the vests, securing them with a series of clicks, they exchanged chest bumps accompanied by Neanderthal grunts that would not be out of place in the chimpanzee enclosure at London's Regents Park Zoo.

At that moment, both women sleepily stood up, exchanged warm hugs with the guys, and enthusiastically pledged to host a celebration the following night upon their return. "But only if you are breathing," joked Siobhan in her soft-spoken, sleepy Dublin accent. "I'm not into necrophilia."

Stepping outside, they were met with an assault of intense light and heat, causing them to wince. The jackets they wore amplified their body temperature, inducing profuse sweating, especially for Grant. Mo, however, appeared fresh and unaffected. Waiting for them were five commandos, lingering around a worn-out Toyota Land Cruiser with a fading yellow and rust, two-tone colour scheme. Despite the lead commando, Jingo, insisting it was one of the latest models, Grant was just grateful they hadn't received an earlier version. The commandos wore oversized coats and furry hats, an odd choice given the approaching 30-degree Celsius temperature. Mo would humorously suggest that mushrooms must be growing in their armpits.

Perched on the battered vehicle, adorned with dents and more than one bullet hole, was a .50mm calibre US-made Browning machine gun, looking as if it had seen more tours than Frank Sinatra. Alongside the Kalashnikov, it was the preferred weapon for conflicts in the developing world. Produced post-First World War, it has played a role in almost every major conflict since, including the Korean War, Vietnam, Afghanistan, Lebanon, and the Iran-Iraq War. Its lethal potential could cleave a man in two if wielded properly. However, Somalis were not renowned for their meticulous weapon care; cleaning wasn't in their fighting vocabulary. Jams due to neglect were frequent, and sight alignment left much to be desired.

The Somalis' unconventional firing technique, executed from above their heads rather than from the shoulder, rendered the sights almost useless. Additionally, there was the khat factor. And Grant could discern from the commandos' eyes that they had recently indulged in a substantial khat session.

Khat, a flowering evergreen shrub, contains cathine and cathinone, producing stimulants with varied effects, not all positive. Locals often referred to it as Abyssinian tea or African salad. Its side effects include mood changes, hyperactivity, aggressiveness, anxiety, depression, high blood pressure, manic behaviour, paranoia, and psychosis. The exhaustive list of African Salad's effects could fill several pages of a medical dictionary. Furthermore, it contributes to trouble sleeping, loss of energy, and lack of concentration. When combined with a teenager wielding an attitude and an AK47, it creates a volatile combination, particularly in conflict zones of the developing world where mental instability is prevalent. The team had learned this through experience. However, an even graver issue was mental instability coupled with a weapon; a potentially life-threatening nightmare.

Somalis were known for their boldness, some even called it stupidity. However, they were also characterised by their deep-seated misogyny and machismo. The prevailing understanding was that challenging a Somali meant risking not just their pride but also the potential for long-lasting repercussions. Grant had heard tales of Somalis seeking revenge years after perceived offences. Farouk had explicitly cautioned Mo and Grant about staying on the good side of the commandos, emphasising the importance of avoiding any form of disrespect.

"As-Salamu Alaykum," offered Grant as he exited the guest house. (May peace be upon you). "Wa alaykumu assalam," Jingo replied, reciprocating the traditional Arabic greeting, even though Somali culture itself wasn't inherently connected to Arabic. Despite this, the majority of the population adhered to Islam. Jingo, the head commando, stood as a formidable figure, a big, tough, and solid man belonging to the Habir Gedir tribe, often labelled as the antagonists in the conflict. His reputation was such that making him lose face was considered an unwise and potentially perilous endeavour.

"Want some salad?" asked Jingo, "or some tea?" A booming laugh escaped him, revealing teeth stained with shades of brown and green, and several noticeable gaps. His eyes bulged, leaving Grant to wonder if it was the result of being high as a kite or simply a peculiar facet of his permanent physiology.

"The commandos and I had some for breakfast." Their expressions, accompanied by bloodshot eyes, betrayed a heightened state of excitement. They were fidgety, hyperactive, and engaged in constant, fast, jerking movements, scanning their surroundings with restless energy.

Jingo continued, "The commandos have been talking, and we think you need to pay more money. Salad is getting expensive here, and we take big risks for you, especially today."

"How much?" Grant asked. "Two times would be good," Ahmed said. "How about an extra $20 per day?" offered Grant.

"Two times would be good," Ahmed reiterated it with increased severity. One commando had retreated to the vehicle, positioning himself behind the .50 cal. The rest of the team appeared fidgety.

"Two times would be good," whispered Mo in Grant's ear.

It was settled; two times it was. Smiles spread across the group, and the commandos' nervous twitches gradually subsided in a form of visual decompression.

"Hey, you poosies," rang out a voice. "What ze fook are you wearing that shit for? Are you men or what?"

Pascal Bourdain, a notorious French radio journalist, was widely acknowledged as a thorn in the side of many. He rolled onto the scene with his squad in a rather unconventional choice of transportation, a battered Citroen 2CV. Accompanying him were three youthful Somalis. They seemed no older than 16.

"Don't laugh," he shouted, "I am on a budget." Positioned atop the vehicle was one individual armed with a browning, while another manned the driver's seat. The third person found themselves wedged into the back seat, tightly gripping an AK47. Fitting into these cramped quarters required the skills of a contortionist, and the prospect of extricating oneself seemed an even greater challenge.

He might have been a bit of a nuisance, but there was something oddly likeable about him. On his door, a bold declaration read: 'Don't waste your bullets on me; I am immortal.' His view on death was peculiar; considering it more of an occupational hazard to be embraced and understood, especially if it happened to someone else. Naturally, he never thought it would happen to him. Who does? He'd defiantly 'spit' at death, laughing in its face. Mo affectionately dubbed him 'Spit the Frog.' He operated as a kind of Jihadist journalist, seemingly unfazed by danger, yet undeniably attracted by the allure of money. Financial incentives awaited those who ventured into the perilous territories that sensible people and established journalists tended to avoid.

Grant and Spit shared a realisation: the more perilous the location, the fewer the journalists. Somalia was a prime example, with most reporters having left along with aid workers and the majority of United Nations officials. Sensible individuals departed at the first sign of danger. Only the resilient, the daring, or perhaps the slightly unhinged remained, those with fractured relationships or no personal connections at all. However, despite the shared awareness of danger, the resemblance between Spit and Grant ended there.

Grant's primary focus was on the unfolding narrative. He and Mo had ventured into Somalia without a specific assignment, bearing their own expenses, and lacking any commitment from news outlets to cover their reports. Their motivation stemmed from the dire circumstances of Somalia, a perilous mix of famine and conflict. In the face of this crisis, thousands were succumbing to hunger, while the toll of the three-month-long fighting had already claimed nearly thirty thousand lives, leaving many more wounded and suffering from rampant malnutrition. The situation was declared the world's worst humanitarian disaster. It was a story he felt compelled to cover. Despite the urgency of the situation, the UN, citing security concerns, was hesitating to provide essential aid. The only relief reaching the affected population was through the efforts of the International Red Cross, but this proved grossly inadequate. Journalists are supposed to be objective. When it came to the UN, it was not hard to be subjective. "UN stands for Unworkable," Grant used to say, although he knew without their presence a bad situation would become even worse.

He looked around him, desolation, destruction, hopelessness, death and misery. It's Mad Max meets One Flew Over The Cuckoo's Nest, Grant thought to himself, but where all the inmates are armed with AK47s.

"So," said Spit, "the first one to the centre of Karaama wins the $100, ok? You remember the bet?" He continued, noticing Mo and Grant's blank faces. "Don't tell me you fookers were too fooking drunk, putain. What fooking poosies."

Many people are aware of the cultural preference among Muslims for cats over dogs due to their perception of dogs as unclean. However, for Mo, the abundance of poosies was overwhelming. "$200," he said. "That's the bet; take it or leave it."

The gauntlet was thrown down, adding yet another layer of madness to the daily grind of chaos and turmoil that defined Somalia.

Commandos from both vehicles rose to the challenge and began trading insults, "Waa kuu wasa," (I will fuck you) said to team 1. "Wasse-fuck, hooyadaa wasse," (fuck your mother) responded Team 2. It was like kids on a playground. Totally surreal.

"Wait," shouted Mo. "I forgot something." He raced back to the room; the two aid workers had fallen into a deep sleep. Bending down, he felt under the bed, and there it was. Snatching it up, he hurried back to the car. Carefully, he placed a 12-inch plastic model of Buzz Lightyear, the lovable character from the Toy Story animation, on the car dashboard.

"What about the white flag?" asked the correspondent.

"Ah shit," came the response. Mo hurried back inside the Rodeo Drive residence and swiftly made his way to the bedroom. Inside, he scanned the room, noting that both women remained sound asleep. His gaze settled on an object lying on the floor beneath Mary's bed. "Perfect," he said, grabbed the item and ran back to the car.

"No problem, my man. Everything is under control." "To infinity and beyond," Mo shouted. As he slid a cassette into the player, the rugged strains of

AC/DC erupted, filling the air with 'Highway to Hell.' Mo possessed a knack for selecting music that perfectly matched their destination, and the enigma of the Bermuda Triangle, with all its mysteries, felt akin to hell itself. The relentless energy of AC/DC, a wild Australian rock band, seemed like a fitting soundtrack for the unfathomable depths of the Bermuda Triangle.

They started driving through the dusty, debris-filled streets. People were everywhere, standing in doorways, inside half-destroyed buildings, and huddled under tarps in narrow alleyways. Their faces looked tired, and their bodies were thin. It felt like they were in a scary movie, like 'Day of the Living Dead.' Somalia seemed full of people who were barely alive, as if they were the living dead themselves. Fear filled the air like a poisonous fog, making it seem like a scene from a disturbing novel by Dante.

The two vehicles split up when they reached the Arco di Trionfo Popolare (Arch of the People's Triumph). This arch stands as a reminder of Italy's past colonial rule in this troubled country. Back then, there was some semblance of order amidst the chaos.

"Arrivederci," shouted Spit. "See you on the other side."

Jingo drove his Toyota down Wadada Wabiri Road towards London Road. They passed the tomb of the Unknown Soldier, then the Mogadishu Polytechnic on the left, which was now a camp for displaced people. They went past the famous Bekara market, where you could buy back items stolen from you the day before. Up ahead, they saw the blackened shell of what used to be the Somali parliament building. They were driving fast, almost like in Star Trek when they talk about warp factor four. The air was thick with sand and dust, making it feel like they were driving through a storm. They took a sharp right turn, feeling like they were only using two wheels, and continued towards the sea and the lush, golden Lido beach. They sped along the coast, passing high dunes, and through the mostly destroyed district of Banaadir until the vehicle suddenly stopped in a wide-open area.

In front of Grant stretched a vast wasteland, just a huge dusty space with nothing in it. Far off, he could make out a row of buildings on the horizon. He couldn't help but wonder why so many people had lost their lives because of this empty expanse.

The car came to a stop at a checkpoint right on the edge of the wasteland. A bunch of young men, with khat in their mouths and holding AK47s, all wearing woolly hats, crowded around the car. They wanted to know where we were going. Jingo told them we were heading to the Bermuda Triangle.

"Iyo Waas," (fuck me) said the one with fake aviator sunglasses and a red Manchester United football shirt. He looked like the man in charge.

"You are crazy motherfuckers," he said in a rather high-pitched voice. "You lookin' for death, man? No one goes to Karaama because of those motherfucking killing Abgal monsters who are destroying our country." He was on a verbal run that was leading to profane diarrhoea. It was clear he didn't like the Abgal tribe.

"We are fighting for our lives, defending ourselves and our poor people as best we can…" His speech was interrupted by a huge outgoing explosion from what seemed to Grant, a 155mm artillery gun nestled in between some buildings close by.

Everyone dropped to their knees right away, even Mo and Grant. The only ones who didn't were those who were still feeling the effects of Abyssinian Tea. The Manchester United fan saw the expression on Grant's face. "Defensive shelling," he explained.

"But I haven't heard any incoming shells," responded Grant. "So I'm not sure why the 'defensive' shelling was needed." Navigating a confrontation with an armed person who's both hostile, high and mentally unstable is always dangerous. Grant understood this well. He spoke cautiously, making sure not to say anything that might provoke or upset the person further.

The man paused, his tired eyes quickly scanning the surroundings as if he were trying to find something, like searching for a dark-coloured object in a black bag. It was clear he was rummaging through his thoughts. Then, suddenly, a smile broke across his face, and he began speaking rapidly, like bullets spraying from an AK47 in full-auto mode.

"Ah yes, they use new types of shells, much silent. Just land and go bang. Russians make them." He was thinking deeply, scanning his brain for more defensive bullshit. "They Russians are motherfuckers, give weapons and arms and guns and silent shells to bad people. Yeah. Bad motherfuckers, killing us good people."

"But you have AK47s and RPGs," answered Grant. "They are Russian."

The wearer of the Manchester United shirt hesitated further, plunging back into the depths of his mental black bag. His verbal flow had stalled, akin to bullets jamming in a gun's chamber. He teetered on the brink of running out of defensive BS to volley back. Then, a glimmer in his eye, accompanied by a relieved smile, and the words resumed in rapid-fire succession.

"But these are…" and he emphasised the word 'liberated'. "These are liberated weapons, and they are being used to save," another big smile. He was delighted with the answer he had provided, feeling satisfied that it accurately elucidated the situation. His contentment stemmed from a sense of assurance in the clarity and depth of his explanation.

Mo was scanning through his English/Somali dictionary. "I can't find any word for insanity in the Somali language," he whispered with a strong note of sarcasm. Grant shook his head and reached for his water bottle, only to find no H2O inside. Instead, it contained pure Egyptian vodka. He anticipated that by day's end, the bottle would be empty. It served as their defence and the first-aid kit against the so-called 'defensive' nonsense.

"Karaama," said Jingo, pointing to the distant buildings. "We will wait for you here."

Grant seemed confused, "But I thought you were taking us?"

"Are you crazy motherfucker or what?" he replied. "The mother's vaginas are Abgal clan and they would kill us. No way, Jose. No kill, no spill. No highway, my way. Other ways of making suicide, and God tell us today, is for salad, not for suicide."

It appeared unnecessary to highlight the disparity in their pay. The peculiar blend of Somali logic, fuelled by the presence of khat and the omnipresent threat of AK47s, served as a formidable deterrent.

"No worry, my man," continued Jingo. "We get you first class and a safe ride to Karaama."

To the left stood a Ford Escort bearing the emblem of SOS Kinder Dorf prominently displayed on its door. Adjacent to the vehicle, an elderly man cast a watchful gaze.

"This is an orphanage organisation, and they have a place in Karaama. This man is from the Hawiye tribe, and they are nootral, so everyone likes them, and no one hurts them. So, good solution for you, my friend. Go now in peace and see you later…..hopefully," and Jingo let out another of his huge laughs.

Mo and Grant exchanged a glance fraught with uncertainty. They found themselves at a critical juncture. The fate of Karaama and its unfolding events held paramount importance for the narrative's progression. Reluctantly, they acknowledged they had no alternative but to align with the enigmatic 'nootral' man and trust in the unpredictable turns of fate. The realm of war reporting rarely offered any assurances or guarantees, a reality that deterred many from venturing into its perilous depths.

They got in the car shook hands with Mr Nootral. He introduced himself as Mustapha. "Onward," said Mo as he placed Buzz on the dash. "Ok, this going to be OK?" Mo inquired to Mustapha. "OK," the old man replied quietly with no smile of reassurance. It did little to instil confidence in the TV team.

Grant gazed down the road towards the infamous 'Danger Zone,' contemplating what James Brudenell, the seventh Earl of Cardigan, and his cavalry must have experienced as they confronted Russian artillery during the historic Battle of Balaclava in 1854 which became known as The Charge of the Light Brigade. This ill-fated charge, born from miscommunication, was akin to a suicide mission, resulting in the tragic loss of nearly half the 600-strong cavalry unit. The event became immortalised through the verses penned by Alfred Lord Tennyson, a literary tribute that Grant vividly recalled from his school days. Among the verses etched in his memory, one stood out with particular resonance.

Cannon to right of them,

Cannon to left of them,

Cannon behind them Volley'd and thunder'd;

Storm'd at with shot and shell,

While horse and hero fell,

They had fought so well,

Came thro' the jaws of Death Back from the mouth of Hell,

All that was left of them,

Left of six hundred.

It seemed apt in a macabre sort of way.

The car moved off to the sound of the commandos shouting and laughing, "Safar wanaagsan aabhiis wasse," (bon voyage motherfuckers). And then they went to chew their 'African Salad.' Fifty metres down the road Grant shouted, "Stop. We've forgotten the white flag, Mo. Did you get one?"

"There weren't any," replied Mo sheepishly. "So I had to improvise." He leaned out of the window and attached a piece of white material to the large car antenna. It turned out to be a pair of Mary's white knickers.

"Really?" commented Grant with a look of mock disbelief. Mo sank deeper into his seat, feeling a mix of fear and absurdity. Grant couldn't help but think that this journey bordered on the ridiculous if it wasn't so unnerving.

Mustapha cautiously approached Karaama, as if adhering to a speed limit. Suddenly, a massive explosion reverberated to the left, its origin ambiguous; whether it emerged from the front or the rear was indiscernible. Yet, proximity rendered the source inconsequential. Moments later, bursts of machine gun fire erupted, unmistakably emanating from somewhere behind, followed by what appeared to be 'defensive' shelling. This sequence mirrored a contemporary rendition of the Charge of the Light Brigade.

"Can you go faster, man?" Mo pleaded.

"Better this way," replied Mustapha, "or Abgal think you are going to attack. Slow good. Fast bad."

There was a certain logic to it, albeit a local logic. He was Hawiye, and he maintained a 'nootral' stance, a stance they had no choice but to accept. However, every metre felt like an eternity. As they neared the perimeter of the Karaama district, they observed fighters dispersed amidst the rubble and within partially demolished structures. One fighter kneeled atop a heap of bricks, an RPG resting on his shoulder. Grant and Mo tensed, anticipating an attack, but the projectile was aimed at something, or someone, behind them. Mustapha continued at the same pace, his expression unchanged, indicating that his concern remained steady, unlike that of his anxious passengers.

An RPG was fired from behind in response. Grant counted fifteen more incoming projectiles. The last one struck a building to the left, causing damage evident from the already-smashed facade and the crumbling, blackened brickwork. It seemed this wasn't the first time such an attack had occurred in the area.

As they came into the district, they were directed to park behind a building. Soon, a group of Somalis, all carrying guns, crowded around them. They seemed young, like a bunch of school boys in the playground. They all spoke at the same time, shouting and gesturing. It appeared threatening.

Mustapha calmly explained the reasons for the visit and who his passengers were and what they intended to do. As he spoke, the tension eased, and the group became more friendly. They were then guided to meet the leader, the Somali interim president. He was once a merchant and is now working hard to save his country. It was clear that he faced huge challenges.

As Grant journeyed, he witnessed a massive amount of destruction, surpassing anything he or Mo had encountered before. Almost every building had been struck, with many completely demolished. However, despite the devastation, people continued to inhabit the ruins. Every few minutes, the ominous sound of another explosion echoed, signifying another shell landing and adding to the toll of death and suffering in a place that appeared forsaken by God.

As they moved forward, they spotted a big cart being pulled by two donkeys. When they got nearer, they noticed it was loaded with bodies, men, women, and even children.

"Daily death cart," explained Mustapha in an almost matter-of-fact way in his quiet, monotone voice. Many people in this place appeared unfazed by shocking events. Instead of being shocked, they seemed to get used to it. It was common to see horror, as if it had become normal. Life was valued more because it was uncertain. But for some, death was a relief from their suffering. This attitude was evident everywhere in Karaama, casting a heavy atmosphere over the area.

"Where's the hospital?" asked Grant.

"No hospital here," replied their driver. "Only houses."

As they heard another shell whistle in Grant asked, "Can you take us to one?"

They had figured out from experience that if you heard a shell whistling, you were safe because it meant it would miss you. It was the ones you couldn't hear coming that made them feel constantly scared and apprehensive.

As they drove, a DIY military vehicle roared around the corner, its technical add-ons were evident. Mounted on its rear was an anti-aircraft gun, its menacing presence unmistakable. With precision and a screech of tyres, it executed a swift one hundred and eighty-degree turn, and the gunner unleashed four rapid bursts of fire with big 20mm shells. Grant knew the sheer power of the weapon. Its intended purpose was clear: to bring down aircraft, but in the wrong hands, it was devastating against human targets.

Mustapha made a right turn then speeded up.

"Why so fast?" Grant asked. "Dangerous," replied Mustapha.

Mo couldn't shake the feeling that if no man's land wasn't dangerous but this was, then it must be incredibly risky. Still, despite the fear pulsing through him, he kept the camera rolling, determined to capture every moment through the distorted lens of the windscreen.

The vehicle navigated through what seemed to be an open garage devoid of a rear wall, then proceeded into a courtyard before emerging onto another street, where Mustapha resumed his cautious pace. As they rounded a corner, they encountered a small patch of land enclosed by dilapidated structures ravaged by bombs. Within this space, a congregation of Somalis, comprising mainly men and women, came into view.

"House clinic," said Mustapha, gesturing to a doorway. Both Mo and Grant stepped out of the vehicle, Mo carrying his camera and tripod while Grant held onto the microphone. As they approached the entrance of the building, they encountered two individuals manoeuvring a stretcher. On it was a body concealed beneath a shawl. Mo immediately began filming the scene, capturing the poignant image of the victim's hand hanging lifelessly from beneath the fabric. It was a small hand, unmistakably that of a child, yet another innocent soul claimed by the tragedy.

As the group entered, their ears were assaulted by piercing screams that seemed to hang in the air, assaulting their senses. The room they stepped into appeared to be a makeshift medical area, perhaps someone's former living room, round and devoid of any decoration. Six tables were arranged within, each occupied by a patient receiving attention. The floor was littered with piles of bloodied bandages and rags, bearing witness to the grim intensity of the situation. Blood stains marred every surface, the floor, the walls, and especially the tables themselves. The only relief from the oppressive heat came from a solitary fan mounted on the ceiling, its feeble breeze offering little respite in the sweltering room.

Mo immersed himself in filming the disturbing scenes before him, absorbing the imagery with a detached fascination. Grant stood frozen, gripped by a profound shock. While he had encountered death and injury in the past, this scene felt exceptionally concentrated, all contained within a single moment. His attention shifted towards the source of the anguished cries. On the table lay a man, his mouth clenched around a piece of wood, restrained by two individuals. A tall figure in a white coat wielded a saw, methodically severing the man's leg as if engaged in a mundane DIY project. Mo approached closer, focusing his gaze more intently on the patient's face than the grisly amputation. Such imagery might find acceptance on TV in the developing world, where there is a higher tolerance for scenes of pain, suffering, and gore. However, based on his experience, Grant knew that such graphic depictions would be censored on Western TV networks, where the portrayal of war is often sanitised to shield viewers from its true horrors, preserving their appetite for an undisturbed evening meal.'

The man, who appeared to be a doctor, didn't seem bothered by the camera crew filming him. People were coming and going; a few men were chatting, and some were laughing at a joke we couldn't hear. The scene was chaotic, but in Somalia, it was sadly common.

"No anaesthetic," he explained while still sawing. He had done this before. He appeared calm and untroubled by the situation.

Grant positioned a microphone nearby as he finished sawing, capturing the haunting echo of metal meeting bone. An assistant swiftly tended to the stump of the severed leg, using stained rags as fresh bandages had been exhausted long before. The amputated limb found its resting place in a sizable yellow plastic barrel, its sides streaked with trails of blood. Grant couldn't help but notice it already harboured two other lower limbs and an arm.

"How difficult is it coping with this number of casualties?" asked Grant.

"We do what we can with what we can," he replied. "But we don't have much. We are almost surrounded, there are hundreds of casualties every day, and we don't have enough medical supplies. The aid agencies do what they can, but the danger makes things difficult. Most of the casualties are civilians. Today, I have carried out four amputations without anaesthetic. I hope we get some in within the next few days. I am not sure how much longer we can last."

Grant noticed an elderly man in the corner of the room. The man had a bandage wrapped around his arm, and he wore an eye patch. It was clear that he had been injured by shrapnel.

"Excuse me," he said. "Are you from Britain?" Grant nodded.

"I remember when the British were here," he said. Grant was impressed with his English. "My father worked for the civil service. I went to the English school. A very good school. Such good teaching. They were the good days," he sighed, "I fear we are forgotten now."

It was largely true. Somalia remained conspicuously absent from the UK's agenda, as it was for any government. To be forgotten, one must first be remembered. Yet, Somalia lingered in oblivion; there were no recollections to forget. To the average Westerner, Somalia was a distant land inhabited by individuals with darker complexions, seemingly disconnected from their daily lives. Grant's objective, through these reports, was to thrust Somalia into the spotlight for EVERYONE. However, he was cognizant that, despite the heart-wrenching narratives, Somalia's plight held no sway over the price of bread or a pint of beer in Britain.

Amidst the mounting casualties being ushered into the villa, they reluctantly departed. Mo, the steadfast, dedicated cameraman, persisted in capturing just one more image, succumbing to the ceaseless plea echoing among TV crews. Eventually, Grant intervened, forcefully pulling him away from the scene. From there they continued for the obligatory meeting with the interim president, an act of diplomacy more than anything else. These encounters typically yielded fleeting albeit necessary soundbites, seldom exceeding twenty seconds, before they could resume their mission: capturing images that resonated with raw reality, untainted by the rhetoric of political figures.

The interview was brief and direct. Time passed swiftly, like a runner in the Olympics. The team needed to finish the shoot and return before it got dark. Time was valuable. Grant realised that life in Karaama wasn't.

They cruised through the district, stopping often to gather more haunting images that revealed the full extent of what was happening. Some were too painful to watch.

They went to a feeding station and witnessed the little amount of food being given to people who were hungry and malnourished. A sense of fear spread as displaced individuals, desperate and weak from hunger, were pushed and jostled as soon as food was available. They wanted anything, flour, oil, and sugar just to survive. Desperation was everywhere.

The hot sun beat down relentlessly, causing Grant to sweat heavily. In contrast, Mo, with his Egyptian background, appeared unfazed by the heat. Despite feeling hungry and thirsty, he had already given away all his food. He understood that his actions wouldn't significantly change the situation or help those in need, but he struggled to eat or drink in front of desperate beings.

A doctor from Médecins Sans Frontières (Doctors without Borders) greeted them. He stood out as one of the few Western aid workers still stationed here, while the rest had been evacuated. Gino, an Italian with unwavering dedication, appeared thin, almost gaunt, with prominent bags under his eyes, hinting at potential exhaustion and stress. Grant couldn't help but wonder when Gino had last eaten a proper meal. With empathy and urgency, Gino guided the journalist through the scenes of suffering, where a multitude of women and children huddled, their faces etched with emptiness, their stomachs hollow with hunger.

"Nearly 70 per cent of children here are malnourished," he explained. "We are giving the children something called Unimix, but we only have enough for ten days, and they are getting less than half of what they need. Thousands are dying. These people stay here because they have a chance of getting food, but the danger from the fighting is greater. It is safer to be outside the city, but the chances of getting food are almost non-existent. It's a lose-lose situation."

Gino showed them Shukri, a three-year-old girl whose right foot had been amputated following an injury from shrapnel caused by a mortar round. Despite her young age, Shukri remained silent, her eyes reflecting a haunting depth. She appeared frail, weighing merely eight kilogrammes, far below the healthy weight of fifteen kilogrammes expected for a child her age. Her stomach protruded, indicating potential malnutrition.

"Kwashiorkor," explained Gino. "It's a severe form of malnutrition caused by a lack of protein and essential nutrients in their diet. Body fluid builds up and causes swelling. It's a big step towards starvation, and then it's followed by Marasmus when they get weak, breathing becomes shallow, eyes become sunken, and muscles shrink before starting to waste away. It's heartbreaking to see."

A tiny child was gently put on a hanging cloth scale for weighing. Grant couldn't tell if it was a boy or a girl. The child looked extremely thin, almost like a skeleton. Gino explained that both parents had passed away. He mentioned that if the child became healthier, they might transfer them to the orphanage, but only if there was space available. This made Grant decide to visit the orphanage later on.

Outside, technicals were driving around in their Mad Max-style vehicles. The team was attracted to a street corner where there was heavy firing. Grant noticed that on the back of a Toyota Land Cruiser, there was an air-to-air missile system, similar to what he had seen on Russian MIG fighter planes. The driver accelerated and turned sharply around the corner, while the gunner launched a missile in the direction the team had travelled from earlier that morning.

There was no possibility for careful aiming. This was completely indiscriminate firing which epitomised the chaos of this civil war, where gunfire, originating from both factions, was killing the innocent more than the guilty. In any conflict, fewer combatants made the casualty lists. The brunt of the dead and wounded always fell on innocent civilians.

Grant found himself increasingly overwhelmed by the stark and grim surroundings. The pervasive presence of death, injury, and suffering, coupled with the relentless destruction, weighed heavily on him. Amidst this bleakness, there seemed to be an unsettling abundance of human folly and a glaring lack of regard for life. However, amidst the despair, some possessed a glimmer of understanding and empathy, extending their assistance to those in need.

At the SOS Kinder Dorf Orphanage, staff endeavoured to offer solace to children bereft of family, yet the environment was stark and devoid of safety measures. This reality wasn't unique to Karaama; safety was a concern throughout the region.

As Mo and Grant stepped out of the car, the explosion struck without warning. There were no whistling sounds, no signals of any kind, just the sudden, deafening blast. It hit them like a physical force, leaving their ears ringing with a high-pitched sound that was disorienting, like an extreme form of tinnitus amplified by the sheer pressure of the explosion. It must have been a substantial shell to cause such devastation. Both men staggered, struggling to maintain their balance as the ringing in their ears intensified. Along with the acrid smell of the explosion, the air was filled with the chilling screams of children and the cries of women, their voices piercing through the chaos.

They rallied their senses, seized their equipment, and dashed towards the billowing smoke and swirling dust at the corner. What lay before them was a scene of unspeakable horror, the aftermath of human tragedy. Fragments of children and women were strewn across the ground and splattered against the walls. Among the debris lay six lifeless women and eight motionless children, their fates sealed, likely claimed by the initial impact. The air reverberated with the agonised cries of several children, their bodies pierced with shrapnel, their faces contorted with fear. Nearby, two males lay prone, their groans echoing in the chaos. Grant's gaze fell upon what appeared to be remnants of brains smeared on a nearby door, and the spilled intestines of a woman, her life extinguished, stretched across the path, compelling him to tread carefully. He met the vacant stare of her lifeless eyes, a silent witness to the brutality of the scene. Overwhelmed, he pressed against the wall, overcome with nausea. Amidst the chaos, a child wailed, his t-shirt stained with blood. Grant, uncertain of what to do, lifted the child into his arms, only for a woman to rush forward and take him away, disappearing into the building.

Mo was relentless behind the camera, capturing a continuous stream of cries, despair, and disfigurement. The scenes depicted the stark reality of what unfolds when communication falters and machismo prevails.

Grant gazed at the gaping hole at the heart of the courtyard, a stark testament to the violence that had unfolded. His understanding of warfare provided him with grim clarity: the crater before him bore the signature of a devastating blow, likely inflicted by a formidable 155mm artillery gun. While to the Habir Gedir tribe, this might have been perceived as defensive shelling, for Grant, it represented something far more chilling: a brutal act of murder, devoid of any semblance of justification or excuse.

In the chaos, Grant and Mo kept working. They were experts at what they did. Their task was clear: show people what was going on. They understood the importance of making others see, understand, and feel the situation in some way. These images would accomplish that, at least for some viewers. Others might remain unaware or unconcerned about the struggles of people in distant, unfamiliar places. They could easily ignore the scenes and continue focusing on their everyday lives.

Mo worked hard to gather every image, even those that wouldn't be shown to the public. These images would become part of Somalia's visual history of death and war, ensuring that no one could deny what happened. Feelings had to be set aside for this task.

Finally, after what felt like forever, Mo released his finger from the record button and looked away from the black-and-white viewfinder. Exhausted, he sank down against the wall. As he glanced around, he witnessed the aftermath of the chaos in vivid detail for the first time in nearly an hour. Until then, the monochrome perspective of the camera had provided some distance from reality. But now he confronted the scene in all its vivid, horrifying colours, and the brutality of the situation struck him with full force. Tears welled up in his eyes as he felt a wave of nausea wash over him.

Medical responders had arrived, tirelessly working to save lives amidst the chaos. Grant and Mo completed their tasks, feeling the urgency as dusk approached. Gathering their equipment, they located Mustapha and knew it was time to depart. The Ford's trunk was swiftly filled, marking their solemn departure from Karaama. The weight of their experiences rendered them speechless as they crossed no man's land, devoid of fear or hesitation. Their departure was accompanied by silence, yet the echoes of the horrors witnessed lingered, likely forever imprinted in their minds. With Mary's white knickers fluttering from the antenna, they traversed without incident, amidst a tense calmness that signalled a temporary ceasefire. Perhaps both sides recognised the futility of further bloodshed, contemplating a moment of respite with the prospect of African Salad.

The SOS car got to the meeting spot, but there were no technicals there to meet them. Since it was risky to hang around, Mustapha suggested giving them a ride back to the Rodeo Drive Guest House.

"But…" began Grant. "Isn't it risky without protection?"

"Don't worry, we are Hawiye, and we are neutral. Everybody respects us, and no one will kill us. Trust me." Reassured, the two agreed.

As they pondered their day's activities, a troubling thought gripped their minds: Where was Spit the Frog? Despite their thorough search, there was no trace of him throughout the entire day.

"He probably bottled out," concluded Mo. "He's hiding low because he doesn't want to pay out the two hundred bucks. Fucking French. Can't trust them."

As they drove off, a kilometre down the road, the Ford turned a bend and encountered four armed Somalis, three with Kalashnikovs and one with an American M16. One Somali wore a furry hat, while the others had their faces obscured by kaffiyehs in a bandit-like fashion. Nervous and jittery, the Somalis gestured for the trio to exit the car. Without hesitation, the men obeyed, stepping out slowly with their hands raised, Mustapha included. They were promptly ordered to kneel. In that tense moment, Grant feared the worst, that they were about to be executed. He closed his eyes, bracing for the inevitable. However, the sound of slamming doors and a roaring engine shattered the silence as the Ford sped away down the road. It became clear: they were after the car, not their lives.

Perhaps it's true that nobody would harm members of the Hawiye clan, but nobody talked about theft. After violence, stealing was common among Somalis. Everyone in Somalia had strong feelings about this.

Mo laughed out loud and was beaming, "Hey man, I got it all. I filmed it all, them pointing guns, you with your hands up, car driving away. Great footage." His excitement was contagious…normally. Not this time. "I just kept rolling."

Grant had a look of pure disgust on his face. "You fucking twat," he exploded. "All the tapes, all the material we shot today and the last 11 days were in the back of that car that you filmed with four carjackers heading off into the fucking sunset. All the risks we took today were for absolutely fucking nothing. It was all a waste of time and effort. What the fuck."

He kicked a box lying by the side of the road.

"Shit," responded Mo. "Big mother fucking ass kicking shit." He sat down on a nearby wooden box, took out a half bottle of Egyptian vodka from his bum bag and offered Grant a swig.

"You know what, man?" he said. "We need another fucking war."

The Hawiye man of peace flagged down a passing vehicle, eager to return swiftly to Rodeo Drive. As they approached their destination, a scene of commotion unfolded around the entrance. A Toyota pickup truck adorned with a haphazardly painted red cross caught their attention; it was a Somali ambulance. Stepping out of the vehicle, they witnessed two stretchers being carefully manoeuvred out, escorted by the visibly distressed guest house owner, Farouk, his head swathed in bandages, his expression fraught with agitation.

"There was nothing we could do," he cried. "It was a direct hit. They are now with Allah, my friend. They are now at peace."

Grant halted the stretcher-bearers in their tracks, his hand signalling them to pause. With a firm grip, he peeled back the vibrant, multi-coloured shawl covering Siobhan's face. On the adjacent stretcher lay Mary's lifeless body. It was evident to Grant that they had been caught in the crossfire, likely a consequence of the defensive shelling originating from their own ranks. A surge of anger pulsed through him at the realisation. As he gazed upon Siobhan's pale features, a profound sense of loss washed over Grant. In the span of just ten days, he had grown closer to her than anyone else. The irony of those who sought to aid others falling victim themselves weighed heavily on his conscience. In that moment, he felt adrift, his strength sapped, and his will to persevere waning like the dying embers of a once blazing fire.

"You know what?" he said, turning to Mo, "I'm not sure I can handle another fucking war."

2

The old man stared down at the book, obediently following the barrage of shouted commands without protest. He could feel the thick tension of hatred in the air, and as he looked up, he saw it reflected in the faces around him. The commands and insults merged into a cacophony of verbal abuse, the words themselves becoming indistinct amidst the onslaught. Though he couldn't decipher the exact phrases, their venomous tone was unmistakable: hatred.

The line moved slowly, revealing the backs of heads and weary bodies. It was a sombre and ominous place. Despite the anxious silence, there was an odd sense of tranquillity in the night air. The book illuminated his surroundings, offering him clarity and a glimpse of youthful vitality. Her voice, tender and inviting, resonated through its pages, beckoning him with a smile. Through the book, he saw her image, and with her, he saw beyond the chaos and fear, into a world of beauty and serenity. He breathed in the atmosphere, felt the presence of birds, and heard their melodious songs, reminiscing on a lifetime of peace and joy. It was as if his youth had returned, accompanied by a gentle spring breeze that caressed his face, carrying with it the fragrance of the fields. He pondered whether he had ever truly noticed these simple pleasures before, whether he had ever paused to appreciate the goodness of life.

Before him, a man started to weep softly. He reached out, tenderly touching his shoulder, offering solace in this bleak moment, reassuring him that he was not alone. Indeed, he wasn't. She accompanied him every step of the way.

They were ushered along by the angry men. He looked down at his book and began to pray.

'In the Name of God, the Infinitely Good, the All-Merciful.
Praise be to God, the Lord of the worlds.
The Infinitely Good, the All-Merciful.
Master of the Day of Judgment.
Thee we worship, and in Thee we seek help.
Guide us upon the straight path.
The path of those on whom Thy grace is,
not those on whom Thine anger is,
nor those who are astray.'

Then they got into the truck.

3

Farley Hudson found himself captivated by the tapestry adorning the wall of the oak-panelled room. He stood in the reception area of the Presidential Palace in Belgrade, his gaze fixed on a depiction of intense animosity. In the scene, a towering figure brandished a massive sword, poised to strike down his foe. The American diplomat couldn't help but feel a shiver run down his spine, as if the bearded warrior in the tapestry were moments away from severing Hudson's head from his shoulders.

The painting depicted a man with a turban and dark skin, seemingly moments away from a deadly strike to his neck. In this frozen moment, the dark-skinned figure, whom Farley Hudson assumed to be an Ottoman Turk, still had his head intact. However, it was evident to the American that many of his comrades had not been as lucky. The artist had captured the gruesome scene in vivid detail, showing several Turkish heads scattered on the ground amidst the chaos of battle, with blood spurting from decapitated bodies and fragments of spinal cords hanging grotesquely, resembling scenes from a butcher's shop.

Hudson pondered that this must have been the fourteenth-century version of a shocking video, reflecting on the disturbing nature of the Serbian depiction. While he had encountered graphic tapestries and paintings depicting scenes from the Napoleonic Wars, this Serbian portrayal surpassed them in brutality. Below the tapestry, an inscription in Cyrillic script caught Hudson's eye. Frustratingly, he couldn't decipher Cyrillic, nor could he read or speak Serbo-Croatian.

Farley Hudson didn't secure the position of US ambassador to Yugoslavia due to his proficiency in languages, expertise in Balkan history, or exceptional diplomatic finesse. Instead, it was his wealth that paved his way. His affluent American lineage, which prioritised pedigree over merit, ensured his appointment. Farley wasn't self-made wealthy; rather, his father, Jerimiah Archibald Hudson III, had amassed considerable wealth, much of which was channelled into supporting the election campaign of his Republican associate and newly elected president, Cole Mitchell. As a result, Farley found himself rewarded with a prestigious diplomatic role as payback for his father's financial support.

Hudson felt no embarrassment about how he secured the job; in fact, he was proud. In American society, he belonged to the upper class, the moneyed elite. While the British had their snobbish accents, prestigious school backgrounds, and grand estates, in America, wealth was the defining factor. His father possessed billions, making him exceedingly affluent. This wealth conferred on him both pedigree and influence. Despite its unassuming appearance, the greenback held unparalleled power and prestige as the world's most coveted currency.

Without his father's influence, Hudson would have merely been a mediocre businessman, clumsily following in the old man's path. This truth was evident to his father, the US administration, and President Mitchell.

Hudson harboured rather ambitious aspirations for the London ambassadorial position. The allure of extravagant banquets, steeped in British pomp and circumstance, the prospect of meeting Her Majesty the Queen, and indulging in fine dining experiences, truly captivated him. Paris, as the second choice, offered similar attractions, albeit without the possibility of meeting the Queen, naturally. Thus, being assigned to Belgrade proved somewhat underwhelming, to put it mildly. Initially unfamiliar with its location, Hudson resorted to consulting a map, which led him to delve into the intricacies of the Balkans region. This journey of discovery extended to learning about the cataclysmic events of the First World War, including the infamous assassination of Archduke Ferdinand, followed by a condensed history lesson encompassing the successive reigns of the Ottoman Turks, the Austro-Hungarians, the German occupations, sympathisers of the Nazi regime, and culminating in the era of Communism.

For an individual whose historical knowledge was limited to statistics from the Dodgers and the NASDAQ, the US stock market, grappling with this extensive past proved to be quite a challenge.

After a three-month crash course in Balkan history in Washington, Hudson managed to fill some gaps in his knowledge and gained a bit of ammunition. Now, when he discussed regional matters, he wouldn't completely miss the mark. However, most of what he absorbed seemed to go in one ear and out the other. Still, Hudson viewed this experience as a potential stepping stone towards the diplomatic elite, envisioning positions in London or Paris.

One of the most surprising revelations for this inexperienced diplomat was the fact that Yugoslavia was home to several million Muslims.

"What the fuck!" he said when he learned that stunning fact. "Fundamentalists in Europe. How the hell did they get there?" His Washington mentors were astounded by his apparent lack of intelligence and the extent of his ignorance. Once again, within the US diplomatic selection process, the perennial question persisted: 'Why him?'

Despite his limitations in cerebral capacity, Farley Hudson possessed a keen awareness of certain aspects of Islamic Fundamentalism. His memory vividly retained significant events, such as the heinous act committed by Arab terrorists who brutally murdered eleven Israeli athletes during the 1972 Munich Olympic Games. He also recalled the devastating attack in Beirut in 1983, where 241 predominantly US Marines lost their lives due to a Muslim suicide bomber. Additionally, he remained abreast of more recent occurrences, including the assault on the Israeli embassy in Argentina, resulting in the tragic loss of 29 lives and over 200 injuries.

Farley was well-versed in his views on Fundamentalist Muslims and the perceived threat they posed to civilization. He didn't mince words or use diplomatic language to describe them; to him, they were simply 'fanatical motherfuckers' who deserved their fate. He believed that any Muslim who attended a mosque was at risk of radicalization and, thus, a potential danger. These beliefs were deeply ingrained, stemming from his upbringing in the Bible Belt of the US's deep South, where his father had instilled in him the notion that Islam was not a religion of peace but rather spread through force. In his convictions, Farley conveniently overlooked the history of Christianity, including the Crusades and the atrocities committed in the name of the Christian God.

Farley was incensed by the presence of Muslims in the US. He couldn't fathom how they had the audacity to reside in what he deemed God's country, obtain US passports, and seemingly disrespect the national flag. He questioned what the nation had come to, permitting them to participate in 'our' democracy. In his view, Arab countries lacked true democracy, with the belief that democracy originated in America and was being disseminated globally.

Coming from a background rooted in the cultural landscape of Louisiana, Farley's upbringing lacked exposure to concepts of tolerance and understanding. He harboured strong disdain for the idea of black individuals embracing Islam, fearing what he perceived as a potential path towards fanaticism and ultimately, civil unrest. Raised in a family where grievances about the Civil War were commonplace, he absorbed narratives of racial tension and division. His grandfather's lamentations about the role of black individuals in the conflict further solidified his views. Now, Farley found himself increasingly troubled by signs he interpreted as indicators of societal shifts that unsettled him.

While Hudson might not have been pleased with his assignment to Belgrade, the Serbs were quite satisfied with the selection of the US diplomat. Made-to-measure, they would remark approvingly.

He remained completely absorbed in the vast tapestry, his mind preoccupied with the looming threat of Islamic fundamentalism, oblivious to the sound of the door creaking open and the approaching footsteps behind him.

"I see you are taken with this amazing work of art," said a voice. As Hudson turned, he found himself face-to-face with President Ratimir Simovic, a commanding and imposing presence. Instantly, Hudson felt a sense of intimidation wash over him. This encounter brought to mind an observation he had made upon his arrival in Belgrade two months prior: the remarkable stature of Serbian men and women. Towering figures, reminiscent of basketball players, seemed to be the norm. Hudson couldn't help but wonder about their diets, speculating humorously that they must include something with horns. Standing at 5'7", the diplomat often found himself feeling physically overshadowed. In the world of diplomacy, as in matters of military strength, size can indeed carry weight.

"This was the battle of Kosovo on June 15th 1387. Outnumbered Serbs fought against the more powerful Ottoman Turks. Some say that it was our finest hour."

"But didn't you get your asses kicked?" responded Hudson. "And your leader killed?"

Simovic's right temple bore a prominent, thick blue vein that pulsed visibly as he braced himself to respond to the question. Farley couldn't help but notice it, contemplating the possibility of it rupturing under the strain of anger.

"Sort of," responded Simovic. "Prince Lazaar was captured and beheaded. His head was put on a stake. But he never wavered nor showed the Turks weakness. It may have been a defeat, but it was crowned with glory. It was the day we told the Turks, finally, that we would no longer endure oppression and brutality. We celebrate this date every year because it shows that no matter what we endure, Serbs will never lie down and capitulate. We will always resist injustice. With the Turks, we resisted for five hundred years."

Farley found it peculiar that anyone would celebrate a defeat with such fervour. Would the losing team in the Super Bowl throw a celebration party? Absolutely not. When the US faced defeat in Vietnam, the entire country mourned for decades. There was nothing to cheer about when you came in second, Farley concluded. Nonetheless, he nodded in agreement with Simovic. He had to be cautious not to provoke that bulging vein to burst, he thought.

"Well, it's a pity you didn't kick Islam's ass once and for all, Mr President," the diplomat said. "If you had, then we probably wouldn't have the goddam problems with the A-rabs that we have today."

Simovic harboured little respect for Hudson, and his sentiments extended to the United States despite having studied there. He perceived the country as a formidable force driven primarily by financial power, akin to a behemoth bully. In Simovic's view, American culture revolved predominantly around the Greenback, lacking the depth and nuance found in historical European class systems. While the British and French possessed notions of class, they lacked the financial prowess attributed to the Americans. Simovic contrasted this with the rich historical consciousness ingrained in Serbian culture, highlighting a fundamental difference in perspectives.

"It's interesting that you say that, Mr Hudson," said Simovic. "There are those that say, not just in this part of the world, that the Islamic ass, as you call it, will need to be kicked and kicked hard in the not-too-distant future. These fanatics are rising everywhere, and of course, Europe has always been a long sought-after prize. In many places, many Arab countries, fanatical groups and movements are declaring a virtual war on the West and our ways." He stressed OUR. "As you know, we Serbs are especially concerned about the rise of fundamentalism in Bosnia. We don't sleep easy in our beds any longer."

"There is talk of an Islamic state here in the heart of Europe, about covering our women, about Sharia law. The concerns among ordinary Serbs are growing, and we are genuinely worried about the future."

His speech was flawless, delivered effortlessly, with every word carefully chosen and emphasised, akin to a skilled actor on stage. However, it was evident that he was speaking to a receptive audience. Hudson had long been aligned with the anti-Islamic Fundamentalist stance, fully committed to its ideology.

While Simovic advocated for restraint and conciliation when addressing Hudson, his rhetoric for the domestic audience took on a decidedly more gung-ho and nationalistic tone.

"I have to inform you that Washington is a little concerned about your recent speeches where you seem to be rallying your people to fight for your nation in preparation for war. The Europeans are concerned, too."

"We will only defend ourselves," was Simovic's angry riposte. "It's easy for Washington to say this and that. They are not living with a threat at their borders. Mexico and Canada are not preparing to take away your way of life. But Serbs face real threats."

He lowered his voice and adopted the air of a concerned and pragmatic politician. "No one wants war, far from it. We are Yugoslavs, and we want Yugoslavia to stay together, united and at peace in the way that our great leader, Tito, created. That's what we Serbs want. But we are not sure about all the rest."

A knock at the door interrupted their conversation. A waitress entered, balancing a tray with a bottle and two glasses. She exuded an air of elegance, her tall figure accentuated by a short black skirt. Hudson couldn't help but admire her long, slender legs. However, his fascination was abruptly disrupted when he noticed what the waitress was carrying. He recoiled momentarily, realising what was about to be served. It was Rakia, a potent drink often likened to alcohol, but Hudson deemed it more akin to gut-wrenching rocket fuel. Among Serbs, it was consumed liberally, used for various occasions ranging from celebrations to mourning, and even as a remedy for ailments or simply for intoxication.

The waitress placed the tray on the table and departed.

"Could I ask you what the policy of the United States is to the question of Yugoslavia?" asked Simovic. It was a question he found himself asking repeatedly, the same one he had posed when the US Secretary of State visited a month earlier.

Farley gave the same answer, "The US still believes that Yugoslavia should remain as Yugoslavia and any break up would lead to instability."

Simovic smiled inwardly. The response indicated a lack of unity between the Americans and the Europeans. There were no threats or warnings directed at the Serbs, no conditions, or uncertainties. Nothing at all. It was precisely what Simovic wanted and anticipated hearing.

He poured two glasses of rakia and handed one to Hudson. He mentally prepared himself for what was to come.

"Givili," (cheers) said Simovic. "Here's to a peaceful future," and he smiled.

4

Yousef Mesic was a devout man, committed to peace. His town, Donji Zelenik, epitomised tranquility, but it hadn't always been so. Throughout history, it had been engulfed in violence spanning centuries. From conflicts involving the Venetians, Ottoman Turks, Chetnik Serbs, Ustasha Croats, Partisans, Nazis, and Italians, to even the likes of Ghengis Khan, the Greeks, Romans, and countless other empires, each had left their mark on this land. Everyone had contributed to the bloodshed that plagued Eastern Bosnia.

But when Josip Broz came with the Partisans and defeated the Germans in the Second World War, driving out the evil, everything changed. He metaphorically built bridges between the Catholic, Orthodox, and Islamic communities. He accomplished this through iron-fisted communist rule, where fear and the future were intertwined. However, his vision of the future meant no more wars, no more bloodshed.

Yousef was a loyal supporter of Tito's regime. He believed that the means employed justified the end result: peace and stability. Publicly, nobody dared to resurrect long-standing hatreds and animosities. Young people grew up without concern for each other's faiths; to Yousef and millions of others, they were all Yugoslavs. While acknowledging Tito's dictatorial rule, Yousef viewed him as a benevolent dictator, the only leader capable of bringing genuine peace to their troubled land. Tito, in Yousef's eyes, had effectively relegated the past to where it belonged: in history. Whenever defending dictatorship, Yousef would jest that it was preferable to have one fool in power than a multitude of them. "Just look at what's happening in places like Italy," he would quip.

Yousef's closest friend was an Orthodox Serb. He enjoyed fly-fishing with a Catholic Croat, shared rakia with people of Roma descent, and played tavla (backgammon) with a Sephardic Jew. It was a testament to religious cosmopolitanism and integration at their finest.

His eldest son, Hassan, was in a relationship with a Serbian girlfriend. Selma, his daughter, was dating a Croat, while her twin brother, Mehmet, embraced modern thinking and leaned towards atheism.

After 33 years of Tito's rule, any conflicts, if they ever existed, were settled through dialogue, not violence. While there were individuals with nationalist aspirations and an inability to move on from the past, hoping for a different future, surely, Yousef had concluded to himself that no one would be foolish enough to disrupt the peace. Would they?

However, that belief began to be challenged at the start of 1991, when Yousef first began to realise that his convictions leaned more towards hope than realism. With the passing of Tito, people became emboldened to speak out, and the future that many discussed seemed intertwined with a past that Yousef believed had been buried by Tito.

Unease permeated Donji Zelenik, even with his friend Milan, the Serb, who grew more distant and less available for their usual afternoon fishing trips. Old arguments resurfaced, becoming more prevalent. Who did what, and for what reason? Who claimed ownership of what? Which regions belonged to whom, and who committed what atrocities? These debates gained momentum, yet Farley refused to fully accept them. Then, everything shifted. Yousef's life, and the lives of millions of others, were forever altered on the day when dialogue and negotiation ceased to exist.

The Drina River served as a natural boundary between Serbia and Bosnia. In Ivo Andric's novel, 'The Bridge Over the Drina,' the Bosnian author delves into the enduring hardships faced by the people of Bosnia from the late 16th century to the onset of World War I. Andric employs the bridge as a powerful metaphor for unity among people and signifies leaving the past behind. This theme resonated well with Tito's Yugoslavia.

Yousef often went fly fishing by another bridge that separated Bosnia from Serbia. For him, fishing was the perfect pastime to escape the haunting memories of a violent past that echoed through Andric's bridge, he believed. But those ghosts hadn't vanished. They still lingered across the river in Serbia, where a form of Christian Jihad seemed poised to erupt.

5

A knock on the door drew Grant's attention, and he opened it to find a waiter with a trolley. The trolley was laden with food and alcohol, far more than they needed for their upcoming journey. Grant figured it was wise to fuel up on calories. They were currently in Zagreb, the capital of Croatia, awaiting their departure for Bosnia. They had stumbled upon their next war, or perhaps it had found them. Grant had managed to confront some of the ghosts of Siobahn and Mary's deaths, albeit only partially. Mo had convinced him that it was his mission to inform and share their story with the world.

"Hey, come and look," shouted Mo.

On the TV screen, scenes of the aftermath of shelling unfolded. It was in the heart of Sarajevo, just outside a bakery where people had gathered to queue for bread. The sight was grim: bodies scattered everywhere. Rescuers worked frantically to tend to the injured, loading them into cars and ambulances. "Thirty dead," announced the reporter, "with many more wounded." It was a scene of utter carnage. The broadcast included a poignant cutaway of a child's toy lying nearby, and a close-up of the small hand of a young victim.

The report from CTN was grim, casting a shadow of foreboding. "And the Serbs are tightening their grip on this besieged city, which has now been surrounded for five months," the reporter concluded.

The grim topic put the two friends off their food, so they focused on the alcohol instead. One advantage of working for a major international network was the generous expenses and excellent room service.

A second report followed, this time focusing on the journalists covering the conflict. It depicted camera teams clad in body armour darting across streets, seeking cover behind shipping containers to shield themselves from Serb snipers. Then, the scene shifted to journalists calmly eating dinner at the city's sole operational hotel.

"Wow, look at all that gear. It's like a science fiction movie. Can we get some body armour with that frontal flap that protects your balls? We didn't have it in Somalia, and man, I need it. Gonna start a family of Mo's one day," Grant ignored the question.

A dark-skinned man was being interviewed, and the caption read 'Ron O'Sullivan.'

"Hey," said Mo. "Isn't that the guy we have to connect with?"

"Shush," said Grant.

"It's a bit like the Battle of Britain in the Second World War," said O'Sullivan, looking directly at the camera. "You have dinner with your colleagues one night and you don't know if they'll be sitting here tomorrow."

"Wow," said Mo. "That was straight out of a Hollywood BS script." Drama and hyperbole were never far from a journalist.

"Yep, he's our man. I am gonna call him."

The TV report persisted, emphasising the peril faced by journalists. It included a scene of a wooden coffin being loaded onto a United Nations plane, serving as a stark reminder of the risks involved.

"The body of ATV producer Chip Fuller being taken back to the United States," said the voice-over. "He was shot dead by a sniper near Sarajevo airport. He is the fourth journalist to have been killed in the last month."

The report returned to Ron O'Sullivan.

"The snipers are deliberately targeting journalists. This is the first war where we have been under serious attack," he said with a look of desperation. "This is the most dangerous place in the world to be a journalist."

Grant couldn't shake the realisation that being Bosnian was also fraught with danger.

"What the Fuck," said Mo. "That Fuller guy, ATV, failed to mention that when they hired us. A staffer gets killed, and then they all go running for shelter. So what to do? Get in the freelancers. A-holes."

Grant experienced a sensation akin to what the Australians might have felt at Gallipoli during the First World War: a sense of expendability.

"Mate, don't worry," he reassured the little Egyptian. "We are experienced, and for the first time, we are on expenses and a good day rate." Mo nodded in agreement, acknowledging that danger itself was one thing, but facing unpaid danger was an entirely different matter.

The subsequent phone call to Ron was brief and costly.

"This satellite phone is costing forty bucks a minute, and Reuters is making a fucking fortune, and the line frequently breaks up, so I'll say this quickly and to the point: my advice to you is don't come, people are dying like flies, journalists are being picked off one by one, the Serbs are strangling this city, and it's only a matter of time before they roll in and clean up big time. To put it bluntly, it's fucking dangerous man."

"So why are you there, Ron?" inquired Grant. "Why are there any journalists, and what would happen if no one reported on the story?"

There was a moment of silence and then Ron replied, "OK, fair point. This is a madhouse, but there is room for more inmates if that's what you want. Let me know what time your plane gets in, and I'll pick you up. And wear your body armour on the plane, as the Serbs are fond of shooting at big, fat, slow targets. And make sure your body armour has a dropdown ball protector; a Dutch reporter lost his last week."

"We are working on that extension," replied the correspondent. "See you tomorrow."

Ron, though cheerful in demeanour, evidently excelled at his job, as attested by the foreign desk. However, it seemed that the desk conveniently omitted mentioning the producer's demise.

Grant looked at Mo's solemn expression, "No matter, my friend. Let's worry about trouble when we get there. Tonight, it's party time, and I have just the place in mind."

Their final hours in civilised surroundings were spent at Zagreb's largest disco, the Saloon, during what was dubbed 'cleavage night.' Mo found the allure of the competition captivating, albeit for purely aesthetic reasons. The contest awarded a bottle of champagne to the girl deemed to possess the most impressive cleavage. Mo found himself overwhelmed by the sight before him. The tall, stunningly beautiful girls seemed to embody perfection, and he felt as though he had entered paradise.

"Oh my fucking God, this is un-fucking-believable. Fuck war. I want peace…a piece of pussy."

Both men were becoming heavily drunk. It was almost a ritual for them before venturing into dangerous territories. "I am never going to leave here," stuttered Mo. "This is the most beautiful place in the world. There is nothing after here." It was 3.00 a.m. and they were the last to leave.

Four hours later, they were packed and waiting at Zagreb Airport, going through UN check-in. Their heads were pounding.

'Welcome to Maybe Airlines,' said the sign. A British flight sergeant explained that 'maybe' meant the planes might take off, they might successfully navigate through enemy territory, and they might evade being targeted by Serb forces, or they might not. The uncertain prospects didn't exactly instil reassurance in the two men.

"Oh fuck," shouted Mo. "We don't have the ball protector body armour extension. I'm never gonna be able to have kids."

They were directed towards an American C130, a four-engine turbo-prop military transport plane primed and ready for departure. Its engines roared with such intensity that conversation became impossible; communication relied solely on hand gestures. Following the loadmaster's signals, they boarded the aircraft and were directed to take seats along the side. They secured themselves with military-grade seatbelts, criss-crossing their bodies, and were provided with NATO-issued earplugs and a sick bag, just in case.

The flight lasted an hour and a half, with forty minutes of traversing Serb territory. Despite no prior incidents of UN planes being shot down, the risk remained ever-present. If such an event were to occur, the likelihood of identifying the perpetrator amidst the chaos of a war zone would be minimal.

Both men drifted off into sleep, succumbing to the exhaustion from their indulgence in cleavage night. However, they both adhered to the three cardinal rules of reporting conflict: eat when possible, relieve oneself when possible, and seize any opportunity for rest.

Amidst the interior of the aircraft sat four pallets laden with essential supplies: emergency tents, blankets, and food provisions. The looming winter added urgency to their mission. It was no coincidence that Sarajevo, with its harsh winters, had once been chosen to host the Winter Olympics.

They woke abruptly as the Hercules descended sharply, preparing to land at Sarajevo International Airport. The landscape below resembled scenes from a developing nation. Grant peered out the window, observing the devastation surrounding the airport: houses in ruins, many without roofs. Tracer shots streaked towards the plane, a stark reminder of the volatile situation below.

The loadmaster offered a thumbs-up and a smile, treating the flight as just another routine day on the job. For Grant and Mo, it was likewise just another day on duty. Despite the bumpy landing, the plane remained intact, a crucial relief. As they came to a stop and the rear hatch opened, the team was swiftly ushered out, half running, half walking towards the airport building, burdened with their equipment. Above the door hung a sign reading, 'Congratulations, you've made it on Maybe Airlines... this time. Have a nice day.' Below it, a big smiley face adorned with a military helmet added a touch of humour. Grant couldn't help but reflect that in a war zone, a good laugh was rare, and this certainly wasn't one.

But in every war zone, maintaining a sense of humour was crucial. The team understood this well; without it, they risked either descending into madness or becoming ineffectual in their roles. After signing the UN's arrivals book, they stepped outside to find Ron O'Sullivan waiting beside a white Land Rover four-wheel drive.

"Dobro Dosli," (welcome) Ron said, extending a hand for a shake. "Now let's get the fuck out of here." He opened the rear of the vehicle for them to embark. It lacked windows and, as Ron cautioned them, lacked Kevlar protection.

"Speed is of the essence," he told them. "But the airport road is a dangerous stretch. That's where Fuller got it, so you should keep low in the back." He put his helmet on and closed the driver's door.

They climbed into the vehicle and settled on the floor, bracing themselves for the upcoming fifteen-minute journey along the back roads. Both were keenly aware that they were vulnerable targets. The Land Rover's flimsy structure offered little protection against bullets or mines.

Mo got Buzz Lightyear out of his bag.

"To infinity and the hotel," he said with a big smile.

The engine roared, and the vehicle surged forward. Grant despised clichés, a sentiment ingrained during his time at a tabloid newspaper where they permeated almost every sentence. Yet, as he observed the Land Rover's swift pace, clichés seemed almost unavoidable. Phrases like 'faster than the speed of sound,' 'breakneck speed,' and 'fast and furious' echoed in his mind, despite the vehicle not being designed for such velocity. Instead, it was engineered for endurance and rugged terrain, leaving Grant with the unsettling realisation that there was no hiding if someone had them in their sights. He felt more anxious than a goat during Ramadan.

The vehicle careened around bends, jolting over curbs and through potholes, tossing the occupants in the back from side to side, their heads and bodies colliding with the interior walls. They resembled pinballs in a machine, ricocheting with each sharp turn and rough terrain. Grant now understood the necessity of wearing helmets, and it wasn't solely due to the threat of Serb snipers.

After they finally came to a stop, they found themselves bruised and slightly battered. The rear door swung open, revealing Ron with a smile on his face.

"Welcome to our little home." It was the underground car park of the Holiday Inn.

"You were right," said Mo. "It is fucking dangerous here." He didn't add that it was because of Ron's driving.

A little boy approached. “Chocolada?” he asked, holding out his hand.

“That’s Igor,” explained Ron. “He virtually lives in the garage. Many just want to survive this war. Igor only wants chocolate.”

Grant apologised and promised, ‘Next time.’ Igor walked away, clearly disappointed.

They proceeded to check in at the reception desk. Upon entering the Atrium, they noticed that all the windows were either boarded up or taped over. “It’s to prevent fragments of glass flying through the air in the event of an explosion,” said Ron. “And there are many.”

“Fragments or explosions?” asked Mo.

“Both,” replied the American.

Hejo, the front desk manager, greeted them with a warm smile. “Did you book directly through the travel agent or through Kuoni Executive Travel?” he inquired. “Just joking, my friends. Welcome to paradise.” He retrieved the register and began scanning through its pages. “Everything above the sixth floor is destroyed. There is no electricity after seven, if we have it, that is, I am afraid, no hot water and no alcohol. Meal times depend on whether we get food and whether any of the staff are still alive to serve it. Laundry hardly works, and you are responsible for cleaning up shrapnel and bullet casings after attacks,” he smiled. “I know I am making it sound much better than it is. But we make do. Will you be staying long?”

A loud woman marched up to the desk. “Hejo, you promised to get me a hairdryer,” she berated him.

“Nema strue lady,” (no electricity), he told her.

“What the fuck kind of a place is this,” she retorted and stormed off.

Ron caught Grant's gaze, "That was Amelia Degusta or disgusted to the rest of us. American journo who gives us all a bad name. Gets stories on room service, stretches them longer than a hippo's knicker elastic and is an Olympic standard shagger. Keep your door locked. It's not the Serbs you have to worry about."

Outside, a deafening crescendo of explosions reverberated in the not-so-distant distance.

"Trebevic," explained Hejo. "Big fighting; it is a mountain overlooking Sarajevo. Most of it is in our hands, for now," he beamed a broad smile.

"If Serbs take it, then we are in bigger than big trouble," said Hejo, smiling again.

"Incredibly dangerous place," said Ron. "Close contact fighting, ever-changing positions and most organisations are banning their people from going there because it is so unpredictable. The Bosnians are suffering a lot of casualties there. You have to be insane to go."

Mo and Grant looked at one another. Danger, challenge, no one else going! It was ticking all the boxes.

"How can we get there?"

Hejo replied, "I have a friend."

"Can your friend come quickly?"

"Very quickly," replied Hejo. "He's our chef."

The chef's inability to speak English didn't hinder communication; war served as an international language, where some sentiments didn't require words. In the realm of television, it was the power of images that held significance, transcending linguistic barriers. As they embarked on their journey, the bullet-ridden windscreen of the car bore witness to the dangers of their surroundings. In the rear of the vehicle, the absence of windows accentuated the sense of vulnerability. Amidst the stark reality of their situation, a weathered car freshener dangled from the rear-view mirror, a poignant reminder of time's passage.

Mo took Buzz out of his pack and put him on the dashboard. "To infinity and beyond and Trebovic," he said, and they headed off.

The car resembled a biscuit tin on wheels, lacking proper suspension, as Grant clung to the backseat door handle to prevent it from swinging open during turns. The engine choked out black smoke, suggesting a filtration issue. Despite the chef's efforts, the vehicle remained stubbornly stuck in second gear, prompting repeated apologies in the only English word he knew: 'Sorry.'

Forty minutes later, the Chef dropped them off about a quarter of the way up Trebevic. He pointed to a path and shouted, 'Gore.' Although the word meant 'up,' to the two of them, it sounded more like 'gore,' evoking a sense of something unpleasant or dangerous.

As they ascended the trail with determination and urgency driving their steps, a cluster of figures appeared ahead, descending towards them. Among them, a solitary figure guided a donkey laden with an injured comrade. Mo instinctively raised his camera to capture the unfolding scene, yet he hesitated momentarily.

"OK?" he asked. The men said nothing, so he continued. Behind came another group of men carrying more wounded fighters.

"Be careful my friend," said one of the fighters, "much danger there. Chetniks everywhere."

"You speak English. Great. How far is the front line?"

"Walk up as far as you see the bodies, turn right and walk for ten minutes more. From there, walk carefully and quietly. Chetniks will be close."

"Thank you."

The ascent proved arduous, with steep sections that made light travel a challenging notion, especially given the essential TV equipment they had to carry, none of which could be considered lightweight. Despite the weighty load, they pressed onward, the cacophony of explosions and gunfire growing ever louder and nearer with each step. Negotiating treacherously narrow paths, they advanced cautiously, their progress measured sometimes in careful inches. Their journey was punctuated by a grim discovery: three lifeless figures sprawled beside a substantial boulder. Adhering to instructions, they veered right and followed a sinuous path, tracing the right flank of Trebevic. Amidst a sudden eerie silence, the echo of approaching footsteps heralded the arrival of additional stretcher-bearers, a solemn procession of four, descending with wounded comrades in tow. They looked at the two foreigners. Most said nothing. One said, "Doberdan" (good day). And they continued on walking. At the time, they were unaware that Doberdan would turn out to be a fortunate day. Amidst the challenges of Mount Trebevic, it appeared anything but auspicious.

Grant and Mo stepped aside, gracefully yielding space for them to navigate the narrow track. Mo adeptly captured the unfolding procession on video, encountering no objections from the fighters. Pressing forward, the air filled with the unsettling frequency of bullets whizzing overhead, a grim reminder of the perilous environment they traversed and how quickly silence can evaporate.

A sudden, sharp sound akin to a plop emanated from just ahead, signalling the presence of a Bosnian 60mm mortar position. This weapon, renowned for its effectiveness within a close range spanning 70 to 3400 metres, told them that they were nearing the heart of the battle zone.

Continuing their ascent, they pressed onward, navigating past a succession of shallow, deserted trenches flanking the path. The imminent arrival of Bosnian fighters, numbering 15 to 20, spurred Mo and Grant to quicken their pace, falling into step alongside the reinforcements. Fifty metres ahead, they arrived at the frontline, where fighters were entrenched in positions, primarily in shallow dugouts. A sudden cessation of gunfire enveloped the mountain in an eerie silence it only serve to heighten the tension.

Mo filmed whatever he could, and no one objected. It was a television war enthusiast's dream. Then, suddenly, heavy incoming fire, followed by three mortar explosions, erupted nearby. The Bosnian lines retaliated with fierce gunfire. A fighter shouted instructions into a hand-held walkie-talkie, growing increasingly agitated. Men hurriedly moved about, and two individuals advanced with Rocket Propelled Grenade launchers. They fired simultaneously, but Grant couldn't discern at what. Mo signalled his success with a thumbs-up, indicating he had captured the shot. Adrenaline coursed through their veins, pure and unadulterated, inducing body-shaking excitement.

Then, the gunfire subsided, bringing a momentary calm to the tense atmosphere.

Grant approached the man holding the walkie-talkie and inquired if he spoke English. The man shook his head in response.

"I want to speak to the Comandante," Grant said in a slow, pronounced way that English speakers adopt when talking to a foreigner.

"Jebiga," responded the walkie-talkie man and gestured to Grant and Mo to move to a shallow trench. Two men were being attended to for what appeared to be minor injuries. In the distance, they could discern the voice of someone shouting.

"Chetniks," said the medical officer treating the casualty. Grant looked confused. "Serbs," explained the medic.

"Oh."

After twenty minutes of waiting, Grant cautiously approached the fighter with the walkie-talkie.

"When will Comandante Jebiga be coming?" he asked. The walkie-talkie man and all the fighters burst into loud, uncontrollable laughter.

Grant was bewildered by the situation. Mo perceived them as individuals with unyielding courage, seemingly fearless in the face of adversity. According to Mo, they laughed defiantly in the face of death, their resolve unshaken by danger. Either way, no Commandante Jebiga came, and the team got what interviews they could do by Grant looking into his Serbo/Croatian phrase book and then shouting words and phrases at the fighters, "Danger? Serbs. What is happening? Are you well? Will you win?"

He held onto hope that their efforts would yield a valuable soundbite for their report.

They recorded another intense bout of action, capturing the harrowing scenes of additional casualties and mortar fire before beginning their descent down Trebevic. Upon reaching the base, they encountered a man waiting in a diminutive car reminiscent of an Italian Fiat 500cc. "Ficho," said the driver. "Great Ficho," replied Grant "I'm Grant, this Mo. Mr Ficho, you-take-us-Televisa please, for Deutsch marks?" waving some notes in the air. The language of money spoke volumes without uttering a word. Unbeknownst to them, 'Ficho' referred to the car, not its driver. Oblivious, they settled into the vehicle, anticipating the gradual, tremulous descent back to Sarajevo, where they would conclude their tale.

The Bosnian TV station served as the hub for all international TV media operations. Equipped with large generators, it ensured a steady supply of electricity essential for broadcasting operations. Additionally, the station housed a substantial satellite dish belonging to the European Broadcasting Union, facilitating the seamless transmission of stories worldwide.

They hurried into the building, guided to a spare room furnished with only a solitary chair, a desk, and windows sealed with tape. It was evident that the Bosnians recognised the potent influence wielded by the foreign media, sparing no effort to accommodate their needs. As they arranged their editing equipment, a sharp rap echoed at the door. Standing before them was a man clad in a crisp suit, adorned with a tie, and draped in a sleek grey Burberry raincoat.

"Welcome," he said. "I am Belmin Mechanic, and I am the Bosnian Foreign Minister. Welcome to Sarajevo. I hope you survive. Many Bosnians have not, but we are grateful you have come to tell the world about the genocide which is being perpetrated against us."

His command of English was flawless. They conducted an on-camera interview, capturing a sound bite to complement the Trebevic footage.

"Our fighters are resisting heroically," he said. "But unless the international community stops the Serbs, there will be bloodshed here on a scale not seen since the Second World War. The arms embargo only helps the Serbs, and without weapons, we will be slaughtered. I hope the international powers can live with that. But we can't."

And just like that, he vanished, swiftly moving on to the subsequent office, the next TV crew, the ensuing interview, and the subsequent plea.

There was a knock at the door. Grant opened it to find a stunning woman standing on the other side.

"Hi, I'm Selma," she said. Grant found himself momentarily transfixed, his gaze locked on her captivating blue eyes and mousy blonde hair, like an Exocet missile homing in on its target.

"Ron said you needed a translator," she said. "I can help you."

"Great," responded Grant, trying to recover from a gawping spotty-faced youth to a mature TV correspondent. "Yes, we definitely need you, we definitely do. How much do you charge?"

She gave him a puzzled look. "Nothing," she said. Grant felt instantly bad but instantly hooked.

Selma was evidently not just beautiful but also intelligent. As an English Literature student, she delved into the intricacies of Shakespeare's works and appreciated the darker themes portrayed in the writings of Thomas Hardy and Emile Zola. She often remarked that their works were depressing to read, yet little did she know that they would prepare her for the hardships of war. Gazing into Selma's striking blue eyes, Grant couldn't help but think that while war was predominantly bleak, it also brought about some unexpected blessings. Selma, he concluded, was one of them.

6

It gleamed in the sunshine like a rare exotic gem. Adorned with stunning burgundy paintwork, striking white-rimmed tyres, and a sleek, elongated body, the sight of the 1932 Rolls Royce Silver Ghost would capture anyone's attention, even those not versed in vintage cars. Its engine emitted a deep, powerful roar, akin to a majestic big cat's purr. This car was more than transportation; it was a statement on wheels, exuding wealth, class, style, and heritage. Impeccably maintained, it held immense value, its worth deemed priceless by its owner. To General Demetris Petranovic, it symbolised power, status, and lineage. Likely unmatched in the entire Balkans, owning such a vehicle made him a true standout.

The luxurious black leather rear seat where he sat had been softened by numerous sessions of moisturising upholstery cream, adding to its opulence.

He extracted a cigarette from his silver engraved handmade case and lit it. It was a Belomorkanal, renowned as the strongest Russian cigarette. He had acquired a taste for them during the Second World War. It was rumoured that just three puffs could coat your lungs and eradicate any lurking germs. However, for heavy smokers, it also carried the risk of developing a husky voice and the early stages of throat cancer. It was considered a cigarette for men, for soldiers. He smoked it with pride, akin to wearing his medals and full dress uniform, the same uniform he hadn't worn in over 40 years, a relic from the days of the Kingdom of Yugoslavia when the Serbs and their military prowess commanded respect.

Young men dressed in fatigues stood to attention as the car passed, saluting the general with an almost overwhelming display of respect.

Most old Serb soldiers would recount tales of fighting alongside the Allies and the partisans against the Germans during the Second World War. However, the General belonged to a rare breed that fought for the Germans. Coming from an aristocratic background, he couldn't tolerate the communist partisan forces led by Josip Broz. Their vision of the future did not sit well with him.

Another reason for aligning with the Germans was to safeguard his community and village. He had witnessed the brutality with which they eradicated partisan supporters and hideouts, and he was determined to prevent such devastation from befalling his canton. The fact that the Germans had honoured him with a medal for bravery after he had eliminated a partisan unit held significance for him. That particular decoration had been concealed in his home on the day Tito and his communist associates seized control of the country. On that day, Petranovic, then a young lieutenant, concealed not only his medal but also his emotions and his car.

He had suffered great losses. Not only had he lost his estate, ancestral home, and possessions, but also his social standing and pride. He endured a year in the Jesenovac concentration camp simply because of his upper-class background, as ordered by Tito for punishment. Jesenovac was one of the lesser-known concentration camps, often overshadowed by infamous ones like Belsen, Auschwitz, and Dachau. However, the atrocities committed there were equally abhorrent. Run by Croatian Nazi sympathisers, nearly 750,000 Serbs perished in that camp. Despite this, no Croatians faced justice at Nuremberg; the guilty vanished to countries like Argentina, The USA, Canada, Australia, and Germany, starting new lives free from accountability.

Upon his release, he became a nobody, stripped of the privilege of holding a passport or attaining any significant position. He was labelled as one of the 'non-people,' marginalised within society.

What saved him were the secret Serb societies, individuals like him, and well-to-do capitalists whom Tito despised. But what troubled Petranovic even more was Tito's suppression of Serb honour and respect, rendering the entire nation void of identity. These societies provided support, finances, and the hope that one day the longed-for Greater Serbia would emerge from oppression, granting Serbs the entitlements they deserved.

The Silver Ghost belonged to his grandfather, and upon his passing, he bequeathed it to his beloved Dimitris. Dimitris carefully stored it in an old shed on the family's former estate, visiting it as often as he could, about once a month, to polish and care for this cherished automobile.

When Tito passed away and Serbs found their voices, advocating for their aspirations and cherished traditions, the General emerged from the shadows. With resolve, he retrieved the car from the shed and embarked on a journey into the dawn of a rejuvenated Serbia, symbolising a fresh chapter in their history.

This day marked the dawn of a new chapter, a pivotal moment in this unfolding journey. It held a profound significance, signifying a fresh start. As the car traversed through the imposing iron gates of the Balsac Military Academy, situated thirty miles east of the Drina River on the Serb side, and two hours west of Belgrade, it symbolised a transition. Two youthful soldiers, likely no more than sixteen years of age, immaculate in their uniforms, snapped to attention, heels clicking crisply together as the vehicle came to a halt. They shouldered their rifles with precision, standing at the ready, a silent salute to the arrival.

The door swung open, revealing a young, bright-eyed subaltern. Stepping aside, he delivered a sharp, precise salute. Without delay, an honour guard snapped to attention with impressive synchronicity, a testament to their rigorous military training.

"My general, everything is prepared," the young man announced, offering one more salute. He pivoted and seamlessly melted back into formation alongside the other hundred young recruits. Trailing behind them, a convoy of ten military trucks painted in a distinctive pea-green hue rolled by, each bearing the unmistakable insignia 'JNA' on top of each registration plate. In the linguistic mosaic of Serbo-Croat, the pronunciation of 'J' rendered it as 'y,' thereby signifying the Yugoslav National Army.

Petranovic ascended a modest wooden podium positioned at the heart of the parade ground.

"Gentlemen," he began, "Today is the end of one chapter for you and the beginning of another, the end of your basic training and the beginning of the Serb fight for the future. This one is far more important, no matter the outcome today. Each of you will have the honour of being part of the New Greater Serbia, which has been denied to us for so long. But whatever course we find ourselves on, the objective will remain the same: the glory of serving the Serb nation, restoring our dignity and the protection of our race and culture."

The gathered men radiated an aura of pride and unwavering loyalty. A palpable sense of anticipation permeated the air as if every breath held a promise of imminent excitement.

Petranovic felt a pang of envy as he looked upon the youthful faces before him, wishing that this rejuvenation had occurred two decades earlier, affording him the opportunity to play a more hands-on role. Regrettably, such a scenario was not his reality. Nonetheless, he found solace in contributing through other means, channelling his efforts in ways that were still impactful.

"Gentlemen," he continued, "You know what you have to do. I wish you all the best. May God be with you."

Three boys commenced a rhythmic beat, pounding their shoulder-cradled drums in unison. Among them, one proudly carried a massive Serb flag, its design striking, a tricolour of red, blue, and white with a radiant gold cross at its centre, each corner adorned with the letter 'C'. In the Cyrillic language, 'C' symbolised 'S', and each 'C' bore profound significance: 'Samo Sloga Srbina Spasava', translating to 'Only Unity Saves the Serbs'. This flag, once outlawed under Tito's regime, along with any symbol of ethnic nationalism, was now unfurled boldly in a new era, marking a shift from the past. Tito's reign had ended, and a wave of change swept through the land.

The young men, crisp in their uniforms, saluted before falling out of line. They boarded the pea soup-coloured trucks, positioning themselves behind the grand burgundy-coloured Rolls Royce Silver Ghost and a dignified General adorned with medals and pride. With the flag and drummers leading the procession, the column set off towards its designated position. Amidst the serene backdrop of singing birds and a clear blue sky, the day unfolded as a picturesque scene of a beautiful spring day. However, the tranquilly was short-lived.

7

Thirty kilometres distant, in the quaint town of Donji Zelenik, the elder men relished the season's first warm sun. Gathered outside the lone coffee bar, they indulged in robust Turkish coffee, puffing on cigarettes, while Yousef, engrossed in a game of backgammon, known as tavla in its Turkish iteration, delighted in soundly defeating his opponent. Yet, amidst his triumph, Yousef remained oblivious to the absence of the village's Serbian men. Had he been more observant, he might have sensed that all was not as it should be.

Every morning began with the ritual of coffee, occasionally accompanied by a glass of Rakia or stock brandy, setting the tone for the day ahead. Meanwhile, the women of the village diligently tended to their domestic duties: washing, cooking, and maintaining the household. Rooted in tradition, this village stood as a bastion of conservative values, unchanged for centuries. Here, the concept of women's liberation held no sway, and the older generation showed no inclination towards embracing it.

Absent from the morning coffee tradition was his close companion, Milan Zubic. Though somewhat unusual, Yousef paid it little mind, engrossed in his ongoing game. With a familiar flourish, he placed a counter on the backgammon board in an age-old manner. Suddenly, a deafening explosion reverberated through the air.

The initial explosion reverberated near the heart of the village, merely fifty metres from the bustling coffee bar. The force of the blast shattered windows, sending a collective gasp through the air. Amidst the chaos, a man crumpled to the ground, clutching his leg as blood spilled forth. Before a word could escape anyone's lips, successive shells followed, each one edging ominously closer to the coffee bar. Reacting swiftly, Yousef instinctively dropped to the floor, drawing from his experience in the Yugoslav National Army. With a keen awareness of the danger, he knew that shrapnel tends to ascend, compelling him to stay low for protection.

Chaos and confusion reigned as smoke billowed through the air, thick with the pungent scent of cordite. The thunderous impacts disrupted any sense of balance and orientation, adding to the disarray of the situation.

Yousef's throat tightened as he struggled to relieve the pressure in his ears. Though his friend's lips moved, their words remained muffled, lost amidst the chaos. It was the sight of blood that jolted Yousef into action, realising that his friend's silent agony was actually screams of pain. Reacting swiftly, he hoisted his friend up and guided him into the nearby coffee bar, seeking refuge and some semblance of safety amid the turmoil.

In the distance, he spotted two motionless bodies near the mosque, along with a donkey that appeared lifeless too.

Then another barrage of shells landed, this time targeting the northern part of the village. Yousef snapped back to reality. North was where his home lay, where his wife awaited him. Without hesitation, he sprang to his feet and sprinted towards his house. Two more shells detonated to his left, sending shockwaves through the air. He staggered but regained his balance, pressing onward up the hill. His sole concern now was for his wife, Sara.

It felt like an eternity to reach the house. The shelling had ceased, but the devastation was evident everywhere. Barns lay in ruins, houses were riddled with large charred holes and broken glass. Shattered concrete littered the streets. Yousef sprinted into his front garden, his breath coming in ragged gasps. He saw the front door and entrance area badly damaged. Calling out Sara's name, he received no response. Stepping over debris into what remained of the kitchen, he noticed a gaping hole in the ceiling and another in the roof, with sunlight streaming through. He would later recall how vividly blue the sky looked. The table lay on its side, scarred by shrapnel. Approaching it, he found Sara's lifeless body, lying still with her face turned to the side, her eyes open but devoid of movement. With a cry, he crouched down, lifting her head in a panicked frenzy, tears streaming down his face. Cradling her in his arms, he began to sob. Fifty years of marriage flashed through his mind: disbelief, anguish, confusion, and above all, the haunting question, "Why?"

General Petranovic issued the command "ceasefire," and in response, the young cadets promptly snapped to attention. He understood the significance of the moment, it marked the commencement of a crucial phase. The eight 155mm artillery guns fell silent, their barrels still radiating heat, while the lingering scent of spent gunpowder hung in the air, a testament to the intensity of the preceding barrage.

Piles of shell casings accumulated behind each gun, evidence of the cadets' practice and precision. Every cadet's performance and accuracy would be evaluated. The initial spotter reports suggested that the shelling had been executed effectively. The final practical exam for the artillery cadets of Balsac Military Academy concluded triumphantly.

On the hill overlooking Donji Zelenik stood Milan, the Serb, the absent friend of Yousef Mesic. He watched in horror as the scene below unfolded, witnessing the devastation inflicted upon the town where he had spent nearly his entire life. He understood that the damage extended beyond mere buildings; it fractured friendships. Milan thought of his Muslim and Catholic friends, now caught beneath the onslaught of artillery, and wondered who had survived and who hadn't. A profound sense of guilt washed over him as he realised he had stood idly by, aware of the impending tragedy. But what choice did he have? He had been swayed by the relentless propaganda portraying Muslim extremism as a looming threat. While Milan had sworn not to take up arms against his friends, he had also failed to sound the alarm. He knew that life would never be the same again.

"Tata, father," said his son. "There was nothing to be done." Darko was a tall 23-year-old wearing a military camouflage uniform and carrying an AK47.

"We had to take action to protect our nation. But don't worry, it will be over soon." Darko displayed no indication of concern or remorse for the recent events. Immersed in Serb nationalism for years, he was resolute in his convictions. He understood what needed to be done.

Down below, a procession of men clad in camouflage clothing began their ascent up the hill.

"By nightfall, we'll be in control, and you'll be able to go back home," he reassured his father.

He pondered what awaited him upon his return.

8

Selma sat in front of the monitors, her gaze fixed on the images flickering across the screens. Every so often, she paused, fingers hovering over the keyboard as she meticulously transcribed the translations. Suddenly, a burst of laughter erupted from her, echoing through the room.

"What's funny?" asked Grant.

"It's about commander Jebiga," and she descended into a fit of uncontrollable giggles.

"What about him? He must be someone important. Everyone keeps talking about him, even the hotel reception staff."

"It's not a name or a person," she said after controlling the laughter.

Grant and Mo exchanged puzzled glances, their furrowed brows mirroring mutual confusion.

"It means fuck it," she explained. "It's a term that everyone uses for everything, including the weather, sports, politics, stubbing your toe, for instance, and having to do things. Jebiga is just a way of expressing yourself. It is perhaps the most common expletive we have in our language."

She smiled, "Serbo-Croatian is one of the richest languages for swearing," she said. "We have some of the best swear words and phrases in the world. You will come to learn that if you stay here for a while." But, she added sombrely, "I'm hoping there won't be a need."

Selma willingly continued collaborating with the two men, finding joy in their camaraderie, humour, and dedication. Mo and Grant painted Sarajevo as a tapestry of stories, teeming with narratives of profound human experiences, tales of tragedy and endurance, yet also of heroism and levity. The Bosnians proved endearing, remarkably so. Many of them possessed a knack for echoing the dark humour of British comedy stalwarts like Monty Python, alongside the more slapstick antics of Only Fools and Horses. They demonstrated an ability to laugh at themselves and extract amusement from even the direst of circumstances. Despite the harsh reality of their lives, characterized by extreme deprivation and a lack of external assistance, they found solace in humour and resilience.

In the days that followed, the team tirelessly gathered every story they could find, often working 18-hour days. They uncovered tales of wounded and killed children, people targeted by snipers, and the shelling of water and bread queues. Amidst the chaos, they also discovered stories of culture and theatre persisting underground. Crafting neatly packaged snippets lasting two to three minutes, they aimed to inform viewers about what was happening and why. ATV eagerly accepted every piece of footage they were given. While part of this eagerness stemmed from the necessity of sharing a story of bloodshed in the heart of Europe, it was also because the opposition US networks were absent. This made it an ATV exclusive. In the competitive world of media, everyone relished an exclusive. As the old adage goes, "If you have it, flaunt it," and in the realm of television, that certainly meant exclusives.

Grant was deeply struck by the remarkable dignity exhibited by the residents of Sarajevo. One particular scene remained etched in his memory: a city centre street ravaged by shells, strewn with debris and destruction. Despite the chaos, amidst the flames being extinguished by firemen and the street littered with concrete and shrapnel, a middle-aged woman strolled along. She was dressed elegantly in a fur coat, with impeccable makeup, donning high heels, and clutching a handbag, as if en route to a night at the theatre. The juxtaposition was surreal, a stark contrast between the desolation of war and the enduring presence of style and culture in Sarajevo and an undying spirit to carry on.

Every day, they made their rounds to the hospitals, which were frequently inundated with wounded individuals, predominantly civilians, including many children. Mo captured footage of a young boy, perhaps just eighteen months old, who had tragically lost the lower part of his left leg in a mortar blast. Despite his injury, he maintained an endearing laughter, gurgling happily and waving his stump in the air. Other than his missing limb, he resembled any typical toddler. In Sarajevo, amidst the occasional humour, tragedy loomed large and often felt insurmountable.

The graveyards became overwhelmed, reaching capacity and overflowing. Sports grounds were repurposed into cemeteries to accommodate the staggering number of casualties. So many lives had been lost that they ran out of the number nine for the date on the makeshift wooden headboards, forcing them to fashion a makeshift nine from an eight.

Driving along the road known as 'Sniper Alley' was a nerve-wracking experience. Even at 180 km/h, Serb marksmen could target drivers. Whenever they travelled along that road or the airport road, Mo would always huddle down in the well of the passenger seat, filming Grant behind the wheel. "Habibi, if you get hit while driving, my footage will make you famous," he said.

"I don't want to be famous," Grant said. "And if I get hit, we'll crash at speed, and then you will be in the shit."

"Habibi," Mo smiled, "you can't decide that. It's in the hands of the Great One."

"Oh, the foreign editor in the sky?" Both laughed.

They featured a story about a young boy rendered speechless by the relentless shelling, the trauma so deeply ingrained that speaking became an insurmountable challenge. Another narrative centred on a 13-year-old boy serving in a unit with his father and brothers. Yet another depicted a harrowing account of a boy who suffered serious shrapnel wounds and had a leg amputated after he shielded his young brother during shelling. Tragically, their father had fallen victim to a mortar attack just weeks prior, as he stood in line, waiting to buy bread.

The family refrained from visiting the graveyard due to its closeness to the positions of Serb Snipers', making it unsafe to venture there.

Grant crafted the story. Malik, just eleven years old, hailed from a family with a background in engineering. His father had been employed across various projects in the Middle East, providing Malik with exposure to the English language at a young age. In the interview, Malik's voice was gripped with emotion. "I miss my father," he said. "I miss him so much." Tears welled in his eyes. Mo's mother sat close behind him, the camera capturing her presence. As tears welled in her eyes, she began to sob softly, her emotions palpable. The scene evoked a mix of empathy and frustration within both of them. It was challenging not to be swept away by the intensity of the moment, witnessing the aftermath of such barbaric acts inflicted upon innocent individuals. Alongside the grief, a wave of rising anger simmered, directed towards those accountable for perpetrating such senseless violence against ordinary people.

The story lacked a crucial element: a visit to the graveyard. However, the inherent danger posed a significant obstacle. Serb shells and sniper fire plagued burials and mourners, particularly at Lion Cemetery, the resting place of Mailk's father. Despite the family's desire to pay respects, it was too dangerous to visit, leaving them bereft of closure. Grant thought long and hard about what to do. He was mindful of the perilous circumstances. And while he couldn't justify risking their safety, he also couldn't fathom concluding the story without a resolution that could do justice to the family's suffering and loss. Grant and Mo knew the profound influence of television and visual storytelling; a compelling conclusion was paramount for maximum impact. So, he resolved to postpone the visit for now.

The Holiday Inn resembled a Club 18-30 holiday hotspot, attracting a peculiar crowd of adrenaline enthusiasts. Wild parties, abundant drugs, copious amounts of sex, and heavy drinking were the norm. In the evenings the motley assortment of an international press corps lounged about, regaling each other with tales of various war zones, as if recounting weekend getaways. The excitement radiated from the storytellers with every anecdote. Journalists egged each other on, with each narrative becoming increasingly extreme and outlandish. It brought to mind the Four Yorkshiremen sketch by the Monty Python team, where each businessman vied to recount his toughest upbringing. With every exchange, the stories escalated, and the exclusives became more sensational. The combination of journalists and alcohol invariably led to conversations that were anything but normal.

As they sat and picked at the sparse offerings that constituted dinner in the Holiday Inn's dining room, a man clad in full combat gear strode past their table.

"He's no soldier," came a voice from a neighbouring table. "That's Mungo de Boer, spelt BORE, a cameraman." The voice belonged to Chuck Brown, an American journalist sitting at the next table.

"He's from Zimbabwe or Rhodesia, as he still calls it. He's a 'when we', when we were in control, when we did this blah blah blah. He is overflowing with BS, has a CV compiled by Walter Mitty, has special forces training, a double first degree, is a multi-linguist, is a classically trained musician and is a military expert. All BS of course. But ageing American correspondents, the ones that dare to come here, love him. He was arrested at Downing Street once for turning up in full combat uniform. I'm told that included his Y-fronts. The guy is a fruit cake. And that's his soundman from Yorkshire, Rodney something or other, who is completely the opposite. They are part of the rich journalistic tapestry that is now woven into Bosnian conflict reporting. Hi, I'm Chuck. Print journo and resident cynic and piss taker."

Chuck Brown served as a paternal figure among the journalists. Approaching sixty, he openly acknowledged his dependence on life support for his liver, a consequence of his long-standing battle with alcoholism. Described as a "functioning alcoholic," his daily routine commenced with a cocktail of pills aimed at mitigating the toll on his liver from his frontline lifestyle. Despite his health challenges, Chuck remained a grounded realist, anticipating the inevitable decline in his health. In contrast to Ron O'Sullivan's pessimistic outlook on life, where doom seemed to loom around every corner, Chuck embodied eternal optimism, except when it came to his personal life, which he likened to a perpetual conflict zone. Chuck approached the turmoil of war with a remarkable level of equanimity, seldom allowing himself to become overly excited by its tumultuous events. His philosophy leaned towards the belief that any challenge could be managed with the aid of a stiff drink or a comforting joint.

"So welcome to Sarajevo. How's it going?" he asked Grant. "Getting settled in with all the death and misery, not to mention the appallingly low stocks of booze?"

"Slowly," replied Grant. "No such thing as a quiet day, scores of human-interest stories to be told, and ATV can't get enough. Long days, though, and I can't get a decent night's sleep. There's a mad machine gunner not far from my side of the hotel, and he keeps letting rip just when I am trying to fall asleep."

"Ah, yes, machine gun Mohammed. He's as regular as your bowel movements after a daily dose of syrup of figs. Comforting in a sort of perverse way."

The protagonist, an American, was the most seasoned veteran among the group, with a profound understanding of the who, why, what, and when of their endeavours. Having traversed through numerous conflicts since the Korean War, he harboured the belief that his own fate was inevitably tied to the next call to arms. Consequently, he adopted a pragmatic outlook, dismissing the notion of dwelling on the uncertainty that looms over him. Instead, he advocated for embracing life in the present moment, urging others to relish whatever time they have left. For him, war served as not merely an escape from personal turmoil but an irresistible calling. Reflecting on past experiences, he nostalgically compared Bosnia to Vietnam, free from bureaucratic hurdles and the ability to hitch a ride on military aircraft to just about any frontline. There were no chopper rides in Bosnia but otherwise you could go pretty much where you wanted. Despite Bosnia's differences, he found solace in the welcoming embrace of its people, a sentiment that underscores the peculiar allure of conflict zones.

He liked Grant. You always had a good first impression of people in challenging situations, particularly journalists. Like a seasoned racing pundit, he provided the Brit with an overview of the participants in the Bosnia Press Pack of 1992.

"That's Grace Barnes," he explained pointing to a plain woman. "She works for British TV. Wherever she is, it's a danger zone, that's because her fucking driving is insane. She's had three accidents so far and got a producer's legs broken. She lives to get awards and is desperate to be wounded. The other day she walked into the French UN medical station at the PTT building and insisted that she had been shot in the toe. They checked and said there was no sign of any injury but she told them to look again. Apparently, she also hasn't been wounded in China, Afghanistan and Libya. But there's always time."

"That's Nerina, a good looker and a good reporter. Good appetite too," he winked. "She works for some nefarious Israeli organisation. We think it's Mossad News."

He motioned towards a hefty man engrossed in a copy of the New York Times. The man resembled a professor, with a goatee beard, rimmed glasses, a prominent pointed nose, and thick, bushy eyebrows.

"Bernie Johnson is perhaps one of the top writers, and his copy is great and right on the mark. But he's as tight as a duck's ass, and beware, when you open a bottle of wine, he's onto you quicker than a surface-to-air missile and much harder to dislodge."

"Georgie there is known as Bunty, apparently named after a character in British Folklore called Billy Bunter. He likes his grub. He's a freelance working for British radio and gets paid by the story. He makes one last longer and sounds more interesting than a series run of Dallas. Don't be fooled by his cherubic facial features and look of innocence. In the business, he's known as the butcher because he can cut up and serve a story in more ways than Jesus created portions with the five loaves and two fishes. He likes to get hammered and phone the world on the Beeb's expensive, sat phone. The other night we called the Brit fugitive Ronnie Biggs in Rio, Tony Benn, the left-wing Brit politician in Chesterfield, and Cindy Whiplash, who runs hookers and likes to 'punish' men in London. Apparently we booked her and some of her gals to come and stay at the Holiday Inn. It was all great fun but expensive. I think he pays for it himself and then claims huge amounts for a so-called shortage of water in the hotel."

"Those guys like to think of themselves as the rock stars of the media world." He gestured towards a group sitting by themselves at a round table. Leica and Canon cameras were spread across the table, resembling a display in a photographic sales exhibit. "They are like the hungry dogs of war, crazy but brave or as stupid as hell, depending on how you look at it. They do an assignment and then spend some time giving lectures about what they did and producing books. Watch this."

Brown shouted out, "Something's happening," in a loud voice. All the photographers were startled, hastily grabbed their cameras, and rushed for the door. Minutes later, they returned, realising it was a false alarm.

"See, fucking crazy," said Brown.

A statuesque woman passed by, a Leica camera hanging around her neck, her face adorned with a broad smile.

"Hi Chuck," she said in an almost childlike, little girl way. "How's it going?" and carried on walking without waiting to hear the answer."

"And that is Tanya Orloff, one of the good old US of A tribe, but don't be fooled by the girlie disposition and childlike voice. She may sound like sweet butter, but she wouldn't melt in the proverbial gob. She is a fundamentalist photographer. She's never without a camera, some say, not me though, because I want to die with my boots on, not my PJs, even in bed, and she is relentless, some say reckless, in pursuit of photographing this war. Her pictures are amazing, but she's nuttier than a bunch of squirrels who are up an oak tree."

He motioned toward a table across the room.

"That's Boris, an ex-officer in the Cavalry Regiment who's been to every conflict and siege since Troy. He's a freelance cameraman, a gun for hire. He's absolutely barking. He is either brave or insane, perhaps both, but he has captured amazing videos around the wars, especially in Afghanistan. I'm not sure how much longer he can last. That's his wife next to him. Brought her here for the weekend. Said they had to get away from the kids."

He made a screwed-up face.

"Bert over there has become known as the godfather of the hacks. He hasn't been a journo for long, was some sort of engineer, but attacked the UN and politicians like a torturer during the Spanish Inquisition. He's not scared of asking the difficult questions."

"Uli is a German TV correspondent." He pointed to a small, blonde-haired man with a pointy chin and large ears. "He's gay. He says he came to Bosnia because he could live as he is, not as they want him to be. Not sure what that means. That's Klaus, his cameraman, or woman if you like. They are like a married couple, always arguing. I reckon it will end in divorce. They have the only armoured car in Sarajevo. That means they can go across the lines in some degree of safety, including the Croatian-controlled areas where you can buy supplies. So if you want to go with them, then you need to be nice."

The rundown of the who's who, describing a mix of general riff-raff, eccentrics, and the intriguing, went on for nearly an hour. Brown was familiar with them all, able to decipher most of their motives. He knew what they were after and what they were willing to contribute to a story, though some were more takers than givers. Brown explained to Grant that some could craft a compelling nine-column spread on suffering based solely on a brief conversation with a colleague over dinner. Others rarely left the safety of the hotel, securing exclusives through room service, a fact Brown used to jest about, albeit not in a humorous manner. For some, merely arriving at a hotel in a war zone was sufficient to garner the recognition they craved so desperately. And this brought him to the last person on the list, the one Grant had already encountered.

"Ah yes, Amelia Degusta, or, as some of us say, Disgusting. She's a real piece of work. Her first story was about spending a week with a family living on the sniper front line. I know her snapper, Bobby. He said they, in fact, spent only an afternoon with the family because they had no running water or electricity. Amelia expects her comforts even in a war zone. But she got a huge centre page spread with a heart-wrenching account of how she suffered with them for seven days. Whisky Tango Foxtrot mate, she is a real Charlie Uniform November Tango."

"Charlie Uniform November Tango?" inquired Singleton.

"Cunt," explained Brown. "She will swallow you whole and spit you out both professionally and physically. She is so at one with the suffering of the people that she takes a UN flight every Friday to Italy for a long weekend in Rome. Yes, a piece of work. She did a first-person piece about being on the front line and then cradling a dying Bosnian soldier in her arms with striking blue eyes who looked up at her and said, 'You are so beautiful', and then died. That's the biggest pile of bullshit I've come across in any conflict I've covered. No one could find the name of the soldier or where the place was he died. She says it's secret because it's from where Bosnian Special Forces operate, and they don't want the place or names revealed."

"She did another about a baby being raped by Serbs, only no one can find a witness or a mother who says that. And this is a country where people open up to you about every conceivable horrific experience they have been subjected to.

They positively invite you into their suffering so you can tell the world. But in war, you can say what the fuck you like about the 'bad guys' because there is no way in hell they are going to the High Court in London or wherever to sue her or any journalist for libel or slander. Wars are a journalistic story-protected environment, and you have a licence to lie. No Dictator or potential war criminal is gonna pursue you."

He swallowed another hefty gulp from the bottle positioned before him, his throat tightening as the liquid burned its way down.

"Nectar," he said. "Fucking nectar."

"I hear she's up for a few awards," he continued, with a look of disgust on his face.

It was a passionate outburst that resonated deeply with any sincere journalist, particularly Grant.

A wide man with a beard and protruding belly walked past. "Not giving the Pro Muslim Propaganda speech, are you?" asked the man. "Remember, there are two sides to every story. The objective of journalism, my friend, is to be objective, not subjective," he said.

"Ah, Stavros, my old Greek mucker," said Brown. "You Orthodox fuckers like to stick together, don't you? What do the Serbs call it? Ah yes, Moi Brat, my brother. Well, if my brother did the things that YOUR brother is doing, then I would shoot the fucker."

Brown was known for his straightforwardness; he never minced words. Once he set his sights on a target, his relentless approach resembled a missile strike. Stavros, a Greek national, was a notable figure in this scenario. It's worth noting that the Serbs received their only major international support, whether official or unofficial, from Russia, Greece, and Greek Cyprus.

"Man, don't give me that shit about victims everywhere and also on the Serb side. They started this mother fucking war. They are not victims. I KNOW about fucking victims. I am half catholic and half Jewish, and you can't get a bigger victim than that. It's almost a fucking profession. And the Serbs are as far away from victimhood as my pecker is from Sharon Stones knickers. But no matter, this noble profession is democratic and balanced unless you live in Serbia, where it's fucking propaganda. But don't you worry about it? You go and get on with your 'objective' support of your highly dysfunctional functional brothers. I hope you have a nice day, but beware of one of those brotherly mortar shells. They can't tell a brother from a stranger."

Stavros mumbled something and walked on.

"What a fucking A-hole," declared brown. "In his eyes, Goebbels was a journalist."

A loud shout went out across the dining room. "Hey, poosies, what zer fook."

It was Spit the Frog, Pascal Bourdain. "I sought you were lost in zer Bermuda triangle."

"We were convinced you were, mate, but anyhow, you owe us $200."

"I have a little admission for you," said Spit, rolling up his arm. "I have a little less immortality now," he explained and threw $200 on the table. "I have to be honest; I never made it to Karaama. We got to a checkpoint where my technical belonged to a different clan, and the other clan decided that zey were not going to 'av it and opened up. The machine gunner was killed, and I got hit by a small piece of shrapnel. We were fooking lucky my friend to get away. But now we are 'ere and safe," he smiled that big crazy French smile. If ever there was a face that said 'insane', it was this one thought Grant.

With Spit present, the dynamics of the Press corps in the Bosnian war zone seemed to be complete, it was now a full deck of cards.

Singleton found solace among a diverse group of journeymen and women, feeling oddly at ease in their company. Describing his personal life as dysfunctional would be an understatement. If anything about his life said stable it would have a couple of horses in it. Relationship after relationship faltered; some partners lacked the understanding to cope with his emotional burden, while others were too intelligent to endure the constant aftermath of the tragedies he covered. He couldn't blame them? He accepted that when the pavement is littered with dog poo, most people choose to cross the street to avoid it.

So Grant found solace in places devoid of pavements, often colloquially labelled as 'shitholes" within his industry. These locales typically lacked proper infrastructure and functional governance. The more perilous and disorderly the environment, the more it diverts his attention from his own dysfunction. His father, a former army officer, harboured mixed sentiments toward his son's experiences, simultaneously impressed by Grant's exposure to more battlefronts than he had encountered yet concerned about his rebellious disregard for authority and the legacy of the British Empire. For Grant's father, the 1950s atlases adorned with swathes of pink denoting territories under British rule symbolised pride and imperial legacy. However, to Grant, these maps served as a constant reminder of shame and the inequities perpetuated by colonialism.

Upon his arrival in Sarajevo, everything seemed to align perfectly for him, satisfying all his expectations. All the boxes were ticked as far as he was concerned. He couldn't deny the allure of the local women, whom he found particularly captivating. He had encountered similar beauty during his time in Somalia, where he believed he had seen some of the most stunning women in

Africa, alongside those in Ethiopia. However, unlike the distant and inaccessible beauties of Somalia, the women of the former Yugoslavia seemed within reach. As if guided by fate, his gaze instinctively drifted towards the grand double doors of the restaurant. As one side swung open, Grant was met with a sight that could only be described as a vision, Selma.

She entered the dining room and approached Grant, her attire consisting of tight jeans paired with a figure-hugging top adorned with a prominent belt. Emblazoned on the belt buckle were the iconic letters "AC/DC," representing one of his favourite bands. As Grant observed her, he began to realise that Bosnian Muslims embodied a unique expression of Islam, distinct from the more familiar traditions of the Gulf States. Their interpretation of the faith seemed to eschew the rigid confines of centuries-old rules, presenting a refreshing and modern approach to Islam, unencumbered by historical constraints.

Selma gracefully settled into the seat beside Grant, her cascading locks and piercing blue eyes captivating almost anyone who beheld them. She noticed the fixed gaze he directed her way, a reaction she had grown used to. Selma, accustomed to attention, was well acquainted with the procession of admirers who sought her favour.

"I want to discuss tomorrow's coverage with you." It broke the spell, and Grant came back to earth."

"Ah, yes," he said in an almost embarrassed tone. "What's on?"

Before she could answer, she found herself drawn to gaze over his shoulder. At the far end of the room, a burly figure sporting a beard and clad in army fatigues stood, his intense gaze sweeping the crowd, as if on a quest to find a particular individual. Selma's eyes met his, a moment of silent recognition passing between them.

"It's my brother, I won't be a minute." She got up and went over to him. After a few seconds, she buried her face in her hands, a gesture of evident distress. Grant observed her turmoil, the furrow of her brow, and the tension in her shoulders. The imposing figure beside her moved to offer solace, but she abruptly withdrew, breaking free from his grasp, and fled the confines of the dining room.

Grant promptly approached the large man.

"What's wrong with Selma?" he asked.

The man introduced himself as Hassan, Selma's older brother. He was previously an engineer, but the war transformed him into a fighter. He was a member of a special unit known as The Black Swans. The transition marked a profound shift from his previous occupation, where he sought to build but now he aimed to destroy and kill.

"You must be Grant," stated the big man, "Selma, I understand, is working with you. I am Selma's brother Hassan. I'm afraid there have been some developments, family developments," he explained.

"Is there anything I can do?" asked Grant.

"No, thank you. We have had some bad news. The bad news is constantly with us, with all of us. We enjoyed too good a life before. The older generation says now that we never appreciated it, and so we are paying for that lack of respect. It's funny, but we watched other conflicts from a distance and always said 'poor people'. Now we are the poor people, and those in other countries are looking at their TVs and seeing us in the same way. Poor people."

Grant extended a glass of Stock brandy to him.

"I hope you are looking after my little sister," he continued. "Not that she needs to be looked after. Selma is tougher than everyone in the family, but maybe you will need help," he smiled. It seemed a forced smile, one to disguise what he was really feeling.

It stopped as quickly as it arrived. "We just heard that our brother, Selma's twin, has been taken to a Serb internment camp, and our close cousin is missing. She is thought to be dead. Our father is living in a place which is under siege. A situation much worse than what Sarajevo is going through. At least we have some supplies. There, they have little."

"I'm not sure if you know, but our mother was killed at the beginning of the war, and since then, we haven't been able to get back to our town because it is cut off. It's in the East, close to the Drina River and Serbia. Not even the UN has been able to get in. So, no one knows exactly what is happening. I should alert you to the fact Selma has not grieved. She can be abrupt, she speaks her mind. But maybe, because of our losses, she might be even more unpredictable. I hope you will understand this and consider it when dealing with her."

He continued, "Well, enough of our problems. I would like to thank you and all the other journalists for coming here to talk about our situation. It means so much."

"You don't need to thank me. It's important to be here to bear witness to what is being done and to remind people that this is a country in Europe. I can't force people to take action, but you know something, they will never be allowed to hide away from the leaders and politicians and say they don't know what is going on. It's being reported in all its blood and gore. I just wish it wasn't always a constant outpouring of bad news."

"Maybe there will be better news tomorrow and a big story for you," he said, downing the last part of the brandy without revealing what the big story was.

"It's what you call secret squirrel stuff, is that correct?" Hassan said.

Grant smiled and nodded.

"Well, I hope the squirrel gets the nuts," Grant said.

9

At the crack of dawn, two enormous explosions rocked the Holiday Inn. The sizable window in Grant's room trembled violently, yet miraculously remained intact, thanks to the tape forming a giant X across it. "That marks the spot," Grant muttered to himself. Grant had strategically placed his mattress on the floor, as distant from the exterior wall as possible. He was well aware of the peculiar and lethal room service by the Serbs: "Two shells and some 7.62mm, please," he sarcastically imagined. Grant didn't fancy being next to a wall when a shell came through.

He swung the door open just in time to witness tracer rounds ricocheting around the atrium, reminiscent of a wayward firework on its last spark. Shouts echoed amidst billowing smoke, followed by an eerie silence that settled like a heavy fog. Without hesitation, he bolted down the stairs towards reception.

"Good morning, Mr Grant," said Hejo behind the front desk. "Another fine morning, the tanks are singing, the guns are chattering from behind the trees and buildings, the Serbs have been helping with our ventilation issues, but most importantly, no one was killed. Thanks to Allah and poor Serb marksmen, of course".

Hejo possessed a sense of humour that bordered on the macabre, reminiscent of the dark wit found in Monty Python, the renowned British comedy troupe, and the beloved Only Fools and Horses series, both of which resonated deeply with him and many fellow former Yugoslavs, including Serbs. Among Muslims like

Hejo, recalling episodes from these shows often seemed easier than reciting verses from the Quran. Despite the grim circumstances surrounding them, Hejo remained an eternal optimist, capable of finding a silver lining even in death itself. His outlook sharply contrasted with that of Ron O'Sullivan, whose panicked shouts about inevitable fatalities echoed through the war-torn streets. Grant couldn't help but acknowledge the grim reality of their situation in a war zone, death was an ever-present spectre.

"Ah, poor Mr Ron," continued Hejo, "He gets so upset and misses all the positives. Some things in this war have actually improved, you know. Not many people report that."

"Like what?" inquired Grant.

"Well, there is no longer unemployment, we don't pay tax, everyone gets free food hand-outs when there is some, and there is a greater sense of community with many more gatherings. OK, they are mostly at graveyards, but afterwards, the wakes are a chance to get together and discuss matters of the day. And there is a growing feeling that maybe alcohol should have had a better understanding in the Koran."

"What was the difference between Auschwitz and Sarajevo?" he asked. "There was gas in Auschwitz." It confirmed to Grant that the humour was blacker than black.

With that, he excused himself with, "I must go now, Mr Grant, as you can see, we have some clearing up to do."

10

Moving the wardrobe proved to be a strenuous task, but he understood that if it posed a challenge for him, it would likely present a challenge for others as well.

This was precisely his intention. The wardrobe itself was a sturdy relic from the turn of the century, a testament to Austrian craftsmanship designed to withstand the test of time, hailing from an era marked by the decline of empires. Against the wall, obscured by the bulk of the wardrobe, hung a large poster, its dimensions rivalling those of a human. Dominating the poster were the five Olympic rings, vibrant in their varied hues, set against a backdrop of snow-capped mountains. Emblazoned across the scene was the year 1984, a significant milestone marking the Winter Olympics hosted by Sarajevo.

With meticulous care, he peeled the material off the wall, revealing a weathered wooden hatch door beneath. His hands, though slender and delicate, bore the marks of someone unaccustomed to manual labour, shielded from the rigours of physical toil. Opening the hatch, he reached into its depths, retrieving a compact radio transmitter and a small, weathered book. Placing them gently on the bed, he regarded the book with a sense of guarded reverence. It was a code book meticulously tailored for his use, its contents known only to him and a single confidant, the solitary connection to his clandestine existence.

He swiftly thumbed through the pages, deftly jotting down symbols and keywords as he progressed. The task consumed a mere ten minutes, a testament to his adeptness. Speed was imperative, a necessary trait in his line of work. Caution, too, was paramount. However, even with the utmost care, the spectre of discovery lingered incessantly. History, particularly military history, had demonstrated that the risk of interception was most pronounced either during transmission or immediately afterwards, before the operator could conceal the apparatus. Over the years, detection mechanisms have evolved dramatically, becoming significantly more sophisticated and efficient.

In Sarajevo, the day unfolded with an auspicious air. The availability of electricity eliminated the necessity of resorting to walkie-talkies, a risky endeavour that could potentially jeopardise operations. Despite the relatively disorganised state of the Muslim factions, employing such a communication device would only heighten the risk of detection.

The Muslims, he observed, were undergoing a transformation; they were gradually organising themselves. Gone were the days of disarray witnessed at the onset of the conflict. Instead, they were beginning to resemble a disciplined army, complete with a clear chain of command and soldiers who could follow and comprehend orders. The emergence of individuals capable of executing tasks efficiently signalled the development of a competent military infrastructure. Reflecting on the failure to capture Sarajevo in the early stages, he acknowledged it as a strategic misstep that could potentially harm the Serbs. Sarajevo had become a symbol of resistance and defiance, attracting the attention of the global media, whose narratives, he believed, were fabricated distortions aimed at depriving the Serbs of justice. Despite their falsehoods, these narratives posed a significant threat.

Serbs had long been recognised for their professionalism within the military sphere. A significant sixty percent of the officer class within the old JNA hailed from Serb origins. They held sway over the majority of military bases and armaments, maintaining strict adherence to proper uniform protocol and exemplifying the expected conduct of soldiers. On paper, it was evident that the Serbs possessed the necessary elements to emerge victorious. However, despite their strengths, they still found themselves in need of his expertise. Victory seemed assured for them, yet with his involvement, it promised to arrive even sooner.

He adjusted the dials, searching for the first of the four pre-arranged frequencies. The first one came through clearly.

"Munja tomorrow late, possibly 4," he said. He repeated, "Munja, tomorrow late 4." Munja was his codename. It meant Thunder, it was also code for strike. He was alerting the Serbs to the fact that there would be an attack against them somewhere around the city.

He articulated a series of terms that delineated the coordinates indicating the location of the impending attack and the numerical strength of the Bosnian force set to be involved.

In the former Yugoslavia, despite the shared language of Serbo-Croatian, distinct dialects emerged within each community, characterised by variations in vocabulary. Among these, "Munja" held universal significance, transcending linguistic boundaries. Its commonplace usage ensured that, if inadvertently overheard by a Muslim radio operator, it would likely not provoke suspicion. Unless actively seeking signs of espionage, such an individual would interpret "Munja" as a mere reference to weather conditions.

Despite potentially missing an opportunity to capture the Bosnian capital early on, the Serbs knew there would be other chances. That was precisely why Munja was positioned there, deeply embedded within the predominantly Muslim administration. His intelligence was invaluable. His presence was a brilliant move in counterintelligence, as he was a spy to surpass all others.

He was less than twenty kilometres, as the crow flies, from the location where his message was received.

"It's Munja, sir," announced the operator. He quickly transcribed the coded message. Upon completion, he sent a confirmation, and the connection was promptly terminated. The entire exchange had taken less than four minutes.

The officer took the message to his office and began decoding it. "Wow," he thought, "this is significant." He picked up the phone, "Condition red," he said, indicating imminent action. The rest couldn't be trusted to the telephone and certainly not to walk talkie. The officer ordered his driver. He had to get to headquarters. He knew they had only hours to prepare.

At the Bosnian Serb Army's district headquarters in Lukavica, General Moimocjelo Pasic and his staff awaited news. Referred to as 'Momo' by his men and the Serb population, who esteemed him as a national hero, the General epitomised old-school military leadership. Having served on the general staff of the former JNA, he was renowned for possessing one of the sharpest military minds. His ability to make swift decisions under pressure was unparalleled; he understood that success or defeat often hinged on split-second choices. Despite the intense pressure, General Pasic had yet to taste defeat; in fact, success seemed to be his constant companion.

He was short and stocky, with a demeanour reminiscent of a Welsh pit pony. Lacking the towering stature typically associated with Serbs, he compensated with other qualities. Among his men, he was adored. Possessing both the means and the weapons necessary to secure victory in this war, he found himself frequently hindered by politicians. In his eyes, politicians were a source of trouble; their actions often created problems that soldiers were left to resolve. Soldiers paid the ultimate price while politicians engaged in endless deliberation. They talked while their own children were sent abroad for education, leaving ordinary citizens to confront danger and make sacrifices. Consequently, he held little esteem for politicians.

During those initial chaotic days in Sarajevo, Momo had the opportunity to seize control of nearly the entire city. The Muslims, ill-equipped and disorganised, remained blissfully unaware of the unfolding events. However, Momo's advance was hindered by the decisions of politicians. The lingering question of 'why?' plagued him, yet he never received a satisfactory answer.

Momo desired to subdue Sarajevo forcefully, disregarding international opinion for the time being and being prepared to justify his actions for years to come. However, the stance of the major powers significantly influenced the Bosnian Serb leaders, leading to a temporary halt on the plan to 'pummel them'.

However, that didn't prevent them from shelling the city to maintain control. A combination of artillery and snipers strategically positioned in elevated areas maintained a firm grip on the city's perimeter. They effectively controlled all major road arteries leading into the city. This control was not incidental but the result of months of meticulous planning.

After Tito's passing, the Serbs perceived an opportunity to reclaim their former dominance and seize control once more. Their plan involved securing the majority of heavy weaponry, tanks, ammunition, and strategic positions, ensuring their position of power. Meanwhile, the Muslims, though numerous, lacked sufficient weaponry to match the Serbs' arsenal.

The situation should have led to an outright victory. However, for Momo, it felt akin to missing an open goal. Instead, they found themselves embroiled in an almost stalemate scenario. But why? His campaign had been flawless, with meticulous planning and excellent execution. This enabled the Serbs to seize nearly sixty-five per cent of the country within the initial weeks of fighting. Then came the order to halt. This directive weighed heavily on the General and his loyal staff. 'Bide your time,' he was instructed. As a devoted soldier and servant to the Serb nation, he complied, albeit continuing his efforts to crush the city and its stubborn resistance.

He famously ordered his men to 'shell them to the edge of madness,' yet despite their efforts, they failed. The resilience of the Bosnians in the city below not only remained steadfast but appeared to strengthen.

As the communications officer decoded Munja's message and relayed it to the General, Munja found himself seated in a coffee bar in Bascarsija, the historic heart of Sarajevo, where many buildings had stood since the fifteenth century. Here, they prepared Turkish coffee using the traditional method, reminiscent of the Ottoman occupation era, a detail that Munja appreciated. Despite any grievances he may have had with the Turks, Munja found solace in the enjoyment of a strong cup of coffee.

General Pasic addressed his staff. "Lightening says there will be a major strike tomorrow at this place," and he pointed to a place called Barice on the map.

"But that's sheer rock in places," responded one officer. "It would be nearly impossible to get through there."

"Which is why they have picked that spot," responded the General. "They know it is lightly guarded, and if they are successful, they would cut off our areas of Lukavica and Grbavica from Pale. It would cut supply routes. It would be a major victory for them. And it is not impossible. Munja says a newly formed unit called the Black Swans will carry out the mission. We know from the last few weeks that this group has been active and has inflicted some casualties and overrun some positions. We cannot dismiss them. They obviously know what they are doing, so we must be ready. Fog is forecast for tomorrow, and that will give them extra cover, plus they will open up with a barrage of artillery and mortars. So we will bring in two extra brigades under cover of darkness. Send a few in at a time, not large groups, so as not to arouse suspicion. I want mortar batteries to cover the east and west sides of the rock face: no smoking or loud talking, and no one fires until the order is given. We need to crush this operation and crush the Black Swans completely. And when their artillery and tanks are exposed, we will smash them. If they broke the siege, they could change the course of the war. That cannot be allowed to happen."

11

Hassan Mesic and his men assembled at the entrance of the tunnel the night before the attack. They were part of a 4,000-strong force divided into groups stationed at the inclines leading to Barice. The rock face was already covered in a moody cloak of fog, a fortunate circumstance, they thought. They had gradually advanced into position from the barns and houses where they had spent the night preparing, smoking Drina cigarettes, and drinking shots of slivavica, the potent plum brandy that was a staple in Bosnia. It was necessary; no man harboured any illusions. This was a perilous yet essential mission. For many, that shot of slivavica and the Drina cigarette could well be their last.

Thick clouds of cigarette smoke filled the air as men checked their weapons and oiled their AK47s. Few among them had been professional soldiers, most were civilians, accountants, lawyers, shopkeepers, and musicians. In the distance, the call to prayer echoed, prompting many, though not all, to kneel and pray. For many Bosnians, their religious practices had been lax until now. Traditionally, Bosnian Muslims enjoyed lively social gatherings and indulged in alcohol. However, faced with the threat of persecution for their faith, many saw fit to embrace their religious identity more fervently, realising that if they were to die for being Muslim, they might as well live as practising Muslims.

Hassan was among them. Despite his father Yousef's devout adherence to Islam, Hassan had never felt compelled to attend a mosque or participate in religious festivals, including Eid, the celebration marking the end of Ramadan. Yet now, circumstances had changed. It struck him as ironic how, in times of scarcity, people like himself were embracing fasting as a gesture of respect for a religion they had previously kept at arm's length. In Tito's communist Yugoslavia, any form of religious observance was frowned upon.

Silently, they all recited the words of the Salah prayer 'A'udhu billahi minash shaitanir rajim.' It means: "I seek shelter in Allah from the rejected Satan." Satan to them were the Serbs.

They wouldn't find much physical shelter in the place they were heading or for what they aimed to achieve. Each man understood the imminent dangers and perils looming ahead. Yet, they were resolute and committed. They saw no other choice. They recognised that success would mean breaking the months-long siege of Sarajevo, a goal worth striving for and worth sacrificing everything for. With no sophisticated radio communications or weapons, they had to rely on walkie-talkies and open channels. Their only hope lay in the element of surprise, hoping that by the time they were detected, it would be too late for the Serbs to react.

12

Twenty kilometres away, General Pasic was delivering his final instructions. Throughout the night, his battle-hardened Romanijan brigades had manoeuvred into strategic positions, establishing new mortar emplacements and ensuring that heavy artillery units stood at the ready further back. Tanks were positioned near the Jewish Cemetery, poised to flank the Black Swans from the rear and to engage any Bosnian armour that emerged once the coordinates were acquired.

The General was well aware of the Muslims' scarcity of artillery and tanks. For the impending attack to succeed, they would need to deploy all available resources, necessitating their emergence from the concealed tunnels and warrens where they typically remained hidden. Previous engagements had demonstrated their cautious use of these assets, with swift actions aimed at minimising exposure. They understood the risk of retaliation, as Serb tracking devices could swiftly pinpoint their positions, often resulting in disproportionate counterattacks.

"I don't want any tank, artillery gun or mortar to return fire for precisely 14 minutes when the Muslim attack begins," Pasic ordered. "We must give them a false sense of where we are and what we have. When the command is given, we will lay down a wall of fire through which no one can pass or escape. Gentlemen, to your positions."

The 10th floor of the Holiday Inn was a haunting sight. Rooms lay in blackened ruins, resembling destroyed shells. Elephant-sized holes marred the outer walls where tank shells had punched through. Towards the back, a wall, once part of a bathroom, was pockmarked with hundreds of bullet craters. Dust and debris covered the floors, and a mattress lay wedged against what used to be a window, its shattered glass strewn across the floor. With each step, the glass broke and cracked into smaller fragments. While noise wasn't a concern, the Serbs weren't close enough to hear; visibility was. Even without night vision equipment, they could be spotted easily, necessitating caution and avoiding an upright stance.

Above the sixth floor of the hotel, the devastation on the south, east, and west sides was extensive. With little to occupy their time, ascending to the tenth floor became a form of relaxation, a peculiar equivalent to a post-dinner stroll. While it might appear unusual to the average person, for hardened war enthusiasts, it served as the ideal way to unwind after another eventful day.

Armed with a bottle of slivavic, a stash of white powder, and several of Bosnia's finest joints, groups of journalists made their way to relax and observe the tracer fire ahead. It had become a nightly ritual. Grant, Mo, Chuck Brown, hacks from one of the agencies, the rotund figure from the Beeb, Spit the Frog, a couple of Austrians, a spirited Australian, and Tanya Orloff headed into what used to be room 1004.

As if on cue, the rapid rat a tat-tat of a machine gun erupted. They cautiously peered through the numerous holes in the front wall, catching sight of tracer fire slamming into the former Bosnian parliament building ahead. Situated squarely on the front line, it remained occupied by Bosnian fighters who drew heavy Serb fire. Tracer fire, characterised by bullets or cannon-calibre projectiles fitted with small pyrotechnic charges in their base, is intended for nighttime combat or low visibility scenarios, aiding shooters in gauging their proximity to a target. Yet, against the backdrop of a burning building at night, there was an eerie allure to them, a perverse beauty similar to a fragment of a fireworks display.

Suddenly, flames erupted from the parliament building, casting an ominous glow against the night sky.

"Wow, bonfire and fireworks, we've got everything, man," exclaimed Chuck. "They have well and truly murdered that building."

As they all imbibed a substantial amount and felt the warmth of alcohol, they found a sense of happiness, albeit within the constraints of a war zone. They raised their glasses to toast a few departed comrades, some of whom Grant had heard of before. With great enthusiasm, they knocked back the sliva, a drink known for its robustness rather than subtlety, a quality that seemed fitting for the Balkans and its inhabitants.

The first shot invariably stole your breath and tensed your throat muscles; the second felt like sandpaper scraping over your tonsils. But it was the third shot where everything clicked. Suddenly, it became smooth, nectar-like, sliding down your throat effortlessly, akin to rain cascading off a windowpane. By the seventh shot, you were typically disoriented, indifferent to your surroundings, and unfazed by your proximity to the war zone's front line. At this point, everyone seemed to adopt the Pascal Bourdain approach to war, spitting in the face of death because they felt immortal.

As Mo started his tape machine, the laid-back sounds of JJ Cale filled the room with 'Cocaine.' At that moment, the little Egyptian companion produced a bag of white powder.

"Courtesy of the Ukrainians," said Mo. "Where would peacekeeping be without them?" Grant produced a metal tray and laid out 10 lines of cocaine.

They each leaned down and took deep, heavy snorts. The sensation was almost otherworldly, a rush akin to a big chill, mental magic mushrooms, kaleidoscope visions, and songs that whispered of liberation. Eager to heighten this feeling, they ventured to what served as the bathroom, where they indulged in something from the Albanian escape 'armoury.' Chuck sat in the bath, lighting up, and took a deep inhale.

"Fuck man, that is good shit," he coughed and handed it around. Bosnia cultivated its own marijuana, primarily in Hercegovina, an area under Croatian control. However, the most readily available and lowest quality variety was Albanian weed, commonly known as Schwag. There was a consensus among locals that Albanians had a remarkable tolerance for inhaling almost anything, a sentiment shared by conflict journalists, who found themselves similarly unfazed by adverse conditions.

The scene unfolded with a familiar rhythm: smoke, drink, snort, and watch. The cycle repeated itself into the early hours, the activities merging into a blur of indulgence. Room 1004 emerged as their sanctuary, the one place where they could shed the weight of daily reality and surrender to hedonistic abandon. Yet, even within those walls, the grip of reality lingered, an ever-present spectre. Humour became their coping mechanism, a shield against the harshness of their experiences. They bantered freely, trading anecdotes of the most appalling moments they had witnessed, treating them with a casual irreverence as if they were seated in the audience of a comedy show at the Hammersmith Odeon, finding solace in shared laughter amidst the chaos.

They exchanged tales of horror and hardship, recounting near-death experiences as if they were commonplace occurrences. Each story served as a card in a peculiar poker game, where the stakes and narratives escalated with each round. While some accounts might have been exaggerated for dramatic effect, most held a kernel of truth or were based on genuine experiences.

Grant recounted his headless in Kabul story, eliciting uproarious laughter, a tale too gruesome for any other setting or with any 'normal' company. Yet among these like-minded individuals, journalists willing to risk their lives to convey stories the world needed to hear felt appropriate. It was one of the few places where troubled souls could temporarily unburden themselves.

Tanya had undoubtedly witnessed humanity's darkest deeds. She narrated her experiences with a childlike innocence, yet her matter-of-fact delivery left many unsettled, even those who were intoxicated or euphoric. Amidst this eclectic gathering, Tanya stood out as peculiar, navigating the peripheries of normality with an unpredictable rhythm.

The Tenth Floor psychotherapy sessions were incomparable. They offered peace, respite, drugs, booze, escape, and the distant sound of tracer fire. For a war junkie, that night was as good as it gets.

At 6:30 a.m., a green-painted, eight-meter-long barrel of a Yugoslav-made 155mm artillery gun emerged from the Draga tunnel north of Sarajevo. Ten young fighters, devoid of any vehicular assistance to prevent Serb detection, pushed it into position. Upon receiving coordinates from the officer, a young fighter peered through the aiming circle, adjusting the dial until the barrels lifted into position.

"Ready," he shouted.

In the silence of the Holiday Inn Grant found himself in bed with Tanya, though he was unsure of how they got there. As they undressed, he noticed her Leica still hanging around her neck, prompting memories of Chuck Brown's introduction. Amidst the sporadic sound of the mad machine gunner, there were no explosions, no familiar cacophony of everyday life in Bosnia. It was an eerie quietude, though Grant soon realised that in Bosnia, silence seldom persisted for long.

At the sound of the first tank shell, he jolted upright in bed, immediately followed by a cacophony of shouting and screeching.

He hurried to the door, flung it open, and was greeted by a barrage of tracer rounds ricocheting around the atrium. Tanya had vanished. Like a greyhound released from a trap, she was in the lobby, half-dressed, snapping at anything that moved or didn't. Then came the deafening roar of another tank round, striking an upper floor. Dust filled the air, and panic ensued below. The gunfire escalated, round after round echoing through the chaos.

A journalist's car became a target for a sniper's bullet as it accelerated up the ramp from the underground car park. Tom, a British photographer determined to capture the unfolding events, sought refuge but stumbled over a low wall, injuring his arm. Amidst the chaos of gunfire, he courageously crawled back to the safety of the hotel.

Grant wasn't entirely sure of the significance behind the intense firing, but he sensed it signified something major, perhaps even monumental. For nearly an hour the sound of the ferocious barrage racked the city. And then quiet.

Less than three kilometres away, Hassan Mesic surveyed the remnants of his unit. The Black Swans had nearly been decimated as they ascended Barice. Despite their efforts, they were met with a relentless barrage of bullets, mortar shells, and artillery fire. With the fog lifting, their lack of cover became painfully apparent. Some soldiers pressed forward in a desperate bid to reach the summit, but the onslaught from both the East and West positions cut them down mercilessly. Hassan, leading the second wave, witnessed half of his men fall to the enemy's fire. Only one managed to reach the top, only to be torn apart by heavy machine gun fire from the tree line. Realising the futility of their situation, Hassan signalled for a retreat, rallying what remained of his men. Among them, he spotted a young fighter with a severe bullet wound to the stomach. Aware of the grim prognosis for such injuries, Hassan wasted no time. He administered a battlefront dressing, securing it tightly around the man's body before hoisting him onto his shoulder in a fireman's lift. Amidst the ongoing barrage of enemy fire, Hassan navigated the treacherous terrain, determined to bring his wounded comrade to safety.

When the firing subsided, and the explosions ceased the painful evidence of their failed mission was evident. It had been an unparalleled disaster. The Remains of the Black Swans regrouped in the same barn where they had sought refuge, where their prayers had once sought shelter from Satan. However, on this day, Satan remained undeterred by prayers or the presence of the Black Swans.

"How could it happen?" Hassan thought to himself. Fog, darkness, surprise, silence, and stealth, all the elements that should have ensured the mission's success, or at the very least, a better outcome than what transpired.

"It was as if they knew," he continued the thought process. "But that was impossible. That would have meant someone would have told them, someone who knew the plans."

Hassan found the prospect incredulous. Indeed, there were Serbs who remained on the Bosnian side, individuals of integrity who had not succumbed to the Serb propaganda advocating for their supposed right to reclaim what they believed was taken from them by the Turks. Yet Hassan was aware that, despite their loyalty, they were under constant scrutiny. Not everyone trusted them. It hinted that someone of considerable authority within their ranks might be acting as a spy. The operation's details were known to only a select few. Alternatively, the substantial Serb presence could be attributed to mere coincidence.

The morning exacted a heavy toll, not only in lives but also in equipment. As they revealed the tanks and artillery, they fell prey to ehe Serbs' advanced weapons tracking systems. Two 155mm artillery pieces, one 105mm howitzer, and two tanks were destroyed. The human toll was grave: two hundred and fifty-nine men lost their lives, and over five hundred were wounded. It marked the deadliest day for the Bosnian forces, dealing a significant blow to their capability, morale, and efforts to break the siege of the city.

"But who?" thought Hassan. "Who gave us away?"

13

They were arranged like corpses awaiting burial, packed so tightly that manoeuvring was a challenge. Once a cattle shed, the space had been repurposed into a makeshift prison, still permeated by the lingering scent of its former inhabitants. The detainees, predominantly Muslim with a sprinkling of Croats, had been rounded up in the tumultuous early days of the war's outbreak. Their homes, distinguished by a damning red X encased in a circle, had been methodically marked before being consumed by flames.

Mehmet gazed up at the corrugated roof of the shed, noticing the few holes that allowed the early morning sun's rays to filter through, as well as the rain on darker days. Lost in deep thought, he found little else to do to occupy his time. The days stretched long, hope was waning, and conditions were growing increasingly bleak. It felt like a surreal world, flipped upside down almost overnight since his time at the Belgrade Institute of Technology, when the once-dismissed predictions of conflict had suddenly become reality. That was the day he came to terms with his identity as a Muslim and watched as his Serb friends and fellow students abandoned him. Taken away abruptly as he sat alone, eating lunch in the cavernous auditorium that doubled as a dining area, he was met with deafening silence, no defence, no protest, only silent compliance.'

It took a few minutes before the shock wore off, but Mehmet reassured himself that the worst-case scenario would likely entail being sent back to his hometown.

'We are all educated people' he thought to himself. Surely common sense would prevail.

There was no sense of logic, only madness. Instead of returning to his hometown and family, he found himself sent to Gornji Polje, a nondescript village nestled within the heart of Bosnian Serb-held territory in the North. It was a place entirely unfamiliar to him, but one that would etch itself permanently into his memory.

'Camp' was a term laden with false grandeur. This was nothing more than a prison, plain and simple. However, Mehmet swiftly realised that it served as a breeding ground for revenge, a reservoir for all the injustices Serbs believed had been inflicted upon them. From the oppression under Ottoman rule to the atrocities committed by the Nazi-backed Croatian Ustasha and Muslim Brigade, to the grievances stemming from the Austro-Hungarian occupation, and the perceived betrayal by their European allies during the Second World War when they resisted the Germans. It seemed as though every Serb carried within them a memory button, summoning forth the horrors they had endured. With each retelling, the stories grew more harrowing. Accounts surfaced of Serb infants impaled by Muslim Nazi brigades during the Second World War, of famine and death during the First World War, and, of course, of Jesenovac, the concentration camp of the 1940s, a place little known beyond the former Yugoslavia and scarcely acknowledged by the majority of non-Serbs. Yet, for Serbs, it stood as one of the foremost symbols of their anguish. Though estimates may vary, it remains an undeniable fact that hundreds of thousands of Serbs, including both combatants and civilians, met their demise in Jesenovac, alongside Jews and Roma. This, at least, was indisputable.

Under Tito's rule after the war, Jesenovac vanished without a trace. The camp was obliterated, fields were ploughed over, and all memory was erased so effectively that subsequent generations remained oblivious to its existence. History books have omitted the horrors and sacrifices endured by Serbs. However, for the Serbs themselves, these memories persisted across generations like haunting heirlooms. To them, it felt as though the events had occurred just yesterday. These traumas were deeply woven into their cultural fabric, reflected in folklore, music, and symbols such as the Gusle instrument and the flag bearing the four C's, alongside the revered but tragic Battle of Kosovo. The past remained disconcertingly present.

In Gornji Polje, Mehmet swiftly grasped that survival knew no rules. Dignity lost equates to losing everything. The guards were keenly aware of this fact. Their methods were often brutal and dehumanising, meticulously crafted to eradicate any traces of civilised existence and to satisfy their own twisted pleasures. Mehmet had become desensitised to the horrors around him. His only prayer was that he wouldn't become their next victim.

Muslims were subjected to beatings and often compelled to assault their compatriots, neighbours, friends, and even family members. Some were coerced into acts of sexual violence, forced into buggery, or forced to rape Muslim women brought in from neighbouring buildings. Remarkably, their immune systems adapted swiftly to the harsh conditions. Rations were meagre and barely edible. Like many others, he shed kilo after kilo, wasting away day by day, resembling survivors of Auschwitz. Some succumbed to madness, seeking refuge in a parallel reality to escape the horrors of their existence.

Mehmet struggled to maintain focus and mental acuity amid the harsh conditions. Despite the near-starvation diet, he persisted in some form of exercise to keep fit. Above all, he battled to contain the anger and hatred festering towards his captors. Like others, he remained stoic, showing no sympathy when one of their own was dragged off for so-called 'interrogation,' which often amounted to torture or severe beatings. Survival meant distancing oneself from such a fate.

Mehmet was no fighter; he was a student. Having never undergone national service in the JNA, he found himself bewildered by the interrogators' relentless inquiries about arms and the number of fighters in his town, questions to which he had no answers. The initial blows from the baseball bat stung, but soon a strange numbness took over, inexplicably dulling the pain.

In the end, like many others, he fabricated numbers and divulged the names of acquaintances to meet the demand for information. Among the prisoners, faces once familiar became unrecognisable as they identified former neighbours, former teammates from football or handball games, individuals once part of their close-knit village communities, and those they once considered friends and colleagues. NOT ANYMORE.

Mehmet's mind drifted back to his village, reminiscing about the simple joys of life they once cherished, when an intrusive voice shattered his reverie.

"Hello, Mehmet," said the voice.

Mehmet glanced up, only to find the imposing figure of Darko Zubic looming over him.

"Good to see you, my friend."

Mehmet was certain: Darko was never a friend, even before the conflict, and certainly not now. His tone carried a mocking edge, tinged with an unmistakable menace.

Both hailing from Donji Zelenik, their fathers shared a close friendship, yet Mehmet perceived Darko as somewhat peculiar, lacking in intelligence, and inclined towards bullying behaviour. At one point, Darko had developed an unsettling fixation on Mehmet's sister, Selma. He would trail her from school and often linger outside the house staring at her bedroom window, leaving her feeling unnerved. Despite Darko's attempts, Selma never reciprocated his feelings. She said she sensed an air of darkness about him.

"How's it going?" Darko continued. "Enjoying your little stay?" Mehmet had never seen anything evil outside of a Hollywood horror movie, but he thought Darko was close to it.

"Not so cocky now are we?" he said. "Not so full of yourself and your stuck-up family's grandiose belief in your self-importance and superiority. So what, I didn't go to college, so what if I didn't have one of those highly paid jobs that all of you Mesics seem to think you'll have? But no chance of that now, eh? And where is that prick tease of a sister of yours, fucking someone with money and power? You Muslims make me sick. You have spent centuries taking from us Serbs. But not anymore, my friend. Those days are well and truly over."

Mehmet remained silent, recognising the futility of speaking up. In this new order, Darko held the reins of power, free to act as he pleased. In war, there were no rules, only the harsh realities of death, suffering, and inhumanity.

Darko spat at Mehmet. "You will never look down on me again," he said with disdain and started to walk off. "Oh, I forgot, I have a little surprise for you later this evening. A little reunion of sorts."

Mehmet knew that whatever it was, it couldn't be good. Yet he had grown accustomed to the notion that nothing could shock, phase, or scare him anymore. Or so he hoped.

As another prisoner was forcibly removed from the premises, Mehmet observed the subdued reactions of his fellow inmates. Reflecting on their dismal living conditions, he couldn't help but compare their situation to that of the barn's former occupants, the cows. The filth and squalor within the barn were beyond deplorable. Three buckets, relegated to the corner, served as makeshift toilets for nearly a hundred men. The stench, exacerbated by rising temperatures, pervaded every corner of the barn, rendering it almost uninhabitable. Due to his status as a student, the guards singled out Mehmet, dismissing him as an 'uppity intellectual' and assigning him the unpleasant task of cleaning the putrid buckets each morning. The nauseating odour threatened to overwhelm him every time he emptied the buckets. Occasionally, the guards would trip the designated toilet monitor as he transported the waste to the disposal trench, or even force a prisoner to retrieve excrement by hand. It was abundantly clear that the guards wielded unchecked power, revelling in their ability to subject their captives to the most degrading and humiliating treatment imaginable.

In an effort to preserve whatever shreds of dignity remained, many prisoners resorted to prayer. However, openly expressing their faith was not an option, as it would inevitably result in harsh punishment from the guards. Instead, they turned inward, silently reciting prayers to themselves. While not everyone was familiar with Islamic prayers, a few of the elder inmates who were devout shared their knowledge. As they passed one another, each man would quietly mouth the words 'Allah Immanet,' a phrase that once held significance mainly for older, traditional Muslims before the onset of the war. Remarkably, it had now evolved into a symbol of solace and unity even among the younger generation of Muslims in the dire circumstances they faced.

Mehmet was taken aback that evening. Inside the room stood a few guards, including Darko, and a woman with her back to him. As she turned around, Mehmet recognised her immediately; it was Hasina, his cousin. Her appearance shocked him; her eyes were red with heavy bags underneath, and her face looked swollen. She seemed thinner than when he had last seen her over a year ago, during a coffee meeting in Donji Zelenik. Despite her changed appearance,

Hasina remained the smart and beautiful cousin he remembered. She was also a talented singer, having performed with renowned Yugoslav musicians and bands like Johnny Stulic and Red Apple.

The guards indulged in swigs from plastic bottles filled with Loza, a potent clear alcohol derived from fermented fresh grapes. As they imbibed, their demeanour grew increasingly boisterous, signalling their progression towards inebriation.

"Hasina has kindly agreed to sing for us," said Darko.

It was obvious to Mehmet that she had been left with no choice. Her appearance was a stark reflection of her inner turmoil, dishevelled and broken, devoid of the vibrant spirit that once illuminated her surroundings with her captivating voice. Sitting beside her was one of the Serb guards, cradling a gusle between his legs, a one-stringed instrument steeped in the traditions of Serbian tales and folk songs. As he plucked a few notes, the sound emitted resembled a mixture of whines and groans. The origins of the gusle have been subject to debate, with differing opinions prevailing. Some contend that it was introduced to the Balkans by Slavic migrants from beyond the Urals as early as the seventh century. Others argue for an oriental origin, suggesting that it arrived in Europe around the tenth century. Regardless of its precise origins, the gusle held profound symbolism for the Serbs, alongside other cultural icons such as Greater Serbia and the flag adorned with the four C's. It stood as a testament to Serb nationhood, deeply ingrained in their cultural identity.

To Mehmet, the sound resembled more the desperate cry of a dying animal than the melodic resonance of a musical instrument.

Hasina began to sing. The melody was chosen for her; it was a traditional Serb song cherished by Serb nationalists, a poignant reminder of the country's history.

Known as "The Downfall of the Kingdom of Serbia," it was crafted to honour the memory of Prince Lazar's defeat by the Ottoman Turks at the Battle of Kosovo in 1389. As Hasina's voice filled the room, its timbre was imbued with melancholy, lacking the vigour and expansiveness that Mehmet fondly remembered and that had endeared her to many.

"Louder," shouted Darko. "Sing with passion, Serbian passion, even though you are not Serbian. You are a whore."

Darko had always been a bully, Mehmet remembered, but he was also a coward, targeting only those who couldn't defend themselves. Here, he thrived, exerting control over those who were powerless. Mehmet felt a surge of disgust as he observed the big Serb's treatment of his cousin and his utter disregard for basic human decency. The situation was incomprehensible, the suffering inflicted upon Hasina, upon Mehmet himself, and upon the Muslim and Croat communities by those they once lived alongside. As Mehmet reflected on his father's admiration for Tito and his vision for unity, he now understood its significance and the role the Dictator played. Tito had prevented this kind of malevolence. Mehmet realised that this evil had lurked beneath the surface, dormant but ever-present, like a dormant volcano now erupting.

He struggled to contain the surge of anger within him. The desire to lash out, to engage in combat, even to kill, coursed through his thoughts. It was a concept that the former pragmatist and advocate for peace had never entertained before. Yet, the old Mehmet seemed to be fading away. In its place, a newfound sense of conviction and inner strength began to emerge. He believed he would endure this ordeal, and when it was over, there would be no more peaceful Mehmet.

Hasina finished the song and the Serbs clapped.

"It's a final show for Hasina. She leaves us tomorrow for more upmarket accommodation, Sonja's," announced Darko.

Mehmet remained in the dark regarding what Sonja's was or stood for, but Hasina knew. She had gleaned details while eavesdropping on guards discussing it during the moments they escorted women away. Hassina was destined for a place known as "The Orchard," a sweet name for a grim establishment. To normal people it was a brothel where young Muslim women and girls were forced to provide sexual services to Serb soldiers. It was not voluntary. Hasina was sombre about her fate, and unable to change its course.

"And now table service," said Darko. Hasina knew what that meant. The two burly Serbs forcefully grabbed the young woman and shoved her onto the table, callously tearing off her underwear. Darko, as the leader, wasted no time and was the first to assault the helpless victim. In a desperate attempt to intervene, Mehmet lunged forward to grab Darko, but two others intercepted him, throwing him to the ground. They proceeded to deliver vicious kicks to his stomach and ribs, causing Mehmet excruciating pain. The onslaught continued for several agonising minutes, leaving Mehmet on the verge of losing consciousness. Eventually, he was pulled to his feet and held upright, unable to escape the brutality unfolding before him.

"Make him watch," said Darko. "Make him see what we use Muslim whores for."

Hasina's face remained impassive, devoid of any emotion, no expression, no tears, and no sign of life. It wasn't the first time she had been subjected to such brutality, and she feared it wouldn't be the last, especially not at Sonja's. But for Hasina, enduring such horrors meant survival. That was what mattered most, or so she tried to convince herself.

Darko finished. Wiped himself on Hasina's clothing, and then, in turn, the other three guards raped her. When they had their way, Darko looked at Mehmet and asked, "Do you love your cousin, Mehmet?"

"Of course I do," he replied, still in obvious pain from the kicking.

"Good. It's your turn. Show your cousin how much you love her."

"I can't do that," said Mehmet. "Please don't make me do that. Have some compassion. What did we ever do to you? Why do you hate us so much? We lived together in peace."

"It was not a just peace," snarled Darko. "That bastard Tito took our lives and nationhood away from us, and you Muslims started the destruction of everything we hold dear. No, it was NEVER a good peace for us, only you and those fucking Ustasha Croats. Now, things are different. We are taking back what is rightfully ours."

He took a 9mm pistol from his holster and put it to Hasina's head, "Now fuck her or I will shoot her."

An ominous expression darkened the Serb's face, prompting Mehmet to recognise the danger. Though the notion was repugnant, the word 'survival' echoed insistently in his mind. Survival. We have to get through this he reminded himself, determined to endure. He lay on top of her. She squeezed his hand and whispered into his ear, "Allah Immanet." A tear trickled down his cheek. He understood that they would endure for the time being, but he realised that life would never be as it once was and that he and everyone else would be forever changed by their experiences.

14

Grant banged on the door hard. "Mo, wake up," he shouted. After a couple of minutes, a haggard-looking cameraman opened the door and stifled a yawn.

"What the fuck, man? It's motherfucking 6:00 a.m. We didn't finish the edit until 1 a.m. What's going on, are the Serbs invading the hotel?"

"Mate, it's foggy," said Grant.

"Thanks for the weather report, but I'm going back to bed," and he turned to go.

"It's fucking foggy, and that means we can finish Malek's story, comprendo hombre?"

He replied, "Oh, OK, why didn't you say?"

Grant entered the room to retrieve the tripod, only to discover a tangle of red hair on the bed, belonging to a naked Amelia Degusta. She lay face down, deeply asleep, with her large, pale backside partially exposed from beneath the covers.

The look Grant gave was pure disgust. "Man, how could you?" he asked.

Mo, putting on his trousers, looked up and said in mitigation, "It's war, man, it's fucking war."

They rendezvoused in the underground car park, where Grant was already behind the wheel of the small Ford, engine running. Mo climbed in, placed Buzz Lightyear on top of the dashboard, and settled into the passenger seat's well, with the camera aimed up at his correspondent.

There was a knock on the window. Grant looked out. It was Igor, the ten-year-old garage dweller. He held out his hand. "Chocolada?" he asked. "Malo chocolada, molim?" (a little chocolate, please?)

"Sorry," Grant replied; "we have none. One day, I promise," he was genuinely sorry. He wished he had some. But chocolate was not a priority in a time of survival.

Igor's disappointment was evident, etched onto his face. In a place where even basic food was scarce, the prospect of obtaining a bar of chocolate seemed nearly impossible. After bidding farewell, The journalist shifted his focus. Departing from the Holiday Inn underground garage always evoked an adrenaline rush. The entrance, situated at the top of the spiralling ramp leading to the garage, was clearly visible to the Serb snipers, positioned less than 150 metres away in a direct line. Given that a Kalashnikov rifle was accurate up to three hundred metres, the proximity was unnerving.

"OK Habibi, I am ready, to infinity and beyond motherfucker," said Mo and began filming. He consistently filmed Grant while driving in precarious situations, anticipating the moment when fate intervened and decided that Grant's time behind the wheel should come to an end, a message ultimately delivered by a sharpshooter from Serbia.

Grant pressed down on the accelerator, coaxing as much power as he could from the 1.4-litre engine. With a sudden surge, the vehicle lurched forward, ascending the spiralling exit ramp. In the dense fog, an ever-present fear lingered that the mist might dissipate abruptly, exposing them to the deadly precision of a sniper's aim. They raced down Sniper Alley, their senses heightened, before veering onto the back roads adjacent to the cathedral. After ascending a hill for approximately a kilometre, they finally reached a point where Mo ceased filming. Here, at this higher vantage point, they were beyond the effective range of any potential sniper threats.

Just after 6:30 a.m., the team knocked on Malek's door. They informed the family that today they could finally visit Malek's father's grave at Lion Cemetery. The boy, acting as a translator for his mother, relayed the message and they hurriedly dressed. As they stepped outside, the thick fog still enveloped their surroundings, casting an eerie atmosphere over the landscape. In a previous reconnaissance mission, they had pinpointed the location of the grave, allowing them to navigate the cemetery with speed. Time was of the essence; they needed to make this visit swift, knowing that the fog would soon lift, obscuring their path.

Both men handed their bulletproof jackets to Malek and his mother, then accompanied them part of the way, indicating the wooden marker that identified the grave. Mo filmed as they walked towards it, capturing Malek, using crutches due to his missing leg, alongside his mother. The Egyptian cameraman ran ahead and waited as the mother and son approached the graveside. Beginning with a wide shot, Mo then zoomed in to capture close-ups. As Malek's mother began to cry, the young boy hugged her tightly, tears streaming down his cheeks. It was a profoundly moving moment, conveying a powerful message about the suffering endured in Bosnia, one that required no words to understand.

"Got enough?" asked Grant. Mo nodded.

The correspondent ushered them back towards the car. Once there, the mother turned to Grant and took his hands. "Hvala," (thank you) she said. He could sense the importance of the moment for them. It was perhaps the closest thing to closure one could find in a war, he supposed. Both Mo and Grant felt a sense of satisfaction. Instead of merely reporting, they had contributed in a small but meaningful way. Dropping them off at home, they then drove to the TV station, where Selma awaited the edit. The report concluded with a poignant close-up shot of Malek and his mother shedding tears at the graveside, followed by a long shot of them walking away, disappearing into the fog. Grant chose to let the shot linger without any accompanying voiceover. It was a compelling story that resonated with everyone who saw it. Compliments poured in from the executive producer, the main news anchor, and numerous others in the newsroom.

A week later, Grant received a call from the Executive Producer, Benjamin Golding.

"Grant just wanted to say that you two guys are doing a great job. Your reporting and filming has been first class, and we sincerely thank you." He also announced they would be giving them a pay rise.

He continued, "That one-legged boy story was tremendous. It touched all of us, and it also touched a multi-millionaire Florida businessman who wants to sponsor the family and get them out of Bosnia. Can you arrange that? He'll take care of visas for the US and travel, etc. You just need to get them out of Sarajevo. I know there is a siege and that, officially, the Bosnian Government is not allowing anyone to leave, but if there were some way you could make it happen, it would give these people survival and a new life."

"I'll see what I can do," Grant said and put the phone down. It would be difficult. Initially, movement through lines was restricted and difficult. Firstly he needed to consult with the family before any decision could be made. But it was almost a forgone conclusion the family would agree and once they did Grant began to hatch a plan.

With no possibility of securing their exit via plane or through an official aid organisation, the only option was to use their own car. The Bosnians wouldn't permit them to use the escape tunnel near the airport either. Grant and Mo would have to smuggle them out. There was a route, but it came with dangers. Southwest of Sarajevo lay a small mountain called Igman, and there existed a dirt track accessible by car. However, a 200-meter stretch of the track would be exposed to Serb fighters armed with machine guns and small mortars. They required an armoured vehicle. Grant needed to approach Uli, the German correspondent and proud owner of the Sarajevo Press Corps' sole armoured vehicle. Uli and his partner Klaus preferred not to venture far from the hotel or TV station, even with an armoured car at their disposal. Nevertheless, they were reluctant to loan it out.

"But vot vud ze Insurance zay if you ver to be hit?" asked Uli when Grant made his request for a loan of the vehicle. "I und Klaus are ze only one's insured to drive."

"Klaus, tell me which insurance company assessor in the world is going to come to the middle of a war zone to verify a claim?" Grant asked him. "Man, it's foolproof, and we will pay you three hundred bucks for the day's hire. What do you say?"

Uli thought long and hard.

"Ya it vud be very difficult for an assessor, would it not? Hmm, ok, but could you give me your one-legged boy story that I can use for my programme?"

"Deal," said Grant, happy that things were falling into place.

"6.30 a.m. tomorrow. OK?"

Uli nodded. "Cash in advance iff you please."

Grant handed him three crisp one-hundred-dollar bills, and in return, Uli handed him the keys. Fewer drinks than normal were partaken in the after dinner tenth-floor social gathering that night. Both Grant and Mo knew they needed to be clear headed and alert.

They woke up early and headed to breakfast. Grant appeared visibly exhausted.

"What's wrong?" asked Mo.

"You know that machine gunner who keeps me awake with his continual rat a-tat-tat every fucking night, the one who doesn't bother you," Mo nodded.

"Well, he wasn't firing last night." "So?" said Mo.

"Well, I kept on thinking that something had happened to him, that he'd been shot or his position overrun or that the Bosnians were running out of ammo or something so that I couldn't sleep a wink."

Mo shook his head and laughed. "You've been here too long, man."

Breakfast at the Holiday Inn wasn't something to eagerly anticipate. The dining room was dimly lit and dreary, with dark wood panels, lacklustre paint, and a carpet that appeared to have seen better days. The morning meal left much to be desired; food was scarce, and the hotel's offerings were meagre at best. Basic fare was the norm, consisting mainly of bread, occasionally verging on staleness, often without butter, and jam that bore little resemblance to fruit. All of this was accompanied by a lukewarm cup of Turkish coffee, more akin to brown-stained water than a robust brew. It was hardly an ideal way to start the day. Meals at the hotel varied between a Russian gulag and a Dickensian workhouse.

Chuck Brown jestingly remarked that he would forward the kitchen's coordinates to NATO, joking that the meals being produced there were violating human rights.

They took their seats and began to nibble on the food provided.

Bernie Johnson entered the room accompanied by a sophisticated middle-aged woman. She was dressed in an elegant fur coat with a silk scarf gracefully draped over her shoulders. They took their seats at the circular table.

"Morning chaps," he said, and then took a flask from his shoulder bag and poured what looked like fresh orange juice into two glasses. It was a captivating moment, yet Mohammed sensed that there was more to come.

Everyone around the table was transfixed by the sight of the juice, almost as much as by the middle-aged woman whom Johnson introduced as his translator. Despite her being Italian and unable to speak a word of Serbo-Croatian, Johnson seemed unfazed by this anomaly. He launched into a discussion about the political story he was writing for the next day's paper. Johnson had a knack for delving into tedious details that most found uninteresting. As one of the top writers, he had the liberty to produce stories of any length he desired.

As people began to mentally drift away, their attention was abruptly captured when a waiter approached the table, balancing two plates in hand.

"Mr Bernie, cooked as you requested," said the waiter and left.

After enduring three months of meagre rations, stale bread, flavourless jam, and coffee resembling an oil slick with the taste of creosote, three fried eggs on a plate captured everyone's undivided attention. A collective wave of salivation swept around the table, akin to a Hawaiian surfing wave in size.

Johnson began slicing the eggs with deliberate slowness, the room silent as he did so. With measured movements, he transferred some onto a fork and raised it to his mouth. However, he paused mid-motion, continuing to speak while lowering the fork back to his plate. He repeated this action three times, the onlookers practically salivating with anticipation. Delicately, he dipped a piece of bread into the yolk, the act resembling a form of foreplay. In Sarajevo, where eggs had become a rarity, the sight of six of them on two plates alongside glasses of fresh orange juice seemed almost surreal, a scene straight out of a dream.

Johnson had a knack for traversing through the lines effortlessly, allowing him to shop in the Croatian-controlled region of Bosnia adjacent to Croatia, known as Hertzag Bosna. Rumours circulated about his room being an Aladdin's cave of culinary treasures. However, it remained just a rumour. No one had ever been invited inside. Yet, those who passed by claimed to detect an aroma reminiscent of a New York Deli emanating from within.

Johnson left the egg untouched on the plate and instead dabbed another piece of bread into the bright, shiny yellow yolk, eliciting further salivation from the group. Once again, he hesitated before bringing the bread to his mouth.

"For fuck's sake, Johnson eat the fucking eggs and put us out of our misery," complained Brown. "There has to be a Geneva convention somewhere about banning what you are doing. Have some fucking compassion, and you and your translator go and eat at another table in the corner somewhere."

The morning's culinary woes, exacerbated by Johnson's torment, were somewhat alleviated by breaking news... the hotel had managed to get their espresso machine working again. They had obtained Italian coffee from a group of Ukrainian United Nations peacekeepers who ran a black-market operation. In Sarajevo, where peace was a joke, they operated under a system where 'peace' took a back seat to a 'piece' of the action.

It didn't take long for the modest breakfast to be devoured. Gathering in the lobby, Chuck and Grant indulged in an espresso each, their first in three months. They cradled the cups, savouring the aroma as if it were a potent drug. Finally, they took a sip, relishing the long-awaited taste.

"Nectar," announced Brown, "Pure, unadulterated fucking nectar."

"Not the first time I've heard you say that," commented Singleton, "But usually, it's to do with alcohol or weed."

Grant nodded in quiet agreement, recognising the significance of small gestures in the midst of war. This contrasted sharply with his experiences upon returning home to London, where people often complained about trivial matters, making it difficult for him to readjust to normalcy.

"So, they are talking about a ceasefire," said Grant.

"Yup, they are talking, but that means diddily fucking squat. The last time there was a ceasefire, four months ago, I spent more time in a shelter than when it was open warfare. The UN described a shelling incident as a violation. The Serbs even shelled the UN HQ. When we rushed in, the commander, an Egyptian, came out of his smoke-filled destroyed office and said, lo and behold, 'There is no cease-fire.' Fuck me, sometimes they are a poor excuse for an organisation. They do the minimum and keep the patient alive. But the long-term prognosis means death. To be honest, though, without the UN and our presence, the Serbs would have taken this place months ago. So they are not totally useless. Anyhow, mate have a good day."

Mo joined Grant in the basement car park, accompanied by Selma, to retrieve Uli's armoured car. As they approached, they noticed Igor, the chocolada kid, lurking in the shadows. Grant gestured to him, expressing their ongoing disappointment over the lack of chocolate, before starting the engine. Igor, understanding the silent communication, shrugged in response and disappeared into the darkness once more.

Mo, usually accustomed to curling up in the well of the passenger seat, decided against it this time. He reasoned that since the car was armoured, the risk of his correspondent being shot was minimal. With no need for a dramatic acceleration, the car eased out onto the ramp, greeted by the first rays of the Sarajevo morning sun.

Their journey to Malek's home was uneventful, taking ten minutes. Malek, along with his mother and brother, awaited them, each holding a small bag containing the essentials for their fresh start. Although modest, Malek's mother explained that it was all they needed for the beginning of their new life. With a final glance around the apartment, she closed the door and handed the key to a neighbour, who would pass it on to newly arrived refugees. In a city familiar with the arrival of victims of ethnic cleansing, their small gesture ensured that at least one family would find solace in a decent new home.

They navigated around Serb-held Lukavica, veering towards Mt Igman. As they neared the final Bosnian checkpoint, they instructed the family to lie flat in the back of the vehicle while Mo covered them with blankets. The armoured Land Rover, lacking rear windows, posed a risk; if instructed to open the back door, they would be vulnerable to detection.

"Doberdan, good morning," said the young soldier when Grant opened the heavily armoured door.

"Where you go, my friend?" he asked.

"We are heading for Split to pick up some supplies," Grant responded.

"Go with God, my friend," the soldier added, and with that, they were through, no checks, no hassle, nema problema, no problem, as the Bosnians often said, even though there were always many problems. The Bosnian people found solace in the media, grateful for its role in broadcasting their plight to the world. Despite their lingering hope that international attention might compel action from world leaders to end the war.

Many, including Grant and his fellow journalists, harboured doubts. Their scepticism was palpable; it seemed as unlikely as the Pope converting to Islam. The reluctance of powerful nations, particularly the United States, to intervene was evident.

As the family emerged from their hiding place under blankets, their smiles were bittersweet, reflecting the sorrow of leaving behind their home, country, and friends.

As their vehicle traversed the desolate track, a sudden burst of gunfire shattered the tense silence. Five bullets pierced the air, all targeting the right side of the car where Mo sat. Although the impact jolted Mo, the reinforced armour held firm, protecting them from harm.

"Let's hear it for Kevlar," shouted Mo. "I wish they could make underpants out of it cos I don't want to lose my winkie tinkie in this or any other fucking war." Selma laughed and just said, "Comandante Jebiga." All three burst into fits of giggles.

As the car swiftly navigated around the bend, disappearing from the sight of the Serbs, they reached the summit, where they were greeted by a youthful ATV producer. Their next destination was Split, Croatia, from where they would catch a flight to Zagreb and then onwards to Miami. After bidding farewell to their family with warm embraces and well wishes, they waved goodbye as Mo retrieved his backpack, extracting a half bottle of vodka.

Mo had the skills of the artful dodger in Dickens' book Oliver Twist.

Grant's look said, 'Where?'

"From the Ukrainian mother fuckers," Mo said. "Sometimes, man, you have to swallow your principles in order to swallow your vodka." Selma downed hers first. She'd been brought up on Sliva. Mo and Grant persevered, although their taste buds didn't quite align with those of their translators. Sampling the local cuisine helped pass the time as they awaited the fading daylight, preparing themselves for the challenge of navigating the return journey under the veil of dusk.

By the time they got back, the party was in full swing. The large conference room had been christened the 'Incoming Club' by the press pack. No electricity so it was lit by candles. Music was blaring out of a tape deck in the corner of the room powered by two large truck batteries, the Clash's "Should I Stay or Should I Go" was playing at full volume. The entire room erupted into a chorus of voices. Many of the occupants were long-term residents, having spent months in this place. Despite their usual sense of deprivation and denial, tonight was an exception. They simply hoped that this temporary release wouldn't be followed by the return of danger in the form of a 7.62mm bullet or a T80 tank shell round. Yet, amidst these concerns, no one seemed to worry. It was time to celebrate. Thick cannabis smoke hung in the air, creating an almost foggy atmosphere near the ceiling. The room was filled with alcohol, and people were forming pairs. Among them, a British correspondent found himself drawn to Grant.

"You've been kicking my arse all week," she said, feigning hostility.

"Such a nice arse," Grant replied, and it was clear to him that she wouldn't mind him getting closer to it. However, his attention shifted as he noticed Selma amidst a group of other translators across the room. Politely excusing himself from the female correspondent, he made his way over to her.

"Hi," he said. "How do you say dance in Bosnian?"

"Ples," she replied and smiled. "Well would you have a ples with me?" he asked.

"That's very nice of you, but I have to go," she said. "I only came to give a note to my friend."

"OK," said Grant, trying to hide his disappointment. "I am sorry about your brother. Hassan told me. If there is anything I can do, please tell me."

"Stop the war. Other than that, there is nothing you or anyone else can do. The Serbs have him, and they will decide what will happen," she said. "Now I must go. I will see you tomorrow."

As she turned and walked away, Singleton rebuked himself for his insensitivity. He realised the inappropriateness of his request for a dance, considering her obvious distress over her twin brother and father.

Mo grabbed him by the arm, "Man, stop standing around, get moving before all the women and booze are taken."

An American cameraman climbed onto the table, removing his shirt to reveal a crucifix tattoo on his chest. Clearly intoxicated, he attempted an impersonation of Jesus on the cross before stumbling and falling off the table. Meanwhile, two other agency reporters, also heavily drunk, attempted to limbo under the table. In a corner of the room, Luc, a French photographer, and Spit the Frog were seen snorting lines of cocaine, provided once more by the Ukrainian peacekeepers.

Spit looked up and shouted to Grant, "Beats the hell out of Khat, doesn't it mon ami?"

Grant saw Grace Barnes in the corner, snogging with a man in uniform.

"That's a British UN soldier," explained her cameraman. "She does like a man in uniform but maintains proper standards. She never fucks anyone below the rank of major." He smiled and headed for a Bosnian translator, lighting up another joint.

At 3:00 a.m. a swaying Chuck Brown appeared and gathered a few together, including Grant and Mo. "Gentlemen," he slurred. "I have here in my hand the key to Eldorado," and he showed a room key with the number 307. "Come with me, and we shall explore together."

Brown took the lead, holding the key in one hand and a small Maglite torch in the other to illuminate the path down the stairway and through three floors. At the door, he stopped and said, "Now let us see what is in Pandora's box."

"Whose room is this?" asked Mo.

"Johnson's," replied Brown.

"Where is he?" asked Grant.

Brown's smile stretched as wide as a Cadilac. "In Rome, probably shagging his translator."

They all broke down with raucous laughter that bordered on the hysterical.

Brown steadied himself and swung open the door. Two candles awaited on the right, promptly ignited by his hand. As the group entered, gasps of amazement filled the room. They stood in silent awe for what felt like an eternity, beholding racks adorned with French wine, Italian salamis neatly stacked nearby, sizable wedges of Parmesan cheese, boxes brimming with pasta, a partially devoured leg of prosciutto, cartons of orange juice, and a grand Italian Panettone cake.

"What the fuck," shouted Mo, there is enough here to feed the whole of Sarajevo."

Bernie Johnson's room did indeed resemble Eldorado. It was adorned with additional lighting and a sofa, likely salvaged from upper rooms in disrepair. Notably, a cable extended from a socket to the bathroom, culminating in a substantial heating element immersed in a water bath. Just then, synchronously with the hotel's power restoration, the bath heater and room lights sprang to life.

"The sneaky fuck," said Brown. "So, when there is power, his element heats the fucking water. No wonder he always looks so fucking clean and polished. And he never shares a fucking thing. But the greedy bastard's never shy to offer his glass when someone opens a bottle of wine at sixty bucks a pop."

British radio Bunty stared in amazement. He hadn't reached his current size without a profound passion for food.

"Fuck Me, mate, there must be five grand's worth of goodies here. This man has shown incredible tenacity in getting around this war-ravaged country and solving the supply shortage. The UN need to learn from him. I think we need to celebrate that," he said as he grabbed a corkscrew and began opening a bottle of Chateau Neuf de Pap.

They each raised a glass in salute, toasting Bernie Johnson. Mistakes often arise in moments of conflict, and Johnson had just made a significant error by leaving his post unguarded to indulge in a weekend getaway to Rome with his 'translator.' It proved to be a costly visit.

"To Bernie," they said in Unison and began a systematic degrading exercise of Johnson's culinary trove. It was plunder, pure and simple. And not one of them felt guilty. War is war, they said as they tucked into every delicacy they could grab.

By 4:00 a.m., they reached a point where eating and drinking were no longer feasible. Each retreated to their rooms, seeking whatever rest they could, clinging to the slim hope that the forthcoming day would be mercifully tranquil, allowing them to recuperate gradually. All but Mo dispersed to their quarters. The little Egyptian, however, swiftly shed his garments and immersed himself in a steaming bath. Adjacent to the tub rested a bottle of chianti, accompanied by Buzz Lightyear perched on the rim.

"Buzz and I would like some quiet time alone if you guys don't mind," he said as he slid under the water. They left them in peace.

Shortly after Grant closed his door, a resounding knock echoed through the room. Upon opening it, his gaze fell upon the Leica before registering the familiar face behind it.

"Forget about me, sweetie," Tanya said and pushed her way into the room. No easing into the day for Grant Singleton, not today.

"I thought for a moment you had forgotten about me."

He closed the door with a look of resignation on his face. How could he forget her?

At dawn, a gentle knock echoed on his door. Standing outside was a Bosnian assistant, employed by Bert, the Reuters correspondent.

"Mr Grant, Mr Grant," she shouted through the door. "Phone call."

Singleton looked at his watch. It was 6:00 a.m. Tanya was fast asleep, snoring like a train. Her Leica camera was lying next to her pillow.

He grabbed his boxers and opened the door.

"It's New York," she said. "They want to speak to you now. They are waiting."

He donned a shirt and descended one floor to the Reuters office, pondering the reason behind the sudden call.

"Hello," he said, picking up the handset. Reuters, though not a humanitarian organisation, imposed sat phone charges that many considered extortionate. Grant estimated that ATV had spent at least $500 waiting for him to reach the phone. In the words of his Geordie ancestors, it was 'small potatoes'.

"Hi, Grant, how are you doing?" it was Benjamin Golding, the Executive producer. He didn't wait for a response.

"Hey, man, I just want to tell you that you are doing an amazing job with top-notch reports, and killing the opposition. The story about the one-legged boy was a real knockout. Amazing images in that cemetery. I want to tell you Peter wants to come and report from Sarajevo."

Peter was Peter Josling Valentine the main anchor of the programme. In the news business, he was a giant. It was like posing a question, 'Where does a 600-kilo gorilla sit?' And the answer was, 'wherever he wants to.' Peter Valentine was a 600-kilo gorilla in the news jungle. He had the freedom to choose his seat, much like a Roman Caesar presiding over the games, wielding the power to determine fate with a mere gesture. In Valentine's realm, careers could be shattered at about the same time. He was the ten million-dollar-a-year man and what Peter wanted, Peter got. And apparently, he wanted Sarajevo.

"Your one-legged boy story was the final thing for him, and he was so moved he said, 'I'm going.' Everyone has tried to talk him out of it, but he's having none of it. He's coming."

"Hmm, that's great," said Grant, not knowing if it was great. Was it a brave move by an anchor with 'soft hands,' or was it a massive PR exercise? Maybe he was being unfair. Grant harboured suspicions despite recognising Valentine's exemplary journalistic track record in the Middle East, even amidst challenging circumstances. And he also felt it was 'his own' story. No one liked to be 'big-footed'.

"He's going to compile a documentary on Bosnia. It will coincide with the Democratic Party announcing that Bosnia will be its foreign policy initiative. It is guaranteed to keep the story on the front burner. He will be in Sarajevo for twenty-four hours. No longer."

"That's great," Grant repeated, thinking that 24 hours for a docco was a little on the short side. "When?"

"Next week."

"Wow, that's short notice. What do you want me to do?"

"Well, keep him alive." Golding laughed at his little joke, but it was a nervous laugh. For US TV news, the charisma of the presenter often held more sway than the content of the stories themselves. Likeable anchors meant likeable stories, which in turn garnered favour from advertisers, leading to substantial advertising revenue.

"Peter understands this is your story, and he doesn't want to step on your toes, but we'd like you to assist him as much as possible while still doing the day-to-day stories. And we'd like you to give him a couple of package ideas as well so we can utilise his presence there, you know, make the most of it."

Grant understood the implications all too well, a media frenzy would ensue, with the ten-million-dollar man becoming the centre of attention, overshadowing the anchors of competing channels. While storytelling was important, triumphing over the competition was paramount. He had conversed with Valentine over the phone on a few occasions, once receiving an impromptu lesson on American elocution in an attempt to modify his British accent to a more mid-western one. Another call was made to inquire about a story he had forwarded, only for Valentine to appropriate, rework, and present it as his own. Someone gave a pissed-off Grant some advice, 'Don't take it personally. He does it to everyone who has a cracking story, so it's a sort of vote of confidence if you like. But never make your intro too good or he will steal it.'

"So, you've got some time to think. We'd, I mean I, would be grateful if you could line up a good heart-rendering story for him to tell. He is an excellent writer, and you know, he respects you. And that's something to be proud of. I'll leave it with you, and we'll get the details to you as soon as we can. But, mum's the word, we can't let the opposition know what we are doing. So be careful who you confide in. Great speaking to you, Grant. You are doing a fantastic job. Keep safe."

With that, the phone abruptly went dead. Babysitting a 600-kilo Caesar-like prima donna anchor wasn't what he had anticipated when he signed up. However, he was beginning to grasp the stark reality of the American news industry, where the demands often felt like navigating an entirely different universe, all for a day's pay.

15

Hassan Mesic strode into the room, greeted by the sight of five men seated at the head of the table. Their expressions were grave, casting a sombre atmosphere over the gathering. It was far from the anticipated celebration they'd hoped. The attack on Barice, their boldest yet, had ended in dismal failure. Two tanks lay in ruins, an artillery piece rendered useless, and the loss of countless fighters left a heavy toll. Caught in what felt like a meticulously laid trap, they found themselves besieged from two directions, akin to an orange squeezed until its pips burst. Only the fortuitous presence of fog had spared them from even greater losses.

Hassan turned to face the five men before him, delivering a thorough report on the extent of the defeat. The five shook their heads in silent disbelief, and no one uttered a word until the chairman of the council asked, "How, how could this happen? We had secrecy, fog, and the element of surprise. We picked an area lightly defended because it was difficult terrain and one from which it was unlikely to launch an attack. Yet they cut us to pieces. How?" he repeated.

"They must have had inside help," offered Hassan. "There is no other explanation. For the reasons you have stated, only someone with detailed knowledge of our plans could have warned the Serbs. Unfortunately, it is looking more and more as if they were warned." He emphasised 'were.' "The sheer amount of hardware they used makes that clear. They were prepared. They did not have this amount of tanks, artillery, and men ready by accident. That means someone inside our command had divulged the plans. It must have been someone high up in the chain of command. I think we have a spy amongst us. It is the only conceivable explanation."

The room was filled with an audible murmur as each man exchanged uneasy glances. Discomfort and disbelief hung thick in the air, almost palpable. For the five individuals present, the notion seemed unfathomable. They had placed implicit trust in the senior command, all of whom were Muslims. Was it one of the Serbs who fought with the Bosnians, who appeared passionate about Bosnia, who pretended they saw this war as Serb aggression? Had they fooled the Bosnian hierarchy? That would have been difficult. They were all watched closely. It would be virtually impossible. But as they had learned in this costly war, the impossible was sometimes possible. It was difficult to countenance the spy being a Muslim. No Muslim would do that. Why would they? What would they have to gain?

The questions and soul-searching began.

Then a large man spoke, "If someone is spying, and I say if, because this could have just been a tragic case of bad luck, I will find out. I have the means. We will get to the bottom of this."

Mohammed Ibrahimovic stood as one of the Bosnian forces' most seasoned commanders, revered for his devout adherence to Islam and feared by both Serbs and fellow Muslims alike. Leading the intelligence and internal police, he commanded respect not for his likeability but for his unwavering dedication to the cause. However, his methods were marked by brutality and inflexibility. Ibrahimovic openly harboured a deep-seated animosity towards the Serbs, advocating for their expulsion from Bosnia and advocating for retribution for their crimes. Despite his religious stature, his stance on revenge diverged from the teachings of Prophet Mohammed, who advocated for forgiveness and mercy even towards adversaries. Unlike the Prophet's teachings, Ibrahimovic showed no hesitation in shedding Serb blood, making him known and feared as the Inquisitor.

"Serbs are behind this, and if they have infiltrated our army, then I will find them. You can rest assured of that. I will leave no stone unturned. There will be an eye for an eye."

He exited the room, initiating the hunt. The others trailed behind, with the exception of General Samir Mujkanovic, the head of the command chain, a seasoned veteran in his sixties. Revered as "Gromo" (Thunder) among his troops for his formidable temper, Mujkanovic's background diverged from the typical military path; he had been a university professor prior to the conflict. Delving into scientific realms such as the Big Bang theory and Darwin's evolutionary concepts, his penchant for challenging established beliefs proved invaluable amidst the chaos of war. Indeed, his intellect and leadership were pivotal in safeguarding Sarajevo from an early collapse during the onset of hostilities. Utilising unconventional tactics, including enlisting the aid of unlikely allies like gangsters and procuring antiquated weaponry from museums, Mujkanovic orchestrated a formidable defence that held off immediate defeat. Yet, as time passed, the siege grew increasingly daunting, with the prospect of breaking it appearing ever more distant and costly, a reality not lost on the Black Swans.

He gestured for Hassan to join him at a small coffee table nearby. As the door creaked open, an elderly woman entered, gracefully balancing a tray with two cups of Turkish coffee, a bowl of sugar, and two glasses of Stock brandy. Her traditional head scarf hinted at her rural origins, marking her as one of the UN Classified displaced persons who had sought refuge in Sarajevo after being forcibly displaced from their villages by armed Serbs.

In contrast to the rural simplicity represented by the old lady's attire, Sarajevo boasted a cosmopolitan flair even amidst the turmoil of war. Here, women adorned themselves with makeup and fur coats, and the city pulsated with nightlife, from parties to discos. Once renowned as a bastion of culture and the arts, Sarajevo embraced modernity with fervour, often leaving tradition and Islamic customs in favour of a more modern lifestyle.

"Givili," said Gromo (cheers). "Although there is nothing to celebrate. We must keep our spirits up and bounce back from this. Morale has been given a devastating blow. We need to resurrect it and move on. Our survival depends on it. Do you have any theories?"

Hassan downed the last of the Stock.

"There were only a handful of people who knew the plan," Hassan began. "A couple outside of this room and the five of you. Commanders who knew were only told the full plan shortly before the attack. At the foot of Barice, they would have no way of revealing those plans to the Serbs."

He continued, "There is one strange thing that happened. Yesterday, we intercepted a radio transmission. It wasn't clear what they were talking about, but it seemed it was coded. But the word 'Munja' (lightning) was mentioned several times. It's the second time in the past week that we have heard this word in Serb communication. Our operator thought this was about the weather. But there has been no lightning or storms lately. It could be a reference to someone or something sending intel to the Serbs. That's a hunch at this stage, but I don't think we can rule anything out. Until we find this leak, if that's what it is, then we can't launch any more meaningful attacks."

The General's face had darkened. He pursed his lips, "Then we must use all means possible to stop this. Otherwise, this will be one more nail in the coffin of Sarajevo."

16

Mehmet glanced around the barn. It was really dark inside. A few men were snoring, and a couple were murmuring in their sleep. Near the end of the barn, a chink of outside light peeked through a hole in the roof, creating a thin beam on the ground. The air was thick with the smell of sweaty bodies, as many men hadn't washed in a while. Mehmet couldn't recall when he last had a shower or cleaned up properly. He always felt dirty. He thought animals probably had it easier.

A hand gently grabbed his shoulder and shook it. Even though his vision was blurred, he recognised Osman's hand. They had formed a quiet friendship, bringing him some comfort. Talking among prisoners was not allowed. However, during the past few weeks, away from the guards' watchful eyes, they had managed to steal moments to talk, fostering a bond and hatching a plan. Their plan was to escape. Both agreed that attempting to escape was better than enduring the daily horrors of Gornji Polje even if it meant facing death in the attempt.

Tonight marked a crucial moment for Mehmet. It was a make-or-break situation, where success meant freedom and failure meant death. He recalled a book by the Greek author Nikos Kazantzakis, which depicted the intense struggle between Greeks and Turks in the nineteenth century. Now, Mehmet truly grasped the significance of that fight for survival.

Both men had realised in the preceding days and weeks that tonight presented the ideal opportunity to escape. It coincided with the celebration of the Slava by one of the guards, a significant event for the Serbs. The Slava was an annual family ceremony honouring their patron saint and commemorating the family's first ancestor to embrace Christianity, along with the saint associated with it. This tradition was passed down from father to son, with only males permitted to conduct its rituals. Mehmet and Osman knew that on this particular night, the Serbs would be consumed with drunkenness and it would render them less vigilant.

They didn't have a watch, but from the shouting, singing, and festivities, they figured it was well past midnight. Silently, they approached the area where the latrine buckets were kept. The smell was almost unbearable. Eight buckets were nearly filled to the brim of urine and faeces. Usually, they were emptied in the mornings. They crept behind the buckets, and Osman pushed a wooden panel. It resisted at first, then, with an extra push, it moved back, creating an opening. The movement caused a loud creaking noise, much louder than in the silent night. They held their breath and stayed still. Nothing stirred, no one shouted, and no guard appeared. But nearby lay the figure of a man, awake and sounding old.

"Sretan put," he whispered (good luck). "Allah Immanet."

The two waved and gave a slight smile. They knew they needed more than luck. They continued through the opening and out into the compound, then hurried to the furthest section between the two lookout posts. Only one post was occupied, but they could tell from his quiet, slurred singing that he had been drinking at the Slava party and probably wasn't the most attentive watchman.

Osman felt around for the piece of wood he had left by the eight-foot-high barbed wire fence. For the past week, he had used it at night to dig a hole under the fence. He covered the hole with a piece of turf he had carefully cut from the grass. He removed the turf and scooped out the remaining earth. The hole was small but big enough for men who had been weakened by a lack of food and poor conditions. They squeezed through the hole, and then Mehmet reached back to put some soil back in the hole and cover it with the piece of turf.

They had two hopes: first, that the guards would be too ill from the Slava celebration to notice the hidden hole or realise two inmates were missing, especially without a roll call; and second, that they could stay hidden in Serb territory without being found. They knew they weren't far from Banja Luka, the main city in the Serb's unofficial state, Republika Srpska. They were deep in enemy territory. They sprinted to the nearby trees, about sixty metres away, and quickly lay down. After a few minutes, they realised they were safe. Standing up, they hugged briefly, knowing that escaping the camp was likely the easy part. The real challenge would be staying hidden and making it over one hundred kilometres to the Bosnian side.

17

The first snows of winter began falling, bringing a biting cold that cut through the air. Bosnian winters were known for their toughness, often harsh and lasting a long time. That's why they hosted the Winter Olympics in 1984. Grant thought about this as he and Mo drove past the Zetra stadium, where Torvil and Dean had performed their famous ice dance to Ravel's Bolero, winning gold. Reflecting on the country's hardships, Grant remembered how half of it had been destroyed by Serb shells. Beneath the surface lay the base of a Danish UN contingent, home to a popular drinking spot called the Viking Pub. Every journalist in Sarajevo longed for an invitation there.

They walked all the way to the top of Lion Cemetery. The place was packed with new graves, each marked with wooden boards and plastic numbers.

They arrived to film a funeral at Lion Cemetery, which was full, so they began digging graves on what used to be tennis courts across the road. Parking their car behind the trees, they cautiously walked past some houses to avoid Serb snipers who might target the funeral, aiming to escalate the death toll. They started filming as the men formed two lines, gently passing the coffins of three family members, a grandmother and two children killed in a mortar attack. The coffins were then laid into the freshly dug graves, while the imam recited prayers.

"Peace be upon you, the believers and Muslims dwelling in these abodes. Allah has mercy for those who left before us and for the ones who come later. Behold, if Allah wills, we shall meet you."

Almost immediately, there was a sudden burst of gunfire, and everyone hurriedly sought shelter. It seemed like the Serbs were ready to attack at any moment. The armed Bosnians attempted to locate the source of the gunfire, but it could have originated from anywhere on the elevated terrain. Swiftly, the mourners sought refuge behind the nearest buildings. Such occurrences were rapidly becoming commonplace in the Bosnian capital.

Selma's voice came on the radio, "Peter is here," she said. "Your boss, and there are a lot of people with him. You'd better come back."

"Shit," said Mo. "The mountain has come to Mohammed."

"He can wait," said Grant. "Let's finish up here. This is more important. Selma, tells him we will be there shortly. Make him a coffee or give him some sliva, lots of it."

Mo focused intently on the scene unfolding before him. He captured every detail with his camera: the prayers, the panic, and the chilling normality of life in

Sarajevo. However, as they made their way back to the TV station, the city fell silent, too silent it seemed. No explosions shattered the air, and no gunfire echoed in the distance. Instead, a serene blue winter sky greeted them, with birds perched peacefully on tree branches. The streets below were flooding with people, bustling like an army of ants. They worked tirelessly, cutting down trees and salvaging beams from destroyed houses for firewood. Nothing went to waste in this city of resilience. Within hours, the once vibrant centre was transformed into a desolate landscape, stripped bare of its trees and marked by the scars of conflict.

It was a warm greeting. Peter was visibly excited to be there.

"I want you to know that this is not a story about me being in Bosnia," Peter stressed to Grant. "It's the story. That is important."

Grant nodded, though inside he harboured doubts. The journalist observed that he was accompanied by two cameramen, one of whom filmed the anchor drinking coffee in the office. Where there's a story, there's often ego, and sometimes they align, he thought. Alongside, there was a soundman, a producer, and an assistant, along with Peter's translator. They required three cars for transportation, all armoured, much to Mo's envy.

"I'm totally in your hands," the anchor explained. "Tell us what to do. I think Ben said there was a story idea for us."

Grant had prepared a very sad story about the elderly residents in a nursing home near the frontline. They were suffering from illness, bullets, and the harsh cold. The UN's response seemed typical of their incompetence. Although they provided stoves for the residents' rooms, they forgot to bring chimneys, making the stoves useless. Grant was aware that the anchor had less than 24 hours to film in the city. The executives at ATV wanted him to finish quickly. Insurance premiums were, apparently, extremely high.

"OK, let's go."

Mo whispered to Grant, "Wait until you see the wheels, man."

Outside the main entrance of the TV station, there were three large, white Land Rovers. They looked shiny and new, with hardly any dirt on them. This contrasted sharply with the dirty grey building, which was riddled with bullet and shrapnel holes. The Land Rovers resembled vehicles you might see in a motoring magazine photoshoot. They were the latest and most commonly used armoured vehicles in war zones. Made by the Courtaulds company in Coventry, UK, each vehicle cost around a hundred thousand dollars. They were designed to withstand most bullets and small fragments of shrapnel.

"A beauty, eh?" said Mo. He looked on in envy and then turned his gaze to their mode of transport, the two-door 1.4lt Ford with flaky paintwork and patches of rust. This vehicle offered minimal protection, nothing close to being armoured. In the realm of armoured vehicles, it provided only as much security as a standard, thin condom. It's unlikely that this Ford would even sell for a thousand dollars if put up for sale.

If the anchor felt embarrassed, he didn't show it. Mo nearly got squashed by the large Austrian cameraman who was filming Peter getting into the vehicle. Another cameraman, a big Irish man, filmed from the opposite side. Everything related to Peter Valentine seemed enormous.

Selma hurried to the car and gave him a black woolly hat. It was the typical winter clothing for many Bosnian men.

Grant looked quizzically. "He wanted one," she explained. "Makes him feel closer to the people," she tilted her head and almost smiled.

Mo muttered "Whiskey Tango Foxtrot" under his breath before stepping into the Ford. Both men noticed the unusual quietness of the city. The absence of explosions and gunfire was noticeable, if not a bit unreal. A war without any actual fighting wasn't what the executive producer had in mind when emphasising the importance of keeping the '600kg' anchor safe.

As they arrived at the old people's home, they spotted an assistant trying to guide an elderly man back indoors. He was dressed in pyjamas and a dressing gown, clearly ill-prepared for the dropping temperatures. Grant realised that the man likely had dementia, which, under these circumstances, seemed like a fortunate situation. He wouldn't know just how bad his life was.

Valentine's car drove around the building and then stopped in front of the main entrance. The driver backed up onto the low steps and parked just before the door, leaving space for the rear door of the armoured car to open. Like a doorman at Tiffany's on Fifth Avenue, he hurried to the back to open the door for the anchor to step out and quickly enter the building, away from any onlookers or potential danger. It only took a few seconds.

Mo and Grant watched with surprise, keeping their reactions in check. It was one of the quietest days they had experienced since they first arrived at the location. No gunfire, no explosions. They speculated that perhaps ATV had made some arrangement with the Serbs. After all, anything seemed possible for the highest-paid and most influential news presenter in the world.

Upon entering, he was met with a sombre scene, a familiar sight for Grant and Mo. The stoves remained in disrepair, and death lingered. Two orderlies solemnly transported a deceased woman on a stretcher through the building's corridors. The stark environment featured bare corridors, concrete floors, and white walls, amplifying the echo of footsteps akin to voices in a canyon. The frigid temperature allowed one to inscribe their name in exhaled breath. Despite the chill, the unmistakable scent of death permeated the air.

"She died last night," explained Selma. "She was eighty-five. She's lucky she's out of this shit now."

They were led to another room, where they found two additional motionless bodies lying on the floor, ready to be removed.

"Where's Peter?" asked Grant. Mo gestured towards a door leading to a courtyard. Outside, the anchor stood, lost in thought, his face showing concern. Grant interpreted it as a sign of discomfort.

"Peter, do you want to come and see this, three dead people, and the situation is quite appalling?"

"No, I'm ok here," he replied, "Just let me know what you see, and please get the names of the dead and something about their backgrounds."

Stu, his producer, shrugged his shoulders and whispered to Grant, "He'll write a brilliant script."

The two friends found it strange that a man who had experienced many events in the Middle East seemed to avoid seeing death. However, when he returned to their office at the TV station and they read his script, it was brilliant, just as Stu had predicted.

Grant admired the quality of the writing, which showed empathy and respect for the deceased. Yet he couldn't shake the feeling that being in Sarajevo wasn't necessary to write it. The story thrilled everyone in New York, and Peter Valentine got five minutes of airtime, almost double the usual duration for most stories. The anchor man was starting to adapt and fit better into his surroundings.

"Grant, thank you so much for today. It was an illuminating experience." He was still wearing the woollen hat. Mo wondered if he would ever take it off.

"I'd like to do one more thing," he continued. "You told me about the gatherings on the tenth floor in the bombed-out room, smoking and drinking while watching the tracer fire. I'd like to join you if I may?"

"No problem, Peter. We'll head up after dinner."

Room 1004 looked just like Peter had pictured it: partly wrecked but packed with meaning, with courageous journalists battling for truth and honesty. However, there was a hitch. The night was silent, devoid of gunfire, explosions, or shouts. Bunty's loud fart stood out as the most notable event. It was a night of unusual quietness, with Bunty's fart being the loudest sound anyone could recall.

"Pity," said the anchor. The disappointment was evident. Grant felt he had failed in some strange way. He whispered something to Mo.

"Excuse me," the little Egyptian said and left the room.

The bottle of sliva went around, followed closely by a joint. Peter Josling Valentine, the war presenter, eagerly consumed both.

"Getting stoned and drunk in a war zone, wow," he said.

All at once, there was a loud explosion, followed by fast gunfire, and then streaks of light shooting across the dark sky. Peter quickly dropped to the floor. Everyone else stayed in their seats. After a moment, the night grew silent again, only to be broken by another burst of tracer fire hitting the building across from the parliament.

"Wow," said the anchor, who, even in the shadows, was visibly warmed by what he was seeing.

"Man, this is war. Shit, we are in a goddam motherfucking war zone."

He went to bed happy. Slowly, he was ticking off the boxes of his experience.

When he'd gone, Brown looked at Mo and Grant. "Strange angle of that tracer fire into the parliament building," he said. "I think the Serbs may have occupied a new forward position," and he smiled. The two friends smiled back and then said goodnight. They descended to the lobby.

"OK?" said Hejo. He was standing at the bottom of the stairs. He was holding an AK47.

"Yes, that was perfect," said Grant. "But how did you organise the explosions? That was the cream on the cake?"

"My cousin had a couple of grenades hanging around, and likes the opportunity to test his arm."

"And the machine gun fire?" asked Mo.

"Ah yes, he was, what do you call him, Mohammed, the mad machine gunner, well he was having a night off to go to a party, and since we help him with, shall we say, refreshments during his night shifts, he was happy to come back for a quick session. That's what friends are for. Did it work?"

"Yes, my friend, it worked perfectly."

The men climbed the stairs, their faces lit up with wide smiles. They felt happy when their plans succeeded, although it didn't happen every time.

The next day, there was an interview with a politician, which Grant was ready for. He wasn't keen on babysitting; he still had stories to write.

During breakfast, they had hard bread, jam without fruit, and coffee with a slick of oil. Suddenly, the building shook from a series of explosions rocking the city. The intensity of the blasts made them realise something serious was happening. Quickly, they grabbed their gear and dashed for the underground garage. Igor didn't get a chance to ask for his daily bar of chocolate. Grant drove the car out of the garage at top speed, making it a difficult target for any potential Serb snipers. He swerved from side to side, then sped around the back of the hotel to the safety of the quiet streets. This routine was always filled with adrenaline and lasted about 25 seconds.

They drove the wrong way down Marsala Tita Street, but in war zones, traffic rules weren't followed. The road and sidewalks were cluttered with debris from shell hits. They continued deeper into the old city, hearing more explosions, maybe fifteen or twenty of them. It was difficult to keep track.

Explosions meant people getting hurt. They had grown cynical. Injuries meant getting attention. They knew this was a chance to show the world what life was like here. It was a sad truth, but sometimes it took violence to get noticed. Foreign news desks never said it outright, but the unspoken message was, 'No blood, no good.'

Their path was blocked by a wrecked lorry. They turned sharply and raced down the final part of Sniper Alley as fast as the car could manage. It wasn't very fast.

"Comfy there?" asked Grant as Mo crouched in the footwell in his normal film-and-famous routine.

"I'm getting used to it," he replied. "But maybe we need to get a beamer or something bigger, and this footwell is a bit cramped, man."

"Sorry you are having to suffer for my potential death scene," Grant apologised sarcastically.

He contacted Selma using the walkie-talkie, instructing her to join them at the French Hospital, which was closest to the centre and typically the first place where casualties were taken. As they approached the old town near the fifteenth-century Gazi Husebv-beg Mosque, they witnessed people running down the street. Despite its beauty, the Mosque made an easy target for Serb attacks.

As they slowed, a man waved them down. He said one word, "Markale". It was the name of the city's main daily market. It was located just a minute away. They sped around the corner, crossing the tram tracks, and saw cars arriving with wounded individuals being loaded inside. Dark clouds loomed overhead, hinting at rain. Grant couldn't help but think of Selma and her belief in Thomas Hardy's idea of pathetic fallacy, which suggested that nature mirrored human emotions. He knew the situation wasn't going to be good.

Mo began filming as they hit the street. Bloodied bodies were hastily placed in any available vehicle, in the back seat or the trunk. A woman knelt on the ground, holding the lifeless body of a young child in her arms, sobbing. Nearby, an elderly man lay slumped over a railing, his head gruesomely disfigured. Grant couldn't help but think of him as a prop from a gory horror movie. Walking past severed limbs and pools of blood, it was clear that some victims were beyond help and left where they fell. The market stalls were riddled with holes from mortar fragments, with poles bent or snapped from the impact. The scene was truly devastating.

Mo took close-up video of everything he could, even the severed limbs he knew would never be shown on TV. There was a sense of controlled urgency as people worked to rescue the living and remove the dead. The shelling had ceased, replaced by a profound sorrow as relatives hurried to the scene.

The anchor and his team arrived just outside the market. They quickly got out of the vehicle, with one man filming the corpses and wounded, while the other captured Peter's reaction to the tragedy. In a matter of moments, Peter began speaking directly to the camera, discussing the horrors endured by the people. His delivery was smooth, confident, and reflected his professionalism. Grant understood why many Americans trusted the news delivered by Peter Valentine.

Grant stopped to hear one line, "And all they were doing is shopping for their daily food, trying to survive in a city under a brutal siege."

The two hurried back to the car and drove to the French hospital. As they arrived, they spotted Chuck Brown and Spit the Frog standing just outside the large glass door, which was now covered with cardboard to keep out the elements.

"The Serbs will be happy today," blasted Chuck. "They've taken out some dangerous three-year-olds and lethal old people armed with shopping bags which could have done real damage with their fucking walking sticks. MOTHERFUCKERS," he shouted at the top of his voice. "Sometimes I want to dispense with journalistic ethics and pick up a fucking gun and give those fuckers exactly what they fucking well deserve."

Scenes like this were distressing, even for those accustomed to war. It was especially difficult when children were involved. Combatants were one thing, but seeing women and children in such situations was particularly unsettling.

Mo filmed a continuous stream of casualties. For the media, Bosnia was always open for business. Death and bloodshed were constant, happening 24/7. Reporters could film anywhere they pleased – from accident scenes to emergency rooms, from operating rooms to scenes of death and dying, even at funerals and in people's homes. You could intrude into people's grief as casually as going for a weekend hike, then casually share snapshots of their misery with the world. No one ever, ever said no. Selma was at the entrance as a little girl was brought in on a stretcher. She was sobbing, "Tata, ochim Tata."(I want my father).

Selma translated, "She's not badly hurt," Selma explained. "Just some glass fragments. Her damage is going to be more emotional when she hears about her father. He's dead."

The two operating theatres were crowded with patients, creating a constant stream of people needing help. Grant couldn't help but be reminded of a similar situation in Karaama, Mogadishu, although there were notable differences. These hospitals had anaesthesia and adequate operating rooms, but they lacked enough surgeons. Junior doctors were forced to step up as surgeons due to the shortage. The air was filled with a strong smell of dried blood and sweat, and the floors and walls were stained dark, presumably from blood. Grant concluded that there was a significant amount of blood being spilled in the hospitals in Sarajevo.

The corridor outside was crowded with people. It felt like a busy street, with everyone waiting to move forward. Moans and shouts echoed through the halls. A senior doctor paced back and forth, checking on each person.

"Triage," he explained to Grant as he walked past the camera. "I'm playing God. I decide who is operated on first. Sometimes it's about choosing who lives and who dies," he explained almost matter-of-fact. Death was a part of life for Bosnians. Grant had encountered moments of 'triage' before and knew there would be more in the future.

The situation was chaotic, but there was a sense of order amidst it. People appeared to be handling things with competence. Doctors had become skilled at performing surgery in difficult conditions, fixing up even those who seemed beyond help, and finding creative solutions for shortages of supplies and equipment.

They kept filming continuously for what felt like a long time, but it was actually less than forty-five minutes. Grant thought to himself, 'Forty-five minutes of chaos for just a three-minute story. What does this say about how we view other people's suffering?' He knew that what happened today would be heavily edited for the news. The final report would make war seem less horrifying than it truly is. All the civilised world seemed to care about were flashy scenes and Hollywood-like action.

They walked to the end of the corridor, searching for a place to sit. A hospital orderly motioned for them to follow him. They walked down a dim, poorly lit corridor and entered a room through a door. Inside was a makeshift mortuary with ten tables, each holding a body. Four of the bodies were fighters, while the others were civilians dressed in regular clothes. Shockingly, two of the bodies were children. Mo began filming each body, capturing wide shots, high shots, pans, zoom-ins, and close-ups of hands, toes, eyes, and wounds. It was a comprehensive visual documentation of the casualties of war.

The orderly beckoned them to the next room. They stood quietly, taking in the grim surroundings. It was a mortuary, but unlike any they had seen before. The bodies within were so severely mutilated that their features were unrecognisable. Grant felt a wave of revulsion wash over him at the sight. This was the reality of war, he realised, a reality often hidden from the public eye. Yet, he couldn't help but think that perhaps people needed to witness this ugliness first-hand at least once in their lives. Among the remains lay a body wearing an Iron Maiden T-shirt, a stark contrast to the gruesome scene surrounding it. It was as if they were witnessing a scene from a horror film, only this time the horror was all too real, created not by skilled makeup artists but by the Serbs brutality of conflict.

He felt nauseous. Leaving the room, Mo followed him. They headed towards the exit for some fresh air. Along the way, they passed two hospital staff pushing a trolley carrying a young girl, perhaps ten or eleven years old. She was swiftly taken into an overcrowded emergency room filled with injured patients. Her eyes showed signs of fading, and she began to struggle for breath, emitting a gurgling sound. Grant had witnessed this scenario many times before; it often indicated that death was imminent. The girl had sustained a stomach injury from shrapnel. A nurse shook her head, indicating chances of survival were grim. Stomach wounds were particularly severe and often untreatable.

Grant instructed Mo to capture a close-up shot. He then filmed her face, completely filling the frame.

"You fucking ghouls," said a voice. "Have you got no fucking respect?"

Grant scanned the room, observing his surroundings. At the rear stood a hefty man holding a notebook. He happened to be a British journalist who recently arrived in Sarajevo.

In an instant, Grant rushed towards the man and tackled him to the ground, firmly gripping his throat.

"Listen, you complete and utter arsehole. You can write whatever you want standing miles away from where something happens. But we have to show what is happening exactly where the fuck it is happening, not a hundred metres or a hundred kilometres away. I don't make any excuses. This war is ugly, but people need to know what is happening and to whom. So, we don't apologise. But this little girl who is about to die is a victim, and my job is to show what happened to her and by whom. So fuck off with your moralising and go and write your shit from a safe distance."

Mo pulled on his shoulder, prompting Grant to stand up. It marked the end of a long day filled with horror, guilt, and frustration. They had endured seven months of it. He felt guilty because, despite their efforts, they appeared powerless. Even after repeatedly exposing the atrocities suffered by civilians, the international community remained reluctant to act. They kept finding reasons to justify their inaction, ignoring the urgent humanitarian need. Grant couldn't help but wonder: What was the purpose of it all? What impact were their efforts really making?

He understood there would be an international reaction, but what kind? Loss of human life, particularly among civilians, would undoubtedly prompt a response. Discussions in the halls of power often revolved around the unfortunate casualties labelled as innocent victims. Yet, these discussions rarely led to concrete decisions; instead, they seemed to meander into more meetings or towards lunchtime. While there were occasional expressions of outrage and calls for intervention, these typically came from opposition political parties with little to lose and often changed their stance once in power. Words, no matter how forceful, paled in comparison to the devastating impact of a 120mm mortar round or the wide-reaching shrapnel from a 155mm artillery shell. Governments would sometimes draw red lines and issue warnings, but they often amounted to empty threats, akin to blanks in a cheap 'Saturday night special' pistol. Maintaining a sense of cynicism was not just easy for a journalist; it was essential.

He walked into the corridor and leaned against the wall, feeling like all his energy had drained away. His mind was swirling with emotions. He was mad, but also on the verge of tears. Mo joined him in the corridor.

"And?" Grant asked.

"She went," replied Mo. As he said, a trolley was wheeled out of the emergency room and down the corridor. The lifeless body of the little girl lay there. A piece of fabric, like a tablecloth, covered her. A small, white hand peeked limply out from under the fabric. Tears streamed down Grant's face as he looked on.

"And I didn't even know her name," Grant cried softly. "I didn't know her fucking name."

The hospitals were too full to handle all the injured people. So, the UN arranged for a big US military plane, called a C130, to fly the badly hurt ones to Frankfurt, Germany, where they could get special care. A line of cars filled with injured people hurried along the small roads to reach the airport. The plane's engines were already running when they got there. They quickly put the injured people on the plane.

Upon returning to the hospital, the anchor's team arrived. Stu, the producer, was a stout man of short stature. His manner of speaking mainly consisted of giving orders and making demands.

"I hear there is a medical evacuation," he said to Grant. "We need to get Peter and a cameraman on that plane."

"I don't think there is a chance of that," responded Selma. "They need the space for the injured, and the plane is about to go. It's an emergency, and time is important."

"Hey lady, what's important is that we get Peter on that plane so he can show the world what has happened here."

Peter walked up. "Selma, can you ask the airport officials to hold the plane for a short time so we can get there? Tell them who I am, and as it is a US-operated flight, they will wait, I am sure."

Selma contained the anger that was building. "They have no idea who you are and don't care either. They care about getting these people to a place where they can be treated and lives saved. That is what is important."

The anchor looked stunned.

"No worries, Peter. It's been sorted," said the producer. "We've been on to the Pentagon, and they are going to make it happen. They will wait for us. But we need to go right now."

There wasn't any chance to say goodbye. The line of armoured Land Rovers quickly drove away, leaving Mo and Grant standing in the parking area, almost unable to believe what they were seeing. They understood that in every media battle, one thing mattered most: personality. And a heavy news anchor like the one they'd just witnessed had plenty of it.

18

In the gloomy basement of the old sports hall, now serving as the Bosnian Military Police Headquarters, Mohammed Ibrahimovic, a devout follower of the Quran, was seeking revenge. The room was dimly lit with a single lightbulb hanging from the stained ceiling, and the walls were peeling plaster, partly covered in dirty white tiles. The air was heavy with the scent of sweat and fear.

A middle-aged man sat on a wooden chair in front of him. His arms and legs were tied to the chair, and he whimpered like a child.

"Why am I here?" he sobbed. "I haven't done anything."

"You know that everyone who has ever sat in that chair says the same thing," responded Ibrahimovic. "But you know what, in the end, it turns out that almost all of them have done something. So, we need to find out what you have done. We can take the easy route or the difficult one." He glanced over at the table positioned along the side of the room. On it lay an assortment of tools: pliers, a hammer, blades, and a drill. This was no DIY collection. This was a toolkit for torturers.

Horror gripped the prisoner's face when he saw the table.

"I am a Serb, but I am a Bosnian too. That is why I stayed here. I didn't agree with what Belgrade has done. This is the truth. I have worked for Bosnia. Me and my family are Bosnians."

Ibrahimovic noticed that the man had wet his trousers and there was blood on his shirt from a cut lip. He described it as an ‘introduction.’ His lip nearly curled as he gazed at this pitiful person in front of him. His dislike and revulsion were evident. His face couldn’t conceal it.

“Listen, you Chetnik bastard, we know all about you, your black-market dealings, your little meetings next to the Verbanja bridge in the dead of night, the fact that you have smuggled Chetniks out of the city. We know everything.”

“But I have helped Muslims and Croats and Jews to get out of the city,” he responded. “It was just a business. It was just money. Nothing else. Something to keep my family alive and fed. Please, you have to believe me. I am a good Bosnian. I am not an enemy.”

“We shall see,” said Ibrahimovic. “We shall see.”

The sounds of the man’s cries echoed up as far as the second floor. People inside the building recognised that the Inquisitor General was busy. Nobody approved of his methods, yet everyone acknowledged that the secrets he uncovered had saved lives. In the basement of the Sports Hall, there were no rules, here there were no Geneva Conventions.

There was a knock on the door. “Enter,” shouted Ibrahimovic. It was a Bosnian soldier carrying a holdall.

“You were right,” said the man. “He had radio equipment and a large stash of Deutschmarks. They were hidden in his garden by a water butt. I think you have a sixth sense.”

The man from Serbia gazed upward with swollen eyes, darkened by the beatings he endured. His right hand was missing two fingers, while his left ear and part of his nose had been severed. The Inquisitor liked to adhere to the traditional methods of torture, reminiscent of the practices employed by the Ottoman Turks centuries ago, where "an eye for an eye" was taken quite literally.

"This equipment is not mine," cried the Serb. "I have never seen it before. Yes, I admit I bought and sold on the black market. But I am not the only one. Muslims are doing this as well. But I never betrayed Bosnia. You have to believe me."

Ibrahimovic found the evidence he wanted. Now, he needed more details: code books, names, contacts, and instructions. He didn't have everything yet, but he was getting close. He felt a sense of excitement, and a small smile appeared on his face.

Four hours later, Ibrahimovic found himself standing in front of General Mujkanovic.

"So, excellent news," said the General. He understood that Ibrahimovic could be harsh, but he also recognised that for Sarajevo and Bosnia, survival was paramount. In such desperate times, drastic actions were necessary. Personally, he wasn't fond of Ibrahimovic, finding him overly zealous in his religious beliefs. However, he admired his commitment to rescuing Bosnia.

"Yes, General, it seems it was him. We found radio equipment and money. Unfortunately, there was no code book. He was a tough man, but he took his secrets to the grave. He died without revealing who his contacts were or the codes. But at least we have now plugged the gap, and shouldn't suffer like we did at Barice again."

The General understood it wasn't an ideal situation. The code books were crucial for deciphering the Serb communications system. Though not perfect, it was a step forward, allowing them to resume planning how to overcome the Siege.

19

Mo and Grant slowly crawled across the ground towards the mound. They were accompanied by three Bosnian fighters and Mujo, the translator arranged by Selma. In front of them lay the Serb-held area known as Otes. Capturing it would enable the Bosnians to access the old road to Ilidza and continue southwest towards Mostar and the Croatian port of Split, providing a crucial lifeline. The biting wind and frozen ground made lying down feel like inviting hypothermia.

"We will attack in a few minutes," said a Bosnian fighter. "You should take a weapon. If the Serbs catch you, man you are big, dead meat," explained the fighter in broken English.

"No thanks," said Grant, "We are journalists, we don't fight. We report."

The fighter looked incredulous. "OK, man, it's your life."

In the distance, the bang, bang, bang sound of outgoing artillery echoed loudly as Mo captured footage of fighters advancing for the attack. Adrenaline surged through them, their heartbeats racing and their mouths feeling dry. They pushed aside thoughts of hypothermia to deal with later. It was a critical moment: survive, and you'd have an incredible story to tell; perish, and you'd be reduced to a tale recounted over drinks, eventually fading into anonymity as just "those guys" among journalists.

'Remember those idiots who played head tennis with tank shells in Bosnia in an insane front line?' the story would go.

Insane, however, was probably right. But idiots....? The next few hours would tell.

Artillery and any form of fire tend to provoke swift responses, a well-known fact for those familiar with frontline warfare. Unlike their adversaries, the

Bosnians lacked sophisticated counter-battery radar, leaving them vulnerable. Consequently, when they launched their attacks, the Serbs swiftly retaliated, often escalating the exchange. The deafening roar of incoming fire reverberated through the air, striking buildings in the vicinity as barrage after barrage descended upon them. Yet, amidst the chaos, Bosnian soldiers pressed forward undeterred.

Suddenly, a mortar shell landed perilously close, causing a machine gunner to clutch his knee in agony, wounded by shrapnel. Bloodstains speckled the pristine snow, a grim reminder of the brutality of war. Moments later, another explosion rocked the area, sending a soldier sprawling to the ground. Though he escaped physical injury, the sheer force of the blast was staggering.

"Let's move," shouted Mo, "They have centred on us." He started running back down the track towards some buildings.

Mo often joked about not being a fast runner, but when someone was firing at him, he could cover 100 metres in about seven seconds. He was fast. His goal was to reach the building and capture footage of Grant and the soldiers returning with the casualties. However, his plans were abruptly interrupted when everything went black. Silence enveloped him, not in the external world but within his own head. His ears rang, and his mind buzzed as he found himself lying on his back. After what felt like an eternity, though it was only a matter of minutes, he mustered the strength to lift his head. Blood formed large patches around him, a few feet away. Despite his efforts to clear his mind, the ringing in his ears grew deafening. Attempting to rise, he was met with a searing jolt of pain, akin to an electric shock coursing through his body. It was extremely painful. Glancing down, he spotted something protruding from his leg, a piece of bone. His trousers bore a sizable tear, with blood flowing freely. The realisation slowly dawned on him: he had been hit, and hit badly. The unthinkable had become reality. Then, another realisation struck him: he had neglected to bring both Buzz Lightyear and the first aid kit. He was in dire straits. Surveying his surroundings, he found himself alone. Everyone had vanished. Completely incapacitated, with shells still raining down, he began to count. Three, four, five, six... Desperation engulfed him as he shouted for help, but his voice was drowned out by the relentless explosions, each one seeming to draw closer.

Struggling against the pain, he managed to prop himself up and tear a strip of fabric from his shirt. With trembling hands, he tightly bound it around the wound, hoping to stop the flow of blood. As he forced himself into a sitting position, the full extent of the injury became clear; it was larger than he had initially thought.

"Fuck man, I don't want to lose my leg," he said to himself. But Mo had seen enough of these kinds of injuries to know there was a good chance that he would if he didn't get some treatment and soon.

Twelve thirteen fourteen, he continued to count.

'Where'd they get all the fucking ammo from?' Mo thought. And where was Grant? Two shells landed perilously close, merely ten metres away. The proximity sent a jolt of adrenaline through him; had he been standing there, the outcome could have been dire. Urgency seized him; he needed to find cover. Yet, amidst the chaos, there was no trace of Grant or the others. Fear gripped him as he contemplated their fate, had they too fallen victim to the shelling? The uncertainty weighed heavily on his mind, a torrent of anxious thoughts flooding his consciousness.

"What if the Serbs overran the position?" he thought and started to imagine that he, a Muslim, would probably be fair game for a Serb. He started to wish he had a gun.

Twenty-three, twenty-four….more and more came in. he heard a machine gun open up from afar. 'Bosnian or Serb?' he thought to himself. Aware of the urgency, he scanned his surroundings and spotted a picket fence roughly thirty metres away. While it offered limited cover, it was better than nothing. Wincing from the pain, he hastily fashioned another makeshift bandage from his shirt and cautiously shifted onto his stomach. Each movement sent waves of agony through him, but he gritted his teeth and pressed on. With every painstaking crawl, he gained only half a metre of ground, his injured leg protesting with each painful inch. Despite the relentless bombardment of shells nearby, he forced himself to persevere, driven by the instinct to survive. The distance to the fence seemed interminable, each moment stretching into eternity as he battled through the excruciating pain. Finally, reaching the fence, he hunched behind it, seeking refuge in its small protection, though the sense of safety it provided was fleeting at best. He lay there in the bitter cold, the passing time marked by occasional cries for help, yet he was growing increasingly apprehensive that he might be the lone survivor.

Another shell came in close. Twenty-six, Mo counted. Then he heard, "Mo, Mo, where the fuck are you?"

It was Grant's voice. "Here, over here, behind the fence," Mo responded.

Grant and two soldiers arrived.

"Where have you been, Habibi?" Mo asked.

"Two of the group got hit, and one was killed," explained Grant. "We were about thirty metres behind you. Now, we need to get you out of here."

Mo continued, "I don't know if I ran too fast into the shell or too slow, and it ran into me."

As a fourth fighter joined the group, the Bosnians displayed their resourcefulness in the face of adversity. With no stretcher available, they ingeniously fashioned one by breaking off a section of the picket fence. With great care, they laid Mo onto the makeshift stretcher, though his agonised cries pierced the air. Together, the group, including the three original fighters and Grant, lifted the fence on the count of three, determinedly making their way towards a row of bombed-out houses.

More shells came in.

"Twenty-eight, twenty fucking nine," shouted Mo. At that point, one of the soldiers stumbled and dropped his corner of the makeshift stretcher. Mo crushed to the ground, the impact jolting through his already injured leg, threatening to overwhelm his senses. The agony surged through him, nearly causing him to lose consciousness. Another piercing cry escaped his lips, echoing into the distance, perhaps reaching even the Serb lines stationed in Otes.

"We have to be quick," said a Bosnian soldier. "There is a spotter nearby, and he has seen us, so we need to move quickly."

In a synchronised effort, the four individuals swiftly lifted Mo, moving with haste across the 40 metres of exposed terrain towards a line of houses, seeking refuge and safety.

"My pack, my pack," asked Mo, "Where is it?" a soldier handed it over. He ruffled inside and came up with a half-bottle of Vodka. He took a swig and offered it to the soldiers and then lastly to Grant.

"Thank you guys very much," said Mo with a smile. He raised the Vodka bottle and said in Bosnian, "givili" (cheers). The soldiers smiled, took their rifles, and went back to where they had come from, back to the battle.

The Egyptian found himself on a flatbed truck, transported a kilometre away from the frontline medical post. A compassionate soldier offered him a cigarette, which he gratefully accepted and lit.

"You don't normally smoke," observed Grant.

"I don't normally get wounded either," said the Egyptian.

A doctor met them at the entrance. "There are some problems," he said, "The Serbs are trying to cut our road back to Sarajevo, and there is heavy fighting. We need to operate on your friend here."

"But this place doesn't have the right equipment," complained Grant. "You don't even have electricity, so there are no x-ray possibilities. How will you find the shrapnel?"

"We won't," responded the doctor.

Grant couldn't conceal his worry. He was acutely aware of the urgency; any delay in treatment heightened the risk of infection, and that meant amputation more often than not.

"Well, are you sure you can do this?" the doctor nodded.

"Have you done this before?"

"Yes, many times. Don't worry," said the medic.

As dusk settled outside Mo was wheeled into a dimly lit room. Grant took another gulp of vodka.

The doctor appeared. "Do you have a flashlight?" he asked Grant, who nodded and followed him into the room.

"Don't let him cut my leg off," Mo whispered to Grant.

"Fortunately, we do have anaesthetic," the doctor announced. A male nurse injected it into Mo, and he quickly drifted into unconsciousness.

"Please, shine on the wound."

The sight left Grant stunned. Up close it was the first time he saw had bad the wound was. It wasn't a pretty sight. The wound spanned about ten inches in length and three inches in width along the calf. The bone lay shattered, the muscle torn away in many places. It looked like a lump of meat on a butcher's slab. The exposed flesh was a raw, crimson display, with loose flaps and bone fragments embedded within. An ominous, elongated cavity ran down the inside of his left leg.

"He was lucky. No artery was hit. There is not much I can do," said the doctor, "but I will do my best. From the look of the wound, I would estimate that there are at least two pieces of shrapnel in there, maybe three." He set about cleaning the wound very thoroughly. The aim, he explained, was to proceed with caution and methodical care to avoid causing further trauma that might result in infection. The doctor emphasised that immediate removal of shrapnel wasn't always the optimal course of action; sometimes, it was preferable to wait.

He meticulously searched for every fragment of shattered bone, no matter how small. With care, he collected these pieces into a tray, working quietly and methodically despite the distant sounds of explosions. Cleaning the wound with alcohol, he remained unfazed by the chaos around him.

After nearly three hours, he completed the task of gathering the bone fragments. Then, he skillfully reconstructed the bone, a little like solving a jigsaw puzzle, although not every piece fited seamlessly. "It doesn't look very neat, but the bone will reconnect," he said. "The human self-healing system is something to behold." He placed the fragments roughly back in place and then tied them with a line.

"Fishing line," explained the doctor when he saw Grant's inquisitive look. "It works very fine."

There was no stitching. The male assistant simply bandaged the calf.

"The main operation to remove the fragments will happen in Sarajevo," the doctor explained. "I hope I have done enough to save his leg. It's up to God now."

"Thanks, Doctor. How long do you reckon he's going to be back on his feet?"

"Well, if he keeps the leg, you are looking at seven to nine months before he can walk unaided. If he's a quick healer, he can be up and running again in six months."

Grant walked back into the small room that passed for an operating room. He looked at his mate lying still unconscious from the anaesthetic. "You dumb Muslim," he thought. "You drank too much and prayed too little."

20

The bustling main dining room of the Holiday was full of journalists, immersed in animated conversations over meals and drinks, exchanging anecdotes and insights. This was Grant's regular dinner venue. The time difference meant scheduling his satellite time to the US after midnight. Suddenly, a tap on his shoulder diverted his attention. Chuck Brown stood beside him, placing a bottle of wine and two glasses on the table.

"Too bad about Mo," he said. "Law of averages and all that. But he's had a good run, and he'll be back. Won't he?"

"I hope so. He was evacuated this afternoon. First Split and then London for skin grafts and rehab. I'm sure he'll be OK. I suppose it was only a matter of time, considering the places we've been and the situations we've placed ourselves in. Bullet with your name on type thing."

"For sure," said Chuck. "They are out there. But shit, man, I ain't scared of those. That baby will find you one day if we keep up this mad, crazy life. But I am shit scared of all those bullets that say, 'To whom it may concern.' There are a lot of those mothers flying around."

"Take a look around this room filled with these wild, wonderful, and weird people. There's more collective scar tissue than a Belfast bomb aftermath, more bullet wounds, phosphorous burns, and shrapnel injuries than the average military unit; more mental trauma than in an asylum; more fucked up lives than the Borgias, more divorces, affairs, and scandals than an American TV soap; more alcoholics, drug addicts, and delinquents than you will ever meet in one gathering and in any other walk of life. What are we if we don't have this? Ordinary fucking people. And we DON'T do ordinary. We have one collective aim: to tell the story of injustice. God, I love this fucking job."

They exchanged smiles, clinking their glasses before downing another shot. It felt akin to sharing a confession in an Alcoholics Anonymous meeting. Yet, encountering a kindred spirit like this always offered a sense of solace, a reminder to Grant that he wasn't alone in his struggles. 'I am a Grant, a war junkie and tomorrow is the first day of the rest of my life....hopefully.' He smiled at the thought.

"Told you, man, it's fucking dangerous here," it was Ron O'Sullivan passing the table and shaking his head. "Fucking dangerous."

"Battle of Britain, Ron, Battle of Britain," both men replied in unison and then burst out laughing. It was abruptly ended.

In an instant, a thunderous shout erupted from the rear of the dining room, capturing everyone's attention. Bernie Johnson, his face flushed crimson with anger, stood there, radiating fury that seemed on the brink of boiling over.

"Which of you spineless, thieving bastards raped my room?" he shouted out.

Johnson possessed a striking appearance reminiscent of a biblical figure, standing at six feet three with bushy hair, a long greying beard, and a voice that resonated like a human loud hailer. While he was esteemed as a talented writer, his demeanour was often likened to that of a Viking on a raiding mission, lacking the delicacy associated with diplomacy. His reputation preceded him, with tales of his explosive temper and aggressive behaviour circulating throughout the journalistic community, becoming the stuff of folklore. Reports of physical altercations with colleagues, confrontations with office managers, and instances of intimidation painted a picture of a figure akin to a monster from a Brothers Grimm fairy tale. Additionally, his tendency towards light-handedness and a penchant for appropriating items ranging from cash to exclusive stories further cemented his reputation, earning him the label of a kleptomaniac in various respects.

"Who was it?" he bellowed to a room that became silent. Even Spit the Frog didn't utter a word, and he always had something to say.

"Some fucker has taken my food and wine and eaten my provisions, and it wasn't fucking Goldilocks and the three fucking bears," he shouted.

Chuck nudged Grant and collected the bottle and glasses. "Retreat, time for a tactical withdrawal," he whispered. "I forgot to tell you the other night that Johnson was a college boxing champ, and a fucking good one, and he's not shy about using his pugilistic skills. Best to give him some space." The two slunk away. Danger was never far away in Sarajevo, inside or outside the hotel.

They polished off the wine bottle in room 1004 on the tenth floor, where their regular group of friends gathered for shared moments of relaxation, laughter, and camaraderie.

"To Mo," said Chuck and raised a glass. "To Mo," the others repeated, and they all downed the slivavic in one. In a synchronised light show, tracer fire burst out, igniting flames beside the old parliament building's window. Mohammed, the relentless machine gunner, unleashed his barrage. Grant couldn't help but acknowledge the fervour, it was a genuine tribute to Mo.

After the sliva and joints were completed and the tracer fire had ceased, Grant made his way back to his room. Hejo remained at the reception, a constant presence behind the front desk.

"Oh, Mr Grant, how are you? So, two more Serb crimes today," he said. "Mr Mo, of course, but the Serbs also committed something far graver…they hit and destroyed the cigarette factory," he said with a deadpan face. "Now, some people could have forgiven the Serbs the killing, the rape, torture, ethnic cleansing, starvation, and the siege, but destroying our cancer supply is something that not even the most forgiving can turn a blind eye to. Cancer was the only way we were going to escape being killed by the Serbs. With cancer, we could go with a smile on our faces. Now, there is no hope."

He rummaged under the counter. "Mr Grant" this is for you. Mr Mo sent it before he left." It was Buzz Lightyear, along with a note. 'To infinity and beyond motherfucker. I may have fallen, but it was with style. I'll be back flying again soon. Love Mo'

The news brought a smile to his face, yet it also made him realise that for several months, he would be without his top cameraman and closest friend. As he ascended the five flights of stairs in darkness, he relied on his Maglite torch, the sound of the mad machine gunner outside echoing in the background. 'Good,' he thought to himself, 'At least I'll rest easier knowing he's alive, well, and still capturing shots.'

He opened the door, and he saw a candle burning.

"I've been waiting." It was Tanya, and she appeared to be highly emotional. She'd just arrived back from R n R in Rome, and she wasn't happy.

"It's not fucking fair," she almost cried. "Just not fair."

"But Mo is going to be alright," Grant tried to reassure her.

"No, not fucking Mo, the market massacre. I wasn't here for it. Can you imagine how that makes me feel? I have been here almost since the start, and just when the biggest event in Sarajevo happened when the first shots were fired, I wasn't here to record it. And did you see those pictures, those agency pictures, pictures taken by people who have no real feeling for a situation? I would have murdered the event. My pictures would have gone around the world, and they would have made a difference."

She started crying. Grant, though drunk, began to regain his sobriety. The ridiculousness of her words slowly dawned on him.

"But this was a truly horrible thing that happened. It's the thing of nightmares, bits of bodies, dead kids, women, and old people. Fucking civilians, for Christ's sake. How the fuck can you be upset because you missed something like that." He shook his head.

"You know what, I think you need help. You are on the wrong side of insanity. We see enough. We don't need to see more. I have witnessed enough carnage and butchery to give my nightmares decent content for the rest of my life. Why would anyone want more?"

Tanya got up and began dressing.

"What the fuck do you know?" she said, "You TV people are just egotistical shitheads who never really go to where it happens. You just pay locals to risk their necks to give you footage that you pretend is yours and then use your makeup kits to make yourself look nice on camera. Your medium is bordering on fucking disgusting. What about your prima donna fucking head honcho Valentine who just swanned in on a PR blitz. Don't you dare lecture me on sanity and what this job is about. I am FUCKING good at my job. My fucking pictures tell stories and get noticed, and there is no substitute for a photographer to be where it is happening. I should have been here that day. Now go fuck yourself."

Grant watched as she stormed out of the room, slamming the door behind her. He acknowledged her competence at her job, yet now he also recognised a hint of instability, confirming his suspicions.

21

Hasina gazed into the mirror, confronting a reflection that felt foreign. The face that stared back appeared was noticeably thinner, with subtle bags beneath sunken eyes, etched with deep lines from countless tears. Grey hairs peeked through, unwelcome reminders of her youth slipping away at just twenty-four. Gone was the Hasina she once knew, the one who shed tears freely. Now, crying seemed futile, a waste of both emotion and energy. In this unforgiving place, tears only invited contempt and disgust from the Serbs, who detested weakness. Her new role demanded resilience, not self-pity. She couldn't help but think of her parents' fate, wondering if they endured a life akin to hers. She prayed it wasn't so.

As the door creaked open, there stood a large, overweight woman. Her jet-black hair cascaded down her shoulders, and her face with heavy makeup and green fingernails.

"Hey bitch," she shouted, "What is taking you so long?"

"I am sorry, Sonja," Hasina replied. "I won't be long."

"You had better not be," she ordered and then left.

Sonja, the daughter of a Bosnian Serb politician, held an unchallenged position of power. She boasted of running the most prosperous brothel in the Balkans, with a clientele that sought out the finest services. Yet behind the facade of success lay a grim reality. Her girls, predominantly Muslim, had little say in their involvement; for them, it was "spread or dead," a stark ultimatum. In the harsh landscape of survival, dignity often takes a backseat, as was the case for Hasina. Enduring repeated assaults, including a brutal gang rape, she learned the cruel lesson of compliance. Resisting meant further violence, so she acquiesced, her silence would be mistaken for consent in the eyes of a hypothetical courtroom.

Beaten and abused regularly, Hasina found a twisted sanctuary in Sonja's establishment. Here, the beatings were fewer, the food more consistent, and the sexual encounters, while still violating, carried a semblance of routine acceptance. Amidst this grim reality, Hasina observed the ignorance of her captors, their skewed perceptions of Muslims, and the events leading to the war. They believed all Muslims, including her, were fundamentalists and wanted to subjugate Serbs to make a caliphate with Sharia law.

'Where did that come from?' she often thought to herself.

Hasina possessed intelligence and education. She held knowledge of history, particularly concerning the suffering of Jews in World War II concentration camps. She had encountered accounts of individuals resorting to extreme measures for survival, even resorting to unthinkable acts such as violence and betrayal. It was only now, in her current circumstances, that she truly grasped the desperation that drove people to such lengths. As she found herself at her lowest point, offering her body in exchange for hope of a future escape to safety, she confronted the harsh realities of survival.

"Odma," (now) shouted out a voice from down the corridor. Sonja grew increasingly impatient as she hurriedly applied the final touches to her make-up. Eager for her girls to begin work, she swiftly made her way down the corridor.

The brothel lacked any semblance of elegance, composed of worn-out couches, scratched tables, and weathered carpeting dominating the room's centre. It exuded a rustic charm similar to an old Wild West saloon, despite the less appealing decor. A Serb flag, bearing the four C's, hung on one wall, while a large stone fireplace with a towering mantlepiece stood opposite, crowned by a painting depicting a formidable brown bear, a common sight in the hills and mountains of Bosnia, often the target of hunters. As one of the other girls revealed, Sonja's was once a hunting lodge frequented by Tito, now repurposed for a different kind of pursuit, one where the prey had no means of resistance.

On the right, a sizable bar accommodated four other girls, while three more lounged on a couch in the corner. Dim lighting enveloped the room, accompanied by soft music emanating from the hi-fi. Hasina cautiously joined them, awaiting the commencement of her evening.

Shortly thereafter, three intoxicated fighters barged in, their drunkenness evident. They emitted wild howls upon spotting the women, accompanied by crude, sexist remarks. Without delay, they ordered a bottle of rakia and settled at a table, indulging in their drinks while assessing the women.

Placing their AK47s against the wall, the trio loomed large in stature. The tallest among them, towering at six feet six, resembled the bear depicted in the painting. He was looking at Hasina and started to blow small kisses while laughing. Despite the unsettling atmosphere, Hasina maintained her trained composure, responding with a polite smile, despite knowing the ever-present threat, 'spread or dead'.

She smiled at the Serb 'bear'. He strode over to Sonja, and they engaged in a conversation. Hasina suspected it was about the price. She had never considered her value in that way before. It was something that was never openly talked about. Besides, she never received any payment. She figured it was probably a small sum. Soldiers didn't earn much. The agreement was swiftly settled, and the 'bear' man made his way closer.

"So, me and you for some fun," he said to Hasina. His breath stank of cigarettes, accompanied by a strong body odour that smacked of neglected hygiene. Hasina couldn't tell when his clothes or body had last seen soap and water, but it had clearly been quite some time. Internally, her stomach churned and her nose wrinkled in distaste, yet she managed to suppress her grimace and muster a strained smile. She rose slowly and found the man impatient. He grasped her by the arm and lifted her. "Time is money," he said and pushed her in the direction of the corridor and her bedroom.

If he possessed any gentle traits they were well hidden, resembling more of an untamed animal. Showing no regard for her or any sense of delicacy, he thrust himself upon her with the force of a wild boar, his imposing figure pressing her into the worn mattress. Despite the ordeal, there was a small sense of relief; his inebriated state lent itself to a hasty climax, followed swiftly by sleep. Lying on her back, she stared at the ceiling, his snoring resonating like a thunderous saw. Summoning the courage to rise, she donned a dressing gown and settled into an armchair across from the bed, her gaze fixed on her assailant. Taking one of his Marlboro cigarettes, she lit it, a habit unfamiliar to her until now, much like the harrowing experience she had just endured. She cast a glance at the 'animal'lying on the bed.

The sense of violation intensified with this Serb more than with most others who had mistreated her. For the first time in a while, tears welled in her eyes, a sensation she believed she had overcome. It felt as though the weight of her suffering was collapsing inward, accompanied by a profound feeling of hopelessness. She questioned the meaning of survival, pondering the cost of her sacrifice, mental and physical, and how much more she could endure. What the ultimate cost would be? Not being a psychologist but a singer, she understood that the trauma she endured would linger long after the conflict subsided. Bodies could be healed, but the scars on the mind were far more enduring.

With disgust, she looked at the Serb lying nearby, his unwashed, malodorous frame dominating her confined space. The urge to vomit surged within her. She went through his jacket pockets, discovering money in a wallet with a photo of a woman, likely his wife or girlfriend. She appropriated some of the money and a few cigarettes.

The bear stirred and woke up. He turned over and Saw Hasina standing over his clothes.

"Hey bitch, what are you doing, you thieving whore?"

As he began to rise, Hasina felt a surge of panic. Under his jacket, she spotted a belt with a holster housing an automatic pistol. Amidst the chaos of her thoughts, she found herself swiftly reaching for the firearm, raising it as the bear emerged from his slumber and advanced towards her.

In that moment, her panic subsided, replaced by a sudden clarity. She comprehended her surroundings, the gravity of the situation, and the inevitable consequences. Moreover, a profound sense of revulsion towards the creature standing before her engulfed her, a creature responsible for ravaging her homeland, her kin, her people and her. Remembering the shared sentiment between the Koran and the Bible, 'an eye for an eye', she lifted the gun.

"What the fuck are you doing, you bitch?" said the Serb getting up from the bed. He began to approach her, yet before uttering another word, Hasina discharged a single round. It struck the large man's chest, causing him to collapse heavily, like a solid block of concrete. She advanced towards him, astonished by her sense of calm.

"Aren't we having fun?" she said and fired a second shot into his forehead from point-blank range. Blood began to spurt from his chest and head, forming a red pool that gradually expanded across the worn carpet. Hasina found herself oddly thinking it somehow improved the tattered appearance of the carpet.

From down the corridor towards the lounge, shouts echoed loudly. With the gun still gripped tightly in her hand, she cautiously approached the door. Two uniformed men came into view, unaware of the weapon at first. With swift precision, Hasina fired two more shots, bringing them down instantly. As she entered the lounge, the women's screams filled the air. Hasina gestured for silence, assuring them there was no cause for fear.

Behind the bar, Sonja rose, her anger evident as her chin trembled and her face contorted in rage.

"What are you doing, you dumb bitch? You are a dead woman," they were the last words she spoke.

Hasina raised the gun and fired two shots into her chest, one through the heart. Death was instantaneous. She collapsed in a heap. Hasina smiled, "Spread and dead," she said. "Allah Immanet," she said to the other Muslim women and then turned the gun on herself. One shot through the head. Her war and torment were over.

22

The historic building, dating back to the seventeenth century, stands prominently in the western part of Sarajevo's old town, easily visible to Serb snipers. Its southern walls, pockmarked by bullets, bear witness to the constant threat it faces. Outside, the remnants of felled trees litter the surroundings, chopped for firewood amidst the chaos. Craters from past shell impacts decorate the main street, creating some kind of surrealist installation. Broken lamp posts further add to the scene, evoking a sense of Armageddon-like proportions. The streets, once bustling with life, now lie mostly deserted. Alongside the building, large shipping containers stand, their surfaces riddled with bullet holes, remnants of Serb attacks, or acts of frustrated aggression.

Within the building's basement lies the headquarters of the Bosnian Government. In the face of overwhelming Serb firepower and strategic advantage, survival seems like an insurmountable challenge. Outnumbered and often outmanoeuvred, they fight fiercely with whatever resources they can muster. Drawing parallels to the biblical tale of David and Goliath, they recognise the power of international media in shaping perceptions. However, they also contend with the realisation that, even as victims, they are not immune to the art of manipulation. Among the cohort of international journalists there began an increasing scepticism towards official narratives there were questions about the government's credibility for the first time since the war began.

Grant and Selma descended into the basement, accompanied by a new cameraman named Jake, a laid-back Australian freelancer. He possessed a carefree demeanour, more concerned with earning his day's pay and having a steady supply of drinks and cigarettes than his surroundings. Grant acknowledged that, in a war zone, beggars couldn't afford to be too selective.

"Who are we interviewing, mate?" asked the Aussie.

"It's the president of Bosnia," Grant replied in a semi-sarcastic way.

"Which side is he on then?" It was a question not worthy of an answer, so Grant didn't answer it. He observed a television crew comprising women near the entrance of the president's secretary's office. One of them, a tall American woman with dyed blonde hair, stood out. She wore a fur-lined coat and matching gloves, with what appeared to be a string of pearls around her neck. Engaged in conversation, she spoke into a satellite phone.

"Yeah, we are waiting," she answered. "I will make the bird." Bird was slang for satellite feed. Planet TV news had its own language.

"No, I won't take any BS," she continued.

Grant was acquainted with her, though they had not met in person. Despite her formidable stature, she possessed a personality that exceeded her physical presence. He had come to understand that she was associated with one of those loud-mouthed American TV crews more focused on appearances than substance. They sought out perilous locales to enhance their reputation and secure lucrative contracts. As she concluded her call, she retrieved her compact makeup kit, a ubiquitous accessory among American TV correspondents. Even Grant had one; it was a standard issue from ATV, bundled with medical supplies and provisions. A producer had once remarked that Grant appeared a touch pallid during a live broadcast and suggested a dab of foundation. Grant knew, though he remained silent, that no amount of makeup could conceal the toll of witnessing the aftermath of crimes such as the deaths of three children, victims of a mortar attack as they innocently played in the streets.

Arriving early for his interview, Grant realised it would likely be another routine session of government-sanctioned dialogue led by a couple of Western-educated ministers adept at delivering soundbites and catchy phrases. Naively, he had assumed he was being offered an exclusive interview opportunity.

Another TV team descended the stairs, led by a familiar woman correspondent whom Grant recognised. She hailed from a prominent French/American background, working for one of the world's largest satellite news channels. Known for her ubiquitous presence and respected stature, she was not one to mince words.

Her appearance evoked images of a classic Hollywood actress from the 1950s. Accompanying her was a diminutive cameraperson, whose scarred face bore the testimony of a past encounter with a bullet. Grant had heard the story: the bullet had shattered her jaw before ricocheting through her cheekbone. While some might have retreated from public view in embarrassment. Not tough-nut-Tina. The American was as tough as old boots. She was also fond of drinking sessions during which she would stick her scarred face into men's faces and say, "Fancy a tumble?" Few did. She was a character. They were both characters.

"Out of the way," shouted the correspondent. "This is my interview. I am in first. I've got a feed in 45 minutes." Grant had encountered numerous challenging situations on the frontlines, yet he had developed a keen awareness of avoiding entanglements with female TV correspondents. As she hurried past him, she exuded an intense energy reminiscent of a hurricane, momentarily leaving Grant feeling intimidated. With a sense of deference, he watched her proceed, and once she had left, the other female correspondent turned towards her cameraman.

"In this business, there are two kinds of women journos, good bitches and bad bitches. I'm a good bitch, but I can tell you that was certainly one hell of a bad bitch."

After the bitches finished, it was Grant's turn. He entered the secretary's adjacent room, accompanied by Selma and the cameraman, before being guided into the president's office, located in the basement. Although small slit-like windows allowed some light, they were all covered with sandbags.

Sitting behind a grand Louis XV-style desk was Bosnian President Mirsad Mehotic, a man of modest stature but resolute character. He was a particular target of Serbs criticism, accused of harbouring ambitions to transform Bosnia into an Islamic state. His unwavering religious devotion to Islam led to imprisonment during the communist era. After his release, he sought refuge in Turkey until the demise of the Yugoslav Dictator Tito allowed his return. The intricacies of politics eluded Mehotic; he felt uneasy facing cameras, wary of the potential misinterpretation of his words. However, he braved media interactions to uphold Bosnia's multicultural heritage, advocating for harmony among Catholics, Muslims, and Orthodox believers. He always gave interviews in Bosnian, and Selma began to speak, outlining the theme of the interview and what Grant was looking for. Though stoic, the president appeared somewhat distant, as if longing for a different setting.

Grant was experienced in conducting interviews, understanding that they lose value if artificially sustained. Obtaining insightful quotes on pertinent subjects was paramount to him. Currently, his focus lay on gathering information about eastern Bosnia.

"Why, Mr President, are you making up stories about eastern Bosnia when no one has been able to get in there? Why should we believe you, considering that several recent government claims have proven untrue?" It was a blunt opening designed to stimulate a strong response.

Selma translated, yet it was evident that Mehotic quickly grasped the question and responded even before she finished.

"We have contact via ham radio," he explained. "They tell us bad things are happening, and many people are being ethnically cleansed. There are reports of many killed and injured, and people have no food. Starvation is looming. Unless something is done, this will be one of the biggest catastrophes of this terrible war. The UN is doing nothing. The Serbs refuse to let them in, and they simply accept this. They say they cannot force the Serbs to comply. By taking this stand and not helping, the UN is being indirectly complicit in the death of thousands of Bosnians."

"But where is the proof? How can anyone act if there is no proof? European politicians are saying privately that you are trying to make this situation seem worse than it is to get the West to come in and solve this matter for you. You have made other claims which have turned out to be inaccurate."

Mehotic didn't wait for the translation. He understood, quite clearly, what Singleton had said. His face reddened and he replied in English.

"By the time the West got proof of what was happening in the German concentration camps, millions of Jews had been killed. By the time the American public heard of the atrocities their soldiers had committed in Vietnam, many more Vietnamese had been killed. How many Bosnians need to die before the West realises what is happening here? It's a dangerous place. We have lost many brave men trying to help the people in the East. The Serbs are well-armed and well-prepared, but we are still continually trying. No one is under the illusion that the West will suddenly change their policy on Bosnia."

He raised his voice noticeably. It marked his inaugural attempt at speaking English during an interview, and Grant discerned that it stemmed from frustration.

"Well, get me in," said Grant. "Get me into Eastern Bosnia, and I will get the proof that the West cannot deny."

Mehotic paused, deep in thought, before summoning an assistant. He swiftly communicated in Bosnian, and the man promptly exited the room.

Selma was sitting behind Grant. "He's just given instructions that you should be linked up with our forces in the north, who will try and get you in," she whispered.

The president looked at Grant and said, "We cannot give safety guarantees, but we will try our best to get you in. There are no promises. If you make it, you will see that everything I have told you is true. You will see. Good luck, Allah Immanet."

"Allah Immanet," replied Grant, and the team left the room. He knew realistically, the chances of him making it to Eastern Bosnia were less than fifty per cent. He also knew that the chances of the president having given an accurate description of what is happening was also probably less than fifty per cent. He was well aware that at that very moment a team of journalists had made a highly dangerous twelve hour hike to another Bosnian enclave because of the same claims. They sent videos and pictures of people fishing and growing vegetables. They had taken a big risk for what seemed a little return.

At midnight, they parked their car outside the Drugge bar, arriving just as three mortar shells fell nearby.

"Great mate," said the Aussie cameraman, "Fireworks." Grant and the Aussie helped Selma through the hole in the wall into full-on, loud blasting music and a party well underway with the countdown to New Year 1993 just starting. Many of the Holiday Inn, journalists were inside mingling with locals, translators and fixers, the atmosphere buzzed with booze, drugs, and high spirits. For Grant, it was a captivating scene, a stark departure from his life in London. In London his girlfriend had left him but in its place Sarajevo had begun to feel like home during his extended stay. Immersed in a journalistic mission, he found himself not yearning for his old life. As Selma raised her glass in a toast, their embrace lingered longer than mere friendship would warrant. Grant couldn't help but notice Selma's beauty, particularly her mesmerising azure eyes. Her intelligence and wit only added to her allure. Enchanted by her presence and the unfolding narrative of Sarajevo, Grant felt himself falling not just for the story but for Selma as well.

'Rock the Casbah' started playing and the whole place erupted in a joyous fusion of irreverent party indulgence.

"You look happy," Grant observed, raising his voice over the music. "I am," she said, "To a point. We had really good news today. My twin brother Mehmet is alive. He was in a Serb prison camp, but he escaped, and he's made it back to my town. He's back with my father. So that is really good news."

They clinked glasses joyfully. Although he hadn't met Mehmet before, if he resembled Selma in any way, he must be equally remarkable.

Grant was unexpectedly bumped into by Hejo from the Holiday Inn, who carried a bottle of sliva in one hand and a glass in the other. Hejo poured a shot and extended it to Grant, who noticed a makeshift bandage wrapped around his head and chin.

"What happened?" shouted Grant. "Tooth problem," replied Hejo. "Not many dentists left working in Sarajevo. But sliva helps. Tell me Mr Grant, what do you get when you have thirty-two Bosnians in a room?"

Grant shook his head.

"A full set of teeth," laughed Hejo, who danced off into the crowd.

Selma and Grant laughed.

"So," Grant said, looking deeply into Selma's eyes, "What are my chances?"

She looked at him, confused. "Chances of what?"

"Chances to get to Eastern Bosnia."

She laughed, "Oh. I thought you meant something else."

"Something like what?"

"Well, I mean…"

Even in the dim light, Grant could see she was blushing. They had been working closely together for weeks. He admired her for her assertiveness; she didn't tolerate any nonsense, not even from him or from the Australian colleague who seemed indifferent to Bosnia. Despite this, she held a genuine liking for Grant, appreciating his approach, his empathy, and his commitment to justice. He didn't view people merely as statistics; each had a name and a story, a perspective in his reports that impressed her. Moreover, Grant was good-looking. New Year proved to be a seminal moment for reasons that would become apparent in the coming weeks. Unbeknown to the two a course was being set but for now it was the party that counted and when the energetic beat of the B 52's 'Love Shack,' broke out the whole room erupted and the war seemed momentarily forgotten. It wasn't death and destruction that captivated the partygoers, it was joy and celebration.

They got back to hotel at 5:00 a.m. The Aussie was so drunk he couldn't make it out the car and so remained slumped in the passenger seat. Selma, though slightly unsteady, remained composed and in control. Grant was losing his control. He lingered in the shadows of the garage stairwell and grappled with conflicting emotions. Like a love-struck teenager he yearned to initiate a kiss with Selma, but he hesitated, fearing the potential fallout of rejection and the subsequent impact on their working relationship.

"Thanks for a lovely evening," she said. "I will try to find my friend who is staying here and stay with her tonight."

"But you can have my room, to yourself, I mean," said Grant in a half stutter. "I can stay somewhere else. It's no problem. I have plenty of possibilities. Honest. Please, take the key."

"Are you sure?"

"Yes, sto per cent," he replied in halting Bosnian. (One hundred per cent.)

"You English are really polite gentlemen, aren't you?"

"Absolutely, we always said excuse me before we invaded a country."

She smiled. To Grant, it was brighter than the sun. She took his hand.

"Thank you so much," I will see you in the morning then."

"Yes, morning," he mouthed and watched her walk into the shadows and up the stairs to room 604."

He felt like a smitten teenager, brimming with joy. It was 5:30 a.m. He made his way back to the car, opened the door, gently nudged the Aussie onto his side, and then squeezed into the back seat.

"Move over, cobber. It's me and you tonight, not exactly what I was hoping for, but, hey, war is war."

23

He had changed fundamentally. The Mehmet of old had vanished, lost amidst the wreckage of a shattered country and a shattered life. In his place stood a new

Mehmet, forged by the harsh realities of a world in chaos. Survival had become paramount, overriding any semblance of order or justice. In this new reality, rules had lost their meaning; the graveyard was testament to the fate of those who adhered to them. It was the rule-breakers, perched upon the hills, who dictated the grim course of existence, raining down destruction with shells and bullets. His countenance bore the weight of this harsh existence, prematurely aged by the burdens he now carried. Taking up arms, he understood that his family, friends, and country were locked in a battle for survival, a fact made painfully clear by the aggression of the Serbs.

Reuniting with his father, Yousef, stirred deep emotions. Yet the man before him was a mere shadow of the vibrant figure he once knew – a man filled with irreverent humour and an unwavering belief in the goodness of humanity. Since the loss of Mehmet's mother, his father had withered, and his vitality had drained away like water from a leaky flask. It was a heart-wrenching sight to behold. Mehmet often accompanied his father to his mother's grave, though the pain of loss made such visits unbearably painful to watch.

His town resembled scenes from Second World War movies, as people flooded in every day with meagre possessions and the few animals they could salvage. Driven out by the relentless Serb advance and bombardments, Donji Zelenik was nestled amidst hills that provided some shelter, but only as long as they remained under Bosnian control. Maintaining this control was paramount for the town's survival. While the Serbs were currently unable to breach its defences, the blockade they imposed prevented essential supplies from entering. With the main road under Serb control, the town was effectively besieged. Consequently, the inhabitants were gradually succumbing to starvation. Previously home to nearly three thousand people, Donji Zelenik now struggled to accommodate fifty thousand displaced individuals. Buildings once serving various purposes, schools, fire stations, warehouses, and sports halls, were now overcrowded, leaving many to seek shelter on the streets. As winter set in, temperatures plummeted, exacerbating the already dire situation.

Mehmet grew resilient in the face of life's hardships and the brutality of the concentration camp. Witnessing the depths of inhumanity, he recognised the absence of boundaries in war. Unlike a regulated sport with referees, there were no signals to halt foul play. Moreover, the lack of witnesses meant no evidence.

In the ensuing weeks, Mehmet transformed into a courageous fighter, emerging as a natural leader crucial for the group's survival. He orchestrated daring raids on Serb targets, becoming a beacon of hope amid the darkness of war. Soon, he garnered the nickname "Pasha," an esteemed Ottoman Turkish title denoting high rank and respect.

He understood the gravity of the situation all too well. The Serb siege had tightened like a vice, making it exceedingly difficult to bring in essential supplies. Despite their best efforts to smuggle provisions through the hills and past Serb lines, for every successful delivery, numerous others were intercepted. Mehmet and Donji Zelenik found themselves without reliable external assistance; the burden of survival fell squarely on their shoulders.

Beside his mother's resting place, he offered a silent prayer before guiding his father back home. Mehmet's resolve remained unspoken as he armed himself with his AK47 and set out towards headquarters. Along the path, he bore witness to entire families eking out an existence on the cold, unforgiving streets: grandparents, grandchildren, the old and weak. Fires dotted the landscape as people burned whatever they could find to stave off the biting cold. Injured men lay on stretchers outside makeshift clinics, their numbers overwhelming the meagre facilities. Treatment was administered swiftly; there was no room for prolonged care. The scarcity of resources forced patients to recover outdoors, exposed to the harsh elements. It was a situation with no alternatives and few choices.

Within the PTT building, serving as the headquarters for the Bosnian fighters, a cluster of men rose to welcome Mehmet with a salute. "Pasha," they said together. Acknowledging the gesture, he made his way to a table covered with a sizable map.

"OK, let's go over this one more time."

Facing a dangerous mission, Donji Zelenik had no alternative. With food stores dwindling to critical levels and ammunition reserves rapidly depleting, survival hung by a thread. To prolong their chances, securing replenishments became an imperative. There was only one course open to them, the solution lay in acquiring provisions from the Serbs. That would mean having to make a daring but highly dangerous breach of Serb lines through heavily fortified positions where supplies awaited. There were no illusions regarding the risky nature of their forthcoming endeavour.

Before him stood Hagija, the ex-policeman, characterised by broad shoulders, a hefty beard, and a perpetual scowl etched upon the visible part of his countenance. Having known Mehmet since childhood, Hagija had previously dismissed him, recalling the times he had remonstrated with him on the streets. In Hagija's eyes, Mehmet had been pigeonholed as a feeble intellectual, lacking the qualities he deemed indicative of true manliness. However, recent weeks had completely changed this perception. Impressed by Mehmet's resourcefulness and courage, Hagija reframed his view. While not acknowledging him as a leader,

Hagija recognised Mehmet as a fellow combatant and well respected by their comrades for his valour.

"The situation is getting bad," he said, "The Chetniks have taken six more villages and about fifty miles of territory. They've cut the last two supply lines. The noose is tightening, and if we don't do something quickly, we'll all be hanged."

Amidst the conquest of villages and loss of territory, the influx of displaced individuals added further strain on already scarce resources, particularly food. Resorting to grinding berries from trees into crude flour offered temporary relief, despite its lack of essential nutrients and protein, merely calming hunger momentarily.

Tensions escalated as fighters received priority rations, leaving others feeling neglected. Mehmet faced the tough choice of allocating resources to sustain the strength of those engaged in combat. Recognising the impracticality of weakened fighters, only fifty men were selected for the imminent attack. The strategy centred on swift execution, striking with intensity, and swiftly fading into obscurity under the cover of night. The element of surprise would be the greatest weapon. After nights of searching, scouts identified the ways through the minefields. It was a now-or-never moment.

"Let's go," ordered Mehmet. "Sretan put," (good luck), "Allah Immanet".

As they stepped outside, they found the fighters prepared, yet the apprehension on their faces was evident. They understood the slim chances of returning unharmed. But the mission was essential. Surrounding them, numerous civilians gathered around small fires on the street. The flickering flames painted their faces with a reddish hue, reminiscent of hell's glow. They appeared thin, worn out, and destitute. Hagija often joked that there were no longer overweight individuals in Donji Zelenik, himself included.

They walked silently in two orderly lines, advancing into the encompassing darkness and ascending the steep hill to the south of town. Their strategy was to execute a strategic 180-degree turn, aiming to approach an area where the Serbs would be least prepared for an assault and where their defences appeared most formidable. The breach would happen by a small Serb village which served as a key defensive position for the town of Vosoka, housing the headquarters of the Serb's eastern forces. Mehmet led the mission. He estimated a three-hour journey to reach their designated attack position.. Gradually, the fighters moved off to be swallowed by the darkness.

They didn't know it but they were being followed.

24

Grant entered the hotel lobby and noticed the body being carried out on a stretcher. He glanced at Hejo with curiosity.

"The fire chief," explained the little man.

"Serbs?" asked Grant.

"No, his lover. Shot him twice through the head because he was going back to his wife!"

'What rotten luck,' Grant thought. Here he was, a man accustomed to facing peril daily as he battled blazes amidst the constant threat of Serb snipers and mortars. The odds of injury were ever-present. Yet, meeting his demise in the safety of his bed at the hands of his lover epitomised the craziness of life in Bosnia.

He searched for Selma and discovered her in the back room by the espresso machine. Unfortunately, the supplies from the Ukrainians had depleted. Her eyes were red, indicating she had been crying.

"What's wrong?"

"My cousin Hasina is dead. We heard today. She was like a sister to me. She'd been forced into prostitution by the Serbs. She finally took her own life after killing some soldiers. One of the other women got word out somehow."

He bent down and comforted her, though she initially resisted before finally accepting the embrace in a prolonged, heartfelt manner.

"You know this war is draining life from us; it's devouring all our emotions. One day, relief and a sort of happiness; the next, tragedy and depression. Do you know your Shakespeare Grant? King Lear Act 4 Scene One. The blind Lord Gloucester says, 'As flies to wanton boys are we to the Gods, they kill us for their sport.' He was so right. So fucking right. We are the sport. When you go to the Serb side, I need you to do something for me. It's something important."

"Of course," said Grant. "Anything."

She nestled further into his embrace, tears trickling down softly. Grant noticed that, despite Selma's usual resilience, she, like many others, had reached her breaking point. Her barriers had crumbled, leaving her vulnerable and seeking solace and safety, almost like a little girl child seeking comfort and protection. She pulled back, wiped her tears, and asked, "Can I stay with you tonight?"

"Of course, of course," he replied, and she relaxed in his arms. Love and war. It seemed never one without the other.

25

An hour before sunrise, Mehmet and his men took their positions, their faces darkened with black shoe polish. Two fighters approached to report that they had found the trail through the minefield. Mehmet had never been religious. In communist Yugoslavia, he was staunchly against all forms of religion, despite his father being a devout Muslim. However, circumstances had changed. Many, like Mehmet, now saw their religion as a source of pride rather than shame. They embraced it openly, realising that if they were to die for being Muslims, they would do so proudly. Mehmet set down his Kalashnikov and began to pray. His comrades joined him, silently reciting the Salah prayer in unison.

Towards the end, they knelt down, shifted their gaze to the right, and softly uttered 'Assalamu Alaikum wa Rahmatullah,' conveying peace and blessings. Then, they turned to the left, repeating the same words to conclude their prayer. With this, they prepared themselves.

Following one another, they began to depart. Mehmet was in the second group of five, while Hagija was part of the third. Once beyond the minefield, they planned to disperse. Each group had a designated objective, whether it was a bunker or a house where Serb fighters were expected to be present.

They navigated the minefield cautiously, marking potential dangers as best they could. A misstep could lead to injury, but worse it would alert the Serbs. After thirty, anxious minutes, they safely passed the mines and Mehmet's group moved deeper into the village, towards a warehouse suspected to house ammunition..

Three of Mehmet's finest comrades advanced towards a house where they could hear voices. Stealthily they crept up to the window, they stole a glance inside. They counted five Serb fighters inside and relayed to their comrades. Mehmet directed his men to encircle the dwelling. Their directive: eliminate the occupants, but silently to avoid attracting additional Serbs.

At that moment, two Serbs exited the house, visibly affected by alcohol, and proceeded to relieve themselves in the bushes. Swiftly and quietly, they were neutralised. They didn't even have time to fasten their trousers. Not a single noise escaped. Hagija, equipped with a silencer, swiftly dispatched each man with a single bullet to the head. Death was instant. Moving on with his group towards the rear entrance of the house, they entered cautiously. The only sounds heard were three 'put' noises, each signifying a bullet finding its Serb target.

The fifty men dispersed, spreading out as they went from house to house along the front. Mehmet ventured deeper into the village in search of the warehouse, which lay just 100 metres away. They moved swiftly and assumed their positions. Surprisingly, there were no guards present. They were complacent motherfuckers, thought Mehmet. They broke the lock and shined a torch. They gasped. It was an Aladdin's cave of weapons and ammunition and machine guns, grenades, 60mm mortars. "Jackpot", thought Mehmet.

Resistance had been minimal. The Serbs had surprisingly few people in position. It was akin to a quick shopping trip for the Bosnian fighters- in and out before anyone realised. However, the reality was different.

As they began removing weapons from the warehouse, an explosion sounded behind them, near the minefield. Another blast followed shortly after, causing confusion among them. Mehmet quickly urged the men to hasten their efforts before darting back towards the houses near the minefield. Shocked, he witnessed a multitude of civilians, Bosnian Muslims, seeking refuge in the houses after following the fighters. They were so desperate for food that they risked traversing the mines and encountering the Serbs. Among them were the elderly and the young as they went from house to house scavenging for food. Tensions rose as some squabbled over bread found on the floor. However, their plight became evident. Gunfire echoed from the direction of the warehouse, where Mehmet's men were under heavy fire. Reacting swiftly, his unit returned fire, and he instructed his men to retreat from the warehouse, grabbing whatever they could carry. Two soldiers were wounded and fell to the ground. Without hesitation, Mehmet and another fighter dashed forward to retrieve the injured, pulling them to safety under covering fire and bringing them back to the safety of the row of houses.

"Belmin and Haris are dead," shouted one of the men. Serbs are pouring into the area."

Hagija appeared. "We need to get out now. Most of the food stocks have been taken out, and there are a lot of ammo and weapons, so let's go; we have enough. The charges have been set. The warehouse will go up in two minutes. We need to go. Now."

The issue lay with the civilians. They continued searching for bits of food, anything to sustain themselves. The threat didn't deter them; their judgment was clouded by desperation.

Mehmet positioned two machine guns to protect the civilians as they retreated. The Serbs were nearing. In one of the distant houses, an elderly man and a woman were feasting on left over burek they had discovered on the table, unaware of the approaching Serb fighters.

"Balija fuckers," one Serb shouted, the derogatory term for Muslims. It meant peasant. And he opened fire. They died instantly. There was no mercy.

The remaining civilians hurried past Mehmet, escorted by fighters, avoiding the mines that had injured two and attracted the attention of the Serbs. Two other fighters swiftly buried additional mines along the established safe passage before joining the others in their hurried retreat.

They listened as two mines exploded with a heavy thud, followed by the cries of two men. Despite the chaos, they remained focused on their duty, providing fighters and civilians with crucial time and space to flee.

Mehmet felt frustrated by the civilians' actions, yet he couldn't fault them. When people are desperate, they act hastily. Despite the setback, they pressed on swiftly through the night. Despite the challenges, their efforts had been largely successful. They managed to secure essential supplies of food, weapons, and ammunition, boosting morale in the process. While they suffered losses with five men killed and four wounded, they succeeded in prolonging the survival of Donji Zelenki, at least temporarily.

26

Hassan Mesic scrutinised the list repeatedly. Twelve names, twelve men, and among them was Munja, the spy embedded within the Bosnian resistance. Hassan was certain of it. Someone from the Bosnian Army's High Command was leaking information to the Serbs. The list included General Mujkanovic, known as Old Thunder. Although it seemed absurd, Hassan concluded that no one, not even the General, the very symbol of Bosnian resistance, could be exempt from suspicion. He combed through the papers again and again, hoping for some detail in the names or backgrounds to provide a clue. It was evident that Munja, the lightning, was still active, and the Serb who perished under Ibrahimovic's torture couldn't have been the informant.

In recent days, there has been an increase in intercepted radio transmissions, coinciding consistently with missions or the movement of men and weapons. The Serbs seemed to possess detailed knowledge of the individuals travelling in the United Nations armoured personnel carrier to the airport, as well as an awareness of the UN's likely lack of resistance if stopped. This became painfully evident when they intercepted an APC, pulled out the deputy Bosnian prime minister, and executed him by the roadside, right in front of French peacekeepers. The ineffectiveness of the UN was a separate issue, what troubled Hassan the most was the leak that had led to the deadly ambush.

The Serbs had located the general area of the secret escape tunnel's entrance and frequently shelled it, resulting in casualties. As a precaution, journalists were prohibited from entering the area. Whoever was transmitting information demonstrated expertise, consistently halting just before their location could be pinpointed.

Of the twelve names listed on the paper, eight belonged to individuals of purely Muslim descent, with no history of mixed marriages in their lineage. Two names were of loyal Serbs, while the remaining two were Bosnian Catholics. One of the Catholics was born of a mixed marriage, a common occurrence in the former Yugoslavia, with a Serb father fighting on the opposing side. Despite scrutiny and surveillance, this individual had consistently proven himself trustworthy. There was no evidence to suggest that he was Munja.

As Hassan's investigation delved deeper into the personal lives of the men he was probing, resentment started to simmer among them. This made him feel uneasy. "What if it wasn't any of them?" he pondered. "What if the Serbs are simply adept at their job, second-guessing every possibility?" Indeed, they were renowned for their military expertise, having contributed nearly sixty per cent of the officer class to the former Yugoslav National Army (JNA).

Munja's actions were proving costly for the Bosnians. Not only had they lost the deputy prime minister they had also suffered Serb ambushes on Bosnian missions. critical intelligence on strategy, troop movements and supply routes were being passed to the Serbs. The routes to eastern Bosnia, including Hassan's hometown of Donji Zelenik, had been severed, and Hassan was convinced that Munja was responsible. What was once a twelve-hour journey through a single Serb line now required a gruelling thirty-six-hour trek through two front lines. With each passing day, the likelihood of survival grew slimmer. Thoughts of his father and brother only fuelled Hassan's determination further.

He had meticulously investigated nearly everyone on the list, leaving only the general and Mohammed Ibrahimovic, the religious zealot, remaining. He harboured little hope of uncovering any incriminating evidence against two of Bosnia's most prominent defenders. These men appeared to be untouchable, beyond reproach.

27

The guard was big and fat. He wore a Chetnik hat. On it was pinned a badge with the four C's and he had an attitude. He also carried a smell that was either Sliva aftershave or he had been drinking. Grant deduced the latter. Beside him was a giant of a woman that the Aussie cameraman instantly christened the 'She-Devil.' She had big lips plastered with bright red lipstick, "like the vulva of a big fucking baboon," said the Aussie. She stood tall, like a solid barrier in human form. Her face was coated with a dark brown foundation, topped with vibrant blue eye shadow. She had a faint hint of a moustache and a few stray hairs covered her chin. She resembled a character from the wild days of 1930s Berlin, reminiscent of the debauchery found in the Kit Kat Klub. Standing at an imposing height of six feet four, armed with an AK47, and wearing a stern expression, she commanded authority not to be challenged. This Serb checkpoint duo surpassed the extraordinary.

The Serbs harboured a strong aversion and suspicion towards journalists. They viewed them as spies and promoters of propaganda, aiming to undermine their nation. However, they were compelled to interact with them as instructed by politicians, in order to present their perspective on the war.

“Get out,” she-Devil ordered. “What have you in the vehicle? Anything to declare?” she made it seem like this was an international border crossing, which is what they wanted the world to think.

“No, nothing.”

”So, what is this then?”

“It’s a camera, mate,” replied the Aussie. “We are TV, so we need a camera to film.”

“But what is this?” she said, unearthing a walkie-talkie from the glove compartment.

“We use that for communicating,” explained Grant.

“Not allowed,” responded She-Devil. “This will be confiscated.”

“And what is this?” It was a bottle of Revlon perfume.

“That’s for you,” responded Grant. He’d been through this checkpoint enough times and dealt with the big Serb enough to know how things worked.

“Really?” she said in mock surprise. Her face instantly decompressed, and a faint smile broke through like a solitary ray of sunlight in a cloudy sky.

"For me? That is very nice. Very well, this time, you can keep your talkie-walkie, but next time, you must get permission. Now your translator is waiting for you over there. Have a lovely day, and I hope to see you soon. But be careful of those Balija bullets. There are lots of them out there."

Zlatko, the translator, wasn't selected for his intelligence. He served as a mandatory companion for journalists visiting the Serb side, purportedly for their 'protection', as per the hierarchy's explanation. However, it was not about control, they insisted.

Zlatko embodied the historical narrative of the Serb nation: their enduring victimhood across centuries, their valiant resistance, and their suffering at the hands of Muslims and Catholics allied with the Nazis during World War II. He staunchly contested the prevalent notion that Serbs instigated the conflict and were engaging in ethnic cleansing on a scale unseen since the 1940s.

"Muslims decided to move to be with their own kind," he explained, "There was no cleansing. That was propaganda."

As they drove towards the Serb-controlled area of Sarajevo, they passed house after house with roofless structures, evidence of past fires. Each building bore a red symbol, a cross within a circle, indicating its inhabitants were Muslim or Catholic. Grant understood that these buildings had been deliberately burned, leaving nothing for their owners to return to. It was clear that the area was now under Serb control.

"What happened to these houses?" asked Grant. "I think that was someone smoking in bed," replied Zlatko.

"What about that one and that one?"

"Again, I think smokers caused them in bed or carelessness in the kitchen," offered Zlatko with a straight face. "Muslims had a big problem of bed smoking."

The team obtained permission to visit the Serb area as Grant aimed to cover the story of Serb civilians residing on the front line. They opted for Grbavica, situated in the heart of Sarajevo, which had been divided during the conflict - part on the Bosnian side, part on the Serb side. Grant empathised with the plight of ordinary Serbs, recognising that not all of them desired the war.

As they drove along the main streets, it became evident that the district had endured significant bombardments, with widespread damage and destruction. Shipping containers cluttered junctions, and apartment buildings bore the scars of bullet and shrapnel impacts, just like on the Bosnian side. Snipers posed a threat on both sides. However, Grant observed that the extent of damage appeared less severe compared to the Muslim side.

"Where is this road called Zvornicka?" asked Grant. "I'd like to get my bearings."

"Around this corner," Zlatko said. Grant made a mental note for later. This was where he needed to do the favour for Selma.

In the streets, individuals were busy clearing away rubbish. A few of them were distinguished by the white armbands they wore. Grant understood that these armbands indicated those who were not of Serb descent. It was straight out of the Nazi-Jew 1930's playbook, Grant thought.

"They are carrying out community duties," said Zlatko very unconvincingly. "It may be war, but we like to keep everything clean and orderly as much as possible."

Grant stifled a yawn, but he pushed through the incoming talk because he aimed to highlight the suffering of Serb civilians. He sought to provide balance and context to the war. They selected a family, a husband, wife, and their two children who resided near the front line. Their home had been struck by shellfire, resulting in the loss of a third child. Additionally, they lacked food and lived in fear. Grant recognised that fear was not exclusive to one side; it affected all. He aimed to tell a compassionate story centred on humanity rather than politics, driven by his commitment to 'objectivity.' However, maintaining objectivity was becoming increasingly challenging, especially with individuals like Zlatko complicating matters.

A frontline journalist had to be everything to everyone in many ways. Some would call it subterfuge others lying. Grant preferred the term white lies but long ago he accepted that to do the job and survive you had to resort to techniques some would find uncomfortable. Diplomacy, hyperbole, disinformation, misquoting, and sometimes distortion. Dealing with dictators and murderers, psychopaths, homicidal maniacs, perverts and schemers called for a different type of approach. These journalists, and Grant included himself, would dive from a great height of moral supremacy into a sea of sycophancy to get the story. The means justify the video. Lies dam lies and statistics. Politicians used them so too did journalists. Pampering the egos of killers by saying 'You've had a bad press,' 'This is your chance to tell people the truth,' or for bloodthirsty war lords who love their kids, they are only 'defending their people.'

A news editor once said, misquoting John F Kennedy, "Ask not what your programme can do for you. Ask what you can do for your programme."

Visiting the Serb side was uncommon. There was a clear and visible distrust and dislike towards journalists, creating an uneasy atmosphere. Though not openly hostile, there was an underlying tension in almost every interaction.

Grant delved into his interviews, hoping to gather material for both future stories and the present one. Yet, he often encountered resistance at every turn. Denials to access frontline scenes, refusals from soldiers, and rejections to visit so called concentration camps which the Serbs labelled as 'holding centres' all contributed to his frustration. Moreover, his encounters with Zlatko, a staunch propagandist, only added to his disillusionment. Zlatko's rhetoric normalised racism, presenting it almost as a recreational activity. Grant recognised that this mindset wasn't a recent development; rather, it seemed deeply ingrained, rooted in a history of perceived victimisation spanning generations. This narrative, perpetuated by extreme nationalists, recounted past grievances as if they had occurred yesterday, shaping the collective consciousness of the Serb people. Grant understood that undoing this entrenched ideology would prove to be a difficult, if not impossible, task.

The streets of Grbavica felt bitterly cold, the air biting against the skin. The buildings, reminiscent of the communist style, stood as large, uninspired blocks, devoid of any imaginative design, merely serving their function. Their dull grey façades mirrored the dreariness of the Bosnian side, blending into the winter's grim weather that afflicted all sides equally. As daylight waned, a thick fog enveloped the streets, akin to a white shroud descending upon the city. Recollections of Selma and her frequent references to Thomas Hardy's use of pathetic fallacy lingered in the journalist's mind. With bad weather often came unfortunate events, prompting him to ponder if such a fate awaited them that day.

Zlatko grew increasingly weary and uninterested. He wasn't the most attentive. Jake would occasionally slip away to capture photos of Serb fighters and positions, while Grant side-lined him with inquiries about Serb history and notable Serbs. Nikola Tesla was his preferred topic. A Serb born in Croatia, he invented the first alternating current motor, which safely provided electricity for homes and buildings. Although a brilliant inventor, Tesla struggled as a businessman and couldn't fully capitalise on his inventions, unlike his rival and former employer, Thomas Edison. For Zlatko, this served as another example of how Serbs had endured victimisation. He maintained they had endured a lifetime of suffering until now, asserting that they had cast off the burden of oppression and were now fighting for their survival.

Grant managed only a nod, feigning interest, while struggling to suppress yet another yawn. It was becoming increasingly challenging. Fortunately, Zlatko had other matters to attend to and opted not to accompany them to the last checkpoint before the airport crossing into the Bosnian side.

"You know your way back?" he asked. "Very simple, just straight down that road for ten kilometres until the airport checkpoint. Don't stop anywhere, and remember, be careful of the BB."

"What's the BB?" asked Grant.

"Balija Bullets, of course," came the reply, accompanied by a deep bellicose laugh.

Grant slammed the door shut and accelerated away. The thickening fog forced him to proceed cautiously, with visibility reduced to mere yards. Getting lost seemed increasingly likely, presenting a daunting challenge. However, Grant remained determined. Despite the headlights offering limited assistance, he pressed on.

After approximately half a mile, Grant made two consecutive left turns. He recognised this route as running parallel to Zvornicka Road, as confirmed by Zlatko earlier. Having surveyed the area beforehand, Grant possessed a clear sense of direction.

As they approached an intersection, the once bustling traffic lights now stood dormant, devoid of power. Two nearby structures appeared to be at rest, their bent forms revealing signs of previous impact. Grant made a right turn, followed by an immediate left onto what he presumed was Zvornicka Street. Navigating through the obscured view caused by the weather, he hoped he had chosen correctly. Fortunately, it turned out to be in the right direction. Passing by the Orthodox Church they had seen earlier, they soon spotted the unassuming building they sought: No. 35 Zvornicka. The structure loomed before them, devoid of charm or character, a stark example of communist-era architecture. It was a soulless creation, one of many erected during the post-war period, promising homes, heating, education, and employment for all. Selma had instructed Grant to head to the top floor, where her aunt Alma resided. He was to look for the name Modic on the door; failing that, apartment 801 would be the destination.

He left the Aussie cameraman in the car.

"No worries," he had said when Grant told him what he was doing and then rolled over and had a kip. He wasn't completely truthful about the dangers or the potential consequences if the Serbs discovered them, but the Australian didn't appear concerned. Ignorance was bliss, Grant surmised.

He ascended eight floors, illuminating his path with his small Maglite torch. The building lay in utter silence and darkness, giving off an eerie sense of abandonment. It felt as though no one resided there anymore, as if they had all departed. The situation was not without its dangers. What if the Serbs stumbled upon him? How could he justify being here alone at ten o'clock at night, without their guide? He forced the worrying thought out of his mind.

He ascended to the top floor, his footsteps reverberating loudly on the concrete, creating an echoing effect throughout the building. A mist of breath escaped his lips, lingering in the chilly air, adding to his sense of unease. What if there was no number, no name on the door? What if he knocked on the wrong door? Too many what-ifs. These uncertainties nagged at him as he pressed onward to the top floor. Amidst the row of doors, he finally spotted 804, its number standing out amidst the uniformity. Several doors bore a red cross, reminiscent of those he'd seen on the charred houses in Republika Srpska. He recalled that they marked the homes of the bed smokers. Passing each one, he reached 801, devoid of any identifying name.

He rapped on the door, initially with caution. He aimed to avoid disturbing the neighbours or anyone else nearby. The significance of this action in Selma's aunt's household didn't immediately register with him. A late-night knock at the door of a Catholic woman married to a Muslim, living amidst occupation, likely evoked a sense of apprehension. Yet, there was no response. He knocked again, slightly louder, but still met with silence. Grant pondered whether they might have left or relocated. With a final attempt, he knocked once more. The resounding sound reverberated through the walls, seemingly alerting the entire building.

He heard movement behind the door. And then the sound of the door being unlocked. After several bolts were undone and a key turned, the door creaked open slightly. In the dim light, he could discern the face of a woman. If fear had a face then this was it.

"Selma," Grant said. "Selma Mesic, tvoja navika." (Your niece). Selma had taught him that.

The aunt swung open the door, her gaze darting past Grant to scan the surroundings for any onlookers before swiftly guiding him indoors. Seated in an armchair was an elderly man, likely Selma's uncle, who appeared frail and unwell. Grant settled into a seat and retrieved a letter penned by Selma, passing it over to Alma.

Through a Serb Croatian dictionary and phrase book he managed to glean that the uncle had been sick and was low on medication. They were visibly scared and though he couldn't understand everything when Alma said Serbs 'nije dobro,' he guessed that meant not good. Their lives must be difficult.

The elderly woman fetched a bottle of homemade sliva and poured him a glass. Its flavour hit the back of his throat with force, and he drank it swiftly. The room was filled with photographs and mementoes typical of older individuals, reminiscent of their past experiences and relationships. Alma picked up a photograph from the sideboard, showing a group of people.

She pointed to a figure. "Selma." She appeared to have been around nine or ten. Next to her was Mehmet, her twin brother. They looked identical. Standing behind was Hassan, and next to him were six adults.

"Moi sestra," (my sister) explained Alma, pointing to a good-looking woman. "Mrtav," (dead) she said and shook her head in sorrow.

There was also a girl in the front next to Selma. "Hasina," said Alma. "Coosin, beautiful," she said in broken English. "Pjevac (singer)."

Grant knew instantly who she was and what happened.

"Mrtav," he said, and Alma began to cry softly. She kissed the photo. She looked up.

"Sara, Moi sestre?" she asked. "Mrtav," replied Grant. This was getting very difficult and emotional for him.

"Yousef?" "Dobro," said Grant, (good). "I Selma, Hassan, Mehmet, sve dobro?" All good, Grant explained, and Alma smiled. Her husband sat in the chair and smiled a little when he heard about the surviving family members but it was obvious he was sick.

Time was slipping away, and Grant felt the pressure of its passing. They were running out of time and needed to depart soon. An antique grandfather clock occupied the corner of the room, its chime marking the half-hour. At 10:30 p.m.,

Grant knew he had to leave. Downing another glass of sliva, he gestured towards the door, indicating it was time to go. Alma swiftly scribbled a note to Selma and handed it to Grant. As he accepted it, he also passed her a thousand Deutschmark note in appreciation. She gasped in almost disbelief and gave him a huge hug. "Hvala ti puno, hvala bog" (thank you so much, thank you, God), and she began to cry again.

She swung the door open. As he glanced back at them, he pondered their fate and the impact a mere thousand Deutschmarks could have on their wretched existence. With a clank, the door bolts snapped shut, and Grant hurried down the stairs. His priority now was returning to the other side, which was still fraught with danger. Yet, amidst the ugliness of war, Grant Singleton savoured one of those rare feel-good moments.

28

It was the night that instilled the greatest fear in the villagers of Velike Donjic. A knock at the door could signal more pain and suffering. Situated 20km from the frontlines, in an area referred to by United Nations peacekeepers and aid workers as the 'Heart of Darkness,' it was a place where Serb fighters sought solace at the end of a day's battle, where they released their anguish and sorrow over lost comrades. It was also where they unleashed their anger, often directed at Muslims in particular. Many young Muslim men had fled at the war's onset, leaving behind the vulnerable, the elderly, the infirm, and the young. When Serb forces suffered casualties, they sought revenge on Velike Donjic.

The village was predominantly Muslim and had been the focal point of prolonged negotiations between the United Nations and the Bosnian Serb government. These negotiations aimed to facilitate the repatriation of the villagers to Bosnian-controlled territory. Aware of the strategic value of the Muslim population as bargaining leverage, the Serbs engaged in protracted discussions. However, unbeknownst to them, this night marked the final hours that the residents of Velike Donjic would endure under Serb control.

Nearly every house bore a red cross inside a circle as a marking. Each dwelling sported a makeshift metal chimney protruding crudely from a wall, while on the opposite side stood an improvised stove for heating and cooking, reminiscent of a bygone era. This method was the sole means of heating and cooking available, as memories of the once-common Yugoslav gas central heating system had long since faded.

At night, in the midst of this bitterly cold winter, remnants of families huddled around the stoves for warmth and light. Food was scarce, despite the UN sending supplies, as most were siphoned off by the Serb military. Contact with the outside world was limited or non-existent.

Leila sat by the fire with her three children, her frail mother and father, both in their eighties. Despite the news that they were to leave the village within the next 24 hours, a mix of hope and dread filled the air. The villagers were cautiously optimistic, but their past experiences had taught them not to place too much trust in promises, especially those made by the UN. Hopes had been shattered before, and uncertainty loomed over their future once again.

A little before 9:00 p.m., the rumble of engines echoed as cars rolled into the village. The engines ceased, followed by drunken shouts and wild gunfire in the air. Leila and her family held their breath, steeling themselves for what might come next. Leila directed her two boys, aged seven and nine, and her sixteen-year-old daughter, Alisha, to the bedroom, instructing them to hide and remain silent. In Arabic, Alisha's name meant beautiful, and indeed she was stunningly so, with striking blue eyes and an almost angelic face. Her beauty and innocence often drew unwanted attention from men. In this moment, fear gripped her heart; she had already lost her husband, a farm worker, in a mortar attack at the onset of the conflict. Now, she dreaded the possibility of losing her children.

She cautiously peeked through the window. Outside, Serb soldiers were gathering in the centre of the village, some brandishing AK47s in one hand while carrying bottles of alcohol in the other. One fighter unloaded jerry cans of gasoline from the back of a truck. Leila felt a sense of dread; if these were to be the final hours under Serb control, she feared they would be far from pleasant.

Leila heard an explosion and saw a flash emanating from a house next to the mosque. Screams pierced the air, followed by three gunshots. The cries abruptly ceased. Leila shuddered, her sons began to cry, and her mother started to tremble. As she looked on, she saw them, the perpetrators, heading towards her house.

"Don't make, don't make a sound," she whispered. "They are coming."

There was no knock; the door was kicked in. Darko Zubic stood in the doorway. He was obviously drunk. His body swayed as he spoke.

"Hello, Leila," he said. "As-salamu alaikum and all that shit. How are we today? Why are those brats crying? Don't they enjoy a little fireworks?"

Two other fighters stood behind him, visibly intoxicated, their eyes scanning the room as if hunting for something. Leila had a hunch about what they were looking for.

"Don't be scared, Leila, that kind of thing won't happen to you," and he pointed to the house near the mosque. "But that bitch's son killed two of my men today. Motherfucker. Now he knows the price, no one to make him Burek anymore." He laughed.

Leila struggled to steady her trembling hands. The boys darted out of the bedroom, sensing her distress. She drew them close, enveloping them in a tight embrace.

Darko took another swig from the bottle, the sound of two more shots echoing in the distance. This time, there were no screams.

"So, you and your fundamentalists will be leaving us here to join the fucking Jihad. Those spineless politicians of ours have agreed to let you go despite everything you have done and WILL do. If I had my way…" and the sentence dropped into a slur and incomprehensible words. Leila, however, was in no doubt what would happen if Darko had his way.

"So where is your daughter?" he asked, "Your beautiful daughter. Alisha. I'd like to say goodbye and wish her well for the future."

The other Serbs bypassed the mother and proceeded into the bedroom. Within moments, they located the hiding place. The burly men forcibly dragged her from beneath the bed, each seizing an arm, and forcefully escorted her into the kitchen. Alisha's tears flowed freely.

"What do you want?" Leila asked in a stuttering voice.

"Oh, I think you know," said Darko with a smirk. "Taxes have to be paid before you leave. That is only right and proper."

"What taxes? We have no money?"

"Physical taxes, Leila, physical ones."

Lines of anguish creased Leila's face. This was her worst fear realised. However, the half-expectation of this moment, lingering for so long, did nothing to ease her pain.

She began to plead, "Please don't. She's so young. She knows nothing. She cannot give you any satisfaction; she doesn't know how to."

Then Leila's voice hardened, and her body straightened. "But I can," she declared. "I have experience, and I can give you pleasure beyond your dreams. But she can do nothing. She has no idea. She will be an anti-climax for you. But I will not disappoint. Trust me. I promise."

Darko thought for a moment. Then smiled. The proposition obviously interested him.

"OK, you know what, I think you might be right. Beauty versus experience. Hmm. Let's give it a go. No harm in trying, is there," and he pushed Leila towards the bedroom.

The elderly couple and the children knelt down on the floor, seeking solace in prayer. The grandfather turned his prayer beads in his hand, silently mouthing a prayer, pondering what they had done to deserve the wrath of God.

They endured the sound of Leila's groans and the feigned ecstasy, each one a painful reminder of the sacrifice made to save her. Leila's daughter sobbed softly, fully aware of the immense sacrifice made on her behalf. Yet, amidst her grief, she also grappled with a profound sense of guilt, feeling responsible for her mother's suffering, despite knowing there was nothing she could have done to prevent it. Her sobbing intensified, echoing through the room.

"Shut up, you fucking Balija bitch," shouted one of the Serbs, "Or you will be next."

A few minutes later, Darko appeared. A big smile spread across his face.

"You know what, boys she was absolutely right. She is the best fuck I have had in years. But don't take my word for it." And he waved his arm in a sweeping welcome gesture towards the room. "Next, please."

He grabbed a bottle of sliva, took a long swig, and patted Alisha on the head, "You've got one hell of a mum, do you know that, one hell of a mum."

Leila persisted in her charade, her actions driven by a mother's desperation to protect her daughter. Though the deception felt repugnant, her daughter's safety was paramount. Leila remained resolute, knowing her daughter's resilience yet acknowledging the potential psychological toll of their ordeal.

"OK," shouted Darko, "get your things, you are leaving. The trucks will be arriving soon."

"Now?" asked Leila.

"Now," replied Darko. "Now or never, though you were so good, I wouldn't mind if you stayed a little longer." His grin was almost evil. Leila thought she could throw up, but she steadied herself and told the family to start packing what they could. With no suitcases available, they improvised with shawls and bedsheets for packing. Despite their sparse possessions, Leila made sure to include photographs and small mementos that captured their life in Velike Donjic, items that would serve as reminders of their village.

They were ordered outside into the centre, where a fresh layer of snow covered the ground and the temperature had plummeted well below freezing. Nearly two hundred people were assembled by the seven trucks parked next to the mosque. Soldiers proceeded to search their belongings, taking whatever they desired, including any gold or silver they came across.

Other fighters began dousing the houses and the mosque with fuel, then hurling lit torches inside. The entire village appeared to erupt in flames all at once.

"You, Balija won't be coming back. This is to make sure. Nothing to come back to," shouted one of the men. Leila looked up. The clear night sky was adorned with countless stars, their brilliance captivating. As she observed a shooting star streak across the heavens, she felt compelled to make a wish. Yet, deep down, she knew that in her world, reality bore no resemblance to wishes.

29

Jake, the Aussie Cameraman, playfully stamped up and down, mimicking a marching motion.

"Fuck, man. This is fucking freezing. When are they coming? My dick has got frostbite?"

Grant glanced at his watch; it was just after midnight. They had been at the crossing for six hours, and yet, there was still no clear indication of when the refugees would arrive. Anxious and impatient, they began to question whether the refugees were coming at all.

"The officials say it is going to happen," said Selma, "but they can't say when. We are in the hands of the Serbs, and you should know by now that they cannot be trusted. They are highly unpredictable."

Jake grimaced but kept marching. Waiting was a routine part of a journalist's job. In newspaper terms, they referred to it as "doorstepping," although there were no doorsteps here, in the remote hills of North Central Bosnia. A sizable press contingent had gathered, anticipating the first expulsions in months.

Amelia Degusta strode past, draped in what seemed to be a luxurious mink coat, its rich fur glistening under the ambient light. Adorning her ears were a pair of exquisite pearl earrings.

"She going to the theatre?" asked Selma.

"Fifth Ave, I think," commented Grant.

"My sources tell me that it's not going to happen, people," said Degusta. "I'm going before I freeze to death." She left. A few others followed.

"Are you sure....?" Grant said to Selma.

"As sure as anyone can be, apart from the New York princess."

For two hours, the sounds of moans and groans filled the air as more parts of the Aussie succumbed to the cold... except for his mouth, Grant noted wryly. Then, abruptly, a volley of shots echoed in the distance, accompanied by red tracer fire shooting into the air. Journalists and aid workers instinctively dove down, momentarily forgetting that the most dangerous shells and bullets were the ones you couldn't hear, they simply struck without warning. However, this knowledge didn't prevent their automatic bodily reaction.

Selma hurried over to a group of soldiers who were listening intently on a walkie-talkie. After a brief exchange, she dashed back.

"They are coming," she said. "Get ready."

Grant nudged the Aussie. "Get your appendages working, mate, except your dick, that is. They are almost here."

The first of the trucks rolled into view, followed closely by seven more. They came to a stop outside a house where UN agencies had established medical and feeding stations. Nearby, a barn had been repurposed into a reception centre, complete with installed stoves to provide heating.

A soldier ascended the back of the first truck and drew back the canvas flap, revealing thirty sets of terrified eyes staring back at him.

"Dobro Dosli," he said (welcome). "You have arrived in the territory of Bosnia and Hercegovina, and you are safe."

Some of the refugees began to cry with relief, while others appeared stunned. Each person was assisted out of the trucks and into the makeshift reception centre. They appeared weary and emaciated, with the children particularly appearing shocked, unable to fully grasp their surroundings and the significance of their situation. Additionally, they seemed apprehensive, likely due to the influence of the uniformed men who had made them feel that way.

Mothers and grandparents comforted the little ones, ensuring they felt safe. Blankets and warm drinks were provided, and aid teams worked diligently, gathering details and providing assistance.

Jake filmed as much footage as he could, relying on the camera light to illuminate the scene. Meanwhile, Grant and Selma spoke to many of the evacuees, listening to their tales of endurance and suffering. Some were able to provide brief interviews, while others were too overwhelmed to articulate their experiences. Most of the evacuees were simple country folk, deeply affected by the magnitude of the moment and their newfound freedom. For an hour, the team captured as many shots and interviews as possible. Grant delivered a stand-up address to the camera, highlighting the misery endured by civilians and the turmoil they had faced. As they began to pack up, preparing to return to Sarajevo to compile a story for the morning news, the weight of the experience lingered heavily on their minds.

A woman approached Selma.

"She wants to give her story. She has something she'd like to say."

It was Leila. She said she wanted to talk away from her family, especially her daughter. They found a nearby house. Jake started to set up a battery light.

"No," said Grant. "We'll rely on light from the candles." He sensed this was going to be powerful.

Leila sat cross-legged on the floor and began recounting her story, about the killings, the turmoil, and how she had given herself physically. Despite the harrowing nature of her tale, there was no discernible emotion in her delivery. Her face remained impassive, her eyes stony, as if she were reciting something she had read rather than recounting her own experiences. Her voice remained almost monotone and matter-of-fact, never wavering or hesitating.

As Selma's narrative unfolded, she found herself unable to contain her tears, silently succumbing to sobs. The woman continued, recounting the harrowing details: the repulsive stench of the fighters, the sexual abuse she endured, and the dehumanising treatment that made her feel lower than an animal. She described how she surrendered herself, performing like a seasoned prostitute, all to protect her daughter. She spoke of her husband, of other women's husbands, and of the pervasive misery and fear that engulfed them all.

Grant refrained from asking any questions; none were necessary. Everything he needed to know was conveyed in one long soundbite. A sickening feeling churned in his stomach as he contemplated, once again, the cruelty inherent in human nature and warfare. As she rose to leave, Grant seized her hand. His expression conveyed gratitude; words failed him.

He crumpled a thousand Deutschmarks note and pressed it into her hand, the entirety of his available cash.

"Something for the children," Leila explained.

The woman said thank you, and only then did a few tears well up in her eyes.

"Thank you," she said in English. "Thank you."

It was a compelling conclusion to the evening, with both the narrative and images leaving a lasting impact. Grant faced a significant challenge: how to condense such a powerful story into less than three minutes?

30

"Incoming," went up the shout as Grant and the team walked into the lobby of the Holiday Inn. He glanced up, only to witness Spit the Frog descending from the sixth-floor corridor railing, abseiling down. If anyone needed further evidence of Pascal Bourdain's insanity, this spectacle certainly provided it. Spit hit the ground with a resounding thump.

"Great Mate," said Jake. "Why not try that on the outside of the building, opposite the old Chetnik snipers? Might make it a little more interesting."

"Zat is not a bad idea," said Spit and began to ratchet himself back to the sixth floor for another drop.

There was scant opportunity for leisure in Sarajevo, unless one considered sprinting across road junctions to evade Serb snipers a form of sport. So, they had to create their own entertainment. Upon entering the breakfast room, they found it only partially occupied. They settled at a table already occupied by Chuck, Bunty, and a couple of agency personnel.

"Fucking strong story," said Chuck. "You should get a good show with that."

"No guarantees," replied Grant. "You can't second guess American networks; they are a bit like the Serbs. Remember that story last Saturday when a mortar killed the three kids after being allowed out of the house for the first time in weeks? Well, it was dropped because of college football. That takes fucking precedence over life and death in Europe. Total tossers."

"But I tell you who did get a good show in the Times this morning, Amelia. My desk faxed me her story."

"She left, she wasn't there when the trucks came nor was she in the reception barn nor there at the end when we left," ranted Grant.

"Well, the story is a first-hand account....as the trucks moved across the lines with their human cargo of misery. It was like a scene from the Second World War. Beaten and tortured people but finally able to taste freedom. Serb gun shots were fired over our heads as we watched the trucks roll up, and then, one by one, they told us their terrifying ordeal of nine months in Serb captivity. Blah, blah fucking blah."

"What a load of first-class BS."

"Gotta admit, my old mucker, she writes beautifully. And it did happen, just not with her there. Don't get worked up about it. That's who she is."

"Yeah, I remember the story about Serbs raping a young toddler, except no one else could find the child or the mother. Not the rape crisis centre, not the Bosnian government, not any aid agency. Nada." Said Bunty.

The agency guys jumped in with their own anecdotes. "Did you read the one when she held a dying Bosnia soldier in her arms? It was pure Barbara Cartland."

"And the mujahideen story in Zenica, the interview with a commander in Arabic about thousands of Islamists heading to Bosnia to fight. She is a woman, but she doesn't speak Arabic, and no self-respecting mad mujahideen man is going to give her the time of day."

"She did get a centre-page spread with that one. She made it sound as if tens of thousands of Islamic extremists were either here or on their way. I know; the only front she's been to is the front row at the Metropolitan Opera House. She gets her stories, her exclusive stories, on fucking room service," said Chuck. "But I also have to throw this into the mix...she's a great fuck."

In unison, the group said, "You haven't, have you?"

"No comment," came the reply.

Selma came into the room and beckoned Grant over.

"OK, the permissions have come through. We can leave for Tuzla tomorrow. Then we just have to find a guide, an army Unit willing to take us, transportation of some kind and a lot of luck. Shouldn't be too difficult, right?"

31

Hassan stood in the shadows opposite the Gazi Husrev-beg Mosque, located in the heart of the old town. This spectacular sixteenth-century Ottoman structure was the largest mosque in Bosnia and one of the finest examples in the entire Balkans. Adorned with ornate arches, marble pillars, and luxurious woollen carpets, it held a revered status in the region. Devout individuals aimed to pray here at least once during the five daily prayer times. Despite the chaos of war, the mosque provided a sanctuary of calm and serenity. Beautifully tiled archways surrounded the minbar, or pulpit, where the imam led prayers and delivered sermons.

Hassan awaited the arrival of one man, known for his devoutness. Surprisingly, his name was also on Hassan's list. Yet he couldn't shake off the incredulity of it all. It seemed impossible. How could Mohammed Ibrahimovic, a deeply religious Muslim known for his mistreatment of Serb prisoners, be Munja, the spy? It defied logic and didn't seem to fit together. However, General Mujkanovic was adamant that everyone with access to top-secret information be investigated, even someone like him. The General emphasised that no one was beyond suspicion.

It was Isha (night), the final prayer of the day, and Ibrahimovic was indoors. It was unusual for him to miss any of the five daily prayers. He was not only a smart man but also an Islamic scholar.

If Hassan were honest with himself, he would find Ibrahimovic a tad intimidating. With his burly physique and penetrating eyes, Ibrahimovic always seemed to make Hassan feel like he was somehow an inferior Muslim.

Hassan found himself at a loss in his role as a spycatcher. Despite his efforts, he had no leads and no solid hunches to pursue. Whoever Munja was, he was cunning. Despite specialised teams deployed to track and monitor, combing through documents and backgrounds, Munja had managed to evade detection. Nothing, absolutely nothing, had surfaced as unusual or suspicious. Munja's intelligence was proving invaluable to the Serbs, enabling them to thwart attacks, dismantle operations, and sever supply lines. He was a clandestine force inflicting significant harm on the Bosnians, surpassing the impact of numerous Serb fighting brigades. And remarkably, he hadn't made a single misstep.

The general went so far as to assert that unless Munja was apprehended and the flow of information ceased, Bosnia's prospects of surviving the war were dwindling rapidly.

However, Hassan's relentless probing, interrogations, and searches were beginning to ruffle the feathers of the officers listed. They started to voice complaints, accusing him of going too far and being overly harsh. 'Where is the evidence?' they would say. Mujkanovic had an answer to that; "Fuck the evidence," he declared, "Probe and probe again and when you have finished probing, probe once more. Munja has to be found."

One thing that weighed heavily on Hassan's mind was the torture and subsequent death of the Serb. Ibrahimovic was known to be an expert in torture, engaging in it almost daily in various forms. Most men subjected to his methods managed to survive for days, but this Serb had died, even after confessing. Strangely, there were no code books found, only a radio transmitter and a stack of money. Everyone Hassan had interviewed expressed surprise at the Serb being labelled a spy. They knew him as a black marketeer who traded with Serb counterparts, primarily for essential goods like food, supplies, alcohol, cigarettes, and gasoline. If indeed he was a spy, it was evident that he was part of a larger network. Keeping him alive might have yielded more information. Now, however, Hassan's investigative trail seemed as lifeless as the Serb himself. One thing remained clear: the Serb was not Munja, whose name continued to crop up repeatedly in radio intercepts.

Ibrahimovic emerged from the arches of the Mosque, located in the heart of Bascarsija, Sarajevo's old bazaar and cultural centre. The area seemed almost frozen in time, evoking visions of Ottoman soldiers marching through its gates centuries ago. Steeped in history, the architecture of Bascarsija reflected its rich past. Ibrahimovic joined a group of worshippers, exchanging hugs and farewells before disappearing into the labyrinth of narrow alleyways that once bustled with shopkeepers and artists. Now, however, most of the shops have been boarded up or severely damaged. Few tourists dared to venture into a war zone.

Gazi Husrev-beg Mosque stood amidst what had transformed into a desolate quarter. Devastation surrounded it, yet the mosque remained largely unscathed. Worshippers like Mohammed Ibrahimovic saw this as evidence that God was on their side.

Hassan trailed from a safe distance, driven by an inexplicable urge to take action, even though he was rapidly running out of ideas. Ibrahimovic ambled slowly along the cobbled pathways, passing by the three-hundred-year-old Serbilj water fountain, an iconic landmark of Sarajevo. Continuing past the site of the market massacre, he ascended the hill. To the right, lay a former park now transformed into a graveyard. He pressed on, passing the Ottoman arch erected shortly after the Turks' arrival in the early fifteen hundred, before disappearing into another alleyway. With no streetlights to guide him, Hassan had to rely on guesswork to anticipate Ibrahimovic's destination, it appeared to be towards his home. Determined, Hassan quickened his pace to catch up.

The spy catcher arrived at the house and once again blended into the shadows, uncertain of his purpose or what he hoped to accomplish. Ibrahimovic was unlikely to leave the premises again, but if he did, perhaps it would raise suspicion. So, Hassan leaned against a nearby wall and waited patiently.

Oil lamps illuminated the house, but Hassan observed no signs of movement. He recalled that Ibrahimovic lived alone with his mother and his father, a devout Muslim who had passed away when he was young. Hassan understood that mother and son shared a close bond.

After an hour of attempting to keep warm, Hassan was on the verge of leaving when he caught sight of a figure. He abruptly halted, holding his breath, as he slunk further back against the wall. The shape emerged from around the corner and headed in his direction. Hassan cautiously retreated deeper into the shadows, pondering how he would explain his presence if discovered. The figure drew closer, passing just a few feet from his hiding spot. It paused for what felt like an eternity before continuing towards the house. Then, to Hassan's alarm, the person stopped and turned, gazing directly at his hiding spot. It was unmistakably the burly figure of Ibrahimovic, carrying a bag. Hassan knew Ibrahimovic hadn't had the bag when he left the mosque. His mind raced through the possibilities. This behaviour was out of character for Ibrahimovic, whose daily routine had been meticulously documented by his operatives. It always followed a set pattern: meal at home, last prayers, then back home again. But now, the routine has changed. What could it signify? Where had Ibrahimovic been, and what was in the bag?

32

Under the full moon, Mehmet perched on the hill, his gaze stretching down to the Drina River, the boundary separating Serbia from Bosnia. Across it, at the distant left end, loomed the Bajna Basta dam. This served as the swiftest and most accessible route for Serbs from Serbia to infiltrate Bosnia, as heavily fortified as it was. Though they always denied aiding their Bosnian Serb counterparts, the falsehood was transparent to all, particularly the Muslims of eastern Bosnia. It wasn't solely the shelling from across the river or the clandestine deliveries of ammunition under the cover of darkness, hidden from satellites and watchful eyes, but also the hunting expeditions. These gatherings of young men, dubbed 'weekend warriors,' would venture into Bosnia for a weekend of hunting and shooting. They transitioned seamlessly from their nine-to-five office jobs to positions where they could take aim at Bosnians, any Bosnian, without discrimination. Yet the prey was overwhelmingly Muslim, perpetually hunted, and subjected to relentless persecution.

The area was steeped in bloodshed, with a history of violence dating back centuries. Blood has been spilled in this region since the days of Ottoman rule in the sixteenth century. The river and the surrounding region epitomised the suffering and cruelty inflicted by humanity. Yet it also symbolised a connection between the West and the East, a unity of sorts. Mehmet recalled studying one of the former Yugoslavia's most renowned books, Ivo Andric's 'The Bridge Over the Drina,' during his school days. The novel vividly depicted the enduring suffering of the Bosnian people from the sixteenth century to the First World War, set in the town of Visegrad, where Andric once resided, less than sixty kilometres downriver from where Mehmet stood. However, unity was now a distant memory, replaced by ongoing suffering. Every fifty years, turmoil engulfed the lives of ordinary people, and survival required strength.

Mehmet had grown immensely stronger since his days as a humble Belgrade engineering student. Life in Bosnia had hardened him; survival had necessitated it. Enduring suffering at the hands of Serbs had transformed him into something akin to granite. Despite being only twenty-three years old, he exuded a sense of maturity far beyond his years. Now regarded as a respected leader, Pasha Mehmet also instilled a certain fear. His methodical approach to killing left some uneasy. His lack of mercy and refusal to take prisoners had earned him a reputation as a warlike figure. He continually repeated that it was an 'eye for an eye'. "They started it," he would say, "We will finish it." He had become a man transfixed in a fight for survival, but it was also a fight to punish the oppressors.

There was no other leader whom his men would prefer to follow. His attacks were frequent and audacious, and his success rate had soared. As a result, the chances of survival for Donji Zelenik had increased dramatically. To the people of Donji Zelenik and the broader region of eastern Bosnia, Mehmet, known as the Pasha, had become a legendary figure, feared by the Serbs.

Behind him stood fifteen of his finest men. This mission wasn't about ammunition or food; it was about revenge, an eye for an eye. With unaided vision, they could easily spot the Serb trucks manoeuvring across the dam, likely transporting supplies to sustain the Serb war effort or perhaps carrying weekend warriors arriving for a shooting excursion. However, they were not the target on this night.

Mehmet gestured with his arm, and the group began to descend the hill, keeping a safe distance from the dam. Carrying three black inflatable dinghies, they moved swiftly and silently. Upon reaching the bushes near a bend in the river, they were shielded from view by the Serbs stationed at the Bajna Bashta. A spotter crawled to the water's edge and signalled for the others to advance; the coast was clear. These men were seasoned veterans, battle-hardened from nearly a year of risking their lives. They had endured losses, wounds, deprivation, and hunger, witnessing first-hand the upheaval of their homeland and the displacement of countless innocents. Their faces were smeared with boot polish, each adorned with a dark woollen cap or balaclava. Armed with Kalashnikov bayonets, hand pistols, and standard AK47 rifles, some even carried Uzi machine guns, all confiscated from the Serbs, they bore the scars of their struggle. While they may have been liberated in terms of cost, the toll in bloodshed had been steep. Each member understood their role with unwavering commitment to the mission ahead, a daring and potentially devastating endeavour.

They swiftly carried the dinghies to the water's edge and commenced paddling, making sure to minimise any loud splashing. Their strokes were gentle and rhythmic, yet the strong wind pushed the boats sideways, requiring the men to exert extra effort to maintain their course.

This mission required meticulous planning as well as an abundance of courage. Their target lay eight kilometres within Serbia's borders. The strike needed to be precise, thorough, and swift. While reaching the target posed its own challenges, returning would prove even more daunting.

Mehmet's scouts had dedicated two weeks to meticulously scrutinising the route, conducting repeated checks to ensure thoroughness. They traversed the river multiple times, identified potential hiding spots, documented Serb positions, and monitored traffic patterns. They possessed a comprehensive understanding of the strengths of various units and their armament capabilities. Moreover, they meticulously scouted back roads and assessed retreat and escape routes. Every detail was meticulously considered, leaving as little as possible to chance. They were as prepared as they could possibly be.

It was a challenging endeavour, but they successfully completed it. The crossing had consumed twenty minutes of their time. The night air was serene, with only the occasional hoot of an owl echoing from somewhere in the trees. After concealing the dinghies in the undergrowth, they regrouped. Dividing into two groups of eight, they set off. With it being ten o'clock, they estimated it would take them two hours to reach the attack point. So far, everything is proceeding according to plan.

33

Grant glanced at the man from top to bottom, then offered a smile before inviting Selma to join him outside.

"You may call me conservative and a little old-fashioned in war reporting, but, really, I would prefer a guide with two legs to get me into eastern Bosnia," said Grant. The man he was referring to was a Bosnia fighter who had lost his left leg after stepping on a Serb mine and, without the prospect of a prosthetic limb, had to use crutches.

Selma smiled. "Wimp," she said. "Don't be silly; he is not taking you to Donji Zelenik, only half way. He only knows the way through the first Serb lines. She will take you through the second line." Selma pointed to a woman standing by the door smoking. She wore high heels, a fur coat and a full face of make-up, including foundation and mascara.

"You are kidding," said Grant. "Thirty-six hours of walking in knee-deep snow, two front lines, crutches, and high heels!! No way, Jose."

"No, she will wear boots for the walk, but I'm not sure about the make-up, and he is a tough man who can make the journey, he tells me, to the first line," explained Selma. "She may not look it, but she is an excellent guide and scout and has been into the eastern parts several times. She has never been discovered. Don't judge a book by its cover, isn't that what you say?"

Grant felt a growing sense of frustration. Despite President Mehotic's approval, the reporter believed that reaching Tuzla after an exhausting eight-hour journey, joining an army unit, and heading into the east would be straightforward. However, a series of obstacles made the trip seem increasingly unlikely. Firstly, Jake, the Australian cameraman, had severely injured his ankle in a fall down the stairs due to alcohol. Then, Bosnian army commanders in Tuzla dismissed President Mehotic's authority over them and showed little willingness to cooperate or grasp the significance of the reporter's mission.

Singleton's optimism hinged on a one-legged fighter and a woman who appeared more suited to Oxford Street than the battlefield. The signs were grim. Grant couldn't shake the feeling that this was turning into a Jebiga (fuck it) experience.

Grant discovered that the remnants of the old communist mindset continued to exert a significant influence on Bosnian society. It was a culture where the default response seemed to be "no," awaiting the question to follow, and where journalists were frequently regarded with suspicion by some and labelled as spies by others. Unlike Sarajevo, Tuzla presented a distinct environment. With less exposure to international media, there existed a considerable trust barrier that Grant struggled to overcome.

“Good news,” said Selma, “There’s a group heading to Donji Zelenik tomorrow from Kladanj, and they say you can go. And I found you a translator who can make the journey.” She pointed to a spotty youth who looked no more than fifteen standing by the door.

“This is Haris,” said Selma. “Haris, this is Grant.”

Haris extended a weak hand for Grant to shake. His expression remained neutral, devoid of any smile or indication of his feelings towards meeting Grant.

“My English not best,” mumbled Haris. “But can help.”

Grant soon noticed that Haris seemed to lack a sense of humour, unlike anyone else in the former Yugoslavia. If his humour were measured on a heart monitor, it would likely show a flatline.

He probed, “Monty Python?” No response from Haris.

“Only Fools and Horses?” the dial of Haris’ recognition monitor didn’t flicker.

‘It’s going to be a long thirty-six hours,’ Grant thought to himself.

“OK, we have to head off shortly to be ready for tomorrow’s departure. I’ve agreed to give a lift to a friend of the guide’s. OK?”

“No problem,” replied Grant.

The surprise was that the friend had some additional company: two chickens and a duck. To Grant, it felt more like a scene from a Marx Brothers movie than the beginning of one of his most perilous missions.

The trip to Kladanj didn’t go as planned, as is often the case with journeys. Instead of the direct half-hour, 30km route, Grant had to take a longer, more challenging path due to Serb occupation of certain roads. Dubbed the “off-piste journey” by Grant, it ended up being twice as long, stretching to four hours. He found it hard to believe that things in Bosnia ever went smoothly. Unlike the precision of Swiss timekeeping, Bosnia seemed to lack the batteries needed for punctuality. Doubts crept into Grant's mind, wondering if the mission would ever come to fruition. He braced himself for potential disappointment.

Their lodging for the night consisted of cushions arranged on the floor of the unit commander's dwelling. The commander, who stood over two metres tall, would be leading the operation. Prior to the war, he had served as a teacher, evident in his demeanour, which exuded a preference for education over combat. There was a distinct aura of gentleness surrounding him. While many warriors sought power and glory in conflict, the commander appeared to possess no such aspirations. He carried himself with mild manners and politeness, resembling more of a librarian with his thoughtful and kind countenance. Internally, Grant harboured the hope that some of his comrades would display a greater level of battle-hardiness.

Selma and sometimes Haris interpreted Izudin's usual Yugoslav discussions when conversing with a Brit about Monty Python and Only Fools and Horses. Additionally, Izudin mentioned Spitting Image, a wacky and satirical British TV puppet show from the 1980s that humorously ridiculed various figures in showbiz and politics.

"Very Good," smiled Izudin, sticking a thumb into the air.

Sleep came easier after a few glasses of Stock brandy, and the morning routine began with a cup of strong black Turkish coffee, followed by another glass of Stock. Despite the intention to depart at 6:00 a.m., as expected by Grant, the departure was delayed. This delay persisted through seven, eight, and nine o'clock. Finally, at 10:00 a.m., a van arrived outside, its driver clad in camouflage gear, signalling their presence with a honk of the horn.

"Let's go," said Izudin. "It is time."

"I give you gun," the commander said, pointing to an AK47 propped against the wall.

"No, thank you," replied Grant. "Me Novinar," (journalist). "No fight. My weapon is camera," he smiled. Izudin gave him a puzzled look. He didn't understand the concept of a man wanting to face the Serbs armed with just a camera.

"Dobro," he said, (good) and walked outside.

Grant gathered his belongings, including the video camera, and his stomach tied itself into knots, much like it always did, before entering potentially risky situations. However, this time, the knot felt larger. He anticipated not just the presence of danger in eastern Bosnia but rather the scale of that danger. Recalling Mo, he longed for his company, remembering the advice of a seasoned photographer who once emphasised the importance of having a companion in war zones to avoid dying alone. Initially repulsed by the notion, Grant now understood its wisdom. Venturing into uncertainty with strangers, he couldn't shake the thought that the next bullet might bear his name. In moments like these, he wished for his friend's reassuring presence by his side.

He shook his head, as though trying to break free from the dark thoughts. Focus on reality and stay concentrated. Stay alert, stay alive, he reminded himself.

No need to hurry. Izudin planned to make a few more stops for chats and cups of coffee before they reached their final destination. Leaving this peaceful spot, they were heading into the chaotic world of frontline war.

The meeting spot lay beneath a railway tunnel. Around thirty to forty men gathered there, armed and ready, with some carrying bandoliers of bullets. Most were smoking and sipping from a plastic bottle, presumably containing alcohol. Observing their fervent consumption, Grant assumed they were avid drinkers, which seemed fitting given their destination. Without hesitation, he joined them in their spirited indulgence.

The guide from Tuzla, usually seen in high heels and a fur coat, appeared at the location. However, she had swapped her usual attire for combat gear and boots while still wearing makeup.

"What's her name?" Grant asked. Haris asked one of the soldiers.

"Dolly," he said. "Dolly is a strange name for a Bosnian woman," the journalist commented mainly to himself, but Haris duly translated that to the soldier who cupped his hands over his chest, clearly indicating a woman's breasts.

"Dolly Parton," responded the soldier and laughed out loud. Into the valley of jokes rode the six hundred, thought Grant and smiled back half-heartedly.

After a few more cigarettes, the group formed a line and trudged up the snow-covered hill. Grant waved goodbye to Selma, uncertain when they'd meet again. Despite his excitement, a hint of nervousness lingered within him. As they walked, the snow deepened, making each step more tiresome. Grant, considering himself fit, had to pause frequently. Dolly, briskly smoking a cigarette, marched past him. The terrain undulated, reminiscent of the children's rhyme about the 'Grand Old Duke of York' who climbed up and down hills. Hours passed in this manner until they reached the top of another hill, where Izudin halted and quietly gave instructions to a colleague, who then relayed the message to the rest of the group.

"No more smoking or speaking from here," said Haris. We are close to the first frontline. Serbs will be close. Our scouts have gone ahead to check the way. We have to wait." One was Dolly, who looked far different from how she had in Tuzla.

The group knelt down, the moments stretching into what felt like an eternity. Immobilised, their bodies succumbed to the creeping chill of the night. A biting wind whipped around them, the darkness enveloping them like a thick blanket of coal. Grant shivered uncontrollably, his body stiffening with the cold. Despite wearing gloves, his hands tinged blue, and his feet grew numb. Chattering teeth betrayed the onset of an intense cold.

Suddenly, a series of shots broke the silence, followed by more. Every man in the group raised their rifles towards the source of the noise and remained alert.

One of the scouts ran forward. “Pomoc,” (help) he said, and two fighters raced to him. Five minutes later, the men reappeared carrying Dolly. She’s been shot in the leg. More shots rang out.

Haris translated what Izudin said. “Big group of Chetniks coming,” he said. “Too big for us to fight. Commander says we must go. Fucking fast.”

“He said fucking fast?” asked Grant. “No, I said fucking fast,” replied a stressed-out Haris.

Five fighters remained to provide covering fire while the group escaped with Dolly. Climbing the final hill through deep snow had consumed two hours, yet the descent only required 15 minutes.

“Slow down,” said Haris. “Commander said we safe now. Chetniks, not come here.”

Dolly escaped serious injury, yet her inability to walk halted Grant’s plans. Realising she was his passage through the second Serb line, Grant faced the abrupt end of his mission due to her incapacitation. Disappointment engulfed him, nullifying the stress and tension of the past 24 hours. All his worry and agitation seemed futile. To access the besieged area, he’d need to endure it all once more.

Selma was waiting at the tunnel when they came down the hill.

"Bad luck," she said. "But I have some better news. There is another way in, by helicopter, an Mi8, but there is a catch."

Grant perked up. "A chopper is great. What's the catch?"

"There is no night flying capability, and it will fly low over Serb-controlled territory for thirty minutes in plain daylight…and it will be packed with ammunition."

"Great, so thirty minutes in a flying bomb with ammo boxes for a seat in broad daylight, so low that any Serb with a pea shooter could hit us. What complete and utter nutter would agree to something as crazy as that?"

34

It marked a rare occurrence, the first instance where everything fell into place as planned. The hotel pickup, the punctual arrival of the car, the prompt assembly of the fighters, and a commander who appeared adequately prepared. There followed a fifteen-minute briefing, followed by a brief respite of five minutes, during which one could indulge in smoking as many cigarettes and consuming as much sliva as humanly feasible. Grant managed both tasks proficiently.

He trailed behind the fighters as they exited the fire station at Tuzla airbase, accompanied by Selma and Haris. Two large Mi8 helicopters stood nearby, their engines humming and rotor blades slicing through the chilly air. Soldiers were busy loading boxes onto the helicopters, while lines of troops formed at the steps leading inside. These Russian helicopters, dating back to the 1960s, were known for their reliability in combat, although a bit sluggish. Grant pondered the maintenance history of the two helicopters, hoping they had been well looked after.

Selma made the decision to return to Donji Zelenik to visit her brother and father, as well as to offer assistance at the clinic, which was overwhelmed with casualties. Having completed a basic medical assistant's course in Sarajevo during the war's onset, her skills were in high demand. It was decided that Haris would remain with Grant.

A man beckoned the journalist up the stairs to the chopper door.

"This to Cerska?" Grant shouted, trying to make his voice heard over the sound of the engines. "I want to go to Cerska," he shouted, but the noise drowned out his words. Even if the helicopter crewman had understood English, the roaring engines and turning rotor blades made that irrelevant.

Grant was aware of the intense Serb assault on Cerska and felt a pressing need to reach the location to document its situation, possibly even its inevitable downfall. Unfortunately, Haris lagged too far behind to provide translation assistance. A crew member directed Grant to the second helicopter, which stood ready for departure. He motioned for Haris to join him, and together with Selma, they boarded the aircraft. Inside, they found it loaded with heavy weaponry, including machine guns, mines, ammunition boxes, grenades, and mortar rounds. Grant observed only a sparse supply of food provisions, consisting of just one or two boxes.

The noise filled the room, making it nearly impossible to hear anything else. Selma attempted a half-hearted smile to ease the tension, but it had little effect. Only Haris remained stoic, his expression devoid of emotion. Seeing that conversation was futile amidst the clamour, Grant retrieved his Walkman, donned his headphones, and pressed play. Bob Dylan's "Knocking on Heaven's Door" filled the air.

"Mama, take this badge off of me

I can't use it anymore
It's getting dark too dark to see
I feel I'm knockin' on heaven's door."

He reckoned that wasn't, perhaps, the best choice of music.

The heavily loaded Mi8 struggled to ascend, like a large animal attempting to rise onto its feet. With a sudden jerk, it lifted off the ground, executing a sharp one hundred and eighty-degree turn away from Tuzla airbase, towards the east, and into Serb territory. The pilot, feeling a surge of anxiety, increased the volume to drown out any ominous sounds, should they encounter danger. Grant couldn't shake the sensation that the aircraft, burdened with its load, was moving far slower than its maximum speed of under 200 kilometres per hour. It lumbered through the air, resembling a sluggish giant. In American terms, it would have been considered an ideal setup for an easy target. Grant's apprehension surged, his heartbeat matching the rapid pace of the chopper's rotor blades.

They descended low, so much so that the treetops seemed almost within reach. Haris, Selma, and six other fighters accompanied them, along with a crew of three. The air was thick with smoke as everyone indulged in cigarettes. Grant glanced out of the window, observing the houses below. He couldn't shake the thought that Serb lookouts might be hidden within, ready to signal an anti-aircraft battery. His thoughts raced, matching the rapid pace of his heartbeat. Selma noticed his unease and gently took his hand, offering a reassuring smile. Here I am, he reflected, an experienced war correspondent, yet she remains remarkably composed while I am almost a blubbering pussy.

He forced a smile, feeling its insincerity as the next song queued up on the tape: Chris Rea's 'The Road to Hell.' Grant found the choice fitting, almost ironic. Seated on his makeshift ammo crate, he couldn't help but wonder about Mo's current comforts, likely lounging in a private hospital bed, indulging in smoked salmon sandwiches while attended to by attractive nurses. Retrieving Buzz from his bag, he silently mouthed ‘to infinity and beyond’ to Selma, who responded with a warm smile. Grant admired her courage, imagining her bravery to be as impressive as footballs. Yet, a niggling thought persisted: perhaps she harboured a touch of madness.

One of the soldiers approached him with a Kalashnikov and offered it to Grant. “No thanks,” he shouted, shaking his head. “Novinar,’ (journalist). ‘No fight, only write.” The soldier gave him a puzzled look and returned to his ammo box seat.

Grant glanced at his watch. It was 2:35 p.m. Thirty minutes had passed since they took off. He had expected a quicker flight to Cerska, given the initial estimate. Nonetheless, it was too late to question the delay now. As the helicopter began its descent towards a snow-covered hill, Grant observed a flurry of activity through the window. Hundreds of people were gathered below, shouting “Hrana” repeatedly and waving branches in distress. Grant swiftly switched to filming mode, capturing the scene as the chopper landed and the people’s reactions unfolded.

Within minutes, the Mi8 unloaded its cargo and was in the air again heading back to Tuzla.

“What’s Hrana?” asked Grant.

“Food,” replied Selma. “They want food.”

“What about the branches? Is that something to do with peace?”

She turned to speak to an old lady.

“No, this is food. The branches are food. They take the berries and grind them down to make a kind of flour. She says that’s all they have to eat.”

They walked along a track to a nearby house. Outside was a little boy with blonde hair, blue eyes, and a cute face. “Hrana?” he asked Grant, holding out his hand. Without any food, the child appeared incredibly thin. Children like this always touched the hearts of even the toughest journalists. They were the innocent casualties in every conflict, yet they bore a significant share of the suffering. Despite being on the brink of starvation, this child still found solace in playing and eating. Grant shook his head as if to say sorry. He had nothing to give and felt bad. He admonished himself silently. Why hadn’t he thought to bring at least one or two bags of sweets?

An elderly man gestured for them to enter from the doorway. Grant captured the moment on film in the kitchen, where a mix of adults and children gathered. Their gaunt appearances were striking. They sat huddled around a modest metal fire, its makeshift chimney protruding through the wall. The elderly man raised his jumper to reveal a belt with several improvised holes, pointing to one added at the end of the belt.

“This was where he was fixing his belt six months ago,” explained Selma. “He says he has lost twenty-two kilos.”

Where is Cerska’s front line?” Grant asked while filming.

“This isn’t Cerska,” Selma told him. “This is an outlying village of Donji Zelenik.”

Grant looked visibly upset.

“But I wanted to go to Cerska,” he spluttered. “I need to get there to record the desperate situation.”

“Don’t worry, you will find enough desperation around here, believe me, and if that is not enough, we can get you to Cerska in the next day or two.”

A small minivan arrived to take the ammo and supplies.

“Let’s go,” said Selma, “He will give us a lift to town.”

Grant occupied the front seat of the van, capturing footage through the window as the vehicle moved along.

“Nema,” said the driver “Zabranjeno” (No, it is forbidden). He couldn’t believe it. Thirty minutes sitting in a time bomb to go and film desperation, and he’s already being told Zabranjeno. It was a frustrating moment, one that called for a cigarette. Retrieving a pack of Marlboro from his pocket, he lit one up. The driver’s reaction was unexpected; he seemed almost eager at the sight. Suddenly, his tough demeanor softened. He smiled a gentle, almost pleading smile. “Ah, Marlboro,” he said in an ultra-mellow tone. “Dobro cigarette, dobro.” (Good cigarette, good). It was plain to see that the man felt the utmost respect for the cigarette brand.

Grant gave him one, and the man was beside himself with joy. He lit up and inhaled long and deep. “Ah, Marlboro,” he said over and over again. It appeared to Grant that this was touching on a sexual experience.

“Uredu,” (ok), said the driver gesticulating to the camera while making the filming action.

“Ok?” said Grant.

It was quite a change. Forbidden until he received a single Marlboro cigarette as a gift. Now Grant had the freedom to film whatever he pleased. With two cartons of Marlboro in his possession, he wondered about their value.

As they approached Donji Zelenik, the van began to overtake rows of people trudging through the snow. Some pushed carts, while others led horses and donkeys carrying their belongings.

“Stop,” shouted Grant. Hurriedly, he got out to film. At the rear of the cart, there appeared to be unwell individuals. Along the roadside, young children trudged through the snow. Grant noticed a woman wearing a headscarf, cradling a baby. He estimated the temperature to be near freezing. The woman glanced at him, her expression devoid of vitality, as she continued walking mechanically. Grant pondered the hardships she might have faced and felt an urge to interview her.

The driver said no, they had to get to Donji Zelenik before nightfall.

"The driver says they are coming every day," Selma said. "There will be plenty for you to film."

As they arrived at the outskirts of the town, night had already fallen. Along the street stood a line of shops, once bustling with people. Outside, hundreds gathered around open fires, casting flickering shadows in the darkness. Grant stepped out of the vehicle to capture the scene on film. For nearly an hour, he filmed wide shots, close-ups of elderly individuals, cheerful children unaware of the situation, and mothers wearing worried expressions. Few were seen eating amidst the crowd.

"Grant, I am going to find my father and brother. The police chief says you and Haris can stay with him tonight. I will meet you at the clinic tomorrow morning," Selma explained. And she disappeared into the night and the chaos.

He glanced around, taking in the surroundings. It resembled a scene straight out of the nineteenth-century East End of London. The enormity of the situation overwhelmed Grant, especially considering the sheer volume of people present. He silently acknowledged that the Bosnian government's claims were accurate. Urgency flooded his thoughts; he needed to share this story promptly. As more displaced individuals trickled into town, the daylight dwindled, making filming increasingly difficult. Grant and Haris set off to locate the police chief's residence, wondering what the next day might hold.

35

The towering wrought iron gates stood tall, surpassing four metres in height, narrating tales of a distant, bygone era. Crowned atop these gates was the emblematic double-headed eagle, representing the national identity of Serbia. Nestled within the gates lay a modest guard post, its presence illuminated by the soft glow of an oil lamp radiating through a diminutive window. With a subtle gesture, Mehmet beckoned one of his comrades to advance. Stealthily, the man approached the post's wall and cautiously peered through the window.

He raised his hand showing two fingers to indicate there were two guards.

Mehmet felt astonished by the lack of security at the military academy, considering the valuable artillery guns it housed. He couldn't believe the Serb complacency and arrogance, realising the heavy toll it had taken. These guns had caused immense harm in eastern Bosnia, resulting in countless casualties, including Mehmet's mother. Determined to put an end to this, he knew the man behind it all had to be held accountable.

He approached the guard post quietly, armed with the pistol and silencer borrowed from Hagija. With swift precision, he opened the door and swiftly dispatched each of the men with two bullets. They were taken by surprise and fell to the ground swiftly. In the corner, a stove simmered with boiling water. Beside it sat a table adorned with a plate of Ajver peppers, Kaimac cheese, and a loaf of bread, accompanied by some prosciutto ham. These were beloved Serbian snacks, now destined to remain untouched.

The two groups advanced along the road towards the main academy building, splitting into two to cover more ground. Mehmet led one group to the right and another to the left, assigning four men to accompany him. Their objective was to locate the artillery guns. Following intelligence reports, they targeted the main Serb barracks, where they believed ten to twenty soldiers were stationed. Maintaining surprise and silence was crucial to their mission's success.

The fighters moved swiftly. Two men positioned mines and trip wires at both the front and rear entrances, while four others located the warehouse housing the artillery pieces. Inside, they found seven 155mm guns and three 105mm howitzers. To their surprise, tucked away in a corner were two T-72 tanks, a valuable discovery. One of the fighters relayed this information to Mehmet while the rest rigged the artillery guns with explosives.

He started to rethink his plan, realising the importance of bolstering Donji Zelenik's defences. After inquiring, he learned that one of his men had operated tanks during national service in the former Yugoslavia. Stealing a tank could greatly enhance their defensive capabilities. Although challenging, it seemed worthwhile. He dispatched the experienced man to inspect the tanks for ammunition and fuel. Upon his return, he confirmed that one tank was fully stocked with shells, machine gun bullets, and fuel, while the other was lacking. Mehmet decided to take the fully loaded tank and destroy the other.

The western wing of the academy housed the young recruits, mostly teenagers. Mehmet viewed them as future combatants, devoid of mercy. The corridors lay silent as men assumed their positions.

He gave the order for the doors to be sealed and fuel to be poured in the corridors.

Mehmet quietly led two men up the stairs to the top floor. There, they found double doors marked with a brass plaque reading 'commandant,' indicating the office. Mehmet was aware that the adjacent room served as the commandant's sleeping quarters, a place where he often stayed overnight, especially on Thursdays, preferring to be near his young students.

One of his men cautiously opened one side of the large double doors, and they entered the expansive office. Moonlight flooded through the window, casting a soft glow. Behind the desk, there were two photos, one featuring the Serbian president and the other the leader of the Bosnian Serbs, and a third painting depicting the sixteenth-century Serbian hero, Prince Lazar.

Mehmet glanced at his watch. It was a little past 4:00 a.m. This marked the beginning of the critical hour for attack, the perfect moment to strike when defenders were typically at their weakest, lost in slumber.

His checklist for the assault was ticked off: Neutralise guards- check. Identify artillery placements - check. Rig them with explosives - check. Secure ammunition caches - check. Set traps in the army barracks - check. Isolate new recruits - check. Establish positions for the machine guns - check. Ensure the getaway truck is prepared - check. Locate General Demetris Petrovic - check. Everything was falling seamlessly into place.

They waited silently as time crept by. With a careful turn of the doorknob, he was met by the soft sound of the general's snores echoing through the room. Mehmet couldn't help but note how peacefully the general slept. According to the plan, the coordinated assault was set to begin at 4:15 a.m, with Mehmet taking the lead. Methodically, he removed the silencer from his Browning automatic 9mm, knowing that stealth was no longer necessary.

Glancing at his watch, Mehmet observed the general's uniform neatly arranged on a nearby chair, every detail meticulously placed. The hat, gloves, and pistol holster rested on the table with military precision, while the highly polished shoes stood proudly in front of the chair, as if awaiting orders.

At 4:14 a.m., the young Muslim walked up to the side of the bed and shook the general from his deep sleep.

"General," whispered Mehmet. "Time to get up."

The General woke quickly but was disorientated.

"What?" he mumbled. "Who are you?"

"I am Mehmet from Donji Zelenik, one of those Muslim Fundamentalists you swore to eradicate," said Mehmet in a voice which started to get louder.

"What do you want?" replied Petrovic.

"Nothing really. I just wanted to ask you a question."

"What?" said the old man, clearly getting agitated and angry in the pompous way that old aristocrats displayed so easily.

"April 12th 1992, remember what you were doing and where?" asked Mehmet.

"How could I remember what I was doing on one day all that time ago?" he stammered.

"Let me refresh your memory. It was the final practical exam for your students on firing 155mm artillery guns. Remember now?" Mehmet demanded. "You came in your lovely Rolls Royce in your lovely uniform with lots of lovely medals and gave the order for your recruits to shell eastern Bosnia. More precisely, to shell my town, Donji Zelenik. And you know what, I guess it was a very successful exam because that day you killed a lot of Muslims. Innocent men, women and children."

"When there is war, innocent people get killed," argued the General.

"This wasn't war, you murdering fucker. This was a massacre of people who never harmed anyone and never picked up a gun or, shot anyone, or threatened anyone. They were not soldiers. Just ordinary people getting on with a simple life.

And one of them was my mother. The sweetest and most giving of all, and you took her life and took her away from me."

"What do you want from me? I'm not going to beg for my life if that is what you want. I am fighting for my people. I am not ashamed of that."

"You should be," said Mehmet. He lifted his pistol and fired two shots into the head of Petrovic. He slumped back lifeless.

As the shots echoed, explosions erupted across the base with booming intensity. The initial Serbs exiting the barracks triggered trip wires, showering them with countless small fragments from anti-personnel mines. Subsequent individuals were swiftly mowed down by a machine gunner. Meanwhile, Molotov cocktails were hurled through the windows of the recruits' quarters, igniting the fuel within. Within moments, flames engulfed the dormitory, and cries of terror filled the air as teenagers found themselves trapped amidst the inferno.

Mehmet raced outside. He looked at the building and heard the screams. "Let them burn," he said.

The ammo dump erupted with deafening explosions, illuminating the night sky like a dazzling fireworks spectacle. Nearby, the escape truck patiently awaited their departure. The tank driver waved farewell before embarking down the road towards the Bajna Bashta dam, their route back to Bosnia. Despite the challenges ahead, the element of surprise and the formidable firepower of a T-72 offered hope for success.

Mehmet silently took his place in the truck's front seat, his expression devoid of a smile as he issued the command to drive. The journey back, which had taken them two arduous hours on foot from the dinghies, now promised to be a mere twenty-minute drive. With a touch more fortune, they could cross the River Drina in time to witness the sunrise from the Bosnian hills. Lost in contemplation,

Mehmet's mind wandered to thoughts of his mother, haunted by memories of her anguish and the violence inflicted upon her. In his pragmatic manner, he found solace in the notion that revenge offered a semblance of relief, an eye for an eye. While it could not erase the pain entirely, it offered a measure of respite, allowing his mother to finally rest easy.

36

"Morgen," said the voice as Grant rose to his feet. He didn't have a bad night's sleep, though the floor felt a bit hard. Haris had already gotten up and was having coffee with the police chief in the kitchen.

Merima, his wife, greeted the visitor at the door. Standing before her was a slender, delicate man, his face adorned with a broad smile and wearing a Turkish fez.

"Morgen," he said again and offered his hand to Grant. "I am Bruno from Germany. So pleased to meet you," he said in heavily accented English.

"Oh," said Grant, "I didn't know any other foreigners were here. Nice to meet you. How is it going, and what are you doing here?"

"I am photographer, taking photos of ze vor. Peeble are ferry nice," he said.

"Wow," said Grant. "I haven't seen any photos of this area in the media. How are you getting your material out of here?"

"I am not," replied Bruno. "I will take everything wiz me ven I go."

Grant was amazed. "But this is a big story, Bruno. You need to tell it and show people what is happening here, how the people are suffering."

"I vill ven I go, maybe soon," he said with a big smile.

Grant perceived Bruno as somewhat absent-minded, as if he were not fully present in the moment. It appeared that Bruno's attention was elsewhere, oblivious to their challenging circumstances. He mentioned that he had arrived in Donji Zelinka after a lengthy 12-hour journey through Serb territory.

"It vos like being in ze boy scouts again," explained Bruno. Make that four coupons, thought Grant.

"Yes, I met a Bossnian in Berlin, and he zed I should go to Bosnia, and zo, here I am."

Grant hadn't seen a smile like that in all his time in Bosnia. How could he be so fucking happy? Haris walked into the room without the slightest trace of a smile and said, "hello." It occurred to Grant that Bruno got Haris's share of the smile gene.

"Heff you a kleine cigarette?" he asked. Grant rummaged around in his pocket and gave Bruno a Marlboro.

"Zey are precious zings here," explained Bruno, suppressing his excitement. "One carton is worth a zousand German marks."

At that moment, Grant scanned the area for his cartons, but couldn't find them. Perhaps he left them in the minivan or somewhere nearby.

Haris said, "We need to go. Refugees coming. Many. You need to film. Let's go."

"Me too," said Bruno.

Grant swiftly retrieved his camera, and together they ventured into the snow, now turning slushy underfoot. Almost instantly, Grant spotted a procession of individuals trekking through the town, guiding two cows along. He zoomed in on them before scanning the surroundings, revealing more figures trudging through the snow and slush, burdened with bundles of belongings and wearing impassive expressions.

"Ask them how far they have walked," said Grant to Haris.

He asked. "Fifteen kilometres," he answered. "They say this is the third time they have moved because of the Serbs shelling. For the last week, they have been living in the woods. But there was no food, so they have come here."

He filmed an interview just as a flatbed truck hurriedly pulled up and halted outside a grey, two-storey building. Six men lay on stretchers at the truck's rear. Some were dressed in camouflage jackets, while others wore regular clothing.

"Fighters who have been wounded," explained Haris.

Grant trailed behind them as they were ushered into the building. Two appeared visibly worse off, while another was audibly groaning in agony. They were gently laid on the floor just outside a room, with Grant diligently filming their every move. Nearby, others lay sprawled on the ground, clearly injured. Among them were two women and a child, no older than six, who sobbed inconsolably. Despite his efforts, Grant struggled to discern the exact nature of their afflictions. The room itself was dimly lit, casting a pall over the scene, while the pervasive scent of unwashed bodies filled the air as usual.

The door opened and out walked Selma. She smiled at Grant but carried on past him.

"Can't talk now," she said and started to inspect the wounded. He grasped that she was prioritising, deciding who was most severely injured, who could receive assistance, and who couldn't. Some argued that this resembled playing God, and it wasn't always straightforward to make the correct decisions, but it remained necessary.

"Him and him," said Selma to two orderlies in white coats. They lifted the first man onto the stretcher. A large portion of his left leg was gone, his sneaker discarded nearby. Grant observed this with a grim understanding that the shoe served no further purpose.

Following the second stretcher, Grant entered a room bustling with activity, serving as the accident and emergency reception. Bodies and individuals filled the space, creating an atmosphere of controlled chaos. Voices clamoured, assistants hurried about, requests for supplies echoed, wounds were tended to, and garments were swiftly removed. Grant paused, observing from a distance. Amidst the commotion, a young girl lay on a trolley, motionless and unattended. Approaching quietly, he captured her face on film. Her eyes, open but unresponsive, held a milky look while she made a faint, gurgling sound, the sound of impending death. Grant referred to it as the 'death rattle.' Examining her hands, he noted a bluish tint to her nails, another sign of imminent death. Ceasing his filming, he reached out to hold her hand, finding it limp and chilling to the touch.

Selma passed by. "Shrapnel in the stomach," she explained quickly. "Sadly, there is nothing that can be done."

"What about her family?" he asked. "They were all killed in the shelling," she said hurriedly and dashed off to help more incoming wounded.

Grant began to grasp the magnitude of the situation: the violence, the pain, and the anguish. Memories flooded back from his time in Karaama, Mogadishu, where he had felt a similar sense of despair. Helplessness overwhelmed him, knowing he couldn't alleviate the suffering.

Suddenly, a door creaked open at the room's far end, revealing a figure in a blood-stained white coat. Clad in surgical gloves and clutching a scalpel.

"More anaesthetic," he shouted in Bosnian and went back inside.

Grant went to the room and knocked.

"Sta?" (What), said a voice. Grant opened the door and eased his way in.

"Ah, good morning, my friend," said the surgeon. "So pleased to meet you. You are the British man who has come to tell the world how we suffer here. Thank you, my friend. I am Nedret. Coffee?"

He was mid-way through extracting a lump of shrapnel from a woman's throat.

"OK to film?" asked Grant. "Nema problema," responded Nedret. (no problem) "Yes, a coffee would be lovely."

Filming carnage and operations while casually sipping coffee with a smiling surgeon amidst the chaos of a war-torn town was a surreal experience. It felt almost bizarre. Just then, Bruno entered with a piece of bread, exchanged greetings with Nedret, and offered Grant some, which he politely declined. Unlike the German, the blood and gore around them didn't stimulate his appetite much.

Grant proceeded to film Nedret conducting surgery. Between sips of coffee, he interviewed him about the challenges he encountered.

"Well, we don't have electricity, so no x-ray, which means we cannot find metal in the body. We do have some anaesthetic left, but it is in short supply. Two weeks ago, we had to perform operations without. I really need another surgeon because on busy days, like today, it is difficult to cope with the number of patients. And you know that some people are dying or losing limbs because they have to wait for treatment. But most of all, we could do with the Serbs stopping shelling us. That would be a big help," and he beamed a big smile.

They both understood the slim likelihood of that happening or the war abruptly ceasing.

Selma was rushed off her feet.

"We'll speak later," she said and hurried off to tend to another patient.

Bruno had that gormless look on his face as if he didn't have a care in the world.

"Mine Freund, any chance off von more Marlboro?"

Having coffee in the operating room was allowed, but smoking crossed the line, especially in Bosnia. Grant escorted the tall German outside, where they could light up.

"You didn't see any cartons of Marlboro lying around when you came today, did you?" asked Grant. After completing his sentence, he noticed the police chief on the opposite side of the street. With a cigarette between his lips, the chief was sharing some with two men. It occurred to him that his cartons of Marlboro might have found new owners. It seemed like they were helping to alleviate the chief's wartime concerns. Two thousand marks could make a significant difference in a besieged town.

"Do you want to come with me to Cerska?" asked the German. "There is a truck leaving, and we can go. I asked the driver."

It was too good an opportunity to miss. "Yes, definitely. I wanted to go there originally," explained Grant, "but they made me go on the helicopter that came here."

"You were very lucky, my Freund," said Bruno. "Zat helicopter vas shot down by ze Zerbs und efferyone vas killed."

Grant drew a sharp breath. Clearly, the imminent threat of a bullet bearing his name lingered, still searching.

The Tata Truck showed signs of age and wear; its exterior was weathered and worn. A tattered canvas cover adorned the rear, marked with numerous holes and tears, evidence of either prolonged use or the harsh toll of conflict. Twenty fighters occupied the back, with Haris among them. Grant and Bruno were ushered to the front seats, positioned alongside the driver. News had spread regarding Grant and his Marlboros. In addition to the fighters, the truck carried vital supplies of ammunition and food destined for the defenders in Cerska. Haris had emphasised the urgency of the situation, stating that the village's defences were rapidly weakening. Time was of the essence; they needed to reach Cerska swiftly.

A kilometre out of Donji Zelenik, the driver stopped in the inside of a right-hand bend.

"Haris, what is happening, mate?"

Haris popped his head out of the canvas on the side of the truck close to the passenger window.

"They do this to fool the Serbs," he explained. "They can see us when we leave the town and then fire when they guess the truck will be passing one bend or another. They know the positions well. So, driver wait for a while and then speeds up. They say it works."

The driver gave a big smile as if he understood what Haris was saying, which, of course, he did not. Then, from his pocket, he took a packet of Marlboro.

'They look familiar,' Grant thought to himself. The driver passed around cigarettes to the passengers, who eagerly lit up. They had barely begun to savour the first drag of tobacco when a deafening explosion shattered the moment. Grant's ears rang as smoke filled the cabin, accompanied by the acrid smell of burning. Shouts erupted from the back of the truck, but they seemed distant and muffled to Grant. He shook his head in an attempt to clear his senses and orient himself. Glancing around, he saw Bruno's lips moving, but the words were lost in the chaos. Smoke obscured his vision, and panic threatened to overwhelm him. When Grant looked down, his attention was drawn to the gruesome sight of the

German's injured hand, part of his thumb hanging limply. Turning his gaze, he saw the driver clutching his neck, blood seeping through his fingers, and staining Grant's jacket. Another explosion rocked the truck, shattering the windscreen into shards. A sharp pain throbbed in Grant's left arm, and he looked down to see blood, realising with a jolt that it was his own. As the senses returned it was clear they had been hit by Serb mortars and were still under attack.

Bruno stepped out of the car, Grant trailing closely behind. The truck's front tyres lay shredded from the explosion. Fighters poured out from the back, hastening towards the town. They halted after a brief hundred-metre sprint to assess the damage. The driver bore the brunt of the injuries and was swiftly ushered into a passing car bound for the clinic.

As Bruno wrapped a handkerchief around his thumb, he noticed Grant nursing his arm, the Marlboro still in his mouth. Bruno marvelled at Grant's feat of sprinting with a cigarette, although briefly. He then realised he had lost himself in the chaos. Tempted to retrieve it, Grant persuaded him otherwise by offering what remained of his own Marlboro followed by a deep inhale.

"Zo goot," he said, seemingly totally oblivious to his dangling thumb wrapped in his neckerchief. They wandered off for treatment, sharing the final flickers of the cigarette. They were well enough to smoke another Marlboro, at the very least, but the real concern wasn't about survival but rather where they would find the next one.

37

In his sixties, General Gaston Leconte, a veteran of the French army, had experienced the trials of some of France's most challenging campaigns and bitter defeats. His journey began at Dien Bien Phu in Vietnam in 1954, where, as a young lieutenant, he witnessed its fall to Ho Chi Minh's forces after a gruelling four-month siege, marking a pivotal moment in the decline of French colonial power in Indo-China.

Next was Algeria, where they faced a significant loss of nearly twenty-seven thousand men during an eight-year campaign. This period marked a public relations disaster for France and signalled the decline of the French empire's prestige. As a young captain stationed there, failure deeply affected him and his fellow officers. They believed they had been exploited and abandoned by ineffective politicians.

As the leader of the United Nations forces in Bosnia, he encountered the same challenges and errors that troubled soldiers and civilians alike.

He inherited his position from a disheartened Egyptian general who, confronted with stubbornness and numerous obstacles, spent his final days in the office, seeking solace in prayer for peace or departure, whichever arrived first.

General Leconte understood that achieving peace in Bosnia was not solely within the realm of the UN's capabilities. However, he recognised the importance of facilitating the process by establishing a framework for dialogue among the involved parties. Taking his responsibilities seriously, he approached his command with dedication and optimism. Unlike adopting a defensive mindset, he actively engaged with leaders and commanders, initiating conversations, gaining insights, and proposing solutions. Despite his age of sixty-seven, he maintained a rugged appearance with thick-rimmed spectacles and a full head of hair.

As a career officer, he couldn't help but admire the Serbs. They resembled a disciplined army with their uniforms, organisation, and structure. In contrast, the Bosnians seemed disorganised and poorly equipped, lacking discipline and the soldierly demeanour he deemed crucial for an effective military force.

Upon exiting the white UN Land Rover, an officer approached and saluted. Leconte reciprocated the gesture, proceeding to shake hands with Major Lars Henriksen.

"Nice to meet you," said the General, "Pity it wasn't under better circumstances."

Outside, a squadron of Danish white-painted Snow Leopard tanks stood parked, constituting the heavy armour of the UN's Nordic battalion, which included soldiers from Sweden, Denmark, and Norway.

The general was led into a room where a makeshift wood-burning stove provided warmth in the otherwise barren space.

He sat down. Major Henriksen offered tea.

"Anything stronger?" asked the General. "I've developed a taste for this local Stock brandy."

A bottle was quickly produced with several glasses.

"Cheers. Now, about this incident," continued the general. He was referring to an attack by Serbs on Swedish UN positions, which provoked a response from the tanks. It had left fifty Serbs dead and wounded and three of their positions destroyed. No UN personnel were injured.

"Now it's been suggested by some in New York that your response to this attack if that's what it was, was disproportionate. You went over the top. Like taking a hammer to crack an egg. Why did you fire 96 shells?"

"Sorry, sir," replied the Major. "We ran out of ammunition."

The other officers smiled quietly at the joke.

Leconte wasn't in a smiling mood. He raised his voice.

"We are trying to win the trust of all sides," he said. "Killing is not the way to do it. You have set back my work big time. I have been negotiating with the Serbs to allow us to take much-needed aid convoys to help the besieged people in the east. This is most definitely NOT going to help."

"Sir, we had no choice," explained the Major. "Our forces were ambushed and could have been overrun had not the tanks been used. Luckily, none of our men was killed. But the story could have been very different had we not acted with force. We have endured sniper attacks and mined roads and barricades as we have attempted our peacekeeping duties to try and help civilians. One drunken Serb with a Kalashnikov at a checkpoint has the ability to stop us in our tracks, and no one here or in New York can change that. We are at their mercy."

"I understand the frustration," said Leconte, "but I emphasise this is a peacekeeping exercise, and we must adhere to that no matter how much provocation and intimidation. Until we get a different mandate from the Security Council we facilitate, we don't fight. So, I order you to show restraint from now on. I am now going to the Serb side to try and repair the damage if that is at all possible."

38

General Novak Kustavic stood at the entrance to the Serb command centre in Bratunac, greeted by a six-man guard of honour standing at ease. As General Leconte's car arrived, followed by two white UN-armoured personnel carriers, a soldier shouted, "Attention!" and the men promptly shouldered their weapons.

It was the type of military greeting that Leconte deeply respected, a display of mutual respect between generals steeped in protocol. Leconte, being old-school, appreciated such formalities.

Kustavic saluted and offered his hand. "This way, General, it is an honour to receive you."

The room exuded warmth and spaciousness. Paintings depicting Prince Lazar, the Bosnian Serb president, and a religious figure, whom Leconte presumed to be a Patriarch of the Orthodox Church, adorned the wall behind a desk, a common sight throughout the room.

"So, General, before we begin, I take it you have come to offer an apology for the wilful killing by your tanks of our men?" said Kustavic in a slightly sarcastic voice.

"Not exactly," said Leconte. "I think this was a misunderstanding, and maybe our forces slightly overreacted. But they genuinely believed they were being ambushed."

"Certainly not," responded Kustavic in a raised voice. "We don't ambush the UN. We know you are here to help. The Muslims engineered this whole thing, they created this so-called misunderstanding, as you call it. Now we have more graves, widows and mourning parents because of this misunderstanding."

The General tried to explain that repeated restrictions on UN movement by Serbs were adding to confusion and frustration and the difficulty of reaching the besieged people in Eastern Bosnia.

Kustavic was almost indignant. "Restrictions are only made because of safety concerns for us and for you. This is a dangerous part of the country. You don't know what the Muslims are doing here. They are responsible for the deaths of many civilians. We are defending our homes, our people. There are parties who are sympathetic to the Muslims and are helping them. Aid convoys bring not only food but weapons, and those weapons are used to kill innocent Serbs. We have to be vigilant."

Leconte made a concerted effort to reassure the general that the UN had no intention of supporting Muslim fighters or providing them with crucial information or weapons to assist their cause. He emphasised that the primary objective of the UN was to provide humanitarian assistance to the people affected by the conflict.

"And that is exactly what we are trying to do," explained Kustavic. "Many of our people have been forced to flee their homes and are now refugees in their own country; where is the UN help for them? Where are food convoys for us? Why is the UN Security Council not speaking about our suffering?"

Leconte anticipated that the meeting would be challenging, but he also understood that if he wanted to gain access to eastern Bosnia, he would need to endure it, express the appropriate sentiments, and listen attentively.

"You know, General, we have suffered here for hundreds of years. Once, we were all Slavs, but when the Turks came, some switched religions. Let us say for tax reasons. But we Serbs, the true Serbs, resisted. That is forgotten by the West, and it is forgotten that we are still resisting. You need to see that."

Kustavic was passionate in stating the plight of the Serbian people and insistent that Serbs wanted to help all and everyone, no matter what religion. But he stressed, "Only the ones who want peace".

Leconte was well-informed about the conflict and could discern that much of the information presented was misleading. Intelligence reports indicated that the Serbs exerted a firm grip on the region, progressively tightening their hold and displacing people, predominantly Muslims, from their homes. He recognised that it was only a matter of time before the Bosnian forces were overrun. His mission, fully supported by New York, was to secure access to Donji Zelenik to facilitate the entry of urgently needed aid convoys.

"Let me make this proposition to you," said Leconte. "For every aid convoy allowed into Donji Zelenik, there will be one convoy for Bratunac and the Serb areas. How does that sound? Furthermore, I will also go into the village to implore them to ease attacks in return for aid?"

He explained an aid convoy was standing by in Tuzla; it could be on the move within a few hours.

"Let me try this," said Leconte. "Let me lead in a convoy, half for you, half for them. Everyone wins."

39

The body lay beside the makeshift graveyard as Grant filmed the scene, a funeral for a young man who had fallen on the frontline. Judging by his appearance, Grant surmised he must have been in his late teens or early twenties, although it was difficult to determine. A man, likely his brother, wept uncontrollably nearby, while an older figure, presumably his father, stood silently, lost in his own world. Grant panned the camera downward and observed the father holding his son's hand, releasing it reluctantly as mourners prepared to lower the body into the shallow grave, marked only by a simple piece of wood. As they turned the body, Grant noticed that half of the young man's head and face were missing, an injury inflicted, he speculated, by either shrapnel or heavy machine gun fire. The specifics were irrelevant; the loss was palpable. The brother offered a few words as the body descended into the earth, while the father remained lost in his grief. Grant's arm throbbed, a reminder of his own recent injury sustained during the attempted trip to Cerska. Although it was only a minor wound requiring three stitches, the shrapnel fragment still caused discomfort. In the world of triage, he would have been waiting for treatment, but in the world of filming, pain was an unwelcome distraction. As the father and mourners dispersed, heading back into town, another funeral came to a close.

Grant had spent three days fully immersed in Donji Zelenik. He had captured a daily stream of suffering, starvation, deprivation, and death on film. Yet, outside this besieged town, few knew the true extent of what was happening. Getting his video footage and reports out was essential. However, since the helicopter was shot down near Cerska, all flights have ceased, leaving Grant feeling increasingly desperate. He had violated one of his cardinal rules of frontline reporting: always ensure you have a plan for both entering and exiting a location. Donji Zelenik, however, posed a unique challenge. Grant had no idea how he and his materials would be able to leave. Having been wounded once already, his mood occasionally dipped into the macabre. What if he were killed before his reports or images reached the outside world? It would render all his efforts futile.

He glanced ahead and noticed a cart approaching. As it drew nearer, he discerned it was transporting two bodies covered in white sheets.

Suddenly, shouts erupted, echoing loudly, followed by cheers. Turning his gaze behind, he spotted a white UN Land Rover with General Leconte inside. It was flanked by two British Warrior armoured vehicles and three APCs (armoured personnel carriers). People shifted to the side of the road, and the cheering grew even more louder. 'Great timing.' thought Grant. 'It's like I ordered them in. Maybe God likes me.'

"We are saved," someone shouted, and hundreds began chasing behind the UN convoy. 'I'm saved too,' thought Grant.

Grant noticed the absence of aid trucks, leaving the cheering people without food. Despite this, he smiled, seeing it as a symbol of progress. The UN had successfully persuaded the Serbs to allow aid through, bringing hope to Donji

Zelenik and to Grant himself. With this development, he knew his reports and videos could now reach the outside world.

40

It was just past 8:00 a.m. when Hassan observed Ibrahimovic's mother locking her front door and heading out. Market day, a Tuesday, drew the elderly in former Yugoslavia seeking seasonal fresh produce. Despite Sarajevo's siege, makeshift vegetable patches offered some sustenance. With her son already at his office for an hour, Hassan acted swiftly. Aware of the limited time before the mother's return, he enlisted a subordinate with a history of breaking and entering, skills vital to accessing the Ibrahimovic house. Curiosity about the bag he glimpsed the previous night drove Hassan, though his actions defied conventional norms. Desperation prevailed in a time when rules held little sway.

The man effortlessly unlocked the latch and swung the door open. It took him a moment to find Ibrahimovic's room. Inside, everything was neat and orderly. A notebook and a diary sat on the desk. Hassan scanned the first few pages. 'May Allah forgive me,' stood out in bold letters, "I must do what I have to do." On the bedside table lay a copy of the Koran, beside a prayer mat tucked in the corner. Hassan rummaged through the walnut chest of drawers while his assistant remained downstairs on watch. The room held only modest attire, predominantly white, along with several cotton Kufi prayer hats. It seemed to Hassan that nearly everything about Mohammed Ibrahimovic was to do with worship. 'Devout, but perhaps a little boring,' he thought. It was the same with the large wooden wardrobe against the wall, filled again with more simple clothes.

Photos of Mecca and Medina adorned the wall, representing two revered Muslim sites. Below hung a small table bearing a prayer mat, prayer beads, a Koran, and bottles of Zamzam water – all souvenirs from the Haj pilgrimage. Nearby lay an airline ticket to Riyad and a bus ticket dated 1979, bound for Mecca. 'It must have been a secret pilgrimage,' thought Hassan. 'During Tito's times, Yugoslavs had to hide their religion.'

On the wall hung photos of Mecca and Medina, two of the holiest sites in Islam. Below the bed lay a large, old suitcase secured with a weathered lock. Hassan retrieved it, revealing its contents: prayer mats, a Keffiyeh, and an Abbaye Muslim garment. Under these items lay a plastic bag similar to the one Ibrahimovic had carried the previous evening. Inside rested a significant find: a scale model of the Masjid al-haram in Mecca, revered as the final resting place of Prophet Mohammed and the most sacred site in Islam. Despite his limited religiosity, Hassan recognised its significance; a framed photo of the same building adorned a wall in his family's lounge. Inside the bag there was a card. It was addressed to Mirsad Mehotic the Bosnian president. Inside was written 'May this Eid bring happiness, fulfilment and victory.'

Hassan shook his head in self-reproach. Ramadan approached, and it became evident that this was intended as a gift for the president at the end of the fasting month. How could he have doubted someone so deeply devoted to their faith? Ibrahimovic's commitment to Bosnia surpassed that of anyone Hassan had encountered. He carefully restored the box to the suitcase, ensuring nothing was misplaced, before turning to leave. A glint caught his eye, a piece of copper wire on the floor. Without much thought, Hassan discarded it in the waste paper bin. Ibrahimovic seemed an unlikely candidate for espionage. The lingering question remained: who was Munja? He was no closer to finding out.

41

General Leconte gathered with the so-called war council in Donji Zelenik, taking a seat at the table.

"The Serbs want peace, too," he said. "They are tired of the fighting." A ripple of quiet laughter swept the room.

"So why are they shelling us and forcing people from their homes?" said one of the council members. "Why don't they let food and aid in? Why don't they let women and children go to safety?"

The general avoided the questions and carried on. "It is significant that we are here, that they let us in. It marks a change in attitude. I am sure of that."

The doctor, Nedret, was at the table.

"General, if they were happy for you to come in, why did they not remove mines from the road." He was referring to one of the UN vehicles that had hit an anti-tank mine, resulting in two casualties. It didn't, however, dampen the general's enthusiasm.

"That was unlucky, and I believe this was not intentional," he said. "But we have set up a line of communication, and there is now a channel to help you. The Serbs have promised to allow aid convoys to come in. The first one is standing by; half will be for Donji Zelenik and the other half for Bratunac."

A collective laugh went up around the smoke-filled room.

"I think you trust them more than we do," said Nedret. "We have learned to be cautious. They are not starving. They have plenty of food and ammunition courtesy of Belgrade. Beware of what they agree to. They never give something for nothing."

Leconte rose. “We will see. Well, gentlemen, it has been a long day, and tomorrow we return to Bratunac to supervise the aid convoy. I bid you good night.”

“General, have you noticed that there has been no shelling or firing since you arrived? But when you go, the Serbs will continue killing us. They won’t stop until everyone is dead. You need to understand that.”

Leconte looked hard at Nedret and thought, ‘I think you are wrong, and you will see. Bonne Nuit.’

Grant had recorded the meeting. After he stopped, Nedret offered him a sip of sliva and a Marlboro cigarette. He observed a sudden increase in Marlboro cigarettes, which he suspected wasn’t just a coincidence.

“What do you think?” he asked the journalist.

Grant replied, “I believe he wants to think everything will be OK, but I don’t think he fully understands the Serbs. It’s interesting that there is no shelling while he is here. Maybe that is the answer.”

“What answer?” asked Nedret.

“Well, maybe he could be encouraged to stay, shall we say.”

“How?” inquired the doctor.

“There are ways,” said Grant and smiled. “Pour me another glass, and I’ll explain what I mean. By the way, where are you getting your Marlboro supply from….”

Upon the break of dawn, General Leconte promptly arose, attired himself, donned his boots, and savoured his initial cup of UN issued coffee, a provision from a Canadian sergeant. As he prepared to depart his temporary post office quarters, he heard the echoing chants emanating from the vicinity.

Beyond the confines of his dwelling, a multitude, comprising predominantly elderly individuals, women, and children, congregated around the UN vehicles. The Canadian peacekeepers exhibited signs of unease, as indicated by the disengagement of rifle safety mechanisms. Observers positioned atop nearby mounds surveyed the scene below with intent. Some carried posters saying, 'Save Us' in English and 'Pomoc (help)' in Bosnian. Others said, 'This is the biggest death camp in the world,' in English. And, 'Do not leave us.'

Leconte instructed the men to board the vehicles and depart, yet none of the crowd obeyed. Despite the efforts of the UN translator to convince them otherwise, the people remained unmoved. The chants grew louder, accompanied by heightened cries of desperation. With each passing moment, more civilians joined the growing human barricade, making it increasingly difficult to proceed.

In a last-ditch effort, the general exited the vehicle and climbed onto the bonnet of the Land Rover, pleading with the crowd to allow them to pass. A UN soldier handed him a loudhailer. "We will come back with food and provisions," he said. "You must trust me."

"We don't trust the Serbs," someone shouted back. "Stay and save us," shouted another.

The surroundings fell silent momentarily for General Gaston Leconte. It felt like a sudden clarity, akin to an epiphany, a profound moment reminiscent of spiritual awakening experienced by the devout once or twice in their lives. Leconte encountered this revelation atop a UN Land Rover in a besieged village, holding a loud hailer. Amidst the pleas of thousands urging him to rescue them, he perceived himself as their sole hope, a saviour. Without any consultation, he shouted out, "I will save you. I will stay here and this place shall be safe, a safe haven for all of you."

After the general spoke, there was a brief pause as his words were translated. Then, cheers and shouts filled the air. The crowd started chanting the general's name and waving enthusiastically. Two women even fainted from the excitement, while others embraced each other in joy.

Among the UN contingent was a Canadian captain and an American major. They looked at each other and mouthed the words, "What the fuck." They realised their commanding officer had deviated from the established path, and there was a significant risk of facing diplomatic and military consequences.

In his role as a rescuer, the general neglected to contemplate the potential reactions of the Serbs. However, that was a concern for another time; for now, he relished the satisfaction of being the one who saved Donji Zelenik.

Grant recorded everything with a sense of astonishment. He had never anticipated that his idea would have such a profound impact. However, after nine months of observing the conflict, he understood that cooperation required participation from both sides.

Leconte announced the town's United Nations protection, raising a flag on a lamp post near the post office. Canadian UN soldiers formed a guard of honour. Celebratory embraces, toasts with glasses, and smoking Marlboro cigarettes filled the air.

Accompanying the unit as a military observer was American Major Benjamin Pratt II. He diligently sent reports to UN headquarters and the Pentagon regarding military activities. However, it seemed he wasn't embracing the role of saviour as enthusiastically as the general.

Grant offered him a cigarette, which he declined.

"What do you make of this then?" Grant asked him.

"Me, I don't trust the motherfuckers, this has all the ingredients of a major fuck up, and when it goes to shit, these people are gonna come for us," he replied. "But know this: I got two clips of bullets for my automatic. That's sixteen bullets in each clip, so if these people turn against us when we can't do what the general is promising, then I am going to take thirty-two of the mother fuckers with me."

It affirmed to Grant that the American military isn't well-suited for travel, and the comprehension level tended to be quite low.

Leconte gave Grant a short interview about his decision and was full of optimism that it was a big step towards peace.

"I want to give you something. I think you journalists are doing a wonderful job," he reached into the jeep and brought out a box.

"A little something for you," explained Leconte. It was an MRE, a meal-ready-to-eat. Not like the American MREs, which were bland and tasteless. Journalists had nicknamed them 'Meals Rejected by Ethiopians.' This was a French MRE, significantly superior to its US counterpart. The French took great pride in their food, even in their military rations.

"Thanks, General, you don't happen to have another spare, do you?" asked the journalist. The general complied.

He promptly arranged for a vehicle to transport him back to headquarters to submit a comprehensive report. Additionally, he authorised the removal of Grant's videotapes, ensuring that his findings could be shared beyond their current confines.

Rushing into a nearby room, he swiftly penned a script. With precision, he narrated it into the camera's microphone, providing clear editing directives and suggestions for video sequencing. Seeking assistance, he enlisted the help of a

Belgian captain named Ronnie to transport the tapes. He meticulously outlined instructions for locating his colleagues in Tuzla.

At last, a way out.

In Donji Zelenik, a newfound sense of calm settled over the town. While many remained sceptical about the permanence of peace or whether the Serbs truly had a change of heart due to the UN intervention, the residents decided to embrace the momentary peace.

Leconte departed in the afternoon, citing the need to facilitate the arrival of the awaited aid convoy. He exuded a quiet confidence, suggestive of a small victory achieved. While enthusiasm could be contagious, so too could pessimism. Meanwhile, Grant met with Selma at the clinic, and together they strolled through the dimming town, relishing the eerie silence.

As night descended, the heavens opened, and Chicken ala King, US MREs, descended from US C130 transporters soaring at 8,000 metres. Thousands of these brown packets rained down, a bombardment of sustenance. People emerged from their homes, tents, and shelters to seize as many parcels as they could. Seeking refuge in a doorway, Grant and Selma shared a moment of laughter. It marked the first instance of external food assistance reaching the town. Despite the occasional landing of Meals Rejected by Ethiopians, residents of Donji Zelenik refrained from making complaints. With the arrival of the general, followed by food aid and the promise of an aid convoy, optimism began to take root.

He looked at Selma and asked, "What do you think about French cuisine and candlelit dinners?"

42

With careful precision, he rolled up the carpet, revealing the imprint of a large shoe pressed into the white powder beneath. His hunch had been correct; Mohammed Ibrahimovic realised that he was under surveillance. The footprint served as undeniable proof. Retrieving the suitcase from under the bed, he opened it, noticing that the card was turned in the opposite direction from how he had left it. A smile crept across his face. If his inquisitors had found anything alarming in the room, he would have surely been arrested or at least questioned. He knew that the search for Munja was consuming the high command's attention. As long as Munja remained at large, the Bosnians would be unable to execute any significant operations capable of altering the course of the war. Ibrahimovic observed that the wardrobe had not been moved. Thus, he concluded that he was in the clear, at least for the time being.

He replaced the carpet and approached the large wardrobe. With some effort, he pushed it sideways, causing a loud, scraping sound. He froze, listening intently. His mother was downstairs, and despite being in her late seventies, her hearing was still sharp. He could hear her singing along to a song on the radio, a routine she followed whenever there was electricity. Gathering his resolve, he gave the wardrobe a final push. It revealed a large Winter Olympics poster and a smaller one depicting the Blue Mosque in Istanbul. Removing the smaller poster revealed a hatch door, which he opened to reveal a large square recess measuring approximately two feet by two feet and one foot deep. Inside lay a Yaesu walkie-talkie, a set of code books, a Morse High-speed Military electromechanical burst encoder, and the tools of Munja (lightening) Mohammed Ibrahimovic was not his real name, and he was not a Muslim; he was Dragan Mihajlovic, a Serb.

Next to the equipment lay a large red tin box, weathered and worn from the passage of time. He retrieved it and pried it open. Inside rested a book, whose once-dark red cover now faded. Atop the book lay an Orthodox crucifix. He kissed the cross four times, making the sign of the cross, before opening the book. In bold Cyrillic letters, the title read: 'The Diary of Dragan Mihajlovic, 1916–.'

Munja was named after his grandfather, whose diary served as a lifeline to the past. Despite the absence of an end date, the diary kept the memory of his grandfather alive. For Munja, it also served as a vivid reminder of the experiences and injustices endured, shaping him into the person he had become, a spy.

He had pored over the diary countless times, attempting to envision Dragan Mihajlovic as the man, the soldier, and the grandfather whom Munja had never met.

For young Dragan, this diary held the weight of a historical document, akin to a bible. It chronicled not only the life and suffering of his grandfather and family but also that of the Serbian people. Dragan found solace in reading sections of the diary after returning from the Mosque, viewing it as an antidote to the Koran. Each time he delved into its words and envisioned the scenes it depicted, he was overwhelmed with levels of anger that were, at times, difficult to contain. Yet his anger and bitterness paled in comparison to his burning desire for revenge. Memories of his father were faint; both he and his grandfather were victims of what he perceived as rabid Croatian nationalism and Muslim fundamentalism, which sought to annihilate the Serbian race. The genocide endured by the Serbs at the hands of the Ottoman Turks and later by the Croats remained a glaring omission in the West's understanding of Balkan history. The brutality inflicted upon them was seldom acknowledged, a testament to the triumph of Catholic and Muslim propaganda. In this regard, the Serbs had lost the battle of perception. But

Dragan remained steadfast in his belief that they would ultimately emerge victorious in the war, and he was determined to play a significant role in it, a feat that would make his grandfather and father proud.

His train of thought was disrupted as his so-called Muslim mother began to sing more loudly. Over the years, he had developed a fondness for her, but he refrained from seeing her as anything other than a Muslim, the enemy who had robbed him of his life and identity. To him, acts of kindness could not erase the predetermined course of destiny.

His memories were hazy, but they lingered. The place where he had resided, which he now recognised as an orphanage, became his temporary home following the death of his parents. Yasna Ibrahimovic had plucked him from that orphanage and embraced him as her own. Together, they traversed various towns throughout Yugoslavia, weaving a new history in each place while erasing traces of the past. Yasna, a spinster with slim prospects of adoption or conception, struck a backroom deal involving money with the orphanage, securing the one thing she desired most in the world: a child.

She was a devout Muslim, and she nurtured Mohammed in the ways of Islam and he became devout as well. Upon discovering the death certificate of a boy approximately the same age, also named Mohammed Ibrahimovic, she realised it was a common name with hundreds of individuals bearing it in the former Yugoslavia. Adding one more Mohammed Ibrahimovic wouldn't draw unwanted attention. To shield her own identity, she concocted a marriage to Mohammed Ibrahimovic, whose grave she had uncovered in a village near her home.

In order to uncover any irregularities in births, marriages, or deaths within the former Yugoslavia, precise information, including names and dates, was essential. Otherwise, such names and histories remained buried in files, tucked away in dark rooms, never to be challenged or brought to light.

They would have been buried alongside Dragan if it weren't for his uncle, his father's brother, who had clandestinely visited him multiple times at the orphanage when he was six years old. It was his uncle who disclosed to him the details of his parents and family history. He presented the boy with a red tin box containing a written account of their past, his grandfather's diary, a crucifix, and several photographs, including one of his parents on their wedding day. Dragan didn't know what became of his uncle; the visits abruptly ceased. Nonetheless, the family history provided by his uncle remained with him, offering the young boy a sense of purpose and destiny. Over time, Dragan came to cherish it as his sacred text. The history of Dragan Mihajlovic was encapsulated within that small, red biscuit tin.

He had adeptly concealed the remnants of his Serb heritage from Yasna and had fully embraced Islam, integrating seamlessly into his new identity. However, the memories never faded. He repeatedly revisited the accounts and diaries, uncovering a painful truth: his parents were killed by Muslims fighting for the Germans during the Second World War. His uncles, and aunts vanished without a trace. In later years, he learned the grim reality that they were victims of Tito and the partisans. In creating the new Yugoslavia they eradicated all traces of nationalism, particularly Serb nationalism.

Later, he discovered that Serb nationalism was not extinguished; it was merely dormant. There existed pockets of like-minded individuals yearning to reclaim their identity and advocate for the establishment of Greater Serbia. With Tito's demise, these groups expanded and grew more vocal, gradually emerging from obscurity. Munja, secretly affiliated with this burgeoning nationalist movement, was valued by those in positions of power. Dragan, a Serb posing as a Muslim, was recognised early on for his potential utility as a secret weapon in their arsenal. And he had proven to be invaluable.

43

Grant heard the screams from fifty metres away as he approached his new home, the semi-destroyed hotel Domavia, which served as the de facto barracks for a unit of Bosnian fighters. Before the war, the hotel would never have qualified for any star rating, with its dirty brown paintwork, shoddy décor, and basic furniture. Now, there was even less chance. It bore the scars of several artillery and mortar hits, with part of the roof blown in and most windows at the rear of the hotel on the north side either smashed by shell pressure blasts or shattered by shrapnel fragments. With no gas or electricity, there was no central heating, giving the place the look and feel of a bleak, cold morgue.

Grant and Haris had been assigned a shared room, which was rudimentary and cold, resembling more of a prison cell than a hotel room. However, given that some people were enduring the freezing temperatures on the streets, they couldn't really complain. Grant hadn't yet met the unit's commander, but he had heard about Hagija, the former police chief. Known to be a tough individual, Grant soon discovered that he was also quite suspicious.

As he descended the steps, he encountered a towering figure with a thick, black, bushy beard and piercing, suspicious eyes. It was Hagija. The screams grew louder, yet the imposing Bosnian appeared unfazed. He nodded at Grant but didn't offer a smile, speaking in Bosnian.

Haris translated, "He says welcome, but he knows you are a foreign spy. He says he will be watching you very closely."

"Tell him I'm not a spy; I am a journalist".

Haris repeated, "Hagija says, what is the difference? Journalists and spies collect information, and use it for their own purposes, but it always helps the other side."

Grant acknowledged the validity of Hagija's point. It wasn't the first time he had been accused of engaging in dubious activities. However, before he could offer any further defence, Hagija walked off into the night.

The screams grew louder, and Mehmet realised they emanated from what was once the manager's office behind the reception desk. He had spent several nights there, indulging in Stock brandy with fighters and locals. Alcohol had become the easiest means of escaping the daily horrors that plagued each day. Yet, there was no escaping the dreadful sound now filling the air.

He opened the door and found a man strapped to a chair, his arms, legs, and neck bound tightly. The man's face was covered in blood, and he had stopped screaming upon Grant's entrance. It became clear why he had been screaming; the man was missing an ear, part of his nose, and his upper lip. Standing to the side was a Bosnian holding a knife with blood coating the blade. He was the torturer. On the table to the right, Grant could see the severed ear, caked in blood.

"Chetnik," explained the tormentor as an explanation as if that justified what he was doing.

"Killer," shouted another.

In truth, Grant knew, as they did, that they didn't need a justification to continue the torture. From reading Bosnian history, Grant knew that this was the way that enemies were treated in Ottoman times. How death was slow and painful, designed to make those who opposed pay in the most horrible way. Sometimes, death could take days, even as much as a week. But that was what happened hundreds of years ago, not the twentieth century. Or so he thought. Reading about it was very different to witnessing it.

A small man approached, “This Chetnik killed many people,” explained the man. “He also was the man who hit you with mortar.”

“Impossible,” responded Grant. “That mortar must have been fired from more than five kilometres away. How come you only caught him then and no others?”

The tormentor, who didn’t speak English, misinterpreted Grant’s expression of disgust as anger directed towards the Serbs. Mistakenly assuming Grant’s hostility, he extended the knife towards the journalist, inviting him to participate in cutting something off the prisoner.

“No way,” shouted Grant in disgust. “That’s fucking barbaric. What kind of people do that kind of thing?” He turned to walk out.

A man standing in the corner stepped forward and blocked his exit.

“People who’ve been killed and tortured in the same way do this kind of thing,” he said in reasonably good English. “That’s the kind of people who can do it. People who are desperate to survive, who have never hurt anyone, people who are afraid and vulnerable and who are being persecuted. That’s the kind of people who do this. The kind of people WE are. This is what the Serbs do to us, and we are fighting for survival here. This prisoner knows information about positions and weaponry, which can help us and which will save lives. That’s the kind of people who are doing this, people who want to save our people from our enemies.”

It was Mehmet, Selma’s brother. He shared the same blue eyes as Selma, but his were not as gentle; instead, they were set in an angry countenance, their intensity like laser beams. Grant felt as though the penetrating gaze had somehow pierced his very essence, making for an uncomfortable introduction. Grant had heard of this formidable fighter and knew he was a key figure in Donji Zelenik's defence. However, he had never imagined that this former engineering student and Selma's twin brother could possess a brutality as bad as that of the Serbs.

Grant walked out, closely followed by Mehmet.

"Wait, I want to show you something." From his top pocket, he took out a piece of paper. "On this paper are forty-eight names of members of my immediate and extended family. Twenty have been killed, including my mother; fifteen are missing, four have been raped, and the rest are in Serb Camps. Don't you have the arrogance to judge me or what we do when the whole world is turning a blind eye and allowing the Serbs to do what they want to us."

"But is medieval torture the answer?" Grant asked.

"Should we waterboard like the Americans, use electrodes like the Arabs or sleep deprivation like the Chinese or instead just be kind and give cups of tea and cucumber sandwiches and hope he sees the light of humanity and tells us what we want to know? Were the British performing a humanitarian gesture when they forged the British Empire? Torture is going on everywhere. Everyone does it, especially the powerful Western countries, but they don't call it torture. They call it interrogation; they call it intelligence gathering. You, my friend, are not living in the real world. In war, there is no black or white, only grey. Most of us were just ordinary people living normal lives. We never asked for this. I know my sister says you are a good man and a good journalist, but you are not fighting for your life. When the shit hits the fan, you leave. We can't, we are here to stay. Perfectly normal people are capable of perfectly abnormal actions. In war, you cross this invisible line going from humanity to inhumanity, and you will do anything to survive. You should thank God you don't have to cross that line."

"So, I make no apologies for doing what we are doing. No excuses. Now, if you will excuse me, I need to return to my 'interrogation'. I suggest you go for a long walk and put your Walkman on."

Grant's mind churned with internal conflict. Mehmet's argument had effectively exposed his overly simplistic stance. Mehmet spoke from the perspective of a normal civilised world, where rules and standards are upheld. However, Grant realised that in war, all rules and standards are swiftly discarded. The first casualty, aside from truth, is humanity itself. The Geneva Convention, revered as it may be in Western countries, amounted to little more than a paper document, lacking in backbone and enforcement power. It was merely words on a page.

Leaving a bewildered Haris behind, he strode down the street, dimly lit by light from oil lamps in house windows, the distant sound of explosions echoing in the night. He soon found himself outside the clinic and entered to find Selma attending to what she claimed was the last casualty—for the time being. The fighter had suffered a minor shrapnel wound to the neck. It took Selma a few minutes to patch him up, skilfully administering stitches before declaring him fit. With her duties done, she led Grant into the kitchen.

"Turkish coffee?" she asked.

"Anything stronger?"

"Only surgical spirits, but I'm afraid that is needed."

"Yep, coffee please. I just met your brother. He was not what I expected; well, bits of him were."

"What do you mean?" she asked.

"Well, he's obviously a tough man and also a capable fighter by all accounts, but I think he is losing his grip on humanity. I know the fight for survival is desperate, but there is something more animal than human about him. That sounds a little crazy. I know he's your twin, and you love him, but he made me feel uncomfortable, not just with what he was doing and what he said, but by how he looked at things. And yes, my view is often way too simplistic, and, as he said, I am not fighting for my life, and I can just walk away anytime I like. But…"

"But what?"

"I am not sure. I just know that this war is ugly, and it is making people ugly."

"Do you know your literature?" asked Selma. "There is this powerful book by William Golding, 'Lord of the Flies.' You must know it. It tells the story of a group of young boys who find themselves alone on a deserted island. They develop rules and a system of organisation, but without any adults to serve as a civilising impulse, the children eventually become violent and brutal. That is war. That is Bosnia today. No rules and no point in playing by rules because they are not recognised and they don't work."

"I am not defending my brother. Like many people, I don't want to know the ugliness that goes into survival, but I want to survive, and that's why I can turn a blind eye and pretend I don't know what is going on. This is not the answer you want, and maybe you will view me differently, but war and the Serbs made my brother this way. The war will end one day. I am convinced of that. But I'm not sure that my brother and thousands more like him will ever be the same again."

She poured the coffee and then embraced Grant tightly. As he held her, he pondered whether he would ever be able to return to his old self once this war concluded. After walking her home, Grant briefly stepped inside the house. In the corner, by the fireplace, sat Selma's father, Yousef. He appeared vacant and emaciated, almost devoid of life. In his hand, Grant noticed a copy of what he assumed was the Koran. Selma had mentioned that he had always been a devout man, but since the war and the loss of his wife, he had become even more religious, perhaps seeking solace and answers.

Pictures of Mecca and Medina adorned the wall, alongside a photograph of Yousef dressed in a white Kebaya during his pilgrimage to Saudi Arabia for the Haj.

"This is Grant, Tata," Selma said to him. "He is the journalist telling the world what is happening here."

Yousef glanced up, offering the faintest of smiles as he nodded his head. Then he returned his gaze to the book, silently mouthing the words of a prayer.

"He is lost," she explained. "Everything has hit him hard, especially the loss of mama. But also, he cannot understand how our Serb friends could wage this war. I think that has hurt and damaged him the most, perhaps beyond repair. He was one of Tito's people, and under his rule, everyone lived together in peace. The killing has hurt him."

"Memet and I try to bring him out of it. We talk about the happy times. But it has no effect. All he does is read the Koran. We lost our mother. He may be breathing, but I think we have lost our father, too."

44

As he approached the Domavia, the relentless bombardment of the typewriter keys echoed down the corridor and into the lobby. Haris was deeply engrossed in his work, creating tirelessly. Grant couldn't help but rue the fact that the end of the war would bring him something he longed for: a decent night's sleep, free from the incessant clacking of the typewriter that invaded his slumber every night now. It was a barrage more relentless than anything the Serbs could inflict. Grant was starting to regret encouraging Haris to write about the ongoing events for Bosnian newspapers. Now, his roommate was like a dog with a bone, tirelessly writing a daily story. Days were spent scouring for stories, followed by even longer nights spent writing them. It felt like a form of Chinese water torture.

"You need to tell Bosnians what is going on," Grant had urged him. In addition to waterboarding, electrodes, and sleep deprivation, there was a new method added to the torture list: Haris typing. The pain was excruciating, driving him to seek an escape. The building was freezing, prompting him to hastily dress and make his way downstairs. Almost simultaneously, a Bosnian sprinted up the steps to the hotel. Grant recognised him as one of the twins who operated the ham radio.

"Mr Grant, dodji (come)," gestured Samir. "Radio." Grant guessed there was now a connection for him.

He raced to the former PTT building which now housed the UN contingent. Samir's twin Fahrudin was speaking into the handset, "Tusam, Tusam," he repeated over and over again, "Are you there?"

"Jasam," came the response (I am here). The twins had succeeded in connecting to Tuzla and ATV and then on to the bureau in London.

Grant took the handset. "Hi, this is Grant," he said.

"Great to hear you," came the reply. It was the voice of Ed Warren, the bureau chief.

"How are you doing?" he asked. "Fine," replied Grant.

"We got the tape, great story; it's gone viral worldwide. Everyone is talking about it, including the UN, governments, and organisations. It's fucking brilliant. The pictures are amazing. You are a star. But we reckon you need to come out as soon as you can. It's too dangerous. Lots of people are dying there, and you've already been hit once. Best not to chance it longer than you really need to."

"Ed, it took me weeks to get in, so I'm not going to leave after just a few days. It's still an important story, but if I leave, who will tell it? I have to stay, and also, there is no way of getting out now."

"But what about the UN? Can't they help you get out?"

"Maybe, but I'm not ready to leave yet. They were great to get my tape out, so let's see how things go."

"OK," replied Warren. "But how are you for doing interviews? Everyone wants to speak to you."

"No problem, as many as I can manage. It's important to get the story out to as many as possible because I'm not sure how long these people can hold out."

The bureau chief handed the handset to a journalist from the Chicago Times, who engaged in a half-hour conversation with Singleton. As the interview neared its end, high-frequency sounds disrupted the conversation. Fahrudin attempted to reconnect the link, but was unsuccessful. Then, unexpectedly, a voice broke through.

"Hey, you mother fucker, telling lies about the Serbs," it was the deep, threatening voice of a man.

"Where has this come from?" Grant asked.

"Serb side," said Fahrudin.

The man's voice continued, "You are all going to die, every last one of you. But we will kill you last. And it will be a slow, painful death, payback for all your lies."

Fahrudin changed the frequency. It sent a shiver down Grant's back. Journalists always enjoyed a privileged position in wars, able to go to both sides.

They were afforded a kind of respect and were accepted although sometimes begrudgingly. But not by the Serbs besieging Donji Zelenik he realised. No invisible cloak of protection. Not anymore.

"I think this was Darko Zubic," explained Fahrudin in broken English. "He from Donji Zelenik. He not good man. He bad. He kill us."

45

Winters in the Balkans could be brutal, with biting winds, freezing temperatures, and deep snow that sometimes lasted for five months. There was a saying: 'Don't burn your gateposts in winter, you might need them in Spring.' Few paid attention to the winter of 1992/1993 any longer. Life was no longer about the cold; it was about survival, about securing food. International aid was scarce, except for the United Nations, which, although present, seemed like a band-aid on a bullet wound—temporarily stopping the bleeding but failing to heal the wound. Against this backdrop, Ramadan posed little difficulty for the Muslims of Sarajevo. With short winter days and scarce food, fasting wasn't a major issue. Nonetheless, Eid al-Fitr, the traditional end of the month of fasting, held special significance. While the celebration couldn't be as grand or widespread as usual due to the war, it was filled with symbolism. Bosnia had defied the odds, standing firm against a formidable Serb War machine, showcasing the spirit and resilience of its people. This resilience was worth celebrating, although in smaller gatherings and through prayers, given the circumstances of war.

In his bedroom Munja was preparing for his own celebration. Before him sat a model of Masjid al-Haram in Mecca, an intricate and splendid model reminiscent of a small child's dollhouse. Also known as the Grand Mosque of

Mecca, it was built to enclose the Ka'bah, the holiest shrine in Islam. A destination of the Hajj pilgrimage that every Muslim aspires to undertake at least once in their lifetime, if possible, it is a site revered by all Muslims. Munja planned to showcase this model as the central display for his celebration of this sacred time. He intended to present it to the Gazi Husrev-Beg mosque in the old town for the main Eid prayers.

Inside would be a bomb, a simple yet potent device containing Semtex high explosives, nuts, bolts, and sharp nails. It would be triggered by a timer, designed to unleash devastation upon much of the old quarter of Sarajevo and tear apart anyone caught in the blast. Moreover, the main Bosnian government and military figures, including President Mehotic and all the senior generals, would be present for the prayers. The prospect of having them all gathered in one location presented a unique opportunity, and Mihajlovic was resolute in seizing it to its fullest extent.

The detonation would be synchronised to coincide with a significant Serb offensive from the western suburb of Ilizda, aiming to sever the city from its northern and western road connections. This strategic move would effectively isolate Sarajevo, creating a stranglehold from which it could not easily recover. Months of meticulous planning had gone into orchestrating this operation.

The Serb general, Moimocjelo Pasic, had grown weary of politicians appeasing international opinion. He believed, as with many historical events, that it was better to take action and then spend fifty years debating the rights or wrongs and the legal intricacies rather than doing nothing at all. Israel had demonstrated this, as had the Americans. Pasic made a unilateral decision to act. He anticipated that Serb politicians would initially object, but once they realised the outcome, he believed, they would come to appreciate his actions. For Pasic, the ends justified the means, and eradicating the Bosnian leadership was essential to his plan.

The model was ornate, a thing of beauty that would captivate any devout Muslim. It struck him as fitting that such a venerable place of worship could be used to deliver such a devastating blow.

There was another crucial reason why this plan needed to succeed, one that held deep personal significance for Munja. It represented the culmination of his clandestine existence, a path to escape, a return home to his own people, the Serbian community. He had been assured that after this operation, he would be granted the freedom to align with the Serb side. After over fifty years of masquerading as a Muslim, he could finally shed the facade and embrace his true identity as Dragan Mihajlovic, fully immersing himself in the orthodox life he had been denied.

Every evening after prayers, Munja would return home via a secret rendezvous point, where a Serb operative would discreetly leave him components of an explosive device. The meeting spot was always hidden and marked by a distinct sign, ensuring secrecy. It was never the same operative, but they all used the same chalk marks to indicate the hiding place. Even if discovered, there were never enough components to reveal their purpose. Different operatives were employed to prevent any single individual from knowing the complete picture of their activities, including what they were transporting and the potential target. None of them were aware that the components were for a bomb. The final piece, the Semtex, would be handed over shortly before Eid. Each part was numbered, simplifying Munja's task of assembling them. It felt like a painting by numbers activity. Munja chuckled to himself.

He was aware that Hassan Mesic had been monitoring his movements and had even come under suspicion himself for a time. Additionally, the footprints under the carpet indicated that his room had been searched. However, it was evident that

Hassan's interest in him had waned. Mohammed Ibrahimovic was no longer considered a suspect. Munja could now operate safely, soon assuming the identity of Dragan Mihajlovic and rightfully taking his place in Serbian society.

46

General Leconte's optimism had been severely tested, but it managed to hold out. Departing from Donji Zelenik for the Serb side, he pledged to return within hours with the town's first aid convoy in six months. However, in reality, it took three days filled with excuses, events, funerals, and bureaucratic proceedings before the Serbs finally permitted the General and the convoy to pass through.

Grant was in the midst of filming wounded soldiers brought from the Eastern Frontline when he suddenly heard cheers. Startled, he turned to see a long line of white trucks, each bearing the letters UNHCR painted on them, winding their way up the solitary road.

They followed Leconte's white Land Rover, and soon word spread throughout the town. Thousands began running towards the spot where the trucks came to a halt near the main central square. It was a misty morning, with a white shroud enveloping the town. People emerged from the mist like apparitions. Mist and fog were welcomed; they meant that Serb spotters couldn't call in targets for mortars and artillery. People appreciated bad weather for its protective effects.

"Hrana (food)," went up the cry. There was panic. People dropped everything. They had gone without for so long. Now, there was desperation.

Grant shifted the camera's focus from a cart bearing two lifeless bodies shrouded in white sheets and the injured soldiers to the aid trucks. Leading the convoy was a smiling General Leconte.

"Success," he shouted to Grant. "You see, I told you I would return with the convoy."

Amidst the clamour of enthusiastic cheers, UN soldiers and Bosnian fighters united to form a human chain, passing boxes of food and medical supplies into a storeroom without windows. The journalist hurried to capture as much footage as possible before moving to the general's car to finalise a script he had started. The returning convoy would provide an opportunity for him to send out his second tape; his network was hungry for more content. This was prime material for TV News.

By the time he had completed the script and delivered it directly to the camera, the convoy had already begun to depart.

'Fuck,' he thought. 'I've missed the chance.'

At that moment, a black Mercedes pulled up. The window was lowered. It was Mehmet.

"Problem?" he asked.

"I need to get my tape to the convoy leader so my story can get on air," he said. "But now we can't reach it," he said with a strong note of resignation.

"Never say never, get in. We will reach it."

"But it's driving into No Man's Land," Grant said.

"Not all men," replied Mehmet. "Get in."

The Mercedes' modified engine roared like a Formula One car on the starting grid. Grant understood that reaching the convoy would require a significant risk; they would be dangerously within sight of the Serbs. He had taken that risk before, and had the scars to prove it.

"How bad do you want to get this story out?" Mehmet asked.

"Bad," came the reply.

Mehmet pointed his finger forward. “Onwards,” he shouted.

The driver revved the engine, and the vehicle surged forward. Grant observed the speedometer from the back seat, noting the gradual climb: 100 KPH, 120, 140, 180, and then at 200 KPH, the vehicle shook violently. Grant couldn’t help but wonder if it might disintegrate. The sound was similar to that of a Second World War German V bomber, but on wheels.

Some journalists would argue that no story is worth risking your life for, but those were typically the ones who relied on second-hand information gathered in hotel lobbies and cafes. Frontline reporting, however, was a different matter, with inherent risks. Mehmet had faced many dangers to reach and remain in Donji Zelenik. He wasn’t willing to pass up an opportunity to inform the world about what was happening.

He attempted to maintain a positive outlook, but he couldn’t prevent the flood of negative thoughts from penetrating his façade of bravado and daring. Would today be the day when a bullet with his name on it finally found him? Or perhaps he would meet his end in a car accident, which would be an ironic twist of fate. The journey was a nerve-wracking experience, a real white-knuckle ride, with the car vibrating as if it were on the verge of breaking apart. The noise was deafening, drowning out any other sounds. At least, he mused, he wouldn’t have to worry about incoming rounds; he wouldn’t be able to hear them over the cacophony.

The Mercedes passed the first few trucks and then found the one with the convoy leader. They slowed as the lorry reached a line of trees, out of sight of the Serbs.

Grant got out and went to the convoy leader. ‘He was Swedish, a frail-looking man with mousy blonde hair and a craggy face. He looked more like one of the refugees,’ Grant thought to himself.

"Please, can you take this to Tuzla?" he asked, "It's important."

"OK," said the Swede.

"But take care the Serbs will be looking for it. Stick it down the front of your trousers. The Serb fighters are all macho. There is no way they will search you if it's in your Y-fronts."

The leader agreed. Got back into his truck, and the line moved off.

"Thank you so much," Grant said to Mehmet. "Nema ne cemu," responded the young Pasha (don't mention it).

They made their way back at a more moderate pace of 180 kilometres per hour. Despite a mortar explosion not too far away, the car's engine drowned out all the surrounding noise. It wasn't until they reached the safety of the town that they exited the vehicle and discovered three bullet holes in the boot.

Bruno approached the car as Grant got out.

"Schiesse," he said. "Zis story iss big I must get my photos out. German press has reached me on ze ham radio."

"That's what I told you," responded Grant. "This is going worldwide. Everyone wants to know about Donji Zelenik and what is going on here. Your best bet is either to wait for the next convoy or ask Leconte for one of his men to take your film out the next time they leave."

Bruno concurred and departed to converse with the UN. Mehmet drove away, while Grant made his way to the clinic. As the mist gradually dissipated, it revealed the town's desolation. Snow transitioned into mud and slush, and the number of destitute individuals living on the streets seemed to increase. However, this day was relatively peaceful, with only a few injuries and no fatalities, a rare success in Donji Zelenik. Yet, as Mehmet reflected, the notion of health and safety was precarious; disaster could strike in an instant. And indeed, it did. The tranquilly shattered abruptly as a small Tata van pulled up. A wounded fighter disembarked from the front seat, while two others lay injured in the back. One of them seemed to be in critical condition. Without delay, two stretcher-bearers emerged from the clinic and swiftly attended to the wounded individuals.

Hagija appeared. “Chetnik attack,” he explained and got back in the car.

“Room for me?” said Grant, and without waiting for an invitation, he got into the back seat, followed by Haris. The van departed, stirring a flurry of activity among the men nearby. Further ahead, an open truck brimmed with fighters, only a few of whom had uniforms. The group comprised a mix of young individuals and older men, some well past retirement age. Among them were also two younger women, armed with a variety of weapons, including AK47s, shotguns, and hunting rifles. Grant harboured a silent hope that their fighting prowess exceeded their appearance.

The Tata van led the way.

“Bajna Bashta,” announced Hagija before Grant had a chance to ask. He turned to Haris and spoke in Bosnian.

“What did he say?” asked Grant.

“He still thinks you are a spy,” explained Haris.

“Serious?” asked Grant.

“Serious,” Haris said with a straight face.

Although the dam lay only twenty kilometres away via a direct route, the presence of Serb snipers necessitated a detour along unpaved tracks, unsuitable for heavy traffic. As they veered off the main road, Grant caught sight of two bodies lying at the roadside.

“Stop,” he shouted. The driver obeyed. Grant got out and began filming the bodies.

“Pazi snaiper,” (be careful snipers) shouted Hagija.

Grant kept low and got as close to the bodies as he could. He could see they were two elderly women wearing headscarves. There was a pool of blood close to one. It looked fresh. A short distance away, he could see the petal-shaped impact on the road of what was no doubt a mortar shell. ‘Mortars don’t discriminate,’ thought Grant.

“Brzo,” (quickly) shouted Hagija.

Hagija says to hurry, “Don’t worry, he says there will be more bodies. You won’t be disappointed.”

He returned to the car and drove another kilometre to a small hamlet where Hagija’s prediction proved correct - there were more bodies. Seven in total, including two women, a child approximately seven years old, and four men. Surprisingly, there was no visible damage from the shells. However, upon closer inspection, he noticed a gunshot wound on one of the men’s right temple. Hagija took his hand and pretended to fire a gun into his head and shouted, “Bang.” He was imitating an execution. He explained that a small Serb group had infiltrated the lines and attacked the settlement.

“No fighters were here,” Haris translated Hagija’s words. “Only civilians.”

Hagija’s men had pushed the Serbs back and were now going to reinforce the frontline positions.

Grant captured as much footage as possible, emulating Mo’s style to convey the gravity of this sombre scene. It was crucial for people to see and comprehend the reality. They often said a picture spoke a thousand words, yet amidst this tragedy, only one word resonated: murder.

Continuing another kilometre along a track, they reached their next stop - Zeleni Jadar, also known as Green Valley, now covered in a blanket of snow.

"Now on foot," said Haris. "You must be quiet now because Serbs may still be in the area." Haris had one expression, and it was always dour.

They advanced in formation, weaving their way through thick undergrowth until they reached the edge of a forest. There, a trench awaited them, manned by some of Hagija's men. Grant couldn't help but liken it to the frontline trenches of World War One. The biting wind and sub-zero temperatures added to the scene's unforgiving atmosphere.

Reinforcements swiftly assumed their positions along the line. Grant's attention was drawn to trees snapped like twigs and blood-stained bandages near a bunker entrance, evidence of recent intense combat. The snow bore witness to widespread splashes of blood, painting a grim picture of the battle's severity. It didn't take long for the threat of further engagement to materialise. A shell tore through the trees, followed by a deafening explosion and cascading branches. The sudden eruption of heavy machine gun fire startled Grant; it felt uncomfortably close. Yet, undeterred, Hagija's men returned fire while Grant continued to document the chaos with his camera.

Nearby, three mortar shells detonated with alarming proximity, sending a chill through Grant's body and numbing his hands. Despite the physical discomfort, adrenaline surged through him as he darted between positions, capturing the intensity of the conflict. His lens framed scenes of tense trigger fingers, the fiery discharge of AK47 barrels, and the anxious expressions etched on faces. Amidst the chaos, Hagija's authoritative voice rang out, directing his men with unwavering determination. While others crouched for cover, Hagija stood tall, his courage, or perhaps recklessness, undeniable. As more mortar rounds fell perilously close, Grant couldn't shake the feeling that danger loomed ever nearer.

"Hi Guys, can I join you?" It was one of the UN contingent, an Irish military observer. "Paddy Monaghan, pleased to meet yer. Bit of a situation you have here."

The Bosnians were too busy to respond.

"They must have three mortars in operation," observed the Irishman. Just as expected, another three rounds whizzed past, this time dangerously close. Even Hagija, startled, dropped to the ground. A big Bosnian swiftly seized Grant, hauling him into the bunker and guiding him through the snow-covered entrance.

"It's pretty good firing," continued Monaghan. "They certainly know what they are doing, so I've got to hand that to them. They must have a spotter fairly close who is calling in the shells."

"Where?" asked Hagija.

"If I were them, I would put him over there," he said, pointing to a rocky outcrop surrounded by some bushes. It was about six hundred metres away from the line.

The Bosnian took a pair of binoculars. "Da (yes)," he said. Two men came forward with a 60mm mortar. They quickly set the range and fired.

"Five metres more," ordered Hagija. They fired again. The big Bosnian smiled, "The motherfucker spotter is running for his life." At least one position was rendered inactive for now. But there were others.

Grant had wisely paused to conserve his battery. Upon reaching the safety of the bunker, he resumed filming. He focused his camera on the face of a young fighter, capturing the fear etched across his features with each explosion. It was evident that this youth was not a seasoned warrior. But then again, who among them truly was?

After an hour and declining battery power he decided he had enough material.

"Let's head back," he shouted to Haris, and they sprinted back through the trees, keeping low. Monaghan followed closely behind. Once they were clear, they walked at a brisk pace. His heart continued to race at an alarming rate, the aftermath of adrenaline coursing through his veins. He felt the lingering buzz of action, his body and mind struggling to return to normalcy. There was a mix of excitement and happiness over what he had managed to capture on film, along with a sense of aftershock, contemplating what could have transpired. He yearned for a drink to calm his nerves. Unfortunately, his camera batteries were too depleted for playback, so he would have to wait until they returned to town for a chance to recharge them. Despite this, he couldn't help but feel excited. This had been an exceptionally fruitful assignment in terms of frontline TV reporting.

Back at the Domavia barracks, it sounded like someone was badly wounded. It was Grant Singleton, a decidedly upset Grant Singleton. "What the fuck," he shouted at the top of his voice. "Fucking idiot." He was sitting in the manager's office in Domavia. This was the day after Grant had witnessed Mehmet and his men 'interrogating' their prisoner. It occurred in what was considered the 'social club' of the hotel, where men gathered nightly to indulge in brandy and conversation, seeking a brief respite from the harsh realities of war. However, for Grant, there was no escaping the horrors he had witnessed, and he wasn't thinking of the torture.

He peered through the camera viewfinder, examining the images captured. Among them were snapshots of feet, legs, men's backs, trees, and the snowy landscape beyond the bunker. However, none depicted the action he had hoped to document. Nothing that remotely suggested he had spent two hours filming in one of the most dangerous frontlines he had ever been to. 'Was it a camera defect,' he thought to himself. 'Or incompetence?' Then it dawned on him. He realised in horror what had happened. The biting cold numbed his fingers, causing him to fumble with the buttons. Unbeknownst to him, in his haste, he inadvertently toggled between record and standby modes. It was a devastating realisation when he discovered that the red record button remained unlit throughout. Everything he had thought he recorded was, in fact, in standby mode, a grave error. Frustration engulfed him as he realised the scarcity of usable footage. All the chaos and danger he had endured seemed futile. He reached for the bottle of stock, seeking solace in its contents. If it had been Mo or any other cameraman responsible for this blunder, Grant would have enacted Sharia law. However, this mistake was his alone to bear.

47

Darko Zubic's countenance was dark with rage. He grappled with a deep sense of unease and discontent, a departure from his usual unwavering obedience to authority. Recent events had left him bewildered, straying beyond the confines of his understanding. Despite his ascent in stature and earning a reputation as a fearless and resolute combatant, he found himself grappling with a growing unrest. Zubic's influence had burgeoned, commanding respect and loyalty from those around him. He surveyed the room, populated by senior commanders overseeing Serb forces in eastern Bosnia.

"Why are we letting the UN take aid to the Balija?" he asked. There was no deference in his voice.

"Why are we allowing them to get strong? There is no reason. We were, we are, winning here. The Muslims are on their knees, and it is, or was, just a matter of time before we overrun them. This is like catching a fish and then throwing it back."

Throughout the gathering, silent nods of agreement signalled the onset of dissent. Suddenly, the door swung open, revealing General Kustavic, the commanding figure of the Serb forces in Eastern Bosnia. His keen observation detected the prevailing mood of discontent among the assembled ranks.

"Problem?" he asked. "Not happy, are we? Well, Gentlemen, I am not happy either, but a course has been set. This has been a political decision, but the overall outcome will be the same: Eastern Bosnia will be ours, of that, there is no doubt. That is not for now. It's the future. But for now, we have to play along as if we are listening to international concerns and responding in a humane way. I know this will be difficult, considering what the Muslims have done here and how many of our people they have killed. But for now, we must hold back."

The men's dissatisfaction was evident, openly displayed through furrowed brows and murmured conversations. Some appeared perplexed, others visibly disgruntled by what seemed to be a shift in tactics, or perhaps something altogether inscrutable. In their eyes, politicians were cunning creatures, forever unreliable, while soldiers were mere pawns in their power games. Though indispensable, they remained expendable, a recurring example in military history.

"Tomorrow, a second aid convoy will be allowed into Donji Zelenik, and that will take out women, children, and old people. That has been agreed at the highest level. No one can challenge that order. No one can stop it, and no one can prevent it from happening. There will also be an airlift by UN helicopters of wounded men."

A louder rumble of discontent spread through the room. They struggled to comprehend why Muslim fighters, who had attempted to harm them and their community, were being granted medical treatment elsewhere. Their dissatisfaction was evident.

"I know this is difficult for you to understand and to accept," continued the general. "But it has to be. This is all part of the greater plan. But I can promise you that there will be a day of reckoning for the Balija of Donji Zelenik, and no one can stop that. Certainly not the UN."

48

It was a mixed day for Grant Singleton. One tape is out and on its way to tell the world, but dramatic front-line scenes are thwarted by cold and lack of care. 'You can't have everything,' he thought, although every journalist wanted just that, everything. He knew there are always setbacks in reporting conflict, the biggest one being zapped, but you had to move on quickly, for everything lost, something else is gained. 'But that's work,' he thought to himself. 'This is something else and, in its way, just as important from the psychological perspective.'

Haris may have been a dull, humourless, individual but if you asked him to do something he did, mostly, without question. If it was within his physical capabilities, he would accomplish it without much hesitation. His scavenging efforts yielded some useful finds for Grant. Among them was a floral tablecloth with delicate lace trim, reminiscent of the 1930s era but suitable for the circumstances of Donji Zelenik, a town under siege with uncertain odds of survival. The candlesticks had seen better days but they still qualified as candlesticks and the plates had that dated blue Chinese design with bridges and birds. They belonged to the budget end of fine dining. But, again, they were plates.

Grant smiled to himself. This was a winner. How could it fail? He set up his tape recorder with batteries freshly charged by the Ham Radio twins Samir and Fahrudin and everything was perfect, sort of, if anything in a war zone could be perfect. Bruno popped his head in.

"Anyzing for me?" he asked. Bruno was the human equivalent of a food-hungry Golden Retriever dog. He could smell a morsel at a hundred paces.

"Fuck off, Bruno. This is not for you," the German slunk away like a beaten animal.

A few minutes later, Selma walked into the darkened manager's office of the Domavia Hotel. On cue, Haris lit the candles.

"Wow," she said. "Very nice."

Grant beckoned her to sit down and moved her chair.

"You are really like an English gentleman we read about," she smiled.

Two glasses were on the table, a bottle of water and two boxes.

"I think I promised you French cuisine and candlelit dinners," he said. "Well, no electricity, so candles and here we have the French cuisine."

She smiled and opened the box. It was a French military ration neatly packaged.

She was amazed once more, genuinely surprised by what she found in the box. Inside were saussice lentils, legumes verts, a piece of camembert cheese with crackers, chocolate Pots De Crème dessert, and a small bottle of red wine. Those familiar with field rations unanimously agreed that French military food packs were without exception the best and certainly miles better than the American and British meals.

Meanwhile, a pot of water sat on the room heater, coming to a boil. Grant added the saussice lentils to it and then opened the wine, pouring it into the glasses.

"Givili (cheers)," he said, and Selma chinked her glass against his.

"How on earth did you manage all this?" she smiled.

Grant tapped his nose. "Contacts," he replied.

He pressed the button on the tape recorder, filling the room with Eric Clapton's "You Look Wonderful Tonight." And indeed, she did. With no makeup on, she wore a simple light grey fleece, a Diesel brand gilet, blue Levi jeans, and Timberland boots. She epitomised the casual yet stylish attire of a war zone.

Selma found herself nearly overcome by the atmosphere and the efforts this eccentric Brit had made. Their connection had been growing, especially as she observed his dedication while working in Donji Zelkenik, her hometown. She had developed feelings for him that differed from anything she had felt for anyone else. She had never been truly in love. But maybe, she thought, this was what her feelings were now: love.

It was a meaningful meal shared with a remarkable individual. Their bond was deepening with each passing day. Initially, Grant attributed their closeness to the shared experience of being in a war zone. He had encountered such situations before, where facing death and adversity forged temporary connections. Yet, there was something unique about his relationship with Selma, something more enduring. Grant sensed a special connection, one that he believed could extend beyond the end of the war – a hope he cherished.

As Clapton's music faded to a close, it was followed by Gloria Gaynor's 'I Will Survive'. They found themselves engaged in laughter-filled conversations about their emotions, life, and aspirations. Despite their surroundings – a war-torn hotel in eastern Bosnia – it felt as if they were seated in a quaint restaurant in London's Covent Garden. They were so taken by the moment that if there had been shelling or firing then probably neither would have heard it.

"This has been so beautiful," she said. "I can't express how this has made me feel. It's like an oasis in the desert. I know you don't like cliches, but I can't think of how to put it. In all this depression and misery, it shows that we can still live and hope."

She took him by the hand and looked him deep in his eyes. "Thank you," she said.

Even in the dim lighting he could still see the blue of her eyes. He moved closer and went to kiss her. She moved back.

"Wait," she said and got up to leave. "I will be back in a few minutes."

Ten minutes later, she returned, "Come, I have a surprise too."

Taking his hand, she guided him through the lobby and up two flights of stairs. With the beam of his torch, he glimpsed partially ruined rooms at the far end of the corridor, while double doors stood at the opposite end. She opened one side.

"Voila, my surprise," she said with a smile.

The room was filled with scores of lighted candles surrounding a large double bed that had pillows, sheets, and a duvet.

"Wow, this is amazing," said the journalist, almost lost for words. "It is an oasis. An oasis of serenity. This is not in a war zone; this is in paradise."

"I had been planning too," she explained.

She turned to him and gently held his face in her hands, pressing her lips against his in a slow, tender kiss. Grant was not one of those overly romantic sort of people who went gaga in relationships. But he swore, at that moment, every part of his being was bouncing up and down like a herd of kangaroos at a punk rave. His heart raced quicker than an Olympic sprinter on speed. He thought he was going to explode with.....with happiness. His emotions were overwhelmed. The kiss lingered, their bodies morphed into one. Selma led him to the bed, slowly and deliberately, unaware of the biting cold, they undressed one another. Her body was sleek and seemed to shimmer in the candlelight. Of course, he had hoped for this but part of him never expected it. Pragmatically the thought flashed in his mind that he was glad he had had a full wash that morning.

They eased onto the bed and their bodies melted along with any inhibitions they may have had. In reality there were none. This was not a wham bam thank you mam. This was a slow, passionate coupling that expressed the love that words could not. It lasted most of the night. For Grant it was perfect. He had never had such a night of beauty and fulfilment. And he knew two things. One he had fallen deeply, madly in love with Selma and Two there was no Haris banging away at a typewriter keeping him awake. Life in a war zones had miserable moments but it also had some wonderful ones. This was one, without doubt.

The reality of where they were, however, could not be held back for long. He was woken at 6 am by Samir.

"Radio," he said, beckoning Grant to go with him. Half asleep, he dressed and followed. Selma slept on, blissfully unaware of Grant's departure into the freezing early morning. At the other end of the ham radio was Ed Warren, the London bureau chief.

"They got the tape," he said. "The mother fuckers got it."

"What?" responded Grant, trying to get his head into shape. Then it dropped like a stone.

"The Serbs got the tape?"

"Yep."

"How the fuck?"

"They searched everyone. They were looking for it. They seemed to know it was coming, and I think they were still smarting from the first report you got out." Grant was angry. "But I told the convoy leader to put the tape down his y-fronts. No fucking macho Serb would search down there."

"Well, he didn't," explained Warren. "He put it in his back pocket apparently, and then Shitsville, they found it."

"All that fucking work, all those images. They were so strong. Fucking Swedish twat."

Warren had a theory. "The radio guy here thinks the Serbs are listening into the ham radio, so he knew who would have the tape. That makes sense. We need a better way," said Warren.

"Yes, we do." agreed Grant. He'd just spent a night sampling the wonderful part of a war zone but now the misery, the other side of the coin.

zone but now the misery, the other side of the coin.

He knew they would have to solve the tape issue quickly because today was going to be a big day, the convoy to take out civilians and then a helicopter airlift of the wounded. These images would be vital to the story and it was essential they got out. But how to fool the Serbs? Grant looked up and saw Paddy Monaghan, the Irish UN military observer walking past the radio room.

"Hey, Major," shouted Grant. "I need your military nous."

An hour later, the convoy entered the square, a line of white Mercedes-Benz trucks bearing UNHCR markings. Laden with medical supplies and aid, they represented a beacon of hope. Their arrival attracted crowds to the centre, eager to witness the unloading. As the trucks emptied, they became vessels for the vulnerable: the elderly, infirm, women, and children. What was intended to be an orderly evacuation quickly descended into chaos, overwhelmed by confusion, panic and desperation.

People had been selected for departure, but the plan had fallen apart. Now, it was a free-for-all, with whoever managed to board a truck given the chance to leave. Desperate civilians clamoured to scale the high-sided vehicles, pushing and pulling in a frantic bid for escape.

Grant filmed as a woman reluctantly handed her child to someone aboard another vehicle, knowing she wouldn't be able to join them. Tears streamed down her face, a poignant mix of sorrow for their imminent separation and relief in knowing her child would be safe. It was a decision many mothers faced, each one equally agonising. Despite the heartbreak, these scenes offered powerful visuals and soundbites. Grant meticulously recorded the expressions of anguish and tears, capturing the raw emotions of the moment.

Haris asked one woman why she had thrown her baby into the truck.

"It is better that at least one of us survived," she replied and her tears flowed even more.

A Bosnian fighter fired his rifle into the air, attempting to restore order, but it proved fruitless. UN soldiers took on the role of porters, aiding as many people as they could onto the overflowing trucks. Relief and tears permeated the air, mingling with sorrow as forced separations occurred.

General Leconte arrived and relayed to the Bosnian leaders an agreement reached with the Serbs: the trucks must depart within half an hour, with no possibility of extensions. Furthermore, after the specified time, no Muslims would be allowed to leave.

Monaghan came by. "Got enough?" he asked.

"Never enough," Grant replied but he knew this would have to do.

"OK this truck," the tall Irishman led him to the last UN lorry. He took a screwdriver and unscrewed the rear right tail light. In between the three bulbs, indicator, brake and night lights was a space. It was the perfect size for one of Grant's Hi 8 video tapes.

"Perfect," smiled Grant. "But how do we let Tuzla know?"

"Leave that to me."

The UN's strength lay in its diverse mission personnel, drawn from a multitude of backgrounds and countries. Although English and French served as the primary languages, Major Monaghan devised a strategy to harness the skills of individuals from less commonly represented nationalities and languages.

"So, we worked out that there are two languages, in particular, the Serbs can't translate quickly or at all. One is Portuguese, and the other is Swahili. In the Military Observers, we have soldiers from Kenya and Portugal. So, from here, we radio in Portuguese to a half way post to Tuzla. We tell them which truck the tape is in by saying the first two letters of the registration number followed by right or left indicating which side the tail light is on. Then, the Portuguese soldier who is halfway will tell his Kenyan colleague the message, and he will relay it to Tuzla in Swahili. Fool proof…I hope."

Grant was impressed. If anything had a chance of success, it was this plan. He couldn't afford to lose another tape, especially considering all the risks involved.

They quickly fitted the tape and then screwed the cover back on.

Leconte shouted, "OK, convoy must leave now. No delays, now, or it will not be able to pass through the Serb checkpoint. No negotiation. Let's go."

People continued to scramble up the sides of the trucks, which were completely full and overflowing. Some women clung desperately to the sides, only to fall off as the trucks drove away. Mothers stood by the road, tears streaming down their faces, as their children vanished into the distance. There was an overwhelming sense of emptiness in the air. Men stood silently, watching, their hearts heavy with the uncertainty of when they would see their loved ones again. Grant felt the weight of the emotion surrounding him but remained focused on filming until the last truck had departed.

A small medical team had arrived with the aid convoy, tasked with assessing the situation and determining the needs of the people. They had brought along a modest supply of essentials, primarily anaesthesia, bandages, and morphine. Though limited, it was a welcome addition to the scarce resources available.

Thierry, the lead physician, wasted no time and swiftly entered the school to assess the conditions and examine the health of children and elderly individuals too frail to depart on the trucks. His evaluation painted a bleak picture.

"These old people will die soon unless they get proper medical attention," he told Grant. "The children have lice, scabies and the start of malnutrition. Many seem to be suffering from dysentery."

Every inch of every classroom seemed occupied, with children, mothers, and elderly individuals filling the space. People sat on desks lined against the walls, while others found shelter underneath them. A large framed photo of Tito adorned one of the walls; he was particularly revered by the Muslims of eastern Bosnia. Grant captured what footage he could before venturing outside for the next phase of the evacuation.

Several Tata flatbed trucks arrived outside the clinic, and orderlies began transferring the wounded onto stretchers. Five British Sea King helicopters were designated for the evacuation operation. Once again, there was a strict time limit they had to adhere to. The helicopters needed to minimise their time on the ground as much as possible. The Serbs had agreed to twenty minutes, but even that was pushing it.

Everyone acted swiftly, and the casualties were swiftly transported to the football field, which served as the designated landing pad. At the centre of the pitch stood a UN air liaison team comprising three members: two French and one British marine. Upon the arrival of the last truck, they signalled for the helicopters to be called in.

They descended low and landed consecutively, the propellers still spinning. As soon as the wheels made contact with the ground, the wounded were swiftly brought aboard. Eight stretchers were loaded onto each helicopter. Grant trailed behind one elderly man, his leg shattered by a mortar blast. The man's face contorted in agony as the stretcher was hurriedly carried, each jolt causing him more pain.

The Liaison team signalled for everyone to step back. One by one, the helicopters lifted off and swiftly departed. The loading had taken a few minutes only. The ground had become crowded with onlookers, and family members were bidding farewell to their loved ones. Despite the lingering bitter cold, the sun cast its warm rays upon the scene, lending an almost relaxed atmosphere. However, as is often the case in war, moments of tranquillity are short-lived, and within minutes, the peace was shattered.

As the last helicopter disappeared, a deafening explosion reverberated across the ground. Grant peered out and witnessed smoke rising from a hillside adjacent to the pitch. Suddenly, another explosion erupted, much closer this time. Grant continued filming, but the picture from his video camera abruptly turned black due to the intense pressure from the explosion. He realised he had been standing only fifteen metres from where the shell had struck, a significant one, judging by the size of the resulting crater in the centre of the pitch. The three-man UN liaison team lay on the ground, ten metres from the impact, miraculously unscathed. Grant found himself five metres further back, still standing, and remarkably unharmed. Amidst the chaos of screams and yells as people fled, Grant remained untouched.

"Medic!" A shout echoed through the chaos. Grant's ears were ringing, and he felt disoriented and confused. Why had the Serbs shelled despite the agreement? As he looked ahead, he saw UN soldiers sprinting down the field. His camera remained black until he noticed two UN soldiers being carried towards him. As they drew closer, the camera picture was restored, and his senses stabilised. Grant shuddered momentarily, realising how close he had come to being hit. Some might call it a miracle, but to Grant, it felt like fate, at least this time. He refocused on the panic around him, filming as the two blue helmets were loaded into a UN vehicle and driven at speed to the clinic.

He saw the American Major on the radio. "More incoming," he said. "There's more incoming." As if on cue, two more shells slammed into the pitch. Grant boarded one of the flatbed trucks and followed the men inside, but he couldn't help but notice their UN colleagues' behaviour. They were beside themselves with concern, pushing Bosnians out of the way and insisting that their friends be treated first. To Grant, it felt as though the locals didn't matter.

Lying on the bed was the same blue-eyed boy Grant had noticed when he first arrived. He lay beside a man whom Grant recognised as his father, both bearing slight injuries from mortar shrapnel. Grant approached them, and the boy looked up and smiled, exuding an aura of sweetness and innocence. Grant shook his head, feeling a pang of nostalgia as the boy reminded him of Igor, the Chocolada kid he had encountered in the shadows of the underground car park at the Holiday Inn.

He couldn't help but ponder whether one day Bosnians would know peace and children would enjoy simple pleasures like chocolate. Yet, in the present moment, amidst the turmoil of Donji Zelenik, such prospects seemed distant and unattainable.

He was beckoned into the emergency room. Nedret, the doctor, viewed the injuries.

"They are not serious. They will live. Don't worry. First people who are badly wounded."

On reflection, it became clear to everyone that the Serb compliance with the operation was peculiar. It later emerged that while the helicopter evacuation was underway, the Serbs shelled the eastern part of town, where the majority of the refugees were sheltering. The area was bombarded by artillery resulting in many injuries.

Grant captured footage of the UN soldiers receiving treatment, panning the camera around the room to capture the frantic scenes. Amidst the chaos, he noticed another young boy lying quietly on a bed, appearing troubled and in pain, as if attempting to cry but unable to. Grant filmed a close-up of him. As Selma rushed past with bandages, he reached out, grabbing her hand, and gestured towards the boy.

"Stomach wound, very bad," she said. "He needs to be evacuated."

For some reason, he asked, "What's his name?"

"Mirnes, and he is three years old. He was playing outside when the shell landed."

The intensity of emotion seized Grant like hands around his throat. It felt as if he were being strangled. He didn't know why he asked the name. It wasn't for identification; it was for connection. He stopped filming and held his hand. It was cold. Grant knew he needed specialist treatment and quickly. He observed as the Canadians grew increasingly preoccupied with the welfare of their friends while showing less concern for others. How their slight injuries were somehow more important than those of ordinary Bosnians. Grant felt some anger. He wanted to tell them to shut the fuck up. To tell them their friends were not going to die but this boy would unless help arrived.

Leconte arranged for another UN helicopter to evacuate the wounded, and he agreed that Mirnes could accompany them.

They escorted the wounded and the little boy to the UN Armoured Personnel Carrier (APC) and began making their way to the football field. However, they were forced to halt halfway there as more shells rained down on the pitch. The French Major, responsible for overseeing the evacuations, found himself in a difficult position and had to make a crucial decision. He waited for what seemed an age.

Grant, who was in the back of the vehicle, shouted, "You must hurry, Major, this boy will die without urgent treatment." The hesitation seemed to last an eternity.

Finally he made a decision. They would return to the clinic, where a plan was devised for a UN helicopter to hover over the town's centre. The wounded would then be winched up to safety. Although a plan was in place, it took nearly an hour before it could be executed.

The Sea King helicopter hovered thirty metres above and lowered down the stretcher cradle. The two UN soldiers were lifted up, and then the cradle descended for Mirnes, but it was too late. He was wrapped in a gold-coloured foil blanket for warmth, but his body had grown cold. He passed away beneath the whirling blades of the helicopter. Thierry, the MSF doctor, checked his heart with a stethoscope and felt for a pulse on the small, pale wrist. He shook his head solemnly and gently closed the little boy's eyes, a silent pronunciation of death. A man stepped forward to retrieve the body, tears streaming down his face. Yet his sobs were drowned out by the deafening cacophony of the helicopter's noise.'

The UN air liaison officer radioed to the chopper, "The boy is dead; you can leave now."

It was a stark and clinical declaration, marking the end of a young boy's life. As the Sea King helicopter ascended into the grey sky and disappeared into the distance, its deafening roar gradually faded away, only to be replaced by the heart-wrenching cries of the man mourning his deceased son. Sitting by the roadside, he cradled the lifeless child, wrapped in a golden thermal blanket. To the journalist, it was more than just the loss of a boy; it felt like a metaphor for the despair engulfing Donji Zelenik and the direness of the situation. Grant realised that these tears would not be the last shed in this town.

49

Hassan raised the night vision goggles and scanned the river bank. There was no firing, no movement, just a deathly silence that often preceded trouble, especially at night. A half-moon hung in the sky, casting its dim light onto the calm waters of the Miljacka River. To the south lay the district of Lukavica, firmly under Serb control. Perched on the hills above were the positions of Serb snipers, from where they could target individuals at will. Though effective in the early days, people had grown wiser and more cautious. Shipping containers had been strategically placed at major junctions and the ends of streets facing the river and hills. The snipers still claimed lives, only not as many.

Not far upstream lies the Princip Bridge, initially known as the Latin Bridge, constructed during Ottoman rule but later renamed after Gavrilo Princip. A Serb, Princip's assassination of Archduke Franz Ferdinand and his wife in 1914 near the bridge's northern end sparked the events leading to the First World War.

Hassan viewed the bridge and was reminded of its history. 'Serbs always cause trouble,' he thought to himself.

He had been waiting for almost an hour, yet there was no sign of movement on land or along the river.

"Are you sure someone will come?" asked the commander.

"As sure as we can be," the officer replied. "Someone comes every few days. It's never the same person, but they use the same dinghy and crossing place. They don't seem to link up with the black marketeers on this side; they disappear into the night and then return a few hours later. This happens regularly. We've tried following them, but they always lose us. They disappear into the shadows, and without street lights, it's difficult to track them. Something is definitely going on."

"We need to find out what," said Hassan.

Lookouts stationed themselves discreetly in the shadows near the old town. They were instructed not to intervene. Hassan was determined to discover his intentions.

Moments later, a silhouette emerged on the Serbian side of the river. Pushing a small, black inflatable dinghy to the water's edge, he swiftly paddled across. In mere minutes, he vanished into the darkness of the night.

"Let's hope at least one of our men picks up his trail," said Hassan.

50

The Princip Bridge held special significance in the life of Dragan Mihajlovic. The assassination of Archduke Ferdinand, the heir to the Austrian throne, and his wife served as a powerful symbol of the Serb fight for independence and stood out as one of their boldest actions. Gavrillo Princip belonged to a secretive Serbian society known as Ujedinjenje ili Smrt, meaning Union or Death, which was a part of the longstanding Black Hand or Narodna Obrana. This society comprised radicals, government officials, military personnel, and politicians. During the early 1900s, they executed a series of sabotage operations and political assassinations. Although the Black Hand never entirely vanished, it retreated into the shadows, biding its time.

Mihajlovic, a member himself, followed in the footsteps of his grandfather, who was also part of the society. Through the diaries passed down by his uncle, Mihajlovic learned that his grandfather had been one of the original conspirators in the plot to assassinate Ferdinand, alongside Princip, Nedjelko Cabrinovic, and Trifko Grabez. This knowledge filled Mihajlovic with immense pride. Over the years, he maintained his connection to the Black Hand through frequent visits to Belgrade, where like-minded individuals plotted and waited for the day when Serbia, and even Bosnia, would achieve independence. Mihajlovic felt that day drawing closer; he could sense it. And just like his grandfather, he believed he played a significant role in the ongoing struggle.

Princip was only nineteen when he committed the murders and was considered too young for execution. Instead, he received a twenty-year prison sentence, but died of tuberculosis two years later in an Austrian prison.

The grandfather managed to evade capture and disappeared, taking advantage of the chaos brought on by the outbreak of the First World War.

The spy meticulously pored over his grandfather's diaries, studying them repeatedly as if they held sacred significance. Through these diaries, he gained intimate knowledge of his grandfather's actions and whereabouts, as well as the hardships he endured, spanning from his involvement in the First Balkan War against the Ottoman Turks to his passing in 1944.

He picked out one entry from the winter of 1914.

His grandfather had written: "It is bitterly cold; some of us don't have enough warm clothing. The Albanians are picking us off every day. We are told we are winning, but it doesn't seem that way. We have lost three hundred men in just over a month. Those too badly wounded to walk have to be left to their fate. Some beg to be shot rather than be captured by the Turks. Our food and ammunition are running out, and we have few medical supplies. This morning, my friend Igor had his leg amputated. I gave him the last of my brandy. They put a leather belt between his teeth, but it couldn't stop his screams. We seem to be on our own. I wonder if I will survive this, I wonder if Serbia will survive."

Reading his grandfather's words always stirred a flood of emotions within him. He pictured himself by his grandfather's side, attempting to empathise with his experiences, though he knew it was beyond his grasp. He had never faced such dire circumstances himself. A profound sense of pride swelled within him as he reflected on the sacrifices made for Serbia by men like his grandfather.

Simultaneously, a simmering anger brewed within him, directed at the injustices inflicted upon the Serbian people.

Whenever he grappled with his sentiments towards Bosnian Muslims and Croat Catholics, he sought solace in specific passages from his grandfather's journal.

September 19 1917. 'I returned home to find the bodies of my mother and father. They had been decapitated, and their bodies mutilated. It was done by Muslims and Croats in the Schutzkorps. My parents never harmed anyone. Why would they do this? They can only be described as animals. I promise that I will avenge the death of my parents and all the innocent Serbs killed by these barbarians.'

The schutzkorps, an auxiliary volunteer militia formed by the Austro-Hungarian authorities, struck fear into the hearts of many as they pursued and apprehended Bosnian Serb dissenters. Some argue that they initiated the earliest instances of ethnic cleansing.

In the end, his grandfather was never able to avenge the death of his parents, nor did he come to terms with the horrors that unfolded in a place that became synonymous with dread and terror: It was called Jesenovac. It's a place that is etched into the memory of nearly every living Serb. It was a concentration camp operated by pro-Nazi Croatian Ustasha. Up to seven hundred and fifty thousand Serbs died there according to Serb historians. Mihajlovic's grandfather was one.

His diaries had one last entry.

Jesenovac April 16th 1943. 'This is a God-forbidden place. I don't know how to put into words the horrors I see every day. The Ustasha do not treat us like human beings. To them, we are less than animals. They seem to treat the Jews better. Death is the only escape.'

The spy pursed his lips with renewed anger. To him, Muslims and Catholics shared equal blame. 'The Muslims will not escape death he vowed to himself. They will pay. I will make them pay'.

As he looked at the model, he smiled, 'And this will help make them pay.'

51

"We lost him," explained the officer. "Fuck," responded Hassan. "We need to find him. It's essential we see where he goes and who he meets. But if that can't happen, pick him up and take him back to the boat. We won't have a choice. We need to know what he was carrying and to whom."

Hassan felt the pressure from the Army command, especially from Gromo. They were eager to break the siege, but with Munja's continued presence, any attempt seemed like a suicide mission. His investigation was hitting a brick wall. There were no clear leads, suspects, or useful intelligence beyond what they picked up from radio intercepts. The situation appeared grim.

His walkie-talkie burst to life. "Command to C3," said the voice, "C3 here, go-ahead."

"C3 requested to H2," replied the voice, "C3 requested to H2," the voice repeated. H2 was the comms centre. Hassan hoped it was good news.

There had been an intercept of a radio communication from Munja.

"We didn't get much," explained the young signals operator. "It was too quick, but we have a general location, around the old town near the Husrev-beg mosque. We need longer to pinpoint the exact position. The radio message lasted less than 30 seconds. It's as if he knows we are listening."

"He does," said Hassan. "He knows everything. And that's a big problem."

Even three floors below ground, they could hear the sound of artillery shells followed by a huge, distant explosion. It was bigger than anything heard before. It was massive.

The comms room burst into activity with a flood of messages.

"Sir," said one operator, "The Dobrinja arms depot has been hit. It's burning, and there have been many casualties."

'Men they could replace,' Hassan thought clinically. But ammunition was much harder. The international arms embargo had seen to that. Unfair but a reality. With every passing day, the Serbs were dismantling their capability not only to attack but also to defend. It felt like this was a build-up to something. But what?

"C3, this Lion 1, Lion 1, package has been located. I repeat, package has been located."

The arrival of the package by whoever crossed the Miljacka that night brought a glimmer of hope. It was the first positive development they had seen.

"Do not intercept. I repeat, do not intercept. Follow the package until it is sent. Lion 2, head to vicinity and wait for my arrival."

Hassan briefly felt uplifted. Perhaps this could be a lead to capturing Munja. However, the optimism faded quickly. The 'package' vanished without a trace. They were left clueless about his whereabouts and, more importantly, unaware that his delivery was the crucial element of Munja's plan - the Semtex meant to strike a severe blow to the Bosnian leadership.

52

Grant was clambering up the hill through the snow when he felt his coat being tugged. He stopped and turned. He saw what seemed to be an old lady climbing up and over him. He recognised the word 'Jebiga'(fuck it) but understood none of the other mutterings of the old lady. She must have been close to seventy Grant thought, but she was moving like an Olympic sprinter with the strength of a weight lifter. He realised that hungry people found an inner strength that defied logic. It was the second night drop of food rations by a US C130 transport plane flying high above. Most of the individual food packets had missed the town falling instead on the snow-covered hills. Thousands of people, most of them displaced, were rushing through the snow to collect as many as they could. A swarm of human beings scavenging for whatever they could, whatever had fallen from the night sky.

A shout went up, "There's some." In the lens of his night vision infrared camera, he could see groups of people heading to the drop spot like a pack of animals to devour a prey. There was no decorum in desperation. Thirty minutes later the old lady who had mercilessly bundled the Brit to one side came back down the hill carrying two armfuls of brown packets. It had been a successful hunt for her. She was panting heavily.

Grant filmed her descent. At the bottom of the hill, there were two armed fighters ordering the people to drop the packets into a large box. The old lady shouted some obscenities but she had no choice. She had to comply.

"Why?" asked Grant "They are hungry, they need food," he said in a slow careful way that Brits adopt when talking to foreigners.

The fighters shook their head and said one word, 'Hagija,' before walking away with the box.

Grant was indignant. He walked quickly to the Domavia where he saw Hagija standing talking to Mehmet.

"Why are you taking food from the people?" he demanded. "They are starving. They need food. This is not right."

"Calm down," said Mehmet. "We all need food, but fighters need it to defend this town. It's not the best situation but you can't have a man too weak to fight. So, unfortunately, we have to prioritise. You need to understand that."

"I do, and I don't," he replied. "They need something. The UN rations that came are not enough."

"Look, before the war, this town and district had less than ten thousand people living here. Now there are sixty thousand. Sixty thousand mouths to feed, bellies to fill. The Serbs are letting in a limited amount of supplies, but it's not enough, so we have to feed the fighters above anyone else."

Hagija had a stern expression on his face.

"He doesn't like me, does he? He thinks I am a spy?" asked Grant.

"Hagija doesn't like anyone. He is a miserable man. No one has seen him smile. But he is a good and brave fighter, so we can put up with the unhappy face. And yes, he thinks you are a spy. That's the nature of your job: you gather information and give it to the world and, in our case, the enemy. So, you don't intend to spy, but that is what you are doing."

It was a sobering thought and not the first time Grant had considered it. But it was true. He gave information away. In the case of Donji Zelenik, he had to be careful what he put in his reports. He understood the necessity of discretion. He realised too that he was subjectivity was starting to creep into the way he viewed this story and it wasn't just because of his relationship with Selma.

Mehmet smiled. "Look we are very grateful you are here and you are reporting on what is happening. You have helped us a lot, so know that you are respected. It's just that not everyone trusts you yet."

"What about you?"

"As a journalist or the lover of my twin sister?" Mehmet asked.

"Both."

"If I am honest, then neither. But we will see. You should just remember that a brother always looks out for his sister in Bosnia. And don't forget that Bosnian brothers are now armed." He smiled and got into the black Mercedes and drove off.

Grant decided to walk through town with Haris.

"Are there any Serbs here?" asked Grant. "Just one," said Haris. "An old man, he's married to a German lady. She is from Dresden and came here during communist times."

Grant knew that Dresden was one of the most bombed towns in Germany during the Second World War. 'If she lived through that, she could live through anything,' Grant thought to himself.

"Let's go and see them."

Their home was behind the Orthodox Church, seemingly untouched by the ravages of shrapnel. Grant couldn't help but wonder if this preservation was deliberate. It took a few moments before the elderly lady cautiously greeted them at the door, after sliding open several bolts. She looked uneasy, there was a hint of fear in heavily wrinkled face but she invited them inside.

Grant, through Haris, asked if he could interview them on camera but they seemed uneasy and politely declined. They emphasised that they were treated kindly, just like Muslims. The elderly man condemned the actions of the Serbs, mentioning that they had fled when the war began, but they chose to remain in their own home.

Haris asked to go to the lavatory. The old lady pulled Grant to one side and spoke in broken English, "Please, we are scared. Some people not nice. We would like to leave. Could you please ask the United Nations if they can take us out? We cannot ask. Please. We are old."

Haris returned, and the old lady quickly changed the subject.

"Thank you for talking to us," said Grant, and Haris translated, "We will see you again."

The door closed and Grant heard the door bolts being slid back into place.

A plan formed in his head to try and get the old couple out of Donji Zelenik. As he returned to the Domavia he saw Hagija and some of his men in the manager's office drinking Stock brandy. He offered Grant and Haris a glass. The translator declined.

"You think I am a spy?" Grant asked. Haris translated.

"Yes, he said, but good spy." Grant thought Hagija was going to laugh, but he yawned instead.

"Can I ask you for a favour?"

Hagija inquired what.

"Can I arrange for the Serb man and the German lady to be taken out of Donji Zelenik? It would be a great favour to me, and they are old. They can do nothing here. It would show great humanity and that you have no ill will towards Serbs."

Hagija's expression didn't change while he listened to Haris translate, and he quickly replied, "Yes, no problem. They can leave if they want."

"Really?" asked Grant.

Hagija nodded.

"Fantastic, that's great. Thank you. I will go and tell them." He finished the remaining stock brandy in his glass and exited the room. Feeling delighted, he eagerly anticipated sharing the news with the couple.

After a brief wait, they reopened the door, appearing pleased as Grant informed them they were free to leave.

The old lady gave a half smile and then asked, "Who gave permission?"

"Hagija," replied Grant. "Oh," she said. The half-smile disappeared.

"It's good news, isn't it?" Grant asked.

"Yes, it is very good news," said the lady, "Very good news. Zank you. You heff been very kind. God bless you."

'Nice words,' Grant thought, but it struck him that there was no excitement in how she spoke them. He wondered whether the surge of emotions she felt was simply shock, a reaction to the possibility of escaping this dreadful place at last. Perhaps, he considered, that was the reason behind it all. He half ran downtown to the clinic. Like an excited little boy, he wanted to share the news with Selma.

As he left the lane a figure stepped out from the bushes and turned towards the house.

53

As Eid approached, Mihajlovic found his anxiety mounting. It wasn't just the imminent attack that troubled him; it was the prospect of escaping afterward that proved equally daunting. There were no certainties. Having managed to evade detection so far, being discovered now, just as he was poised to deliver a devastating blow to the Muslim leadership, would be catastrophic. It would set back Serb plans significantly, perhaps even years.

For Munja, it was often the solitude that weighed heaviest on him. The inability to share his thoughts, seek advice, or engage in casual conversation left him feeling isolated. There was nobody with similar beliefs and goals with whom he could discuss his plans, aspirations, or apprehensions. He was truly on his own. Communication was limited to coded messages, and even then, it was mostly one-sided. He couldn't help but envy his grandfather, who had comrades he could trust and confide in, comrades with whom he carried out operations. Munja longed for the camaraderie that such bonds fostered. In his world, serving and fighting for one's people represented the pinnacle of purpose.

He opened the old tin box, carefully revealing his family history within. The weathered red tin bore the label 'Deutsche Biscuit', dating back to pre-World War I times. These biscuits were beloved not only by Austrians and Germans but also by the British, including the Scots. Despite the anti-German sentiment during and after the war, the brand was cleverly renamed 'Empire Biscuit' to navigate the changing times. However, some things, especially food, transcended ideologies, remaining cherished regardless of political shifts. Yet, rebranding could fool in the short term.

He retrieved another photograph from the box, his only other memento aside from the wedding photo. It depicted five men, three seated and two standing, dressed in full Serbian Military uniform. The image was worn and torn, suggesting its age, yet the added image captured a moment frozen in time. The men wore hats adorned with the Serb national badge, featuring the iconic four Cs and plumed feathers. Their jackets were draped over their left shoulders in a traditional fashion. Each man sported a moustache, and three proudly displayed a single medal pinned to their left breast.

Mihajlovic wasn't entirely certain about the identity of his grandfather, yet he had a strong inclination that the man standing at the back was indeed him. There was a resolute aura surrounding him, exuding pride and strength. Seeing this figure, Mihajlovic couldn't help but see a reflection of himself. He longed for the opportunity to have known his grandfather, even if only for a brief moment, to understand his essence, his actions, and his motives. While he could speculate, it wasn't quite the same. He often felt a pang of self-pity. Although he didn't particularly yearn for his mother, the absence of his father and grandfather weighed heavily on him. These were the kind of men who formed the backbone of the Serb nation. None of the five men present wore a smile, and why would they? They were warriors engaged in a covert battle for the Serb nation, constantly confronting death and danger. Almost all of them paid the ultimate sacrifice.

As he sifted through the contents of the box, a tattered piece of paper fell out of the box. He picked it and saw it was his grandfather's pledge of allegiance to the Serbian nationalist cause.

He read:

'I, Dragan Andrea Mihajlovic, by entering into the society, do hereby swear by the sun which shineth upon me, by the earth which feedeth me, by God, by the blood of my forefathers, by my honour and by my life, that from this moment onward and until my death, I shall faithfully serve the task of this organisation and that I shall at all times be prepared to bear for it any sacrifice. I further swear by God, by my honour and by my life that I shall unconditionally carry into effect all its orders and commands. I further swear by my God, by my honour and by my life that I shall keep within myself all the secrets of this organisation and carry them with me into my grave. May God and my brothers in this organisation be my judges if I should wittingly fail or break this oath at any time.'

There was a faded signature at the bottom which was more like a scribble and what looked like a dark thumb print. The spy speculated that it was sealed with blood. Among the contents was a small booklet titled, 'Constitution of Ujedinjenje ili Smrt' (Unification or Death), containing 36 articles advocating violence and actions against any nation opposing Serb independence.

At the bottom was the organisation's seal showing an arm holding a flag of unification with a skull and crossbones and to the side a bomb, a phial of poison and a dagger. Encircling these symbols were the words 'Unification or death.' Dragan Mihajlovic held history in his hand and pride in his heart. It was the raison d'etre to everything he was doing.

54

Hassan anticipated that the upcoming meeting wouldn't be enjoyable. General Mujkanovic, also known as Gromo, had a reputation for having a fierce temper and little tolerance for incompetence or mistakes. Hassan realised that not having any leads on who Munja was would likely be seen as a failure by the general.

The general didn't look up when Hassan entered his office.

"So, what have you to report?" he asked.

"I am sorry, General, there is a little new. We followed a Serb operative but lost him, so we don't know where he went and what, if anything, he brought with him. But we can conclude that he wasn't a black marketeer. We picked up his trail later, but we lost him again. Anyhow, if they are planning something his arrest would have shown we are on to them. I just hope that he comes back again, and this time we will be lucky."

"Not good, is it?" said Gromo rhetorically. "We think they are planning something, but we don't know what and when. We know someone is spying from inside our organisation, but we don't know who, and we know secret documents or materials are being brought over the river, but we don't know what. We actually know fuck all."

There was a knock at the door, and a young soldier entered.

"Radio activity from the last 24 hours, sir," he said, placing the report in front of the general.

Mujkanovic scanned the entries.

"Anything of note?" inquired Mesic.

"Not really," replied the general. "Nothing from Munja, nothing significant and just some ramblings from some drunken Chetniks on the hills who were obviously bored."

"Can I take a look, sir?"

He glanced over the report swiftly. As he reached the part about the drunken Serbs, he paused, focusing more intently. It was common to come across drunken chatter on the radio waves. Serbs stationed for extended periods on the hills surrounding Sarajevo frequently turned to excessive drinking while engaging in walkie-talkie conversations with fellow soldiers nearby, sometimes teasing Bosnian troops across the divide. Their discussions ranged from football and women to politics, and of course Balija.

Gromo noticed Hassan looking more closely at one section in particular.

"What is it?" he asked.

"It might be nothing, but there is one exchange between some men when one says the hand is back or black. The operator wasn't sure because the Serb seemed to be well drunk and was slurring his words. But, I'm thinking if it was the hand is black, then could this be a reference to the Black Hand. I might be clutching at straws, but…." Gromo sat up straight.

"You mean the Serb nationalist movement?"

Hassan nodded.

"But that was wiped out by the Ustasha and Tito, and it has never been heard of in nearly fifty years. Any members left alive became non-persons and were never allowed to hold any senior positions, certainly not in the military or government."

"Or maybe not," said Hassan.

The general went to his bookcase and brought out a book titled, 'History of the Balkans.'

He went to the Index and then flicked through pages until he reached one titled 'Cerna Ruka' (Black Hand).

"Are they operating again? Are they behind the espionage, the subversive operations? But, even if they are, what good can it do us even if we know Black Hand is operating again? We don't know who they are and, more importantly, where they are. We are no closer to finding out if Black Hand is involved in any plot. This is like pissing in the dark and hoping it finds the pot."

Hassan examined the page closely, focusing on the seal of the Ujedinjenje ili Smrt, which meant Unity or Death. He recognised the Black Hand as the organisation's military branch.

"I've seen this sign somewhere before," he said, "Or elements of it, and recently. I need to check something if you will allow me, General."

He saluted his commanding officer and promptly exited the room, his mind focused on the solution lying somewhere in the old town, where he had recently been while searching for Munja.

Night had fallen and Hassan drove to the point where he had previously watched Ibrahimovic and followed him. There was an eerie quiet on the streets that were devoid of people and movement. Only those who had an official duty or were returning from the mosque had a reason to tread the streets after dark. Of course, he had lost Ibrahimovic that night, believing that the intelligence chief had gone home. Only he hadn't. He arrived back an hour later.

Hassan retraced what he thought was Ibrahimovic's route that night, navigating through the winding, cobbled alleyways lined with centuries-old houses. Oil lamps flickered behind polythene-covered windows, and smoke billowed from makeshift chimneys protruding from walls. Some buildings bore scars of partial destruction, lacking windows or doors. Approaching one such building, Hassan noticed a closed door secured only by a chain between two holes. With a tug, the chain yielded without a padlock in sight. As he directed his flashlight to the left of the door, he observed bullet and shrapnel holes alongside graffiti markings. 'Die Chetniks,' was written and 'We will win.' But next to it, there was a drawing of a skull and crossbones.

He stepped into the courtyard, the door creaking behind him. Across from him, another door stood partially ajar. Beside it, scribbled messages, mostly anti-Serb, adorned the wall. Adjacent to the graffiti, a crude drawing depicted a hand clutching a banner or flag. . Carrying on he could see that someone had been here. There were cigarette butts on the floor and they looked fairly fresh. He pressed on through the door, his flashlight scanning the room.

Towards the far end, a sizable concrete structure caught his attention, resembling a trough for livestock. It was evident that this place had once provided shelter for animals. On the trough was another drawing in black, probably charcoal, of a dagger and a bomb. They were hard to notice unless you were looking for them. And Hassan was. He touched the writing and the charcoal came away easily suggesting it had been recently applied. There was a connection.

Hassan's realisation hit him like a bolt of lightning: all the drawings were part of the symbols of the Black Hand. It was too much of a coincidence. He directed his torchlight around the trough, revealing deep scratch marks on the floor. He pushed the trough. It was heavy but not immovable. He put the torch to the side and started to pull the trough towards him. It resisted at first but with each of Hassan's efforts, it gave way a little more until it finally, came away from the wall completely. Hassan shone his torch and there was a bag. Someone had gone to great efforts to hide it. Was this the place where the Serb had come with his secret contents? He went to reach for the bag and then suddenly his world went black. One blow to the back of the head and he collapsed unconscious.

An hour later, he awoke, feeling the dried blood on his temple and the pounding headache. Struggling to piece together what happened, he examined the trough's hollow space. The bag had gone and with it also any clue to what it contained, who it was for and whether it had any connection to Munja. But his gut feeling was that it was connected to the spy. There was no other explanation.

The dots began to connect, gradually forming a clearer picture. Although still somewhat distant, one thing consoled Hassan, he felt he was edging closer to uncovering the truth and identifying those responsible. The pursuit of Munja seemed to be nearing its conclusion, or so he hoped.

55

Leconte was brimming with optimism; his mood was positively buoyant. Singleton found himself torn between amusement and incredulity, unsure whether to chuckle or simply shake his head in disbelief. Meanwhile, Haris remained unmoved, either unable to believe what he was hearing or simply being his usual self.

"Yes, they do want peace, and they will negotiate to make things better for everyone," the general continued. "I really believe that we are moving towards the end," he said with a little smile.

He turned to stroke the little yellow budgerigar in the small cage on his table.

"Isn't that so mon petit oiseau?" The locals bestowed the small bird as a token of appreciation for his efforts to transform Donji Zelenik into a sanctuary, albeit without the safety aspect. This cheerful yellow budgie soon became his trusted companion, often joining him for a drink. The general developed a fondness for both Bosnian Stock Brandy and his feathered friend.

Leconte cherished his gift, engaging in conversations with the tiny creature more than with most people. The Frenchman seemed lost in thought, soaring mentally to unknown destinations.

As he savoured a sip of brandy and drew deeply from his Cuban cigar, the room filled with billowing smoke and the rich aroma of tobacco leaf.

"But General, are you sure you can trust the Serbs?" Singleton asked politely. "After all, they are still shelling the outlying areas, civilians are still fleeing from their homes in front of Serb advances, and they are still stopping aid convoys getting in and civilians getting out to safer areas."

"Details mon ami, details. They cannot, of course, stop things overnight. These things take time; everyone has to be on board. But around this area, the Serbs want peace. I am convinced of that."

Optimism or naivety, Grant couldn't decide which. 'The general was, in essence,' he thought, 'a good man who wanted well for everyone. But he seemed to be ignoring reality.' From the journalist's viewpoint, the general's perspective differed greatly. It wasn't only the Serb attacks that cast doubt on optimism. Grant also detected animosity when his radio exchanges were intercepted by someone he dubbed 'Lord Haw Haw,' reminiscent of the notorious German WWII propagandist. Each burst of anger was filled with strong language, directed both at him and Muslims in general. The individual recited alleged Muslim atrocities from history and issued threats of imminent revenge. He always finished a diatribe with, 'We are going to kill you all, but you will die last.'

With each smuggled report and every exclusive story revealing people's suffering, Serb anger and threats escalated. It's an understatement to say that he wouldn't be warmly welcomed on the Serb side anymore. He began to think that when he went to the frontlines, he should reconsider the offer of an AK47. Hagija always told him that, "Serbs don't have respect for journalists. They will kill you just as quickly as a Muslim. They remember what happened to them hundreds of years ago. They will not forget what you said about them in your stories yesterday. But hey, my friend, it is up to you. Your life."

Journalists weren't combatants and must never be regarded as such; otherwise, it would endanger the safety of every journalist from potential reprisals. Grant firmly believed in this, even as doubts about this reasoning crept in more frequently.

"Thank you for the drink, General. We will see you tomorrow. Bonne nuit."

The general was deep in thought, stroking his budgie, and never noticed them leave.

As they left the room and closed the door, Haris turned to Grant. "He is on another fucking planet," he said. "He will still be saying they want peace when they carry the last motherfucking body out of here." Haris never spoke much but this was perhaps the most profound thing he had said and his longest sentence to date. Grant was impressed.

As they descended the stairs, Major Pratt was coming up.

"Hi Major, how's it going?"

The American took him to one side. "Man, this is a clusterfuck. It's all going down the John and us with it. The general thinks he is Mother Teresa in fucking uniform, and he thinks the Serbs are aiming for the Nobel Peace Prize. It's going to turn ugly. But there is one good bit of news. I got another clip of bullets today, and I can now take thirty-two of the motherfuckers with me when they turn. And they will fucking turn. Take my word for that. My advice to you is to get yourself a weapon." He paused and then added, "But don't quote me, OK?"

He trudged up the stairs, embodying the contrast between optimism and pessimism, akin to the Yin and Yang of Leconte and Grant. Grant leaned towards Pratt's perspective, recognising the unfavourable odds, with the exception of the locals' potential support. The situation in Donji Zelenik appeared bleak to everyone but General Leconte.

"Drink?" asked Major Monaghan as he passed the departing Pratt. "You should take no notice of yer man dare; he could make the allied advance on Nazi Germany sound like Custer's Last Stand."

Paddy Monaghan possessed an inherent Irish charm that rendered everything as mere facts of life, devoid of undue distress. Unlike Pratt, he could even frame

Custer's Last Stand as a casual gathering at the Little Bighorn, suggesting a cool approach to daunting situations.

Grant accepted the invitation.

He got out a bottle of Jameson's Irish Whiskey. "I was saving this for a special occasion," he said. "But I've concluded that if I waited for a special occasion in Bosnia, I'd be almost teetotal by now."

He took out two glasses and filled them with generous measures.

They exchanged cheers.

"So," Grant started, "Do you share the general's optimism?"

"Well, off the record, No, I don't."

"Why?" he responded.

"Well, from what I have seen and what I have heard from the Serbs, there is a deep-rooted anger aimed at the Muslims. Not just from now, but this has been going through the generations, being handed down from one to the next. They may talk about peace but it has to be peace on their terms. No one can give them that. And you know, yer men here, der muzzies, well dey have done some damage too. And yer boyos over dere want some retribution. So I tink it won't end well."

"So?"

"So, they will take it. They are not stupid. They know it will take a lot for the international community to take definitive action to stop them, especially when dey have Russia behind them. I don't believe this will end peacefully. And I can see that the odds are in the Serb's favour. More men, better and more powerful weapons. They are in the driving seat. And, as I said, Muslims have done bad things in these parts. Serb Civilians have died, too. Now, you can argue what came first. The chicken or the egg? But at the end of the day, each side looks at the number of dead chickens, not why they died."

He continued. “Do you know yer UN history? In The Congo in 1961, in a mining town called Jadotville, 155 Irish UN soldiers held off a 3000-strong Katangese force for seven days until they ran out of ammunition and water. They inflicted more than a thousand casualties on the Katangese besiegers. I was one of them. It was my first taste of combat, and it terrified me. But the thing that was clear was that our position was impossible. And I think the position here is impossible, too. The Muslims cannot win. The only way they will survive is through surrender or a negotiated settlement, and the latter is highly unlikely, believe me.”

“So, you are not an optimist?” asked Grant

“On the contrary, I am. I come from a family with fourteen kids, I rolled out of bed one night and couldn’t get back in, so I went to the UK to find work, and when I made some savings and reached the age of eighteen, I joined the army. I believed that when I left Ireland, I would make it somehow. So, I am an optimist, alright, but I am also a pragmatist. As a military man, I can see the strengths and weaknesses. Yes, some of these people are brave; desperation makes you brave. But most are not soldiers. They don’t think like soldiers, and they make mistakes. Above all, they need to know that for all the general’s optimism, the reality is far different, and they need to plan accordingly, though I am not sure how.” He refilled the glasses.

“Here’s to…” and he halted and thought hard. “Here’s to survival.”

They downed it in one. “One for the road?” he asked.

Grant made a strong swallowing sound and took a deep breath. “No thanks, I’m going to a party,” he said with raised eyebrows and a smile.

56

Back in Sarajevo, there was a general panic in the lobby of the Holiday Inn that hadn't been seen since the booze stocks almost ran out in the early days of the war. The press corps shared a strong comradeship during major conflicts, fostering relationships, marriages, and bonds akin to family. Everyone, or nearly everyone, supported one another and wished each other well, but not too well and not to the extent of getting world exclusives.

And that was what Grant Singleton was doing on a daily basis in a place that was the hottest news story in the world. But for the international press pack it was as inaccessible as the furthest planet in the universe. Everyone had wished him well, just not that well. When rivals get exclusives, foreign desks ask questions and make demands. Usually impossible demands. "Get there as quickly as you can; it's only four inches on the map. Can you get close enough to do a live? How big a minefield?" For media, common sense was one of the first casualties in war zones when losing out to exclusives.

Planet news is not for the faint-hearted. Journalists are orbiting 24 hours a day and the beast needs to be fed. It can be a cut-throat business especially when it comes to exclusives. In Donji Zelenik one journalist was pumping them out. In the Holiday Inn scores of others were walking round like inmates in an asylum trying to work out how to get in on the act and appease desperate Foreign Desks. And that was not an easy task.

Some, like Amelia Degusta, had already penned numerous accounts based on information from elusive radio sources. Others, frustrated by the lack of direct contact with people on the ground, struggled to make meaningful connections. With helicopter flights no longer an option and Serb control making overland travel perilous, access was severely limited, if not impossible. In such circumstances, the prevailing wisdom was to get as close as possible to the action, even if it meant taking considerable risks.

Chuck Brown was on the sat phone with his agency.

"Eight hours minimum," he repeated.

"No, we can't take the main road you can see on the map. Yes, I know it's only a few inches on the map, but several of those inches are held by drunken Serbs with bad tempers and lots of weapons."

He turned to a colleague. "Four inches is about the size of his dick on a good day," he said, shaking his head. The stupidity of foreign desks was legendary in international journalism.

"One, it's mined, two, bridges have been destroyed, and three, Serbs are just waiting for idiots to attempt to drive along it so they can reward stupidity with a bullet to the head. It would be like a turkey shoot. Do you get my drift?"

"No, not fucking coal mines, mines that go fucking boom and disperse bits of your body into the fucking hinterland." He shook his head in frustration. The person on the other end of the phone seemed oblivious to their own lack of insight, persisting with unrealistic ideas.

"What about a helicopter? Can we hire one?" came the anonymous foreign desk ignoramus, at which point Chuck Brown almost puked and slammed the phone down in its cradle.

"Assholes," he said. "Total, unambiguous assholes."

Competition was challenging, especially in the United States. Unlike many other countries with more traditional news cultures, the US was driven by financial incentives. Having exclusive stories meant attracting more viewers, which in turn meant increased advertising revenue – more dollars. Anchors earning ten million dollars a year needed to justify their salaries. Currently, ATV dominated the news landscape, attracting significant advertising revenue. Chuck Brown called it corporate copulation where people adjusted news coverage according to the amount of the greenbacks it could earn. He said anchors and executive producers had resorted to performing a kind of corporate cunnilingus.

Now, as the other US networks scrambled their units in pursuit of exclusives, they found themselves playing catch-up on Donji Zelenik.

Outside Sarajevo's Television Station, the journalistic convoy stood ready to embark. Twenty-four-by-fours revved up, poised for the eight-hour cross-country journey to Tuzla, aiming to get as close to Donji Zelenik as possible. The closest place with decent hotel accommodations served as their destination. Not every journalist was eager to undertake the journey, given the inherent risks and discomfort. Some, like Degusta, opted to 'monitor' from Sarajevo. There exists a group of journalists who perceive a war zone as such, regardless of whether they spend most of their time in a hotel. War is one thing; comfort is another. Yet, once on the ground everyone adopts the esteemed title of war correspondent.

Mungo DeBoer stood outside the TV station among the throng of journalists. His correspondent, a woman of imposing stature matched only by her ego, stood alongside him. She held the cameraman in high regard for his extensive military knowledge, finding solace in his expertise amidst the uncertainty of their world. Rodney, the soundman from Yorkshire, however, seemed disinterested, his worn parka and indifferent expression suggesting his mind was elsewhere, perhaps on Whitby Pier rather than in the midst of a war zone. He casually finished his breakfast, sipping from a can of Yorkshire bitter obtained from the Ukrainian UN black market, while distant sounds of bullets and mortar shells echoed in the background.

"7.62 mm AK47 fire," explained DeBoer confidently to his correspondent. "And also 81mm mortars, probably Russian," he continued. The statuesque correspondent felt reassured.

All of a sudden, nearby, there was a massive explosion. The Zimbabwean hit the muddy floor. Rodney was still standing. He finished off the dregs of the can of beer and belched. " You Twat, that were outgoing lad."

Brown couldn't contain his amusement, finding the English word 'Twat' particularly funny. He considered DeBoer to be a prime example but believed he was well-matched with his correspondent. DeBoer rose, brushing the mud off his military-style camouflage jacket, though his embarrassed expression lingered.

Igor, the Chocolada kid, approached with his hand outstretched. Brown, feeling apologetic, offered him a piece of gum, as it was all he had. Although it was not what Igor desired, it was better than nothing. The American started the engine and into the back seat entered Tanya.

"Can I join you? We've got to get there man; we are missing out. I can't believe Singleton never told me where he was going. Fucker."

Brown turned and looked at her. "Have you been crying?" he said and then thought better of pursuing the line of inquiry.

They navigated through the hills, avoiding the frontline and pre-warned Serb positions. The snow-covered roads proved challenging, causing Brown to switch the car into four-wheel drive mode, but it still began to skid despite the snow chains. After reversing cautiously, Brown opted for a different route forward. Suddenly, the continuous blare of a horn caught his attention, prompting him to halt. Passing on the left was a small yellow Yugoslav-built car called a Zastavo, reminiscent of a Fiat 500. Laden with bags and cases on its roof rack and four occupants squeezed inside, it lacked four-wheel drive and snow chains. Yet, it effortlessly overtook Brown's car. Some things in Bosnia just defied logic.

About 400 metres uphill, Brown's lips gave a small smile at the sight of the Zastavo nestled in a patch of snow by the roadside. Without fuss, the four individuals exited the car, each taking hold of a section of the front and rear bumpers and effortlessly hoisting the vehicle back onto the trail. With a nonchalant air, they resumed their journey, as if such occurrences were routine.

The car took a different track and disappeared into the snow. They drove up to a Bosnian checkpoint. "Be careful when you go this way," said the young soldier. "Serbs are not far away. There is much danger. Better if you go another way."

"Is there another way?" asked Chuck. "No" replied the young man. "This is the only way to Tuzla."

"Then we have to go this way," said the journalist.

Their progress was abruptly halted less than a kilometre ahead by a deafening explosion. The Land Rover keeled over onto its side. Tanya's cry pierced the air. Unseen beneath the snow, they had struck an anti-tank mine. Tanya was thrust forward, her chin colliding with a camera body. Brown, bewildered, felt his head connect with the door as the vehicle capsized. Attempting to move, he cried out in agony.

"My ribs are broken," he shouted. "Fuck. What a fucking bummer."

Blood was spurting from Tanya's chin, and she was holding her wrist.

"I think it's broken," she said. "It's my camera hand. I can't use my camera now." She started to cry, her tears filled with anger and frustration rather than pain. Their conflict had hit a temporary obstacle. Brown remained still, confident that assistance would arrive. Retrieving a flask from his top pocket, he took a deep drink of Sliva. Then, from another pocket, he produced a joint, lighting it and inhaling deeply.

"War sucks," he said, "War really sucks."

57

It was 5 AM, and a fierce, biting wind cut through the air, feeling like a slap from a giant, powerful hand. The temperature hovered below freezing, and Grant found himself stamping his feet in the snow to ward off the chill. Knocking on the door again, this time louder, he observed chinks of light from oil lamps seeping through the makeshift curtains of nearby houses, casting an eerie glow in the darkness. As a curtain shifted, revealing a larger beam of light, Grant caught sight of the silhouette of someone peering out from within. Other curtains followed suit, revealing more suspicious and wary eyes peering into the darkness.

Eventually, the interior door bolts were drawn back, and the door creaked open slightly. The face of the German lady emerged.

Haris broke the silence with a greeting of "good morning," which was followed by Grant. As she glanced around, Haris noticed the figures in the illuminated windows, causing her discomfort. She swiftly ushered the two men inside, eager to leave the exposed area.

Haris translated for Grant.

"It's ok, everything is ready. There is a car, a UN car, waiting to take you out," he said.

"Nein," replied the woman, and spoke to Haris in Bosnian.

"She says they have decided not to go," he said. "They want to stay in the town with their friends and neighbours."

"But why?" asked Grant. "Last night, they really wanted to leave; what has changed?"

Haris asked. The woman's face was almost blank as she explained to Haris.

"They prefer to stay here, in their home, with their friends," he translated. "She says it was wrong for them to think about leaving after everything people have done for them."

Grant felt disappointed. He had secured all the necessary permissions from Hagija, from the UN, and indirectly from the Serbs. This was supposed to be a heart-warming story, a kind of happy ending for two elderly individuals caught in a difficult situation.

"Is anyone making you stay?" Grant asked.

"Nein," the woman responded almost robotically. "No one is making us stay. We want to. Thank you for trying to help. But you must go now."

She swiftly opened the door and ushered them out, almost as quickly as she had welcomed them in. The sound of bolts shutting echoed behind them as they exited. Grant glanced around and noticed human shadows retreating from the windows, with curtains swiftly closing.

"What do you think?" Grant asked.

"Sometimes it's best not to ask," Haris said matter-of-factly and walked off through the snow. The dejected journalist followed slowly behind, confused and nonplussed.

As they vanished into the darkness, a figure emerged from the bushes across the street. Hagija observed the departure of the journalist before turning and walking in the opposite direction.

58

The device was compact and fairly neat, prompting Mihajlovic to stare at it with a sense of admiration. He marvelled at how something so small could wield such devastating power. Despite his lack of expertise in bombs or bomb-making, he had diligently followed the instructions and assembled the device laid out on the bed. One thing he did know, however, was that homemade bombs were often unstable once the timing device, wires and detonators were connected. They could explode prematurely or fail to detonate altogether. That's why he waited until the last possible minute to insert the detonators. Now, with the final delivery of Semtex in hand, the last piece of the puzzle was in place.

To Munja, the device was a thing of beauty. The explosive material was contained in a large block, resembling something a child might use to mould miniature figures. It emitted a faint scent reminiscent of almonds or marzipan. Adjacent to it, securely taped down, was a simple clock serving as the timer, with a designated spot in the block for the insertion of the small copper detonator. Plastic bags filled with nails, nuts, bolts, and shards of glass were meticulously arranged around the Semtex. Though compact in size, the bomb possessed the potential to decimate the entire Bosnian Muslim leadership, a devastating blow that could mark the end of the war and secure victory for the Serbs.

He smiled, patting himself on the back in self-congratulation. He was aware that this action would elevate him to hero status among the Serbian people. It would serve as the culmination of his grandfather's legacy, allowing him to emerge from the shadows. The lifelong goal of his grandfather and others like him would finally be achieved, a true tribute to those who had made the ultimate sacrifice for Greater Serbia.

He meticulously affixed the top of the model to the base housing the bomb and secured the clips. With just one day remaining, he programmed the timer to activate during the mid-afternoon Eid prayers. After carefully placing the religious replica in a holdall, he prepared to deploy it today. The unsuspecting Imam would then position the model in a prominent location within the mosque, in tribute to one of their most devout brothers, Mohammed Ibrahimovic.

59

From the exterior, it appeared to be an ordinary, unremarkable house. However, in the case of Donji Zelenik, it bore the scars of war, pockmarked by an array of weapons fired by Serbs: mortars, artillery, and tank rounds, leaving behind the scars of conflict. Yet, inside lay the entrance to a place of refuge, a sanctuary from the brutality of war, where death and chaos seemed temporarily suspended. It was a nuclear bunker, one of many scattered throughout Yugoslavia. Tito, a communist leader, had defied Stalin's authority, charting his own path for revolutionary socialism. Despite numerous assassination attempts sanctioned by the Russian dictator, Tito remained steadfast, leading Yugoslavia on his terms, much to the envy of other, more compliant communist nations. However, this did not guarantee Tito's safety. He remained wary and prepared for any eventuality, including defending his country against nuclear threats, not only from the capitalist West but also from the Communist East.

Tito was a shrewd leader, evident in his ability to confront Stalin and emerge unscathed. However, survival necessitated staying vigilant and remaining one step ahead of potential threats. He initiated an extensive nuclear bunker construction project, scattering installations throughout the country. The bunker in Donji Zelenik was relatively modest compared to the grandeur of the Amrijska Ratna Komanda (ARK), known as ARK, situated southwest of Sarajevo. ARK, the most clandestine military installation and one of the largest underground facilities, was initiated in 1953 and completed a year before Tito's death in 1980, at a staggering cost of $4.6 billion. While Donji Zelenik's bunker paled in comparison, it boasted similar build quality and safeguards as ARK, featuring thick, impenetrable walls, long corridors with a series of 1.2-metre metal doors, and being located deep underground. ARK descended 280 metres into the earth, whereas Donji Zelenik's reached only half that depth. Nevertheless, despite the absence of nuclear weaponry, those who entered knew their safety was assured for the day.

Grant stepped into the house. Before him stood another metal door, with another just a few metres ahead. They were both heavy and difficult to move. He began his descent down the spiral staircase, illuminated intermittently by oil lamps. About halfway down, he heard a throbbing sound. As he descended further, he recognised it as the heavy metal music blaring from a room ahead. Opening the door, he was hit with the full blast of Metallica. He recognised the song 'One,' the band's famous anti-war protest anthem.

"Oh, please go help me," it went.

'Darkness imprisoning me
All that I see
Absolute horror
I cannot live
I cannot die
Trapped in myself
Body my holding cell'.

As he entered the room, the finale erupted: a crescendo of machine-gun guitar sounds, a musical equivalent of a New Year's fireworks display that assaulted the eardrums and seized control of the body. The room was teeming with young people. He noticed Selma deeply immersed in heavy rock-style gyrations, and as the final notes faded away, the youth took command of their bodies, drenched in sweat, and exhaled deeply. It was a poignant song that Bosnians were increasingly embracing.

Selma saw him and immediately ran over and hugged him.

"Drink?" she asked.

"Stock brandy?" he replied.

"Stock all gone....but" and she smiled. "We have something fitting for a nuclear bunker."

She handed him a plastic tumbler with a clear liquid in it.

"And luckily, we managed to find something civilised to go with it."

She produced a bottle of Coca-Cola.

"Compliments of the UN Canadians," she explained and poured some into the tumbler. "Not too much, because this has to go round a little; now try."

He had never tasted a cleansing agent before, but he imagined this experience wasn't too dissimilar. As the liquid seared his throat, mouth, and chest, his senses recoiled one after the other. His mouth felt ablaze, and it took a full minute for him to regain control of his speech and his vision. It was as if his throat was being scraped with sandpaper.

"What the...what was that?" he asked with a pained expression, trying to regain control of his larynx.

"Surgical spirits," Selma replied. "Desperate times make you have desperate drinks," she laughed. "What was that quote about drink never having made a man better? But a man thinks it was better. Same for us, it's not making the situation better, but it's making us think it is better…at least for a short time."

"Givili," she said, cheers, and Grant laughed. He began to feel a sense of improvement, as if he had been transported to a different realm. He surveyed the room around him, realising that it must have been the control room in the event of a nuclear attack. However, there was no semblance of control present here. Instead, teenagers and young adults in their mid-20s to 30s were drinking, dancing, and engaging in the activities typical of a night out. Despite the abnormality of the situation, Grant found solace in the idea of mind over matter. Tonight, the details didn't matter, and it was heartening to witness Selma's unbridled laughter, a sight he hadn't seen in quite some time, not sicne the commander Jebiga episode.

He glanced towards the far side of the room and noticed one of the Canadian UN contingent, a captain, who appeared visibly overwhelmed and lacking any sort of control over the situation.

"Mucho rocket fuel," Selma explained. "He popped in to say goodnight two hours ago and I hear he's just proposed to one of the nurses." And she let another wholehearted laugh.

Grant found himself falling deeper and deeper in love, and for a brief moment, he attempted to push aside the reality of their surroundings and the escalating situation. However, he knew all too well that such distraction was almost impossible. It was evident to everyone that the situation was deteriorating rapidly. Despite General Gaston Leconte's belief that the Serb forces truly desired peace, they continued to fire and probe, further exacerbating the tension.

Selma saw Grant was deep in thought. "What is it?" she inquired.

"Things don't seem to be getting better, despite what Leconte says."

"I know, Mehmet says the Serbs are bringing in more men. He believes they will launch a big attack soon. Leconte refused to believe him. He has been fooled into thinking that they are just normal, peace-loving people who love kids and animals…just not Muslim ones. He says there is a big fight coming that could decide the fate of Donji Zelenik."

She saw he was troubled. "No matter, for one night at least, we are going to forget the war and all its horror and pretend that we are in London at a club. We are dancing and happy and thinking of where we are going to go on holiday, to somewhere warm where we will only have to worry about what factor sun cream to put on. Donji Zelenik will not be in our thoughts. Only love." And she smiled again.

Bruno, the German, stumbled over, his fez half-cocked in a rakish sort of way. He had a tumbler of rocket fuel in one hand and a piece of bread in the other. "Alles ist gut," he said. "Ziss is und fantasiche party mein freund." He staggered off, closely, followed by Haris, who smiled at Grant as he passed.

"Is he pissed?" Selma nodded. 'Miracles do happen,' Grant thought to himself and smiled. Maybe one will happen for Donji Zelenik.

They settled on the floor as the heavy metal music faded away. Positioned in the centre on a chair sat a young man, likely in his late teens, with long hair and dressed in a combat jacket. Next to his chair lay an AK-47 and a guitar. He picked up the instrument, strumming it gently before launching into a song.

'There's a lady who's sure
All that glitters is gold
And she's buying a stairway to heaven
When she gets there she knows

If the stores are all closed
With a word she can get what she came for'

It was Led Zeppelin's 'Stairway to Heaven.' As the music played, everyone in the room settled down, their bodies swaying gently to the rhythm. Some knew the words and sang along, while others simply hummed along. For Grant, it was an intensely poignant moment, and he felt a profound sadness wash over him. He struggled to control the tears welling up inside him. In all the places he had reported from, he knew that this assignment would always stand out as the most memorable, yet also the most painful. It felt as though he were trapped in a nightmare, unable to wake up. Despite his efforts, he couldn't envision a happy ending here. He glanced around the room, pondering how many would survive this ordeal and how many would ever be able to return to a semblance of normality. But then he realised, how could anyone ever be normal again after enduring such horror?

The singer continued.

'And it's whispered that soon
If we all call the tune
Then the piper will lead us to reason
And a new day will dawn
For those who stand long
And the forests will echo with laughter.'

The next few drinks went down swiftly. The rocket fuel no longer carried the same punch it did with the initial gulp. He welcomed the alcohol, embraced the circumstances, and for one fleeting night, he embraced a semblance of peace that he wished would endure, though he understood it was unlikely to last. He held

Selma's hand and then kissed her passionately. 'Que sera, sera,' he thought. 'Whatever will be, will be.'

60

He couldn't recall how he had ended up in bed, but the sudden explosions jolted him awake. The first blast felt distant, as if echoing in his dream. The second was much closer, rattling the hotel. By the time of the third impact the room shook, Grant was sitting upright in bed, his senses alert despite the freezing temperature that had plummeted unnoticed.

Haris shouted out, "Attack, Serb attack."

Grant had no time to dwell on the almighty hangover that descended upon him like a Panzer division charging into battle. Hastily, he slipped on his boots, snatched up his camera and bag, and bolted outside. Chaos reigned as men scattered in every direction. If this wasn't outright panic, it was the closest thing to it. Amidst the frenzy, Grant spotted Mehmet.

"What's happening?"

"Big attack. I think this is The One. They want to take the town. This is the end of the bullshit they have poured out to Leconte. He has been naive and stupid. The UN can't save us. It's up to us now."

"Where are you going, and can I come with you?"

"We are heading northeast to Zeleni Jadar. This is where the main attack is coming from. Come if you like, but it will be dangerous, and we won't have time to look after you."

"Understood," said Grant.

"Take this." Mehmet offered him an AK47.

“Thanks, but I am a journalist. Remember, we don’t use weapons; we report on people who do.”

“Fine, I hope your camera and notebook give you good protection. Don’t forget to wave your press pass when a heavily armed Serb stands over you with a rifle on the battlefield. I am sure he will respect that.”

Outside the Domavia, three open-backed trucks were parked, filled with men. Half of them were dressed in civilian attire. As usual, not everyone had a gun.

A UN jeep pulled up, and General Leconte rolled down his window. Spotting Grant, he motioned for him to approach.

“I don’t think this is a serious attempt to take the town,” he said. “I believe it is just a little bit of action ready for some bargaining in the coming weeks. You shouldn’t worry too much. I am going to speak to them.”

Grant speculated that if Leconte had been in General Custer’s position at the Battle of the Little Bighorn, he would still be under the impression that Sitting Bull desired peace.

“General, what’s not serious about waves of shells being fired into the town?” he asked, but the words wafted into the atmosphere as the general’s vehicle turned and headed south.

Heavy machine guns, 60mm mortars, and crates of ammunition were being loaded onto the trucks amidst shouting and gesturing. More men clamoured aboard, while lines of civilians scattered in all directions, desperately seeking refuge. It was evident to most that there was no safe haven to be found.

The UN captain, who just six hours earlier had been indulging in heavy drinking in the bunker and proposing marriage to a nurse, approached Grant and inquired about the destination of everyone.

"Not exactly sure," said Grant. "But they said it's going to be hot so I reckon we won't have a problem getting rid of our hangovers."

As helping hands lifted him into the back of the truck, it lurched into motion, departing from the town. They passed by the mosque and then the Orthodox church, once symbols of coexistence among people of different faiths. However, the distant sound of shells now painted a different narrative. The streets were flanked by half-demolished houses, with fresh debris scattered all around. Explosions echoed in the distance, punctuating the grim reality of the situation.

It wasn't clear how long the journey would last, but the sound of incoming shells was growing closer. He surmised they weren't far away.

The truck came to an abrupt halt, accompanied by loud shouting. Soon, everyone began to disembark, including Grant, who followed suit. They proceeded in a long line along the snow-covered path, flanked by trees, leading to a small valley where a half-ruined house stood. Men dispersed in different directions as Grant followed Mehmet and a small unit towards the front of the house. A fighter swiftly set up a .50mm heavy machine gun while Mehmet scanned the area using binoculars.

"See anything?" said a voice. It was the Canadian UN captain. He was a designated military observer who had followed them up.

Mehmet shook his head and continued looking. You can never hear the shell or a bullet that hits you. You only hear the ones that pass. The first shell that landed was, as Americans would say, 'Bang on the money.' The explosion rang out, deafening in its intensity. Cordite lingered in the air, and once Grant regained his senses, he was greeted by the sound of screams. He noticed that the machine gunner had been struck in the knee, blood gushing out onto the otherwise pristine bed of snow.

Mehmet reliably informed him that it had been an 81mm mortar shell as he continued scanning the area. He was aware that there must be a Serb spotter observing them, but the question remained: where?

A second shell exploded very close.

"Ow," shouted the Canadian Captain. He was lying on the ground, holding his leg. But there was no blood.

"Are you hit?" shouted Mehmet. "I'm not sure," he replied.

"No hit, captain, this was pressure from explosion. You are ok. We need to move. They know where we are, and the fuckers are good at their job."

Two fighters hastily lifted the wounded machine gunner in a chairlift and rushed down the path. Grant dashed ahead to capture the scene on film when, suddenly, two more shells slammed into the vicinity.

"Let's move faster," he shouted, "Brzo, brzo" (faster, faster). His voice was laced with panic. He'd been in similar situations before, but anyone who said they weren't scared would be lying. Fear was a constant companion in war.

He had barely gone 20 metres from the group when an explosion hurled him into the air. Crashing against a small wall, the deafening blast left his ears ringing and his vision blurred. He felt as if he were floating in a dream, until the shock subsided and the reality of the situation sank in. More mortars pounded the area, exacerbating his disorientation. It wasn't until he had run another ten metres that he felt a searing pain in his arm. Glancing down, he noticed a hole in his coat, blood pouring from the wound. Acting swiftly, he tore off a piece of his shirt and applied it to the injury. Amidst the chaos, shouts echoed behind him, but he couldn't locate the rest of the group. Racing ahead, he sought cover at the end of the wall. Lying low, he peered around the corner, extending the camera to capture the unfolding events and record the explosions' sounds.

A sharp pain erupted on his face, just below his left eye. Something trickled down his cheek, and he instinctively wiped it away with his jacket sleeve, only to realise it was blood. He had been struck in the face. Though not severe, he didn't believe it was significant at first, but soon, a stinging sensation set in. With every touch, a burning sensation intensified.

Mehmet and the others rushed towards him. Two fighters were carrying the machine gunner, while two more were assisting the UN captain.

"He's been hit in der ass," explained one of the fighters in heavily accented English.

"It hurts like fuck," shouted the captain, who was lying face down arse upwards.

"Can you take my belt pouch?" he asked Grant. "There's medical stuff in there, bandages and some morphine. I need morphine."

Grant rummaged through the pouch until he located the morphine. Removing the cap from the small morphine syrette, he inserted it directly into the Captain's upper leg, near the right buttock. Though the relief wouldn't be immediate, within a few minutes, the captain would enter a state of delirium, significantly reducing the pain.

More fighters emerged from the tree line, followed by a mortar unit. Swiftly, they set up and began firing mortars into the areas they suspected the spotter to be in, as well as where the Serbs were mobilising for an advance. Grant captured what footage he could, but he realised it was time to tend to his wounds.

The UN captain was loaded onto the back of a flatbed truck, and Grant climbed up to join him. The driver steered the vehicle back towards Donji Zelenik. Along the way, they passed more trucks transporting fighters towards the battlefront. The sound of shelling grew increasingly intense, and the southern part of town bore signs of more impacts. People emerged from their houses and temporary shelters, clutching a few bundles as they hurried northwards towards the UN base at the PTT building.

At the clinic, wounded fighters were being brought in, with the captain being carried into the building, followed closely by Grant. Inside, nearly every available space was occupied by injured men. Grant's attention was drawn to two civilians in the corner and a small child who had been struck by shrapnel. Without hesitation, he began filming the scene with his camera.

The door to what used to be the emergency room swung open, revealing Selma tending to wounded men. Oblivious to his presence, she continued her work. Meanwhile, Nedret, the doctor, hurried out of the door to assess the new arrivals.

"Yes, yes, no, no, yes," he shouted, dispensing instantaneous triage according to injuries and what medical supplies he had to help. He saw Grant.

"Not again," he said, beckoning him forward. "I thought Bruno was the grenade magnet. Are you trying to beat him?" He quickly checked Grant's wounds.

"So upper face and arm," he said, "But the other arm this time, very convenient. It's not too serious, I don't think, but the eye may be a problem. I have at least two big operations and a lot of patching up to do. Selma will clean your wounds, and I will take a closer look later. OK?"

Grant acknowledged him with a nod as Selma attended to his wounds. The arm bore a small hole, roughly the size of a coin, which she cleaned with alcohol before applying a gauze bandage. The same procedure followed for his eye. After giving him a quick kiss and a smile, Selma promptly returned to the emergency room. An elderly lady then handed Grant a cup of Turkish coffee. Finding a seat, he listened to the UN captain's groans and nonsensical murmurs, induced by morphine. Grant's grandmother would have described him as 'away with the fairies' as he drifted into unconsciousness.

As more shells exploded in the distance, providing a macabre soundtrack to the war, the room was filled with a symphony of human groans from the wounded. The air was heavy with a strong metallic smell, reminiscent of copper. It was the unmistakable scent of blood, which ordinarily isn't overpowering, but when exposed to oxygen, it emits a potent odour, strong yet strangely sweet. For Grant, sitting there with a very passable cup of Turkish coffee, it had become a familiar scent. 'There were weird moments in this war,' he thought to himself.

"Cool, man, we made it. It's nice here." The morphine had truly worked it's magic and the captain had gone some distance with the fairies. He was mentally surfing all kinds of nice thoughts.

It took two gruelling hours for the fighting and shelling to finally ease. While occasional shells still fell and sporadic bursts of machine gun and rifle fire echoed, Grant sensed that the Serb advance was halting. Mehmet entered and confirmed his suspicions.

"The work of Leconte?" asked Grant.

"More that the Serbs didn't envisage such strong resistance, and we made them think twice," he reasoned.

"Did you lose many men?" Grant asked.

"Losing one is too many," came the reply. "But we lost a few and many more wounded, as you saw. I hope my sister takes good care of you."

61

In the hills opposite, across the valley from Zeleni Jadar, Darko Zubic kicked the floor in acute anger and expressed his frustration. "Fuck those fucking politicians, they are selling us out again."

This was the day he received the order to capture Donji Zelenik and bring it under Serbian control. However, just as the final advance was about to begin, the order came to a halt. Little explanation was given, except that the UN had intervened. As he gazed at the houses around Zadar, he envisioned Donji Zelenik. It felt tantalisingly close yet frustratingly out of reach. The excuse offered was that victory was inevitable, but impatience threatened to undermine their efforts. Zubic burned with a desire for triumph and retribution.

General Mujkanovic, the leader of the Serb forces, shared his frustration. Two hundred kilometres away, at the hilltop headquarters near Pale, he slammed his hand forcefully on the table and unleashed a barrage of expletives, a display of anger that few of his subordinates had witnessed before.

"Why?" he asked the dour-looking man opposite him. "Why, when we are close to winning, why? This makes no sense."

His face reddened with anger. The scarlet patch birth mark on the right-hand side of his face glowed like some kind of nuclear reactor. His voice almost broke into a tremble.

"Please explain."

The solemn man was not a soldier; he detested violence. However, Kresimir Anjic was a politician and a pragmatist. He lit a cigarette, inhaling deeply and releasing a cloud of smoke filled with the scent of cancer, a ubiquitous presence in every military room and establishment.

"Because if we don't, then the West will finally get involved, and we cannot fight them with weapons. We need to fight them with intelligence. They certainly don't want to get involved after the disastrous Gulf War. But with all these anti-Serb stories in the world's media, there is growing support for intervention. That is what our sources tell us and our Russian brothers. We need to be realistic."

"But to move our big guns away from Sarajevo will make us vulnerable," moaned Mujkanovic. "They could break the siege and then, who knows, carry on to Pale and beyond. These weapons are our defence. They are essential."

Anjic took another drag of the cigarette and immediately coughed. Russian cigarettes had that effect, strong and carcinogenic but also affordable.

"We have had initial discussions with the UN, including Leconte, and the agreement would be that we remove some but not all. They recognise we need a strong defensive capability. But, as I said to you, we fight with our brains, not just guns. And the best of this is that there are no conditions, no red lines or no go areas. That means Sarajevo may be untouchable in the future, which we guessed might be the case if we are honest, but the East is not, and that is important because it connects to Serbia. That allows us to link up and, finally, create the Greater Serbia we have always dreamed of. In effect, what is being intimated, and what we believe, is that in return for Sarajevo, the West is, in fact, sacrificing the Muslim-held lands in the East. This could not have worked out better. So, General, begin your planning for the final phase and the defeat of the Balija in the East. All that stands in our way is Donji Zelenik and a few small towns and villages. Victory is in sight. I propose a toast to Greater Serbia, which is now a reality and no longer a dream."

For a moment, Mujkanovic hesitated, processing the politician's words. Then, a realisation dawned: perhaps this was the solution. He raised his glass in celebration, a smile spreading across his face. The once prominent birthmark seemed to soften, and there was no longer a need to pound the table. For once, a politician had begun to make sense.

62

Nedret shined the light into Grant's wound just beneath the eye. The doctor looked long and hard.

"There's nothing I can do for this," he said. "Without electricity, I cannot perform an x-ray, and without that, we can't determine how deep the piece of shrapnel is. It could be superficial, but we can't take that risk. Even the minutest shards could be dangerous in this area. With capillary action, any fragments could eventually move towards the eye. It doesn't matter how small. It could cause blindness. Now, maybe that would never happen, but I advise that we cannot take the risk."

"So, what does that mean?" asked Grant.

"It means you need to get to a hospital with the right facilities as soon as possible, locate the shrapnel and have it removed. There is no alternative."

The disappointment was clear on the journalist's face.

Nedret saw it. "I know you don't want to leave, and we are all very grateful that you came here and told the world how we are suffering. It has made a difference. But you need to think of yourself now. We are going to survive. We have become tough people. But I can't guarantee that you will retain your sight in that eye unless you leave and get it sorted."

"But I can't leave by road because the Serbs will take me."

Nedret replied, "The UN is sending in a helicopter to take the Canadian captain out. He still has a lump or two of shrapnel in his ass which needs to be removed, or it will make taking a dump a little uncomfortable. They will take you as well. Leconte has given clearance. Departure will be in two hours."

As he exited the room, a wave of numbness and emotion washed over him. He noticed the door slightly ajar beside him and hesitated. Peering inside, he saw the Canadian captain lying face down on a bed. Without a second thought, he entered the room.

He was still recovering from the effects of the anaesthesia, and the lingering sense of delirium persisted.

"I saw St Peter," he mumbled. "He was standing there, and he spoke to me."

"What did he say?" asked Grant. "Did he say anything about Bosnia or Donji Zelenik, anything about survival and peace?"

It didn't register. The captain continued. "I saw St Peter, I saw him; he was in the clouds. He saw me. I saw St Peter."

Grant smiled despite the throbbing pain from his wounds. Nedret had patched up the hole in his arm and removed a small piece of shrapnel, but the discomfort in his face seemed the most agonising, perhaps due to the uncertainty looming over him. He hesitated to leave after investing so much time, but he knew it was necessary. His gaze fell upon Selma, who was attending to a young fighter nearby. Beside her, a bucket overflowed with bloodstained clothes and bandages. Wiping her brow with her arm, strands of hair fell across her face as a ray of the winter sun illuminated the left side of her face. In that moment, she appeared to Grant like an apparition, something out of a biblical tale. Never had she seemed more beautiful to him, and he felt a reluctance to part ways with her. Catching his glance, she offered a brief smile before returning her attention to stitching up the young fighter's wound.

He waited until the last of the wounded had been tended to before pulling her aside to inform her of his imminent departure.

"I know," she said. "Nedret told me. You have to. I understand."

"But I will come back, I will, I promise. I don't know how, but I will make it happen. I'm good at that."

"I know you are, and I believe you. There is talk of a ceasefire, and more UN soldiers will come in, so people are feeling a little more optimistic. We are tough people. I think you know that by now."

He smiled. "Tough and beautiful," he said. Their kiss was long and full. Grant didn't want it to end. God, he loved her.

He turned and headed to the door. Then he looked back.

"I will be back. I will. No matter what. I will be back."

63

With only two days remaining until the Eid celebrations in Sarajevo, Hassan found himself grappling with the challenges of Ramadan. While some claimed that the scarcity of food made this Ramadan easier, For Hassan this was not an easy time. He was no closer to uncovering the identity of Munja, and most days felt like he was pursuing shadows, searching for ghosts, and imagining scenarios. Meanwhile, radio intercepts from Munja had surged, adding to the sense of impending events. Although they had yet to crack the code, the increased activity suggested that something significant was on the horizon, intensifying the urgency of their situation.

Gromo had issued strict orders to leave no stone unturned. Like Munja, he sensed that something significant was looming on the horizon. Munja's intelligence had inflicted considerable damage upon them, and they were determined to prevent any further harm. They understood the urgency of the situation. However, the question remained: how could they counteract a threat that remained invisible and elusive?

There was a knock on Hassan's door. A tall man with long black hair walked in. He had a pronounced limp. His name was Arif, a former police detective before the war and a good one by all accounts. But he had been wounded by shrapnel wounds in frontline fighting action. Hassan had him transferred to his unit. It was under protest. Arif wanted to remain part of his special forces unit. But his injury clearly made that impossible. And Hassan needed the expertise, the incisive detective's mind that he clearly didn't have. In a nutshell he needed the investigative nous that could uncover what he had so far been unable to do. A man of Arif's ability could maybe make the difference. He could help stop the biggest threat to Sarajevo and Bosnia. And Hassan was desperate.

Arif approached the desk and laid some papers down.

"Take a look," he said.

Hassan scrutinised the document closely. It was a birth certificate. He reviewed it several times, shaking his head in disbelief. His investigation had expanded to encompass comprehensive background checks on the twelve men with access to top-secret information, delving deep into their pasts.

"OK, I give up. It looks like a normal birth certificate. What am I missing?"

The birth certificate belonged to Mohammed Ibrahimovic, the devout Muslim known as the inquisitor, whose impeccable Muslim lineage seemed unquestionable.

"Well, it's not what is on the birth certificate, but possibly, what's not," Arif said.

"What do you mean?" he replied.

"Well, something is a little strange. It says he was born in Klucna in 1948. His mother was born in Grosnik. She always lived in Grosnik until she moved to Sarajevo in her late forties. Now, there is one good thing about communism, which I am sure you don't appreciate yet, but you will, and that is there are records on absolutely everyone, down to hobbies, activities, medical history, travel, interests and achievements. God Bless communism. Now, the records, which thankfully were not destroyed when the main central archive was hit, show that his mother came to Sarajevo in 1955 to take up a teaching post at the Marshall Tito Junior School. And that is when Ibrahimovic was enrolled in school. There is no record of him being in any other school here. So doesn't it seem strange that he started school at the age of seven when there is no prior medical reason for a late start?" Hassan thought. "Well, maybe she moved back to Groznik and didn't work, and he attended school there. What's so strange? Have you checked school records in Groznik?"

"Yes, but they were destroyed in Serb shelling. Mrs Ibrahimovic is a widow. Her husband, according to the school records, died shortly after the boy was born, but I can't find a death certificate, although the father was from a village north of Groznik. There is no trace of Mr Ibrahimovic dying in 1948. His first name was Alia. Now I've done some digging, and I have found that there were 15 Alia Ibrahimovics born in the Groznik area between 1920 and 1930. These could have been the father of Mohammed. Of these, nine are dead, three are now living out of Bosnia, and three more are, according to the last records, still living in Sarajevo. I have their addresses."

"OK, I think it's a long shot, but we have nothing else, so go-ahead. You check those, and I think I will go and have a word with Mrs Ibrahimovic. We need to tick all the boxes, no matter how improbable.

64

The door stood tall and imposing, a typical feature of classical Ottoman architecture. Its twin doors boasted large metal doorknobs and two rows of decorative knuckle studs. Above the portal, an arched stained-glass window casts coloured hues, with an inscription in Arabic adorning the space.

'Hathihe aldaar 'adha'at bahjaten Watajalat farahan lilnaazirin
Koteba alsaedu alaa 'abwabiha 'Adkhuluha bisalam aminin
This residence is radiant with joy,
And cheers those who look at it,
Good fortune is inscribed on its thresholds. Enter therein, in peace and serenity.'

Hassan was aware that this property was upscale and would fetch a high price in peacetime. While there was no nobility in Communist Yugoslavia, he knew that before communism, aristocratic families would inhabit houses like this. He approached the door and rapped on it using one of the large, ringed metal knockers, producing an almost mediaeval sound. Receiving no response, he knocked again, this time with more force.

There was a loud creaking sound as it was slowly opened. From behind it, the face of an old woman peered out suspiciously.

"What is it?" she asked. Her tone was not friendly.

"Mrs Ibrahimovic, my name is Hassan Mesic from Army command. I need to talk to you. In private."

"What about?" she asked, almost aggressively.

"It's better inside," he said.

He sensed her reluctance to let him in, suspecting that she might have refused had he not been wearing a uniform. The older generation was raised to respect and even fear men in uniform, as it symbolised authority and power. Refusing an official request was simply not customary.

Her face was small with a pointy chin. She wore a head scarf but Hassan could see strands of grey hair falling out. He noticed that her back was arched probably an advanced form of sclerosis which causes the spine to curve. It can also affect the brain. But Mrs Ibrahimovic seemed mentally sharp.

Her walk resembled more of a shuffle as she guided him into the sitting room, with its lofty ceilings and tiled mosaic floor adorned with a large, intricate Turkish carpet. A large, multi-coloured chandelier hung from above, its design reminiscent of the Ottoman era, a style Hassan recognised from a visit to the Grand Bazaar in Istanbul during a university trip. The walls were adorned with photographs capturing various moments of her and Mohammed's lives: snapshots of him as a young boy, posing in front of a mosque in Sarajevo, enjoying ice cream at the coast with his mother, and on his graduation day. Mohammed's framed degree took pride of place above the open fire, surrounded by these visual milestones that charted his journey from boyhood to manhood.

Hassan scrutinised the photos repeatedly, sensing that something was amiss. Then it struck him. There were no photos of Mohammed as a baby, and notably absent were any images of the father, her husband.

"What is it you want?" She asked. "Mohammed is in his office; you can contact him there."

"I don't want to speak to Mohammed. I want to speak to you," he replied. "I come here with the authority of the Bosnian Army High Command. Don't be alarmed; there is nothing to worry about, and there is nothing sinister in my visit. I am simply updating our records for security reasons. Everyone is included, even the senior generals and politicians. It is just a formality, and I won't take up much of your time."

The old lady appeared to relax slightly, yet she remained perched on the edge of her seat. Rays of winter sunlight filtered through one of the windows, a rare sight in Sarajevo, where most windows were boarded up or covered. However, this particular window faced away from the Serb positions.

"Mrs Ibrahimovic, there are a few gaps in our records, and I was hoping you could fill them out. We understand you lived in Groznik, and your husband died shortly after Mohammed was born?"

"Yes, he died of tuberculosis. Mohammed, of course, never knew him, and I think he has suffered because of that, for not having a man in his life. But he sought solace in God who filled the hole in his life and his heart."

Hassan nodded. "We can't seem to find your husband's death certificate."

Mrs Ibrahimovic fidgeted in her seat. She looked uncomfortable.

"I'm afraid I don't have a copy. It must have been left behind in Groznik. Before Mohammed was born, I worked with children, but after he arrived, I became a housewife after a short time working in a school here in Sarajevo. It is the right place for a woman to be at home to care for her family and her children. For the short time after Mohammed's birth, Alia adored his son. It was tragic that he died so soon after he was born. But it was the will of Allah."

She began to cry. "I have tried to be a good mother and make up for him not having a father."

"No one is saying you are not a good mother, Mrs Ibrahimovic," Hassan interrupted. "I don't mean to upset you. Just one or two more questions, and then I will leave."

She wiped her eyes. He felt guilty for making her cry.

"You had Mohammed late in life?"

"Yes, I had begun to give up hope. But then God gave me the gift of life, and it changed our lives. He is everything to me. Is there something wrong? Is there a problem with Mohammed? Has he done something wrong?"

The question surprised Hassan. It seemed to come from nowhere.

"No, of course not. As I said, I am just updating our records. We are at war, and everything has to be checked. Does your husband have any surviving relatives?"

"No, he was an only child. All his family have sadly passed away."

"And where is he buried?"

"In the graveyard in the village of Klucna north of Groznik," she said.

He expressed gratitude to the old lady and departed. While the meeting yielded no concrete evidence, several details troubled Hassan: the absence of baby photos, the lack of images featuring the husband or Mohammed, the absence of a death certificate, and the apparent discomfort of the elderly woman. Could she be concealing something, and if so, did it relate to Munja? Such a possibility seemed highly improbable. However, one thing remained certain: Mohammed Ibrahimovic, though an improbable spy, could not yet be ruled out of the investigation. Not at this stage.

65

The moment he returned to headquarters, he summoned Arif to his office without delay.

"Get a map; I need to know where the village of Klucna is."

The former detective spread out a large-scale map on the table, pinpointing Groznik before tracing a path north-westward to the village of Klucna. Two lines were then drawn, one extending north and the other south.

"It's in no man's land," said Arif. "It looks like less than a kilometre from Serb positions."

He picked up the phone and spoke to a colleague for a few minutes. "Hvala, thank you," he said, and put the phone down.

"So, apparently, the village was overrun in the early days of the war. But we pushed the Serbs back. They control high ground overlooking the valley where the village is, and it is too dangerous to hold."

Hassan went deep into thought, 'I am not sure what part Klucna plays in this investigation, but it could hold the key to whether Ibrahimovic can be eliminated from our inquiries or if he needs further investigation. However, I know it won't be easy or safe, but we need to get to the graveyard.'

66

Getting dressed was always a hurried affair, but the real challenge lay in mustering the courage to take the first step and leave the comforting warmth of the sleeping bag. Mornings were bitterly cold, with no heating in the shabby rooms of the Domavia. Temperatures plummeted below freezing at the break of dawn, causing warm breath to form frosty patterns in the icy air.

Grant swiftly unzipped the bag and hurriedly dressed himself, minimising the time his partially clothed body was exposed to the harsh winter mornings of the Balkans. "Hypothermia for breakfast," he thought wryly. Despite the challenges, discomfort, and danger, Grant would miss Donji Zelenik, and not just because of Selma. He had settled into a routine and learned to adapt to the hardships, but more importantly, he felt a sense of purpose in informing the world about the situation in eastern Bosnia and the struggles of ordinary people. It gave him a sense of fulfilment, especially during the bitter winter months. Although he wasn't sure of the impact of his reports, given the international community's inertia in the face of continued Serbian shelling and civilian casualties, he believed in the importance of his work. Despite leaving for treatment for his eye, he was determined to return, driven not only by the pursuit of the story but also by his connection with Selma.

He left Haris sleeping soundly and made his way down to the front office. Mehmet was seated behind the front desk, a large pot of Turkish coffee at hand. Gesturing to a nearby seat, he poured Grant a small cup of coffee, followed by a glass of Stock brandy.

"This will warm you up," he said. "My sister will be sad that you are leaving."

"I will come back," said Grant. "As soon as my wound is fixed. You can count on that."

"It may not be so easy, my friend. The Serbs are still taking territory. It's now too dangerous for our helicopters to fly and it will take at least two days by foot through numerous Serb lines. The odds of you getting back here are slim to nothing. The only way would be with the UN. But I think that once you are out, the Serbs won't let you or any other journalist in here. They don't want Donji Zelenik to feature on prime-time news anymore."

"We will see. But if I can't it won't be for lack of trying."

The noise was deafening, prompting both men to instinctively drop to the floor. A huge, head-shaking boom reverberated through the room, causing it to tremble. As they struggled to regain their bearings, one of the few remaining windows in the lobby shattered into thousands of shards, hurtling through the air. It was unmistakably a shell, a sizable one, landing not far from the hotel.

"Artillery," shouted Mehmet. "Big artillery, maybe 155mm."

One shell after another rained down, each impact resounding loudly and relentlessly. The building shook violently, as if the entire Donji Zelenik were trembling. Even by Bosnia's standards, this onslaught was significant. Amidst the explosions and the cacophony of falling debris, shattered windows, and breaking glass, screams and shouts echoed throughout the area, some loud and piercing, others barely audible murmurs. Grant rushed outside with his camera to capture the chaos. In the middle of the road lay a massive crater, three feet deep and four feet wide. He could see a house forty metres away, engulfed in flames, with a gaping hole in its roof. Further down the town, more shells slammed into buildings. Two people emerged from a house, carrying an elderly woman. Her jumper was soaked in blood, and one of the men held a blood-stained tea towel to her head. They hurriedly placed her in a car and drove off.

He captured the chaotic scene and the panic-stricken people on video. This shelling was undoubtedly the most severe the town had endured since the onset of the war.

A young fighter ran to the hotel. "Igraliste," he said, panting. "Skola." (School playground).

Grant started to run. The shelling had ceased, or perhaps it was just a temporary pause. Was there more to follow? Either way, it made no difference. Grant was aware of his duty to document and report. His pace quickened. The school was close to the clinic. He thought of Selma; she would likely be there. Determination surged through him, propelling him to run even faster. Rounding a corner, he abruptly halted, confronted by a scene of utter devastation, human devastation.

Bodies littered the playground, many of them children. Some cried out in pain, while others lay motionless, surrounded by large pools of blood. As he began to film, he noticed limbs detached from bodies and children with devastating injuries. The sight was nauseating, but he continued filming, unable to look away. The memories of a similar tragedy in Karaama flooded his mind when the orphanage was struck by a shell. Grateful for the viewfinder's black-and-white display, he remembered Mo's horrified reaction when he saw the graphic scenes in full colour. Despite capturing everything on camera, he couldn't shake the thought that these images would be too graphic for Western television. It was not the kind of footage one would want to watch during dinner, Grant reminded himself.

A woman lay lifeless by a football goalpost. Grant immediately recognised her as a teacher he had previously interviewed about the importance of maintaining school during wartime. She had emphasised the need to provide children with a sense of normality. But what constitutes normality in the midst of war? Grant surveyed the scene around him. This, he realised, had become the new normal.

A man frantically searched the playground, moving from one lifeless body to another, desperately seeking his son or daughter. His anguish was palpable. Then, amidst the devastation, he recognised a familiar bag. Clutching it tightly, he began to weep uncontrollably until another man approached him and urgently shouted, "Clinic." Fuelled by newfound hope, he wiped away his tears and rushed to the clinic.

In the centre of the playground, two large shell holes gaped, deep and wide. Surrounding them, a pattern of smaller holes radiated outwards like a macabre rosary, a sight Grant had sadly become all too familiar with. He pictured the countless razor-sharp metal fragments ejected by the exploding shell at terrifying speeds, potentially reaching thousands of feet per second. There would be no time to react; death and injury would be nearly instantaneous. Everywhere he looked, he saw the grim aftermath of those deadly fragments.

People emerged with stretchers to assist those who were injured but still alive. Grant panned the camera and captured the heart-breaking sight of a mother sobbing beside the body of a young girl. Holding the shot, he then moved closer, zooming in on the mother and then the little girl. Grant estimated her to be around eight years old. Despite the chaos around them, the girl appeared peaceful, as if in slumber, with no apparent injuries to her head or upper body. However, as Grant lowered the lens, he witnessed the mother's hand covering a large, gaping hole in the girl's stomach, with part of her intestine protruding. The woman desperately tried to keep it in place, offering her daughter some semblance of dignity in death.

"Animals," the mother said. "They are nothing but animals. What did Lydia ever do to them?" She bent over the body, and her sobbing became uncontrollable.

He glanced around and spotted General Leconte and a few of his men strolling around the playground, assessing the aftermath of the carnage.

"This is terrible," he said in understated anger.

Grant was engulfed in a whirlwind of emotions: anger, remorse, and a deep sense of distress. His body trembled, his mind reeling from the sight before him. Though he felt the urge to cry, he knew he had to focus on his work. With determination, he marched towards the general. Anger triumphed over his other emotions as he aimed the camera at the Frenchman.

"What the fuck, General, do you still think the Serbs want peace? These are just murdering bastards. They want to kill everyone. Peace, it's a goddam fucking joke, and if you are honest with yourself, you will see that too. Maybe you will also see that they are just jerking you around. They have only one intention, and that is to overrun this place, and they don't care how many people they have to kill to do it, men, women and children. When will you see that? This is just plain fucking murder. Tell them that when you next have a glass of fucking brandy and talk about them wanting peace. What the fuck?"

The journalist came to the realisation that this was not an interview; it was a statement, a statement of pure disgust. The language used was entirely subjective, reflecting the depth of emotion that had been building up over months. Like a dam struggling to contain rising waters, the journalist had suppressed his inner emotions. However, in the face of such callous violence and bloodshed of the innocent, the dam had completely disintegrated. The pain burst forth in an uncontrolled torrent of words, a raw and impassioned rant.

The general remained silent, absorbing the verbal onslaught without offering any defence. He understood that no words could adequately convey the gravity of the situation, except for one: murder. The journalist's accusation resonated with Leconte; it was indeed pure, unadulterated murder. Yet he couldn't bring himself to admit it, nor could he excuse it. As was often the case, Leconte and the UN found themselves caught in the middle, lacking the power and, often, the will to take the necessary action. In this instance, silence seemed to be the most prudent approach. It was the only option, particularly when dealing with a journalist.

"The UN can do nothing to help these people. If this doesn't prove it, then nothing will."

He had never addressed a general in such a manner before. However, he recognised that those words needed to be spoken, despite doubting their effectiveness.

He left Leconte visibly shaken, his face drained of colour as he gazed into the abyss where moments ago children had been joyfully playing. It served as a stark and brutal reminder of how swiftly death could descend upon Bosnia.

He hurried to the clinic, where bodies were strewn side by side on the floor, leaving no space unoccupied. Nedret and Selma rushed around, attending to the wounded amidst the chaos. It was another round of triage. He moved through the scene, pointing and making quick decisions. Selma distributed packs of bandages and organised the injured into lines, forming a queue of suffering and despair, a relentless procession of injury and disfigurement. Children cried out in a mixture of panic and pain, some still in shock. The pervasive odour of unwashed bodies and discarded blood-soaked bandages filled the air, yet the clinic remained warm inside. Helpers bustled about, carrying buckets of clean water and fresh linens, diligently cleaning the benches and floor amidst.

"No coffee today," Nedret said and moved fast into what was used as the operating room and his first patient, a young boy with half his left leg missing. The door closed. The job of saving began.

Mehmet entered the room, assisting an elderly man with shrapnel wounds in his back. Carefully, he laid him down on the floor.

"What does your bible say?" he asked Grant. "An eye for an eye? Pretty much the same as in the Koran but more detailed. "Life for life, eye for eye, nose for nose, ear for ear, tooth for tooth and wounds equal for equal. There's no room for misunderstanding."

His expression was resolute, with a chilling determination underlying his words. Grant began to understand the gravity of this sentiment. He had heard the rumours, and he knew what Mehmet's resolve meant. Someday, somehow, Mehmet would seek vengeance. Grant anticipated it would be ruthless, much like the Serbs. In that regard, they were alike.

He exhausted the last few minutes of tape and stepped out into the cold embrace of the winter's day. It provided him with a momentary sense of relief; the brisk bite of nature temporarily washed away the sensations and odours of the carnage. Yet, nothing could completely erase what he had witnessed. It could never. Those memories would forever linger in the depths of his mind, adding to the ever-expanding collection of horrifying images he carried with him. He understood that much of his material would never be used. It was much too horrific. But, he thought, 'Maybe, one day, people would demand to know what war was really like, and he would have the proof.'

Bruno approached, his tear-stained face revealing his emotional turmoil. His red eyes spoke volumes. Despite being a photographer, he was first and foremost a human being. Grant couldn't help but wish he could share Bruno's sentiment, but throughout the horrors they had witnessed, his sole motive had been to document. Someday, someone will have to be held accountable for these atrocities.

Bruno retrieved two Marlboro cigarettes from his pocket and extended one to Grant. They both lit up, the act not a celebration of survival but rather a sombre acknowledgment of the dead and injured. Then, from his other pocket, Bruno produced a small bottle of white liquid and handed it to the Brit. Grant took a sizable gulp, feeling his throat recoil at the fiery taste of homemade slivavic. Neither man spoke; to both of them, words seemed insignificant and futile.

67

The journey back to the relative safety of Tuzla was quicker than expected, but not in the manner he had anticipated. The Canadian UN military observer remained heavily sedated, still rambling about Saint Peter, while being accompanied by wounded adults and children in need of treatment beyond the capabilities and resources of Nedret and his team. Just outside the football ground, he bid farewell to Selma with a kiss. As he opened his pack, he retrieved Mo's Buzz Lightyear doll.

"I want you to have this; don't go anywhere without it. It was my friend's lucky mascot," he said. "Was that the guy who was wounded?" she asked. They exchanged smiles, and Grant shrugged before walking away. Halfway, he glanced back at Selma. She waved, and he couldn't help but wonder when he would see her again.

The British Sea King helicopter could transport twenty-eight fully equipped troops, but only fourteen casualties on stretchers, and even that was pushing it. Most of the wounded looked severely injured. Grant couldn't help but wonder how many would survive and, if they did, how they would cope. Healing the body was one thing, but healing the mind was an entirely different and challenging endeavour. While PTSD, or Post Traumatic Stress Disorder, provided a simplistic explanation, it failed to capture the complexities and turmoil of the mind when confronted with shock and horror. Mental wounds were not something that could be bandaged and left to heal; they could fester and haunt individuals for life, seeping out like pus from a festering wound, causing invasive and lasting damage.

Grant reflected on his journalist friends who, like him, ventured into the heart of conflict, witnessing the inhumanity of man first-hand. However, PTSD was not confined to those who braved the frontlines; it was ubiquitous among journalists, even those who didn't stray far from safety. Some seemed to acquire it almost as a status symbol, while others developed it for seemingly trivial reasons. Journalism, despite its noble intentions, was not immune to bullshit; it often found itself at the forefront of it.

He filmed as much as possible before venturing into the cockpit area to capture images of the pilot. As the chopper lifted off, Grant was provided with a headset to listen in on the radio traffic.

Instantly, the radio cackled into life. "Sea King Five Zero Zero Two, you are ordered to land immediately in Zvornik. Repeat, you are ordered to land. Do you copy? Over."

A chill ran down Grant's spine. Zvornik was a Serb stronghold, and if the helicopter landed there, it would signify two things: first, casualties would be deprived of vital assistance, a matter of life and death; and second, he would likely be arrested by the Serbs. The consequences were uncertain but ominous. They were well aware of his identity; the radio interruptions and threats had made their disdain for him and his reports abundantly clear. Grant didn't hold much hope for his chances. The UN was notorious for its tendency towards appeasement, and Grant suspected they would comply with the order. This would mean that the footage of the playground massacre would be confiscated, and the world would never bear witness to the horrors inflicted. He began to remove his tape, preparing to hand it over to the pilot. However, it turned out he shouldn't have bothered.

"Hello, Zvornik air traffic control. Nice to hear from you, but sorry we cannot comply as we have landing gear difficulties. Repeat, we cannot comply so we must continue on planned course. Have a nice day. Over."

The British pilot remained remarkably calm and brave. Grant let out a small sigh of relief, sensing that he was calling the Serbs' bluff. However, uncertainty lingered regarding their potential response. The Serbs had a history of acting unpredictably, often disregarding logic and common sense. Some believed they could act recklessly without facing consequences, shielded by an invisible barrier of impunity that war seemed to provide.

"Sea King Five Zero Two, you must comply," came the agitated reply over the radio. "Repeat, you must comply and land in Zvornik. You are in violation of the air space of the territory of Republika Srpska. Land now or face the consequences. I repeat, land NOW or face the consequences."

It was becoming a game of brinkmanship.

"Hello Zvornik air control, sorry old boy cannot comply for reasons previously stated, and according to my manual, Respublika Srpska is not a country; therefore, you have no legal jurisdiction over the air space. And can I point out that there are two NATO F-18 jets currently flying at ten thousand metres armed with some pretty decent air-to-surface missiles which have kindly offered to help us into Tuzla. Over."

The radio went dead; there was no response.

"Let's see what they do," said the Pilot. "Five more minutes over Serb-controlled territory."

The tense moments stretched into what felt like an eternity, but thankfully, there were no incidents. The Serbs eventually yielded, perhaps out of respect for strength or maybe out of fear of it. Once the helicopter safely landed in Tuzla and the casualties were unloaded, Grant approached the pilot and warmly shook his hand.

"I want to thank you," he said. "I think what you did saved some lives today and saved me from arrest and who knows what. Thanks again."

"You are most welcome. You've done a fantastic job there. What I did today was nothing compared to what you have been doing. So, thank you."

Grant smiled. "Can I ask you, was it true about the NATO jets?"

"No, total bollocks, old chap. But I find bullshit is useful sometimes; I think some journalists are prone to it too." He smiled.

A young woman hurried towards the helicopter. The blades had ceased spinning, and the surroundings had grown noticeably quieter.

"Grant, I am Rebecca, I am a producer from London sent to help you. Ed said we must get you to the hospital in Split as soon as possible to get that eye sorted."

"No, let's go straight to the edit suite. I have a very big story to get sorted first."

68

The story made headlines worldwide, with ATV branding it as a world exclusive, and rightfully so. The tragic toll from the playground incident was immense: fifty-six lives lost, including fourteen children, and seventy-three others injured. This report sparked discussions in homes and political arenas globally, leading to widespread outrage. Government hotlines were inundated with calls from the public demanding action. Finally, the world, including Europe, began to acknowledge the devastation unfolding nearby. Pressure mounted on the Serbs, focusing on Belgrade and its president, known to hold influence over events in Bosnia.

Emergency meetings were convened at the UN Security Council, the European Parliament, the Arab League, and NATO. News headlines and opinion pieces bombarded the Serbs, echoing the intensity of artillery fire. Politicians who had previously remained passive, asserting that the issue belonged solely to Yugoslavia, now joined the chorus condemning the Bosnian Serbs. Many called for intervention, or at the very least, an end to the arms embargo that had inflicted significant harm on the Bosnians.

The outcome was a ceasefire for Donji Zelenik. Although it was achieved through violence, it provided a break, allowing people to live safely, at least for the time being. The future remained uncertain, but that was a concern for another day. The ceasefire brought immense relief, not just to the crowded town's residents but also to Singleton. It was rare for him to see a story making a tangible impact, and it felt satisfying, but with caveats, many of them.

69

Ed Warren was a man of the corporate world, not a journalist. He grasped the importance of business and ratings, being well-versed in such matters. Referred to by Chuck Brown as one of the corporate copulators, Ed wasn't deeply familiar with the intricacies of sourcing and presenting news stories. However, he recognised the immense public interest generated by Grant Singleton's reports, which translated into valuable advertising revenue for the network. For Ed, Grant was indispensable, despite his unconventional approach, leading Ed to regard him as somewhat eccentric. Since Ed had recruited Grant, he basked in some of the reflected glory, and it was crucial to him to keep Grant happy. So any constructive criticism of Grant's reporting had to be gently managed.

"Hey man, great news about the eye."

Grant replied, "Yes, it wasn't a threat to the retina, and they managed to extract the piece of shrapnel. The right-hand side of my face is a bit sore but should be ok in a few days. No pieces to camera though for about a week."

"Look, man we think you should come out for a while. You've been there way too long. You are starting to go native."

"What do you mean?" said Grant.

"Well, maybe the balance is kinda missing a little because, and it is understandable, you are getting a little too subjective because of what you are experiencing. The executive editor took out a couple of your stand-ups in one or two reports because you were clearly emotional, and it came over a little like you were anti-Serb."

"I am anti-murder actually. I can't NOT get emotional when standing knee-deep in the blood of women and children. Who can prevent that? I challenge anyone not to."

Grant paused, took a deep breath, and reflected on what the bureau chief had said. Maybe he had a point. Maybe he was getting too involved. Maybe he needed a different approach. But what approach? He always reported what he saw. Maybe there was some innuendo or hidden direction that led his reports. But, overall, he only ever reported what had actually happened, what he had witnessed.

Warren continued. "Look, this is no big problem, my man; your reports are great, and we are in awe of what you have done. But we reckon that the Serb side to all this has been lacking a little, just a little. I know they are not easy and don't throw out the welcome mat for the media, and they are dangerous, deranged motherfuckers, but even deranged, dangerous motherfuckers have a side to a story that needs to be told. I know you are trying to get back to Donji Zelenik. That would be a great story because no journalist has been able to get in since you left, but can we try and do something with the Serbs in the meantime? The Foreign minister has been visiting the US, and he made the point about the lack of balance and the feeling in New York is that we need to do a couple of stories from their side. That way, we can't be accused of being biased. What do you think? I'll leave it with you. I'll email you the contact details of someone on the Serb side who the foreign minister said can facilitate a visit and interviews?"

Grant reflected. To himself, if he had to be honest, then maybe he could be accused of being a little biased. A lot if you were on the Serb side, of course. After all, he had never reported about the torture of the Serb he had witnessed in Donji Zelenik. He had weighed that up very carefully before deciding not to. He concluded that the swaying factor would be used to label Bosnians the same as the Serbs, that they were all as bad as one another. That would affect how the outside world viewed both sides. The fact that people react to brutality and loss is not the same as perpetrating it. So, Grant had left it out. He was being selective, not objective. But his conscience was clear. Overall, the Bosnians were quite clearly the victims of this conflict. Grant did not doubt that.

70

It took three attempts before the operator managed to link the Ham radio connection with Donji Zelenik.

"Tusam Tusam?" (Are you there?) He said. Finally, Grant recognised Fahrudin's voice. "Jasam," he said, (I am here.) Grant took over the handset.

"How are you, my friend?"

"Good, Mr Grant. Good. No bombard, so good, very good. Your friend here. Bye for now."

"Hi there, how's your eye?" It was Selma.

"All good, no danger and I just have to wear a bandage for a week or so and then I can come back."

"If they let you in. The Serbs are not happy with you. The playground story really hit them. It was horrible and bloody, but it finally got a ceasefire. It shows that if enough people die, then the world acts, at least if there is video evidence they can't ignore. I just wonder how many more Bosnians will have to die before the big powers take a grip. For now, we are enjoying the quiet."

"The Canadians left today and have been replaced by Dutch UN. They don't seem too friendly. They have started building a compound down the road in Potachari. There is a lot of barbed wire, concrete blocks and lookout towers. They are scared we are going to attack them or something. Also, your friend, the American major who had thirty-two bullets to kill us 'Muslim motherfuckers', left. In the end, he never shot anyone. He must have been disappointed."

They both laughed.

"Well, I am trying to get back. I am hoping to hitch a lift with a UN chopper, but they are saying no for now. Apparently, it was a condition laid down by the Serbs for agreeing to a ceasefire that no journalists would be allowed in. So far, it's holding, both the ban and the ceasefire. But I will get there. I promise. I miss you very much. I never realised I could miss someone so much. It has never happened before. Honest."

She laughed again. "Sure."

"Trust me," he said. "I am a journalist."

The line cackled, and Selma was lost for a moment. A voice sounded out, loud and menacing.

"You motherfucker, you come back, you die. Everyone dies. You last. Motherfucking liar and Muslim lover. I will be waiting for you."

The radio operator hurriedly started changing frequencies to lose the hostile voice. Fahrudin did the same on his set. After a few minutes, they linked up again to a new setting.

"Who was that?" asked Grant.

"That was Darko Zubic," answered Selma. "A really bad individual who used to be a neighbour. He's now a killer, and he's deranged. Ignore his threats. He was, and is a bully, only, now, a bully with a gun and a sort of cause."

It seemed that real anger never stopped. It always lingered, hidden in the shadows, and Darko Zubic, along with others like him, had plenty of it. It was like a slow-spreading wound.

"I must go now. I have to go and do a story with the Serbs about balance. Two sides to every conflict, my bureau chief said, and there must be perfectly good fucking reasons for killing women and children," he said sarcastically. "They love kids and animals and have been forced to commit atrocities because…what the fuck, I am not sure how I am going to do this. I don't want to, but I have no choice. This is going to be hard."

71

The once-pristine snow had now transformed into a muddy brown slush, revealing glimpses of green on the hillsides. Grant and Jake, his Australian cameraman, navigated their worn-out Ford up the hill. As they approached, they spotted a barrier guarded by a lookout post and sandbags, with a figure peering over one and an AK47 barrel visible. Passing through a Serb checkpoint was always an adventure, but the one on the road to Pale, the reputed capital of Republika Srpska, stood out. Encounters ranged from drunken soldiers demanding cigarettes to encountering the imposing figure of Vesna, known as the She Devil, who was to human kindness what Genghis Khan was to philanthropy.

As their car arrived, Mrs 'Unphilanthropic' stood guard. Vesna, towering at six feet four and weighing one hundred and twenty kilogrammes, positioned herself in front of the vehicle. She took pride in her role, which had injected excitement into her previously mundane life before the war. Unlike her days at the small Konzum supermarket in Pale, her current job granted her status, admiration, and authority. Clad in her standard blue overall uniform, she wore a holster with a pistol attached to her belt, embodying an unfeminine appearance. However, her face bore layers of makeup, resembling a Japanese Kabuki character with thick foundation, bright red lipstick, and light blue eye shadow, presenting a striking image.

She didn't acknowledge the team that had given her perfume during their last visit. Vesna thought it was just another day and another gift. If she wasn't fond of someone or was feeling grumpy, getting through the checkpoint could take as long as sitting in a traffic jam in California. Searching vehicles took up a lot of time, and body searches could feel intrusive. But Vesna didn't mind either, especially the latter.

The Aussie cameraman opened the window and leaned out.

"G'day Vesna, how's it going, darlin'?"

"I not your darling, I not your friend. Where is your mouth from?" Vesna understood the concept of an accent, but having grown up in a humble rural environment, her exposure to English was primarily through movies. To her, 'mouth' simply referred to speaking, and she found the Aussie talk somewhat excessive for her taste.

"Australia luv, hey, what are you doin' tonight? Wanna catch a movie or summin'?"

Vesna also didn't have a sense of humour. "No movies in Pale, only Belgrade. War here. We suffer."

Three UN-Danish Leopard tanks arrived at the barrier. A Serb soldier emerged from a dugout, appearing unsteady on his feet, possibly due to alcohol. He held a Kalashnikov rifle and displayed a confrontational demeanour.

"Wait there," he shouted at the squadron commander. A single intoxicated Serb, armed with an assault rifle, could hold authority over a four-person crew operating a 55-tonne tank equipped with two 7.62mm machine guns and a 120mm canon capable of piercing armour from a distance of four hundred metres. Grant couldn't help but notice the irony; it was a metaphor for UN's lack of effectiveness.

Jake took something out of his pocket. "Well, will this help the suffering?" he handed her a tube of lipstick. It was Fire and Ice by Revlon. Vesna may have been an uneducated country girl, but she knew Fire and Ice.

"Wow, for me? Many zanks. I have the perfume too?"

"Yeah, that's right, I brought it for you last time," explained the Aussie.

She was like a pig in the sty and waved the car through without checks. To Grant life could be entertaining if it wasn't so sad. Who would want to live with people like Vesna. If there were many like her then maybe it was better to live in a divided country.

The road to Pale was winding and lined with rows and rows of tall evergreen trees. As they climbed you could see the Serb positions on the hills overlooking the city. It was a shock to see how close they were and how easy it would be for snipers to find targets. They noticed the yellow-coloured Holiday Inn and Grant could see the bombed-out tenth floor. He shuddered and wondered if he had ever been in the cross hairs.

In the distance they could see a figure on a mule. As they got closer, they saw he was an old man. They stopped the car. The old man was wearing an old Serbian hat with the four Cs on. It was a traditional Chetnik hat. He had a long, bedraggled beard and hair that was matted. It obviously hadn't seen a bottle of shampoo in some time. The man was clearly drunk, almost to the point where he could hardly stay on the mule. The talk in Sarajevo was that the Serbs spent more time drinking than sniping and if ever alcohol stocks were to run out then the body count in Sarajevo would rise dramatically. This Chetnik was harmless. He smiled to reveal crooked, brown-stained teeth. A number had succumbed to dental abuse leaving more than a few gaps.

The elderly man mimicked the act smoking with two fingers pressed to his lips, grinning once more. Jake lowered the window and handed him two cigarettes.

"Hvala," (thank you) said the old man. He put one behind his ear and the other in his mouth. He lit up and kicked the mule into movement. 'If only all Chetniks were like him, then there would be no war,' Grant thought to himself.

It felt strange driving into Pale. There was the odd pockmark in some buildings maybe caused by bullets and shells at the beginning of the conflict but Pale looked like a normal small rural town getting on with life. They passed a small road with market stalls, women walked with shopping bags of vegetables, men sat at coffee bars. All fairly insignificant. At first glance there was nothing to suggest that this was the headquarters of the perpetraters of the biggest conflict Europe had seen since the Second World War. Nothing except the men in uniform, the armoured personnel carriers and military vehicles parked in nearly every street. The men drinking coffee had AK47s by their feet, pistols in holsters and some even wore hand grenades attached to webbing belts alongside pouches of ammunition magazines.

The cameraman parked beside a coffee bar near the municipal building they were heading to. Stepping out, they felt a tense atmosphere, reminiscent of an American Wild West saloon when the piano falls silent. Hostile gazes met them as they unloaded the camera gear and ascended the stone steps of the imposing, grimy-coloured building. Above, the Serbian flag fluttered on a tall pole in the gentle breeze.

As they entered the room, familiar looks greeted them, looks filled with hatred and distrust. Grant recognised these gazes all too well; they had encountered them many times before. It was a lesson in vigilance, a reminder to stay alert. Over time, he had become adept at observing body language and tone of voice, gaining a sense of what might transpire. He had also learned the art of defusing tense situations before they escalated, most of the time, at least.

“Bit edgy here, mate,” said the Aussie. “I reckon we shouldn’t hang around after dark, or we may get a bit of a rogering.”

Jake was the master of understatement.

Grant approached a large wooden desk, where an exceptionally attractive dark-haired woman sat in a blue camouflage uniform. She had high cheekbones, a broad face, coarse shoulder-length black hair, small eyes with downturned lashes, and dark skin. Her appearance struck Grant as more Asian than European, and he found himself wondering where he had seen those features before.

"Yes?" she said in perfect English.

"I am here to see General Pasic," responded Grant.

"One moment," and she picked up a phone.

It hit him. She looked Mongolian. That was it. She was a throwback to the days of Genghis Khan whose armies reached all the way to the Danube in the thirteenth century. He left death and destruction everywhere he went. He also left something else. 'The Mongols had obviously had R n R in Serbia,' he thought. Grant recalled an article discussing a genetic study suggesting that the infamous warrior, known for his brutal campaigns of rape and pillage, was also a prolific lover. Studies of Y-chromosome data indicated that as many as twenty million people could be descendants of his. This woman bore a resemblance to one of them.

Behind her desk loomed a large door, presumably leading to the General's office, alongside a wall adorned with the ubiquitous Serb portraits. These included the Bosnian Serb president, the Serb president, a figure with a black hat, a long grey beard, and a crucifix around his neck, whom Grant assumed to be the patriarch of the Orthodox Church, and the adored hero of Serb history, Prince Lazar.

"You can go in now," she said, pointing to a door behind her. "But you first. The cameraman must wait. The general prefers a quick talk before the interview."

Grant knocked on the imposing, three-metre-high door and was gestured to enter. The general rose from his seat and approached, extending his hand for a handshake. He was a diminutive, slightly overweight man with strikingly large green eyes. He wore fatigues devoid of any insignia indicating his rank.

"I am glad you could make it," he said. "Please sit."

'His English was halting but passable for an interview,' Grant thought. This was one of those meetings that Grant had experienced countless times: encounters with individuals who bore the stains of blood on their hands, yet politeness was required, even when one longed to label them for what they truly were: murderers. Journalism often straddles the line between diplomacy and objectivity. The General bore ultimate responsibility for the atrocities unfolding in Bosnia, the siege of Sarajevo, ethnic cleansing, the slaughter of innocent civilians, and the recent playground massacre Grant had witnessed first-hand. This was the same man who had advocated for shelling Sarajevo to the brink of madness. As a journalist, Grant had to suppress feelings of revulsion.

"Thank you for inviting us," he said with rigid formality.

"You are most welcome. I wanted to speak to you before the interview and set out a few things. I know with American prime TV, time is limited. What is the average duration of a story? About two to three minutes? So, I think it is difficult to convey feelings and situations in a short space of time and that means sometimes a story can be, how shall we say, distorted or lost. Wouldn't you agree?"

"Not exactly, General. I always try to get balance in a story and offer all sides of an argument."

"Ah yes," the general responded. "I saw your so-called balanced reports from Donji Zelenik."

He smiled. "Look, I think it better to be frank and honest, and I don't want to beat about the bush as you say, but you don't like us, do you?"

"Pardon?"

“Serbs, you don’t like us, Serbs? I think that is pretty obvious from your reporting. You seem to think that we are just plain killers. We got up one morning and decided to kill all Muslims and Croats.

“Not at all, General. That’s not accurate.”

“You know, you have just come to this country, but this country has been here for a long time, and many things happened here in the past. A rich history, you might say. But a history bathed in blood, and it didn’t start last year. It started long ago. But let’s forget the past, the Ottoman Turks, the Austro-Hungarians and the suffering of the Serb people. We only have to go back fifty years to see how and when the problems we have today really began.”

The general spoke passionately, delivering an impromptu history lesson. Grant realised he wasn’t the first journalist to receive such an education, nor would he be the last.

“Are you aware of this man?” He showed a photo of a man in a Nazi-style uniform.

Grant nodded in recognition. He knew that the portrait depicted Ante Pavelic, the Croatian leader of the pro-Nazi Ustasha movement, who had ruled over Croatia from 1941 to 1945.

He displayed another photo, this time of a poster depicting a German SS soldier standing alongside a Bosnian Muslim soldier adorned with SS insignia and a Croatian Ustasha flag. Boldly printed on the poster were the names of Ante Pavelic and Adolf Hitler.

“So, Nazi Croats and Muslims served in the German army, the Waffen SS mountain division. And these Ustasha and Muslim Nazis all killed Serbs. I am not going into all the details of what happened in the Jesenovac concentration camp, even though that was a horrific crime which has largely gone unpunished. But I want to address the matters of today."

He took a breath and opened an article from a newspaper. It was written in Serbo Croatian.

"This says, 'Entry forbidden to all Serbs, Jews, Gypsies and dogs.' The Ministry of the Interior, led by Andrija Artukovic, issued the following decree: 'All the Serbs and Jews residing in Zagreb, the Capital of Croatia, must leave the town within twelve hours. Any citizen found to have given them shelter will be immediately executed on the spot.

"This was a decree from the Second World War issued by the pro-Nazi Ustasha government. Here is a copy for you so you can check the accuracy of the translation. So, we are there with the Jews and dogs. That was from 1941. How good is your Serbo-Croatian?"

Grant shook his head.

The general pulled out another piece of paper. On it were the words Srbe na Vrbe.

"This is from today. Know what that means? It means hang Serbs from the willow tree, as they did in the Second World War. And you know what, when all this Croatian Independence movement started, pushed by the Croatian Diaspora, most of whom are the descendants of the pro-nazis that fled after the war, they sang it again in rallies in Zagreb, on Revolution square, in 1991. Srbe Na Vrbe. So, what do you think Serbs living in Croatia felt?"

The general paused and reached for the phone. Grant recognised the words 'rakia' and 'kava'. After hanging up, the general offered Grant a cigarette, which he accepted. It was Marlboro Red. Grant lit it, and a few minutes later, an attractive assistant entered the room carrying a tray. On the tray were two gold-rimmed shot glasses, a large decanter filled with white liquid, and two small cups of coffee. She placed the tray on the table and exited the room.

"Turkish coffee," he explained. "Some Turkish things were good. Givili," and raised his glass. Grant followed suit, but he felt uneasy. The general extinguished his cigarette, gulped down the rakia in one swift motion, and encouraged Grant to do the same before refilling their glasses.

"The point I am trying to make to you," he continued, "Is that nothing is black and white. Serbs felt threatened, and what we are doing is defence. Many were scared that what happened fifty years ago was going to repeat. The bottom line is that this is all about PR, and the Serbs don't have good PR. Jews have good PR, and so too do the Croats and Muslims. People like you call them victims. No one remembers what the Nazi Croats or Muslims did in the Second World War. About mass executions of Serbs at a place called Karitska. The catholic church, which is now, this day, so critical of alleged atrocities, was in total support of the Nazi Croats. Who has held any of these to account? Pavelic is still a hero. Ustasha, who fled in 1945, still comes back to Croatia on holiday every year to swim in the Adriatic and walk over the graves of their Serb victims. Where is the justice? Tell me, where is it?"

His face flushed with realisation. He halted the diatribe and reached for another cigarette, inhaling deeply as he took a moment to regain his composure.

"But General, the past doesn't excuse what is happening today. Innocent civilians are being killed daily. Atrocities are being committed, there is widespread ethnic cleansing from Serb controlled territory and...."

He couldn't finish the sentence. The general interrupted his face now puce, the eyes almost bulging.

"Innocent Serbs are being killed as well. Many. Do you report that? And ethnic cleansing? The Croats started that, but we Serbs didn't. If people want to leave, they can, but if they want, they can stay. I don't have a problem with that".

At this moment, Grant came to the realisation that arguing was futile. The general's perspective seemed to veer dangerously close to propaganda and appeared unmovable. 'Fanatic' wasn't an unfair description. A sense of nausea churned in Grant's stomach, and though he wanted to vocalise his discomfort, he found himself unable to do so. He drew a parallel with Goebbels, the mastermind of Nazi propaganda, who was convincing and equally fanatical. Peering into the general's eyes, Grant didn't see a man guided by reason and honesty; instead, he saw a killer. He resolved to conduct the interview on camera and depart as swiftly as possible. Sometimes balance could be difficult to stomach.

72

Chuck Brown sat in the dining room nursing his broken ribs and an opinion. He waved Grant over. "I hear you ventured over to the heart of darkness today to be 're-educated'?"

Grant's face contorted into a grimace. It was an answer enough.

"I know, man. They are something. What do the Chinese call their re-education camps? Ah yes, vocational training. Brain fucking is what I call it. If the Serbs were a bank, they would be morally bankrupt, and their humanity account would be in deficit. They are living in the fourteenth century and are using everything bad that has happened to them in the last five hundred years as a justification for what they are doing now and how they are doing it. It really fucking annoys me. Imagine if a couple of fucking Inca descendants rocked up in Madrid and started killing Spaniards in revenge for what they did in South America during the Inquisition! Give me a fucking break."

He paused and changed tack, "But I can help your pain. Dr Brown can give you partial healing."

He bent down and opened a bag. First, he brought out a bottle of white firewater, sliva. Then, a bottle of red wine.

"Vranac from Montenegro, the best red you'll find in these parts," explained Brown and then pulled out a plastic bag filled with clumps of fine green leaves. He imitated a drum roll.

"Lebanese gold," he said proudly. "Not the Albanian schwag shit that we normally smoke. This is pure quality. I have not been wasting my time while you have been away. Don't ask how I got these goodies or how much. A journalist has to protect his sources. But a visit to the tenth floor is in order after gruel, and then you can fill me in on life and love and what it's like to be a journalist who is hotter than molten lava."

Grant smiled. "It's a date big boy." He looked up and saw a figure at the door waving. It was Hassan Mesic, Selma's brother. "But first, I have to go and see someone. Can I borrow the sliva?"

Brown complied, and Singleton approached Hassan, shaking his hand and gesturing for him to join him in a corner of the lobby. Singleton retrieved two glasses and poured alcohol into them. From his bag, he retrieved a letter and handed it to Hassan. It was from Selma.

"Thank you," said Hassan. "And thank you on behalf of my people for your brave reporting in my hometown. You really made a difference. We owe you a debt of gratitude. How is my brother, sister, and father?"

“Your father seems not to have recovered from the death of your mother and what is happening. He is seeking solace in God. Your sister, of course, is doing a wonderful job, and your brother is a strong and brave fighter. He has helped save the town.”

“Wow, my little brother is turning out to be a hero. Who’d have thought?”

“Your sister is worried about him. She says he has changed a lot, and he will not be what you remember. There is a hardness about him that Selma finds difficult. War has changed him.”

Hassan took a breath, “You mean that war has made him a killer, is that it?”

Grant didn’t reply, but he didn’t say no.

“It’s strange how life turns out and how we turn out in life, isn’t it? Mehmet was always the weak one in the family, the studious one. I was the sportsman and the fighter. Selma was born about a minute before Mehmet. He came out smaller and weaker. It was Selma who always looked out for him, not the other way round. If he ever got picked on it was Selma who stepped in and kicked their asses. She was his backbone and support. Not in a million years could you imagine that Mehmet would become a fighter. That’s like fiction.”

“What do they say the first casualty of war is? The truth. Then, the second must be dignity. You lose your dignity, and once you lose that, you are capable of anything. My brother is doing what he has to survive. There are no rules, as you must surely know by now. And judgement by people sitting in the safety of European capitals is unfair. People are not the same, but war can make them the same, if that makes sense. Every man must believe he is doing the right thing. Sometimes wrongs become rights, fighting for what is good for him, his family, and his country. What do you fight for, Grant? Justice? What is justice, and whose justice is it?”

Truly, Grant couldn't answer that simply. He said, "I just find it amazing how people, who are so seemingly alike, same humour, same language, relatively well educated, can kill each other. How friendly neighbours have become deadly enemies. It's really beyond me," said Grant.

"This is the Balkans. There is no sensible explanation. It's just the way we are. We live life passionately, and we kill passionately, too. In our case, we didn't want to but if we had turned the other cheek, pretty soon, there would be no face left. As I said, nothing makes sense, not even to us who live here and understand better than most. I'll give you an example. One of the most famous Yugoslav poets was Ivan Goran Kovacic. He fought against the Fascists in the Second World War and wrote what is perhaps one of the most famous poems, Jama, the pit. It was a message against torture and war crimes. It stands the test of time. But my point is that he was killed by Serbs who were also fighting Fascists. It seems that in war, we get the red mist, as you call it, and the need to kill overtakes the need for humanity."

He downed his sliva and stood up. "I'm afraid I have to go. Lots to do. We will meet again. And again, my thanks."

Chuck Brown awaited with the Montenegrin wine, accompanied by the usual motley crew: Bunty BBC, Spit the Frog, the ever-traumatic Tanya, and the prophet of doom, Ron O'Sullivan.

"Ron says it's all going down the toilet, so I reckon we'd better drink as much as we can before that happens," said The American. "To Bullshit and diplomacy and the human cost that incurs. Cheers." They raised their glasses.

Amelia Degusta was passing. "Actually, guys, my sources tell me there will be an intervention. Governments have been moved by our stories. I have had feedback from the White House."

"They must like fiction if they are reading your stuff. But great first-person piece INSIDE Donji Zelenik. When did you get back?"

Her face reddened. "I never said I went there. I said this is what it is like. There is a fucking difference, you moron. And the US cares."

The group burst out laughing.

"Like fuck, the US cares." Responded Brown. "You don't have to go back far in history to know that is a pile of big steaming BS. The USA, the great moral father of the world, which decides what is good and bad. It doesn't help people because it wants to help people; it helps people to protect its interests. Look at the 1991 Gulf War. Peace came with a no-fly deal to stop Saddam from flying his fighter jets. But that deal didn't include the helicopter gunships. And after our smart motherfucker president encouraged the Kurds, Shiites, and democracy-seeking Sunnis to rise up and take destiny into their own hands, what happened? Well, they were slaughtered, and what did the US do? Fuck All. They stood and watched and then issued strongly worded press releases condemning the situation. So do me a favour and get real."

The Vranac had gone and so had Degusta.

Grant got up and took the bag of Lebanese Gold. "Gentlemen, I think this committee should be reconvened on the tenth floor so we can deal with any other pressing issues of the day. Onwards and upwards."

73

The knocking was loud and persistent, breaking the peace of the late hour. It was ten o'clock at night, an unusual time for visitors. Mrs Ibrahimovic hesitated behind the door, uncertain of the unexpected caller's identity.

"Who is it?" She asked. "Nasser," came the reply, "from the Mosque. I am sorry to trouble you, but I need to see effendi Mohammed. It's important." She opened the door, and the man looked upset and troubled. "Please. I need to see him."

She showed him to the sitting room, and she went upstairs towards Mohammed's room. "Mohammed, there is a Nasser here to see you. He seems desperate and says it's important."

She heard a scraping sound from behind the door. "What's that sound?" She asked. "Nothing" came the reply. "Just moving my bed a little. I'll be straight out."

"Make it quick, please. It's late, and I want to lock up before going to bed. Come now."

Mohammed stepped out, closing the door firmly behind him. Unseen by Mrs Ibrahimovic, the large wardrobe had been shifted away from the wall. Little did she know, Munja had been exploring his hidden stash, keeping secrets concealed within.

He walked into the sitting room. "Nasser, my friend, what is it?"

"They want to take my son to serve on the front line in Otac. He is only Seventeen, and you know how dangerous that place is. He's not a soldier. Can you do anything?"

"Calm down, my friend, and let us see what can be done. Have faith in God and me." And he closed the door.

Mrs Ibrahimovic, a former teaching assistant, had honed her ability to observe people's behaviour, particularly children. However, she found that understanding adults posed a greater challenge due to their complexity. There was something about how he had come out of the room, shutting the door so tightly that it made her think, 'Was he trying to hide something?' As she sat in the kitchen, troubling thoughts consumed her. His frequent late returns from the mosque, where he claimed to discuss the Koran, his prolonged stays in his room, and his occasional cold demeanour and conversations with her weighed heavily on her mind. Despite his responsibilities in security work, she couldn't shake the feeling that there was something peculiar about him, especially after overhearing women gossiping about his supposed cruelty. Something didn't feel right to her. Maybe it was this investigation that was going on. This Hassan Mesic asking difficult, invasive questions. What was happening? She was confused. But then she focused on his room. What was that noise? It didn't sound like the bed. What was it?

She entered the hallway and caught snippets of the conversation between Mohammed and Nasser. Then she climbed the stairs to her son's room. Upon opening the door, she noticed the large wardrobe shifted away from the wall and a poster lying on the bed. Approaching the wardrobe, she spotted an opening in the wall. Drawing nearer, the elderly woman spotted the book 'Diary of Mihajlovic' written in Cyrillic script. All Yugoslavs had been educated in the Latin and Cyrillic alphabets. She knew what the words were. Then she noticed the radio equipment accompanied by a book filled with unfamiliar letters and symbols, along with a gun. Retrieving the diary, she settled onto the bed and flipped open the cover. Inside was the inscription: 'To my beloved nephew Dragan Mihajlovic, Once a Serb always a Serb.' She shuddered. He knew. He knew he wasn't her son; he knew he wasn't a Muslim. He knew the history. How? How did he come by this diary? Who had given it to him? And why did he keep it a secret that he knew? But what was the radio equipment for? Why was it hidden? Questions raced through her mind. Questions but no answers, only confusion. The door was ajar, and she heard Mohammed say goodnight to Nasser.

"Don't worry, I will do what I can."

She hurriedly returned the book to its place and swiftly left the room. She walked down the corridor to her room just as Ibrahimovic reached the top stair. He heard her door close quietly. His concern started to grow. Quickly, he went into his bedroom. Everything seemed in place. He went to the small carpet close to the wardrobe. He lifted it and, in the powder, he saw several footmarks. They were small footmarks. He knew that they were from the old woman. He sat down on the bed and sighed. He knew now what he had to do, and quickly. Eid was two days away, time was of the essence.

74

Her body was sprawled across the sitting room floor, her legs and arms splayed out, and her eyes wide open as if she had been in shock. It seemed as if she had witnessed something terrifying. Police and soldiers were mingling in the entrance area when Hassan arrived. A subordinate approached him.

"It looks like she has been strangled," the policeman said.

Hassan entered the room and surveyed the scene. There were signs of a disturbance. A chair lay on its side, a table was overturned, and broken pieces of crockery littered the floor. His gaze fell on the old lady, he recognised her as Mrs Ibrahimovic. Nearby, the telephone hung off its cradle, and beside her right hand rested a photograph of Mohammed Ibrahimovic as a young boy, approximately seven years old. The skin around her neck showed discolouration, appearing blue-black in hue. At first glance, it seemed that his assistant's assessment was accurate.

"There are signs of a break-in. A kitchen window is broken, and it seems things have been taken from the cabinet. At first guess this seems like a robbery. There have been a number in the area in the past few weeks. As people get desperate, they resort more to theft and it's well known that we don't have the resources to track them and certainly not stop them. We have sent word to her son. He will be able to fill in some of the blanks.

"Out of my way." Hassan recognised the voice of Mohammed Ibrahimovic. He hurried into the sitting room, where he encountered the sight of the lifeless body. He just stood and stared for what felt like an endless moment before he succumbed to overwhelming emotions, collapsing in despair. In that moment, the stern Inquisitor was transformed into a vulnerable, grieving child.

"Mama," he cried. "Mama," and the crying got louder. He stooped down and carefully lifted her body. Although it disturbed the crime scene, no one voiced any objections. He embraced her tightly, tears streaming down his face as he wept inconsolably. He kissed her pallid skin and cradled the lifeless body in his lap. Over and over again he sobbed, 'mama.' Onlookers observed the heartfelt sorrow of a devoted son. Hassan reproached himself for thinking Ibrahimovic could be Munja. He gently placed a hand on the man's shoulder to offer comfort and strength.

"I am so, so sorry," Hassan said. "This is just too terrible. My humblest condolences. We will do our best to find out who is responsible. I don't want to interrupt your grieving, but we need to know what happened. We think the motive was robbery and that your mother disturbed whoever it was, but we need to know what was taken so it can help us in our investigation."

Ibrahimovic carefully placed the body down, then stood and approached a large sideboard. He opened a drawer and began searching towards the back.

"It's missing," he said. "The valuables box is not there."

"Are you sure? Could it be somewhere else?"

"No, it is always kept there," he replied.

"What was in it?"

"Money, mostly Deutschmarks and her jewellery, a ring and a necklace given to her by her mother, my grandmother. I think there may have been a bracelet as well, but I'm not sure. I hadn't seen inside for a long time, so I can't be positive. And yes, all the documentation."

"Documentation meaning marriage, birth and death certificates and that sort of thing?"

"Yes, I think so," replied Ibrahimovic.

"Had you noticed anyone suspicious hanging around the house in the last days or weeks, anything that looked out of the ordinary? And what about someone who may have wanted to hurt you because of your position and what you do?"

It wasn't beyond possibility that this could have been revenge dressed up as a robbery by someone wanting payback. Ibrahimovic, the Inquisitor, was well known for his cruelty. Nothing could be ruled out.

Ibrahimovic shook his head.

"When you get a chance, could you make a list of items that are missing together with a description or, better still, any photos you may have that can help us."

"Death is estimated at around 8:00 a.m. Can I ask where you were and when did you last see your mother?"

Ibrahimovic shot off a look that seemed to say, 'insult'.

"What, you suspect me of killing my own mother?"

"Not at all," replied Hassan. "It just helps us in pinning down a little more precisely when she died before we can get an accurate pathology report."

Ibrahimovic's anger subsided.

"This morning about seven. We had breakfast together. She said she was going to the market and then was going to have coffee with some ladies from the mosque."

"And you?"

"I was at the Mosque in private prayer. These are troubled times, and I was seeking direction from Allah. It is only he who can guide us."

"Was there anyone with you?"

"Nobody, I prefer the solitude of prayer in the morning before embarking on my day. It is a time for a man to be alone with his God."

Hassan gave an inward hmm. He expressed gratitude to Ibrahimovic and assured him of regular updates. Exiting through the kitchen door into the rear courtyard, he observed the towering walls enclosing the area. Any intruder would need considerable agility to breach them. Surveying the ground beneath the window, he noted a mix of mud and snow, devoid of footprints. Directly beneath the shattered window lay a heap of glass. Returning to the kitchen, he spotted only a few glass fragments on the sink's surface. Despite his determination to pursue the investigation, Hassan acknowledged the grim reality: the absence of a fully equipped forensics department drastically reduced the chances of apprehending the murderer. The destruction of the sole DNA testing laboratory and the exodus of most scientists from Sarajevo compounded the challenge.

A policeman walked in carrying a small metal box and handed it to Hassan.

"That's the box," commented Ibrahimovic. "All the items were in there."

"Did you find anything other than this?" Hassan asked the officer. He shook his head.

"No papers, certificates?"

"No, nothing, Sir, it was behind the wall leading to that small mosque. There are no windows that look over that area. I have knocked on doors, and no one heard or saw anything."

Ibrahimovic walked over to Hassan. "I know you will need to talk to me more, but now I need a little time to myself. We can talk at length later. I just need a few hours for reflection and contemplation. Thank you."

He moved to the sideboard and retrieved a small prayer mat. Heading to the far corner, he laid it out and commenced his prayer, reciting the Quran fluently in Arabic. Some officers also joined, paying their respects to the devout Muslim's loss in a solemn moment.

75

Two hundred kilometres away, ex-police detective Arif and two fighters lay flat on their stomachs, gazing at the neglected graveyard ahead. It was tangled with overgrowth, deserted by the villagers who had escaped the Serb advance. Klucna sat in a desolate stretch, less than a hundred metres from Serb territory, serving as a passage for attacks and reconnaissance missions. The local commander had warned against venturing there without a clear purpose, emphasising its perilous nature.

Arif had a clear purpose. He followed his intuition, the kind that an experienced detective would get. He'd had them before. Mostly they were right. In his previous life he had learned that a strong hunch should never be ignored.

After dawn broke, dark clouds loomed overhead, accompanied by a touch of morning mist. A light dusting of snow veiled the graves, creating a wintry scene reminiscent of a winter photo. All it needed was some holly and mistletoe beside a pile of neatly wrapped presents and it could have made the cover of a Christmas card. They were startled by a clump of snow falling from a tree. It dropped to the ground with a heavy thump. The sound seemed to be amplified. All three held their breath and strained their ears wondering if the Serbs had been alerted by the sound. They hadn't, but it didn't lessen the sense of apprehension. They continued to lay without movement, with only the occasional whisper of communication. It didn't take long lying on the frozen ground before the chill began to permeate their bodies. But the time to move had to be right.

Arif observed a solitary red flower resting against a gravestone, a touching symbol of someone's enduring affection. Despite the dangers, at least one person deemed it worthwhile to honour a loved one's memory. His attention then shifted to movement amidst the bushes beyond the graveyard. A uniformed figure emerged, accompanied by two others. Arif quickly gestured to his companions, and together they minimised their presence, their white ponchos aiding their camouflage. With bated breath, they aimed their weapons. The Serbs, as silent as the surrounding graves, continued on, oblivious to the hidden figures nearby unaware of how close they had come to death.

Arif waited a few minutes to make sure they had gone. "OK, let's move," he whispered, "Keep low, move fast, check every grave. Signal if you find anything."

They rose to their feet, their bodies hunched as they advanced. Arif had split the cemetery into three sections. It wasn't a big burial ground but many of the gravestones were covered by snow. They would need to be wiped. If the Serbs came back they would see that, if they were observant.

They moved swiftly and smoothly, sometimes crawling, then rising to their knees to brush off the snow and read the inscriptions before moving forward to the next grave. They went from grave to grave. No signal, no recognition. Hope began to fade. Arif moved to the far end of the graveyard. It took him to within seventy five metres of the Serb positions. He could hear a radio playing in the distance. The graveyard was open ground. If they were spotted, they would be easy targets.

He rose to his knees and brushed off the snow, a relieved smile lighting up his face. This was it, exactly what he had been searching for. The inscription, though in Arabic, displayed the deceased's name in Latin script: Alia Ibrahimovic, born in Klucna in 1913 and passed away in 1940. Beside the main headstone, there stood a smaller one. On an impulse Arif wiped the snow away. He smiled again. This may be the answer. He signalled to the other two to head back. Their mission had been completed. He may have found the key to revealing who Munja was. He needed to get back to Sarajevo as soon as possible.

76

In the dimly lit Pale Municipal Building, thick cigarette smoke filled the air, reminiscent of a firefighter's drill. General Moimocjelo Pasic had gathered his top commanders from across the territory, spanning from the western Krajina region to the northern sector along the Sava River and extending southwards near Mostar and eastwards near Donji Zelenik. Among them was Darko Zubic, newly emboldened after challenging the motives and tactics of his senior officers. Pasic was keenly aware of Zubic's growing discontent, as well as that of the younger men who admired him. He understood the need to address their concerns, and today he intended to do just that.

"Gentlemen," started Pasic "Thank you for coming. And thank you for your patience. I know many of you have become a little confused with our sense of direction and our goals. Some of you may have even thought that those goals had changed, our ideals had dissipated, and we were ready to abandon our ultimate aim of achieving Greater Serbia."

By a slow sweep of their faces, he could see that many had, indeed, started to believe this.

"Well, today, I can tell you that this is not the case. These goals and ideals are the very oxygen which our nation breathes. You are here today to learn how these aims will be achieved and soon."

There were murmurs of agreement, and a tone of excitement was raised. The general continued.

"In two days, it will be Eid, the Balija's big celebration. It will also be our big celebration, of a different kind. We will consolidate and extend our western, southern, and northern borders, and we will take the last piece in the jigsaw puzzle, Donji Zelenik, the final obstacle to making the entire eastern Bosnia connect Republika Srpska fully to Serbia proper."

"Plans are in place, and it will coincide with the annihilation of the entire Muslim military and political hierarchy in one go. I cannot tell you more for security reasons. But rest assured, all of this is the result of many months of planning. The politicians are on board, and we know that the international community, especially the Americans, will not act. They cannot save the Muslims. No one can. Each of you will have specific plans and objectives. These are all contained in the documents you are now being handed. The troop build-up will begin tonight during the hours of darkness. We need to keep this secret until the last possible moment. Go back now to your units and prepare. In two days, we attack. For God and Serbia."

"For God and Serbia," the gathering repeated. The room emptied. The commanders were elated.

Pasic called Darko Zubic back.

"A word, if I may," he said.

"Yes, sir"

"The east around Donji Zelenik has been a thorn in our side for a long time and the Balija there have hurt us greatly. They have killed many Serbs. They need to learn a lesson and to learn that they are not welcome any longer in eastern Bosnia. After their defeat, there will be talks, negotiations involving foreign governments about the so-called rights of these Muslims. But we need to ensure that these rights to return are not taken up. And I am relying on you to achieve that. You need to show the Muslims why it's in their best interests to stay out of Serb sovereign territory, and you need to be strong. This is no time for weakness. It is up to you how you achieve this, but the one thing I will say is that a dead body has no rights."

Zubic nodded. He knew what that meant; it was clear what he had to do, and he knew he was being given carte blanche to do it.

77

Seven thousand kilometres away and twelve hours later, five men gathered in a dimly lit conference room on the highest floor of the Pentagon building in Arlington, Virginia. Known among insiders as the 'Supreme Court', this room was where crucial and sometimes irreversible decisions were made. Throughout its history, it had been the epicentre of choices that bolstered wars, revolutions, dictatorships, covert operations, and even assassinations. Where orders for nefarious activities had been unleashed and where a blind eye was turned to the brutal activities of despots and war criminals as long as they served US interests.

Civil rights groups criticised them as cruel and contrary to the basic principles human rights. However, the individuals in this gathering belonged to a powerful unit responsible for determining which rights were deemed acceptable and which were not. Each person had in front of them a classified document labelled Top Secret, along with a folder containing black and white photographs. Positioned at the front of the room was a large white projector screen. All attendees held high-ranking positions within the US armed forces, representing the Army, Marines, Navy, and Air Force. Adorning their chests were colourful rows of decorations earned from various conflicts they had participated in, symbolising their dedication to duty. These were patriotic Americans committed to safeguarding America's interests, regardless of the sacrifices involved.

Towards the rear of the room stood a man dressed in ordinary clothes: a neat grey suit, a blue tie, and well-shined shoes. On his lapel, he wore a badge with the American Stars and Stripes flag. He was CIA. His name was Edward Manners. The irony of his name wasn't lost on those present. Despite being called 'Manners', his demeanour lacked any such niceties. He was among the most experienced CIA operatives, known for his directness and having no time for small talk, which he referred to as 'pussy-footing around'. He was originally an operative who spent time in countries like Cuba, Congo, Iran, and Lebanon. Places where so-called 'un-American' activities were happening. He stood at the forefront of American operations, often straying from conventional methods. In the complex realm he operated in, Manners never questioned the unconventional approach. Aware of the unspoken rules of espionage and counterintelligence, he understood that sometimes the righteous path required dubious actions. To Manners and his comrades, adorned with various accolades, the USA represented the beacon of righteousness. His initiation occurred in Latin America, where he and the CIA played a pivotal role in a significant event, the support of General Augusto Pinochet's coup against the socialist Chilean president Salvador Allende on September 11, 1973. It was the beginning of a military dictatorship. Manners learned then that human rights of other countries didn't count, American ones did.

The Marine general started speaking first. He called up the first image on the large screen.

"So, this is the first satellite image taken this morning at 0800 Bosnian time. It shows several tanks and military vehicles near a farm about twenty-five kilometres north of a place called Donji Zelenik. This is the corresponding photo taken yesterday showing none of those vehicles.

"These are a series of photos showing the area to the east of Donji Zelenik close to the Bajna Basta Dam taken a little before dawn. Those are tanks moving across the bridge from Serbia into Bosnia. We estimate that at least four squadrons have moved in over the last twenty-four hours. That's sixteen Russian-built T72s."

He pressed the remote, and a series of black and white photos appeared on the screen. The images showed trucks and soldiers.

The general continued. "In addition, AWACS surveillance footage shows significant Serb troop build-ups in the east, west, north and south. Gentlemen, we haven't seen anything like this for a long while. It suggests a major offensive, and that is totally at odds with what the Serb political leadership has been saying and is still saying to the UN as of yesterday."

The Air Force general joined in. “There is also intel about more artillery being moved into position around the eastern part. They’ve tried to disguise it, but we can see quite clearly in this photo 155mm artillery guns being moved from Pale to Bratunac. It looks as if they are going to attempt to take the entire eastern part.”

The brass all nodded.

“This is dynamite intel,” said the Navy admiral. “There are fifty thousand plus Muslims crammed into Donji Zelenik. Any major offensive will result in massive loss of civilian life. That will be unavoidable. We saw what happened when the playground massacre happened. There was massive international condemnation, and pressure was put on the Serbs to agree to the current ceasefire. If this offensive happens, and it looks pretty certain it will, then there will be moves from many governments for outside intervention. And, of course, that would be heavily reliant on us. Morally, however, we need to inform the Bosnian government what is happening so they can mitigate the offensive as much as possible, which probably won’t be enough to save the town.”

Manners got to his feet and walked to the front of the room in front of the slide screen.

“Morally, we need to do fuck all,” he said. “This fight has nothing to do with us. Publicly the administration is supporting the Bosnian government, but privately, we just want this whole fuck fest to be gone. This is Yugoslavs killing Yugoslavs. Muslim Yugoslavs. They should sort it out themselves. Cleansing is happening on both sides; water finds its own level. The feeling is that if we enter this war, then it will be a clusterfuck, and we will be dragged into a long, drawn-out conflict that will be time-consuming and expensive. The bottom line is we really don’t give a flying fuck about eastern Bosnia, and as soon as the Muslims realise that, they can get around a table and talk real peace.”

Senior officers were not used to that kind of tone being aimed at them.

"So, what you are saying is, we pretend we haven't seen these satellite images and allow eastern Bosnia to fall?" asked the Marine general.

"That's exactly what I am saying; it's what this administration is saying. This intel will never reach the Bosnian government. The Serbs will clean up, and two or three days later, after the mopping up has finished, we jump in and say, 'Hey guys, you'd better talk peace or else'. Job fucking done, back to the bar for a beer and a burger. Condemnation doesn't cost American lives, but intervention does. No one wants that for a bunch of ex-commies who can't sort their shit out."

The air force General, who was head of the military intelligence department, shook his head.

"We can't do that. There are thousands of civilians who will be killed. We can't sit back and watch that happen without trying to do something."

Manners appeared angry. "That's exactly what we are going to do. Remain blind and schtum. Quiet and ignorant. These pictures and intel remain classified. Highly classified. And that comes from the very top. Yes, civilians will be killed. That will be unfortunate, but as you gentlemen all know from your long, distinguished careers, in any conflict, there is always collateral damage. Which one of you has not given an order that has directly or indirectly cost civilian lives? Dead civvies is sad, but it's a fact. That's always going to happen in war. Now we need to move on and talk about Iraq and chemicals and that asshole Saddam Hussein. He's a much bigger problem to us than the goddamn Serbs."

78

Hassan knocked twice on the door, the second time with more force. He had been informed that the elderly occupant was partially deaf and rather irritable. As he prepared to knock for the third time, the door creaked open slightly. A face appeared in the gap, a vision of an old man with thick, pebble-rimmed glasses and tufts of nasal hair.

“What is it?” he half shouted. “Who are you? What do you want?”

“Mr Zivanic, I am Hassan Mesic from the Bosnian army. I need to ask you some questions. Can I come in? It’s important.”

The old man widened the door and gestured for Hassan to enter. Leading him through to the kitchen, he revealed a fresh pot of Turkish coffee on the table alongside a plate of half-eaten burek.

“Do you live alone?” Hassan asked. “What?” shouted the old man.

“Do you live alone?”

“Yes, my wife died twenty years ago. What do you want?”

“You were principal of the Sarajevo Gimnasia School from the 1940s to the 1960s, weren’t you?”

“Yes, that is correct. It was the best school in the city. Excellent teaching staff and fine curriculum. I was very honoured to hold that position. We sent many fine young people on their way with an excellent education.”

“Do you remember a teaching assistant by the name of Nina Ibrahimovic?” Hassan asked.

The man replied immediately, “Yes, of course. She was excellent, had fine knowledge and was well-liked by children and staff.”

Hassan marvelled at the old man’s memory.

He continued, "She came to us in the middle part of the forties, just before the war ended. Her husband had died, I'm not sure how, I presumed, during fighting or bombings, but she had a son, and they were both devout Muslims."

Hassan told him the basic details of how she'd been murdered, and the old man looked stunned.

"Who on earth would want to kill her? She was such a lovely, gentle person."

"We are investigating her death and looking to see if there are any clues in her background. We think she may have been killed after a bungled robbery, but we are not sure, and we have to probe every possibility. Do you know of anyone who may have wanted to harm her from the past?"

The teacher shook his head. "Not at all. She was a person who exuded goodness. She always worked with children. First, as a teacher, and then I seem to remember she was a matron in an orphanage. I think in Groznik. Then she came to Sarajevo. She came with excellent references. Said she wanted to give something to those who had been denied by fate and circumstances."

Hassan sat up straight. "An orphanage?" he asked. The old man nodded. "How old was the son?" "I think he was about seven," the man replied. "He started in the elementary school which was the feeder for the gimnasia. I remember him well. He easily passed the exams for my school and was an excellent pupil. Mohammed, I think, was his name. Very sharp. Could quote passages of the Koran at a very young age."

"So, you never met the father?"

"No, as I understand it, he died shortly after Mohammed's birth. A real tragedy for a boy to be brought up without a father. Nina only worked part-time for a few years. She devoted herself to that boy. She said he was home-schooled for the first few years. He must be devastated. Poor man. Who on earth could kill such a nice person? This whole world is changing, and not for the better. Years ago, you would never have murders. That was unheard of. Such a shame."

Hassan stood up and offered his hand to the old principle. "Thank you, Sir, you have been a great help. I must go now. Allah Immanet."

As the door closed behind him, Hassan felt a lingering wave of excitement. He began to discern a connection between Mohammed Ibrahimovic and Groznik, the absence of death and marriage certificates, and a history that appeared to commence after Nina Ibrahimovic's arrival in Sarajevo around 1945. Now, he had unearthed a connection predating that period, notably involving an orphanage. Piece by piece, the puzzle was coming together, offering glimpses of clarity. Hassan instructed one of his men to return to headquarters and contact Arif. He wanted Arif to investigate the orphanage in Groznik.

On his way back to command, Hassan made a diversion to the Gazi Husrev-Beg Mosque to seek out Mohammed Ibrahimovic. He had a few matters to clarify. As he entered, he observed the unusual tranquilly, no shelling, no gunfire. Though out of the ordinary, it wasn't entirely abnormal in these tumultuous times. Hassan brushed off the thought and proceeded inside, scanning the Musallah, the prayer area. It wasn't prayer time, yet a devout few were engaged in prayer and Quranic recitation. Suddenly, a door opened, and the imam emerged, holding a model of the medina.

"Hello, imam," said Hassan. "I am looking for Mohammed Ibrahimovic. Has he been here?"

"He was here earlier. It is a difficult time for him, of course. He came to pray and to give us this wonderful model of the Medina ready for Eid prayers tomorrow. Even in this time of grief and devastating loss he is thinking of others. He is truly one of Allah's people."

The imam carefully positioned the model of Masjid al-Haram in Mecca on a small table at the bottom of the pulpit steps. It appeared to be heavy, and he struggled slightly with it. Hassan stepped forward to assist him in placing it properly. With the model in place, the imam began to pray. Hassan quietly exited the mosque. He had to locate Ibrahimovic; there were pressing questions that needed answers.

79

Mohammed Ibrahimovic grew increasingly impatient. He longed for tomorrow to arrive, eager for the decisive blow to be dealt to the Bosnian leadership. He yearned to shed the Muslim identity he had worn for so long and embrace his true self, Dragan Mihajlovic. He craved, or rather, needed, to live as a true Serb. Though he would maintain his religious beliefs, his devotion would now be directed towards the orthodox church instead of Islam. The moment was drawing near, yet this did little to assuage his growing discomfort and nervousness. Suspicion was mounting, with too many questions being asked, particularly by Hassan Mesic. Mohammed wondered how much Mesic knew and how much he had pieced together. He concluded that it wasn't enough, or else Munja wouldn't be walking free. Nevertheless, Mohammed knew he had to remain vigilant, tread carefully, and be ever watchful.

He continued driving, fully aware that if he were discovered at this juncture, the entire plan would unravel, with potentially dire consequences for eastern Bosnia. The Serb military relied on Munja to eliminate the entire leadership, a move intended to sow disarray and confusion, facilitating an easier offensive. And that would save Serb lives.

He steered his Lada Niva four-wheel drive off the track and onto a narrow path barely wider than a footpath. Bringing it to a stop beside a large bush, he paused, scanning the surroundings to ensure he hadn't been observed. Satisfied that he was alone, he stepped out of the vehicle and scrutinised the area meticulously, searching for any signs of life. All remained creepily quiet.

He retrieved a green tarpaulin from the trunk and draped it over the vehicle, then covered it with branches. He had meticulously scouted this location multiple times. It was selected for its remoteness to the west of Sarajevo, the challenging terrain that would hinder pursuit, and its proximity to the river, which would serve as his escape route. He had rehearsed the plan repeatedly. During the chaos in Sarajevo following the mosque bombing, he would make his way to this secluded spot. Situated near the district of Otes, where heavy fighting had occurred, it was not easily traversable, an intentional choice. Though not without risk, it was a calculated risk. His escape plan involved using a dinghy to cross the river at the point where the Miljacka River met the River Bosnia. Thick foliage extended almost to the water's edge, and the chosen crossing point was one of the shortest. The strategy entailed hiding out until dusk after the bombing, then making a swift paddle across the river. The nearest Serb position on the other side was the base in Ilidza. It would be a perilous crossing, with Muslim forces scattered throughout the area. He banked on two factors: the confusion afforded by the aftermath of the bombing and the unlikeliness of Otes being considered an obvious escape route if he were identified as the bomber. Instead, they would likely anticipate him taking the more perilous but quicker direct route to the airport. Speed and surprise were paramount.

He pressed on through the dense bushes, thirty metres from the river's edge. As instructed, there was a plastic bottle tied to a bush. Moving to the left, he found a tree bearing the Black Hand symbol. He knew where to look now. The bush was dense, and despite knowing what awaited, it was impossible to see. The hiding spot was expertly concealed. Stepping into the bush, he pulled some branches to reveal a dark green canvas cover. Under it was a black dinghy with two paddles. Inside lay a bag containing a pistol, an AK47, spare ammunition magazines, hard biscuits, and a handheld radio. The plan was unfolding perfectly; everything was in position. However, for the plan to succeed, Munja had to remain in the mosque until the last possible moment. Departing prematurely would raise suspicion and increase the risk of discovery, rendering months of intricate planning futile. Earlier that morning, before prayers, he had set the bomb's timer in motion. No one suspected what lay within the Eid gift. Time was ticking, quite literally.

80

The assistant stood before Hassan Mesic, presenting the daily intelligence report. "There was suspicious Serb activity reported around the River near Otes. The local commander thought there was going to be a raid, but it turned out to be nothing. There was no sign of any enemy infiltration.

"Anything more?" he asked. "No sir, apart from a radio intercept. One message which said, 'Munja Gotovo." (Munja finished).

Hassan thought long and hard. 'Why would Munja be finished,' he thought to himself. He may have been the most valuable asset to the Serbs. Either I am getting close to him and he escaped, or there is something significant being planned. Ibrahimovic kept preying on his mind. There were aspects that didn't sit right with him, and there were too many inconsistencies. Yet everything led to a dead end. There was no concrete evidence, nothing tangible, just suspicion.

"Have you heard from Arif?" he inquired. The subordinate shook his head.

"He's been held up by heavy fighting, which cut the road. There was poor reception because he was in the hills. We heard something about Groznik. It wasn't clear. Nothing more."

"Let me know as soon as you regain contact." He dismissed the man.

A profound sense of unease enveloped Hassan as he attempted to piece together the puzzle before him. The reduction in firing and fighting around Sarajevo, minimal radio communication from Munja aside from announcing he was finished, the mysterious death of Mrs. Ibrahimovic, along with missing birth, death, and marriage certificates, and the absence of any history of Mohammed Ibrahimovic before the age of seven, what did it all signify?

Upon returning to base, he proceeded directly to General Mujkanovic's office.

"General, I think you should cancel Eid prayers tomorrow. Something is going on. I have an uneasy feeling. I think it's too much of a risk to have all the leadership together in one place."

The general requested evidence.

"I don't have anything concrete, but I am uncomfortable. There has been a decrease in fighting, and it's almost as if the Serbs have moved their artillery and tanks. And I know there is no intel to show that, but something is going on."

The general paused and then replied, "No, Eid prayers will go as planned. The footage and story it represents is important. That's been decided by the President, who, as you know, is very religious. He believes it will be symbolic and will rally people. It will lift their spirits. God knows they need some good news in all this misery. I don't agree, but this is a done deal. Just make sure we have security which is discreet and make sure there are no mass arrivals. People should not come in one group but individually."

Hassan was aware that the next twenty-four hours were going to feel interminable.

81

Mehmet Mesic sat in the radio room of the PTT building in Donji Zelenik, listening intently to the radio traffic. Fahrudin moved the dial from one frequency to another, each connection bringing forth more dialogue from the Serbs.

"Something is going on," said Fahrudin. "There's never usually this much activity. But in the last twenty-four hours, it's hardly stopped. Of course, we can't break the code, but I am not sure this is good news. Just one word was repeated on several of the frequencies: Munja."

Mehmet summoned all the local commanders to gather together.

"This might be nothing, but it could be something, and if it is something, it could be big. We need to prepare. Get out all the mortars we have and place them in the east. If a big attack comes, then it will be from there. Get all the men in the positions that we have previously designated and make sure this mobilisation is done quietly. We don't want to alarm people, and we don't want to give the Serbs a sign that we know they are up to something if they are. I am going to see the UN."

Mehmet endured a twenty-minute wait before being granted entry into the newly heavily fortified UN compound in Potachari. He underwent a thorough search, and his weapons were confiscated. The compound occupied the premises of a former transportation company, partially destroyed during the early days of the war. Inside, the Dutch commander Captain Marco Van Gost, occupied what was once the manager's office. He didn't appear friendly to Mehmet. He got the opinion he didn't want to be there, that it was a reluctant posting.

"Captain, I think the Serbs are planning something," Mehmet said directly. "There has been a lot of radio communication and we are concerned. You have made us give up some of our heavier weapons and without these, we are extremely vulnerable."

The captain smirked. "So, you have no evidence but just a hunch. And what do you expect me to do? I have thirty-eight men, and I don't have a mandate to protect a herd of cows, let alone sixty thousand people. We have seen no signs that the Serbs are planning anything. If there was a build-up of forces, then for sure, there would be satellite pictures showing this, and I would be informed. So, I don't think your hunch is correct. We have visited the Serbs and it seems clear they are more than happy with the ceasefire. I think they are more than content with things to stay the way they are."

Mehmet got up to leave. He turned and said, "Captain, you have been here five minutes, and you have no idea what the Serbs are planning and what they are capable of. If your assessment is wrong then it won't be Dutch peacekeepers paying the price. It will be Bosnians."

And with that, he departed, slamming the door behind him.

82

Hassan awoke at the first call to prayer, signalling the break of dawn. The first rays of light filtered through the window, marking the transition from night to morning. It was Eid, a significant day for Bosnian Muslims. He hurriedly dressed and made his way to headquarters to obtain the latest intelligence reports. Despite his anticipation, there was little change, and he still had no news from Arif.

As he drove to the mosque, he sifted through everything he knew and didn't know in his mind but still couldn't find any difinitive answers. With prayers set to begin in two hours, he felt a profound sense of helplessness, an uncomfortable feeling that weighed heavily on him.

Soldiers had been discreetly stationed in nearby houses and within the grounds of the Mosque. As dignitaries, commanders, and politicians arrived one by one for the ceremony, they performed the traditional Wudu (ablutions), cleansing themselves by washing their hands, faces, arms, and feet before entering. It felt as though hundreds of eyes were fixed on the mosque and its worshippers. Soldiers occupied every rooftop and lurked around every corner. Every conceivable inch was under surveillance, not just around the Mosque, but throughout the city.

Spotters all radioed in with the same message, 'All quiet, no movement.'

It was the same message in Donji Zelenik. Mehmet's men were in position, but they saw and heard nothing.

Mohammed Ibrahimovic arrived at the Mosque, one of the last worshippers to do so. He was warmly greeted by many, receiving handshakes, hugs, and kisses, particularly from the imam. Hassan attempted to approach him, but the Inquisitor swiftly moved away to engage with another group.

Just as he thought he had found his opportunity, his assistant entered the mosque and caught his eye. Urgently, he waved him over.

"It's Arif, he's been wounded. You'd better come he wants to speak to you. He says it's urgent. He says it's about Munja."

Hassan trailed behind him as they stepped outside. The call to prayer had begun. He made his way towards the car and then climbed in.

"Headquarters, quickly."

As the call to prayer, known as the adhan, faded into silence inside the mosque, the imam ascended the six steps to the pulpit. Turning to face the congregation, he commenced the special Eid Ul Fitr prayer, reserved solely for this occasion.

"Allahu akbar, Allahu akbar La ilaha illallah, Wallahu akbar, Allahu akbar wa lillahil hamd, Allah is the greatest, Allah is the greatest, there is no God but Allah." The congregation repeated.

At headquarters, Hassan raced up the stairs to the radio room. "Get me, Arif, now," he ordered. It took a few minutes to connect.

"Arif, are you there? Are you there? Are you over?"

"Yes, I am here, sir."

"Are you OK?"

"I'll live. We hit a mine, taking a detour to avoid the fighting. Leg is a bit messed up. No big walks for me for a while."

"Have you got information regarding Munja?"

"Well, I can't say for certain, but there are some interesting revelations. We found Ibrahimovic's grave in Klucna. But something more interesting. Beside his grave was that of a seven-year-old boy, Mohammed Ibrahimovic. He was born on the same date as the Inquisitor. People in Groznik remember Mrs Ibrahimovic and how she moved from Klucna to become matron at the local orphanage.

"But there is something that is even more interesting; on the day she left for Sarajevo, adoption papers were drawn up for a seven-year-old boy. I went to the orphanage, and they had their records, thankfully. The boy's name was Dragan

Mihajlovic. He was adopted by Mrs Ibrahimovic. I think Dragan Mihajlovic is Mohammed Ibrahimovic."

"The boy was a Serb?"

"Yes."

Hassan drew in a deep breath, realising that if this information was accurate, there was a strong possibility that Ibrahimovic was Munja. If that were the case, what was his agenda? Moreover, if he turned out to be Mihajlovic, then he was Serbian, not Muslim.

"Great work, Arif, great work. Heal soon, my friend and get back safe. Over."

He raced back down the steps. He needed to get to Ibrahimovic and quick.

As the Eid worshippers immersed themselves in prayer, Ibrahimovic quietly slipped away through the imam's office at the rear of the mosque. Glancing at his watch, he noted that there were less than twenty minutes before the bomb was set to detonate. He needed to put distance between himself and the mosque, but first he had to retrieve his belongings from the house.

Hassan's driver drove as if his life depended on it. He didn't know it, but it did. They couldn't rely on walkie-talkie connection. That might alert Ibrahimovic. Five minutes later the car pulled up. Hassan ran out and spoke to the guards inside the walls of the mosque gardens.

He entered the grounds of the mosque. Outside every space was taken, men were on their knees deep in prayer. He slipped inside. It was completely filled with more men in prayer, every space taken except for one, one empty place. It was glaring. He scanned the room and couldn't see Ibrahimovic. He knew that the empty space was his. He was missing. It was suspicious. A man so devout would not miss a second of such a solemn occasion. Everything seemed to add up and pointed to the fact that Ibrahimovic was Munja.

Hassan dashed outside, signalling for three men to join him in the car, and swiftly directed the driver to Ibrahimovic's house. The eight-minute journey felt agonisingly long. Arriving, they found the front door slightly ajar. Drawing his pistol, Hassan instructed one man to accompany him while two others went to the back of the house. Carefully, they entered through the door. There was no sign of Ibrahimovic and no sound. It was eerily quiet. They checked the downstairs rooms. In the sitting room all the photos of Ibrahimovic and the woman who pretended she was his mother were lying on the floor in pieces.

Hassan ascended the stairs cautiously and quietly, taking each step with care and pausing after each one to listen for any signs of movement. Silence greeted him at every turn. Upon reaching the top, he found all the doors closed except for one, the same one he had sneaked into a few weeks prior, belonging to Ibrahimovic. With his gun drawn, he positioned himself beside the doorway before swiftly entering the room. His heart raced with anticipation, but to his surprise, the room was empty. His gaze fell upon the wardrobe, which stood away from the wall. Upon closer inspection, he noticed the poster hanging by a single pin, revealing the hidden compartment. Inside, he found only a piece of paper. On it was written 'The greatest Eid present.' The carpet had been moved. Hassan saw that there was powder underneath and the smudged outlines of what were footprints. 'Of course,' he thought to himself, 'The tactics of a spy. He must have known his room had been searched.'

He ran downstairs. The two soldiers met him.

"Sir we found this in the back metal bin." He held up a burnt book. It was the remains of the code book. "And also, some radio equipment which had been fairly well smashed up."

Hassan pondered deeply. He was convinced that Munja was behind this. Knowing that Munja was Mohammed Ibrahimovic and realising that Ibrahimovic was actually Dragan Mihajlovic, Hassan couldn't shake the feeling that Munja had orchestrated something. But what exactly had he planned?

Then he remembered the piece of paper. 'The greatest Eid gift,' he said to himself over and over again. 'What could it be?' He racked his brains. And then the realisation. 'The model, Masjid al-haram in Mecca. That is the gift,' he thought. His mind raced back to when he first searched Ibrahimovic's room and he found the small pieces of copper wire. It hit him like a hammer.

"Fuck, it's a bomb, and it's in the mosque. Quick, we must get there. Don't bother with the roads, he told the driver go through the pedestrian area."

"But what about the snipers?" asked the driver.

"Fuck the snipers, this is much more important."

The minutes raced by faster than Hassan could comprehend. He had no idea what kind of device, how big it was and what kind of timer. But he remembered how heavy it was. He had no idea how long he had got. But he deduced that Ibrahimovic had planned this well, it must be a bomb big enough to kill most of the Bosnian political and military leadership in one go. He knew he had to prevent it, at all costs.

The car screeched to a halt. Alerted Guards raced to the gates, scared the mosque was under attack.

"Out of the way," shouted Hassan. And he rushed through the gates and into the mosque. Prayers were still in full swing. He looked around and shouted, "Everyone out. There is a bomb. Leave the building calmly and in order, but quickly."

The imam looked shocked.

"You too, imam."

He spotted the model and approached it cautiously. Gently lifting the top off, he revealed the bomb, a seemingly basic device yet packed with enough Semtex to obliterate not only the mosque but also a significant portion of the entire district. Bending down, he noticed the countdown timer displaying four minutes on the digital readout. After carefully replacing the top, he realised there wasn't enough time to defuse it. They had to dispose of it, but where?

"Give me room," he said in a mild, controlled voice, trying to limit the panic. "Bomb coming through."

He went out to his car.

"Driver, get to the closest part of the Miljacka that you can."

"But Sir that's the most dangerous part of the river, that's the closest part to the Serb snipers."

"Fuck the snipers. If this doesn't get into the river in precisely two minutes, there will be no one left to snipe at. But drive carefully; I don't know how unstable this is."

The driver had panic written all over him. He stalled the engine.

"Take your time," Hassan said as calmly as he could muster, "but please, hurry up."

The engine started on the second try. The driver accelerated swiftly along the most direct route to the river. From that point onward, the Serbs would have a clear shot from less than eighty metres away.

Hassan looked at his watch, a minute and a half left to go.

"Hurry, man, foot down. There's a minute to go."

In the last minute, time seemed to paradoxically slow to a crawl and speed by in a blur for Hassan. Despite the urgency of the moment, he felt a relative sense of calm. 'I am a Muslim. I am in the hands of God,' he reminded himself. 'He will look after me…he hoped. It's funny,' he thought, that when a man faces death, he reaches out for God, even an atheist like him.

Hassan could see the stone wall by the river and, to the left, the Princip Bridge, where Archduke Ferdinand and his wife met their end. As he contemplated his own fate, he wondered if he was about to meet a similar demise. The driver abruptly stopped the car, positioning it squarely in front of the wall. Two shots rang out, shattering the silence. The bullets struck the car's windscreen, causing the driver to duck instinctively. Hassan exited the vehicle cautiously, clutching the model tightly. He crouched down, moving forward from the safety of the car to the protection of the wall next to the river. Two more shots pierced the air, slamming into the wall. Sensing an opportunity, the driver opened the front doors of the car to provide a bit of cover. Hassan waited for the right moment to act.

As the seconds ticked away, he was acutely aware that the snipers had him in their sights, anticipating his next move. Placing the bomb carefully on the ground, he removed his hat and grabbed a nearby piece of wood. Placing the hat on the makeshift stick, he waved it further along the wall, hoping to distract the snipers. It was a crude tactic, but one he had seen used in movies, and sometimes it proved effective.

More shots echoed in the air. One struck the hat, sending it flying off the stick. The diversion had succeeded. Hassan swiftly rose to his feet, hurling the bomb into the river in one fluid motion, then dived back towards the rear door of the car. He estimated they had less than 20 seconds remaining. Bullets continued to pepper the vehicle.

"Leave the car," Hassan shouted, "run." The two men sprinted across the street, zig-zagging to make themselves harder targets. They reached the safety of the buildings and braced themselves. The noise was deafening as the bomb exploded beneath the dark waters of the Miljacka. A massive spray of water shot high into the air as if half the river had erupted. Both men were blown off their feet, and the car was catapulted thirty metres into the air. Rows of buildings on both sides of the river were partially demolished, and chunks of brick and concrete were hurled around like confetti. The Serb snipers had ceased firing, likely as stunned as Hassan and the driver.

Their ears were ringing, their balance was lost, but they were alive. Munja's plan had been foiled; the leadership had been spared. However, it had been a close call. As Hassan regained his senses, he remembered Munja and wondered where he could be. He got to his feet, wiped the dust from his uniform and said, "We've got to find the bastard. He'll be trying to escape."

83

At the exact moment the bomb detonated in the Miljacka River, the first barrage of Serb shells descended upon Donji Zelenik. It marked the beginning of a relentless and intense bombardment. Strategic positions and facilities were systematically targeted, including the clinic, the headquarters housed in the PTT building, and the Domavia Hotel. Each Bosnian trench and bunker was subjected to precise attacks. Shell after shell pummelling the area, leaving death, injury, and devastation in its wake. Those who could seek refuge deep underground clung to whatever hope they could find in prayer.

Mehmet had established a command position to the east of the town, nestled within a dense cluster of trees at Zeleni Jadar, or Green Valley. However, the valley appeared more smudged with brown and white patches from melting snow than green. He recognised that this wasn't an isolated shelling incident; it was the precursor to a major attack. Mehmet sensed that their struggle for survival was about to face its most formidable challenge yet.

Men rushed in with frontline reports, painting a grim picture. The Serbs were mobilising thousands of men and employing tanks to support their advance. Sustained bombardments aimed to weaken Bosnian positions, causing casualties among Mehmet's units. He knew that repelling the attackers for more than a few hours would be impossible. It was a fight for their lives and for the survival of Donji Zelenik. The young engineer dispatched small groups of fighters to launch lightning strikes on Serb forward units, aiming to slow their advance and provide cover for civilians to take shelter. Amidst the chaos, Mehmet remained composed, understanding that panic would only hinder their efforts. He issued orders, knowing that some of the men would not return. In the early moments of the attack, it became clear to him that they needed to consider escaping. If the offensive unfolded as he feared, it was only a matter of time before the area would be overrun. Escaping from a besieged town would pose significant challenges and perhaps even prove impossible. While there were gaps in the Serb lines, they were not large enough to facilitate the evacuation of thousands of fighters and civilians. One thing was certain: options, like time, were rapidly dwindling.

Hagija stood waiting at the Domavia, where flames engulfed the manager's room. The building had taken at least one direct hit. Men were being carried out on stretchers.

"We need to leave," he said to Mehmet. "We cannot hold. The town will be lost soon, and if we stay…."

Mehmet interrupted his words. "I know, I know. Gather as many men as we can and supplies. Take only as much ammo as you can carry. Don't bother with food. We won't be eating today. This is about surviving."

He rallied his senior fighters and outlined the only plan available to them. It wasn't intricate; it was simply to fight their way through the enemy lines to the northwest and head towards Tuzla, hoping that Bosnian forces from there would arrive in time. He volunteered to stay behind and cover the escape. When he asked for volunteers, fifty men stepped forward. They all understood that this mission was almost certain to end in sacrifice, but they were determined to buy time and delay the Serb advance.

They proceeded to the UN depot near the PTT building, where their heavier weapons had been relinquished, and commanded the UN guards to step aside.

"You can't come in here," responded a Dutch peacekeeper.

"And who is going to stop us," spat Mehmet. They poured into the building, pushing the peacekeepers to one side and grabbed whatever they could: RPGs, mortars and heavy machine guns.

"Thanks for everything you have done for us," snapped Mehmet. "But we must be going now."

He made a stop at the PTT building and headed straight to the radio room. Inside, Samir and Fahrudin were seated by the radio set, with Samir holding the handset.

"Radio Sarajevo and tell them we are lost. It is only time before the Serbs over run us. Tell them we are escaping and if they can send help, as much as they can. Tell them…" he hesitated. "Tell them Alu Akbar."

Mehmet ran to his house. His father was sitting by the fire reading from the Koran.

"Tata, we must go. The Serbs are coming, and they will kill us."

His father looked up. His face had the innocence of a child. He showed no sign of understanding what his son had said and he said nothing, just returned to his reading.

Mehmet lifted his father up slowly, trying to muster some respect in the desperation of the moment.

"We have to go. Come," and he ushered him through the door.

Selma was running up the street to the house. She hugged her father.

"Take him to the UN compound," said Mehmet. "There is some safety there, I hope. He cannot come through the lines; he's not strong enough, and there will be a lot of danger. You go with him and stay with him."

"But there are many wounded; Nedret needs help. We can't just leave."

"I'm telling you, listen to me. It is finished. We cannot hold out, and we don't know what the Serbs will do when they get here, but I am sure it won't be good. Republika Srpska hasn't signed up to the Geneva convention on human rights. You must now think about our father. Go now."

Selma acknowledged the truth in his words, but accepting it didn't make the situation any easier. She gently guided her father down the street, their surroundings marred by shell damage and engulfed in flames. Amidst the chaos, people hurried past, clutching whatever belongings they could carry. As she turned to watch her brother and his men depart for the battle, Selma felt a pang of worry. Mehmet paused, turned back, and flashed a trademark smile before disappearing into the trees.

Samir was on the handset trying to find a frequency the Serbs weren't jamming. He found one.

"This is Donji Zelenik, this is Donji Zelenik," he said, repeating the sentence over and over, his voice wavering. "We are finished. We need help. The Serbs are coming. The Serbs are coming."

A Serb voice interjected Samir. "Yes, you Balija bastard, we are coming, we are coming."

84

Hassan sat beside the radio operator. One by one, the Bosnian spotters radioed in their reports. Each gave the same response. 'No sign of Ibrahimovic, the Serb spy.' Hassan had instructed for every potential crossing point to be closely monitored, with particular emphasis on the airport, which served as the quickest route to the Serb side but also posed the greatest danger. Despite their efforts, there was no sign of him anywhere. While the Serbs had their snipers, so did the Bosnians. In the sobering reality of daylight, attempting an escape over the Miljacka River or down the airport road would have amounted to a suicide mission.

Frustrated, Hassan pored over the map of Sarajevo, searching for potential locations where Munja might have fled. He was certain there must be an escape plan in place, a starting point for it. But where could it be? As he traced the river out west, noting its narrowing path, he paused, lost in contemplation.

"Where are those last intel reports about Serb activity around the Miljacka?" he asked his second in command. A pile of papers was produced. Hassan hurriedly read through them, then abruptly stopped. His eyes darted back and forth across the lines. And there it was, perhaps Munja's escape route.

'Serb activity reported Bosnian side of Miljacka in area of Otes' the report stated. 'No one found, no signs of sabotage, no attacks or shooting.'

"Otes," Hassan shouted out loud. "He's escaping via Otes. For sure, he will cross the river somewhere there. Get twenty men, and let's go. Quickly, there isn't much time. We can't let him get away."

85

As Munja approached Serb-held territory, he felt himself drawing closer to his true identity, to Dragan Mihajlovic. It was as if he were undergoing a transformation into a new man. Upon hearing the massive explosion in Sarajevo's old town, he smiled contentedly. He had achieved his goal; Dragan Mihajlovic had dealt a devastating blow to the Muslims. His sacrifice had not been in vain. However, thoughts of escape now consumed him. He knew it was only a matter of time before Hassan Mesic pieced together the reasons and timing behind the attack. Munja hoped that, amidst the chaos of the bombing, it would take longer to determine his whereabouts. He guided the car further into the bushes, knowing there was no need to conceal it any longer. This was the endgame. By the time the car was discovered, he would be long gone, safely in Republika Srpska, embracing his new, true life.

He made his way down the narrow, mostly overgrown path towards the spot where the dinghy was concealed. Pulling back the branches, he revealed the dinghy and equipment exactly as he had left them a few days earlier. Switching on the radio, he double-checked his AK47 and glanced at his watch. The plan was to wait until dusk, when a barrage of fire and mortars would strike the southern side of the river, to cover his escape. Thirty minutes remained before darkness enveloped the surroundings. Nervous yet exhilarated, scared yet determined, he knew his moment was approaching. Reflecting on what he had accomplished, he remained unaware in the bushes west of Sarajevo that his deadly plan had been thwarted. Hassan Mesic had outmanoeuvred him on that front.

The Serb crouched low in the bushes, clutching his orthodox crucifix and the biscuit tin containing his cherished antecedence. In that moment, he felt a profound connection to his God and an even stronger bond with his people. The anticipation was palpable. Glancing at his watch once more, he couldn't shake the feeling that time was moving in reverse. Suddenly, he heard a noise nearby. Cocking his AK-47, he assumed a firing position, attempting to control his breath and remain undetected. He was beginning to feel what fear really meant. 'There was no way they could have found him so quickly,' he thought to himself. Then he heard the fluttering wings of a bird as it burst out of some thickets, and he heaved a huge sigh of relief.

Five minutes before the designated escape time, he began to position himself. The dinghy wasn't excessively heavy, but neither was it light, making it difficult to manoeuvre through the dense bushes. With approximately thirty metres separating him from the river's edge, most of it across open ground, he advanced cautiously, moving in stages of five metres at a time. Each interval required a brief pause for rest, catching his breath, and listening intently. He wasn't the fittest of men; years of consuming burek and heavy Bosnian food had taken their toll. As he neared the river, a sound caught his attention, the snapping of a branch or twig, not a noise typical of birds in the bushes. It was the sound of something considerably heavier. Soon after, he discerned voices speaking in hushed tones, Bosnian voices, Muslims. Crouching down, he was faced with a flurry of choices racing through his mind: wait until they passed, stand and fight, or attempt to cross the river before the diversionary fire began.

He couldn't afford to waste time. Despite the risk of getting caught in the shelling, he opted to wait and observe. Attempting to regulate his breathing, he struggled against the controlled panic coursing through his body. Retreating from the dinghy, he doubled back and concealed himself behind a tree, patiently waiting. As the voices drew nearer, he estimated there were likely two men, though their demeanour suggested no sense of urgency. He pondered whether they were hunting him or simply conducting a routine patrol.

The two young Bosnian fighters were oblivious to the presence of someone nearby. Devoid of radios, they remained unaware of the frantic search for the Serb spy, Munja. For them, this was simply another routine patrol, a task they carried out twice daily, every day. Suddenly, the lead fighter halted in his tracks, signalling for both men to kneel down. With a gesture, he directed his comrade to move to the left. They paused, listening intently, before cautiously advancing. As they approached the dinghy, one of them noticed a bag and a radio; the latter unexpectedly turned on and cracked into life.

"Munja, Munja, pet minute," the voice said (five minutes). The soldier had heard of Munja, knowing him to be the most wanted man in Bosnia. He speculated that perhaps Munja was present. His comrade inspected the bag and discovered the ammunition and a compass.

With no time to process, his comrade fell in an instant, clutching his neck. The soldier turned to find Mihajlovic standing there with the ferocity of a wild animal, brandishing a bloodied knife. Desperately, the soldier reached for his Kalashnikov, but he was too slow. The knife pierced his chest, and he crumpled to the ground. Ibrahimovic stabbed him twice more before seizing the radio and the bag of ammo. Stepping over the fallen soldier, he retrieved the dinghy. Suddenly, a shot rang out, followed by a sharp pain in his upper left thigh. Collapsing, he realised a bullet had passed through his leg. Turning over, he saw the dying Bosnian clutching the gun. "Jebece," he said (fuck you.) Mihajlovic shot four rounds, and his body slumped lifeless in the grass.

The pain surged through him. With no bandages at hand, he knew he had to stem the flow of blood. He had been shot, but he was reasonably certain the artery hadn't been hit. Blood seeped from the front of his thigh, and though he was grateful the injury wasn't more severe, he knew it could have been. Drawing from his military training, he understood the importance of halting the bleeding from both entry and exit wounds. Tearing off strips of his shirt, he packed them into the front and rear wounds. The rear hole proved more challenging, but after several attempts, he managed to address it. Though the makeshift solution wasn't perfect, it would suffice until he reached the river. Despite being patched up, he moved slower. Yet, the escape remained imperative. Limping back towards the river, each step was a struggle, with the last ten metres proving the most agonising. The gunfire would have alerted anyone nearby, and time was of the essence. He needed to cross before the covering fire commenced, mere minutes away.

86

Hassan's Jeep pulled up just as the four shots rang out, signalling the death of the young Bosnian fighter.

"It must be the spy," shouted Mesic. "Spread out and head towards the river, but be careful of sniper fire."

They raced through the bushes and halted abruptly when they came across the bodies of the two young fighters.

"He's gone this way," shouted Hassan, seeing the track the dinghy had made. "He's going to cross the river. Quick, we've got to stop him."

Mihajlovic fought against his injuries, his willpower overriding the pain. Blood seeped through the makeshift bandages as he lowered the dinghy into the water and grasped the oar, propelling himself forward with all his might. The going was tough; he battled against a fierce current whipped up by a northerly wind. It demanded every ounce of his strength to keep the dinghy on course. A lesser man would have faltered, but Munja summoned every muscle in his body, fuelled by sheer determination.

He was near his destination, only ten metres away on the opposite shore when the diversionary fire erupted. The onslaught was fierce. Mortars, artillery, and machine gun fire tore through the bushes with devastating force. Hassan and his men dropped to the ground, lying motionless as the chaos unfolded. Two members of the group were struck by the onslaught, with shells raining down and shrapnel scattering all around them, rendering movement impossible. But Hassan couldn't allow the spy to escape. Disregarding his own safety, he dashed through the bushes towards the river's edge, where he spotted Ibrahimovic about to reach the bank. Despite the incoming shells, he pressed forward.

He knelt down, lifted his AK-47, and took aim. The first shot missed, followed by the second. He observed as Ibrahimovic exited the dinghy. With only a few seconds left, Ibrahimovic would soon vanish. Once he reached the shelter of the trees, his escape would be assured. However, his limp impeded his progress. Despite his size, he remained a substantial target, even from seventy-five metres away. Yet he teetered on the brink of vanishing into the foliage.

Hassan shouted out, “We found the bomb. You failed. You didn’t kill anyone. It was all for nothing.”

It was worse than a wound. The towering Serb came to an abrupt halt, unsure if he had heard correctly. Turning around, confusion etched on his face, proved to be a fatal mistake. Mesic wasted no time, unleashing a volley of shots. At least two bullets found their mark, causing Mihajlovic to collapse backward, releasing the dinghy rope. There was no final breath, no moment of victory. Serb soldiers emerged from the bushes, providing cover, while two men dragged Mihajlovic away. But it was too late. Munja, the spy, lay dead.

Hassan had no opportunity to celebrate his success. Under a barrage of gunfire, he sought refuge in the bushes. Keeping his body low, he regrouped with his men. Hidden among the foliage, he observed as the Serbs retrieved the body and witnessed the empty dinghy being carried back by the wind and current to its origin. As the Serbs withdrew, the covering fire diminished. After a few tense moments, Hassan and his men cautiously advanced. They returned with the two wounded fighters and the bodies of the two who had fallen victim to Mihajlovic’s attack.

Hassan took a moment to catch his breath, his mind still racing and adrenaline still coursing through his veins. One of his men approached, holding out a red biscuit tin.

“It was in the dinghy,” he explained.

Hassan examined it closely. The words ‘Deutsche Biscuit’ were written on the lid. Upon opening it, he discovered a diary and several photographs belonging to Munja’s grandfather, revealing his allegiance to the Black Hand and the Serb nationalist cause. Here lies the answer to the identity of Dragan Mihajlovic, also known as Munja the spy, and the motivations behind his actions.

As they reached the vehicles, Hassan's radio sprung to life. "HQ to Black Dog, HQ to Black Dog," the voice said. "Code Red, Code Red. Immediate."

'Black Dog' was a code reserved for the direst emergencies. Hassan understood that the activation of this code, along with 'Code Red,' signified a grave situation. It indicated that somewhere, something terrible was unfolding. This realisation cast a shadow over the subdued celebration of extinguishing the threat posed by Munja and the relief that no more Bosnians would perish at his hands.

87

Mehmet's hit-and-run tactics were effective in buying time. The Serb advance had slowed and even halted in some areas. However, it was evident that they were on the brink of being overwhelmed. He understood that timing was crucial, knowing when to hold ground and when to retreat. He made the decision to launch one final coordinated attack to sow chaos and inflict casualties, providing his group with a valuable head start. Mehmet and his men lay low at the edge of the treeline, overlooking Zeleni Jadar. From this vantage point, they could observe the cautious advance of the Serb soldiers. Mehmet had divided his forces into three groups: one facing the Serbs directly, with the other two positioned diagonally on the right and left flanks. The plan was to lure the enemy in, unleash overwhelming firepower, and then swiftly retreat.

Each man understood the importance of timing; their breath was held and their fingers were poised on triggers as the first wave of Serbs advanced. Faces were etched with fear and apprehension, yet each felt the surge of adrenaline as contact neared. The Serbs cautiously moved forward twenty metres, followed by the second wave. They spread out across a fifty-metre-wide expanse of pasture, numbering three to four hundred men. Mehmet realised he was vastly outnumbered. Behind him were three mortar positions, each armed with small 60mm Russian-made mortars capable of firing in confined spaces. Mehmet signalled. The first wave of mortars exploded among the ranks of the third line of Serbs, hitting their mark. From three sides, the Bosnians unleashed a barrage of concentrated fire with AK47s, heavy machine guns, RPGs, and grenades. The air filled with the anguished cries of wounded Serbs as they fell under the onslaught. Orders were shouted out amidst the panic. Then one word, 'Nazad,' (retreat). It was repeated several times. Mehmet's plan had unfolded flawlessly. They observed as the Serbs hurried back, aiding the walking wounded but leaving others where they lay.

"Shoot to wound, not to kill," ordered Mehmet. He knew that one injured man would need two to help. That would be two more men taken out of the fight.

Darko Zubic stood amidst a cluster of trees, his gaze fixed on Mehmet Mesic as he organised his men. Anger surged within him like a volcanic eruption, fuelled by the shame of defeat and the sense of ignominy. If anything, this only heightened his resolve to exact punishment on the Muslims and emerge victorious. 'Mehmet Mesic, I will be seeing you again,' he thought to himself. 'You can be sure of that.'

Mehmet issued the order to retreat back to the town, having successfully slowed the enemy's advance at this juncture. However, the conflict persisted throughout Donji Zelenik, and Mehmet realised he lacked the manpower and weaponry to cover every area effectively. Five flatbed trucks awaited them on the roadside, and the fighters quickly boarded, heading back into town. Meanwhile, plumes of smoke rose into the air, and civilians fled with crying children in tow, while explosions echoed in the distance. Amidst the chaos, a UN armoured personnel carrier (APC) appeared, but despite the attempts of a group of civilians, primarily the elderly and children, to flag it down, the APC sped past without pause. Whether they were overlooked or disregarded, the result was the same: Chaos was everywhere. The UN was not.

The young Mesic stood up on the back of the truck and addressed the civilians and the fighters.

"The Serbs are coming," he declared. "We cannot stop them. There are two options: surrender or run. I recommend civilians go to the UN compound in Potachari and ask for protection, but I strongly think all fighters should try and escape. The Serbs want to settle scores, that is certain. Those that want to leave, meet me by the mosque in five minutes."

His words only heightened the prevailing sense of panic. Civilians hurriedly descended the winding road towards the UN compound, clutching whatever belongings they could carry. His men swiftly made their way to the mosque, where the imam awaited. Together, they all began to pray. Mehmet knew it was a time for God and guts and more than a little luck.

88

Grant Singleton sat inside the Sarajevo Presidential Building, his nerves on edge as he waited anxiously. After twenty minutes, Hassan Mesic emerged, his expression tired and stern-faced.

"Hassan, what's happening? I hear Donji Zelenik is under heavy attack and it's serious?"

"I can't say too much right now," Hassan replied. "But yes, it is serious. That's all I can say."

"Are Selma and Mehmet OK?"

"No one is OK," he replied, his voice almost solemn.

"Come on, man, level with me. I love your sister. I need to know whether there is anything I can do."

Hassan took him to one side. "Look, it is serious. It seems as if the Serbs are going to overrun the town if they haven't already done so. Communications have been cut. Mehmet has given the order for civilians to go to the UN compound and fighters to escape over the hills. We are sending a force from Tuzla and the surrounding area to try and link up with them and save as many as we can. The rest is up to the international community. They need to stop this attack and save lives. The Serbs have hidden behind a pretence of a ceasefire. The world needs to see that. The world needs to fucking well act. Go and report that and quickly."

Hassan was losing his composure as the desperation of the situation became ever too clear.

"Are you going with this force?" Grant Asked. Hassan nodded.

"Can I come with you, not firstly as a journalist but as someone who wants to help?"

Hassan looked at him and shook his head. "This is not your fight. My people and my family are there. They are not a story to me. They are what I am. I need to help them."

"Let me help, please. The story will come later. I am talking to you now, not as a journalist but as someone who loves your sister. Survival comes first, and I need to help. I need to help your family, your sister and your people. Please, Please. Hassan, you can't say no. I love your sister. I really do. You need to believe me."

It was the first time he had uttered those words, but now, at this pivotal moment, he realised their undeniable truth. The conflict in Donji Zelenik had become his own personal war.

Hassan thought deeply. "OK. Grab your equipment and then be here in five. If you are not we will not wait. Understand?" Grant nodded and rushed off.

Five minutes later, a truck arrived, and Hassan and thirty men got in. He gestured to Grant to climb up.

"Where exactly are we going?" the journalist asked.

"As close to Donji Zelenik as we can," Hassan replied.

89

Outside the gates of the UN compound in Potachari, chaos was escalating to monumental proportions. People screamed, others shouted, and children cried. The elderly wandered around in a daze, uncertain of the unfolding events, some oblivious to the imminent dangers they faced. The compound was fortified with towering fences crowned with spirals of razor-sharp barbed wire. Massive double metal gates stood closed, flanked by tall posts armoured with rows of sandbags. Large, triangular concrete blocks were strategically placed to thwart suicide bombers and vehicular attacks. Young Dutch peacekeepers, armed with automatic rifles, wore expressions of deep concern.

But the peace they once sought to preserve was now shattered. Old couples were separated. Wives begged for their husbands to be allowed in. Their pleas were swallowed in the chaos. A blue band of UN soldiers stood at the gates and pushed back the growing tide of human desperation that was trying to get in.

Capt. Van Gost, the UN commander, barked instructions to his men. "Only allow in the elderly and women and children. Absolutely no fighters."

One by one, the elderly, the young, and females were permitted to enter the compound, while male teenagers were turned away. Despite pleas from parents to allow them entry, Dutch soldiers remained unmoved. Some begged, others shouted, but their efforts were futile, and the answer remained a resolute no.

Many of the young men had discarded their camouflage jackets and weapons, now placing their trust in the security provided by the UN and relying on the mercy of the Serbs.

The radio operator twins, Fahrudin and Samir, lingered on the outskirts of the panicked crowd, which continued to swell in size. Despite the chaos surrounding them, they remained silent observers, almost as if they were spectators at an unravelling drama. Meanwhile, explosions reverberated from nearby districts, accompanied by sporadic rifle shots echoing from the hills and occasional bursts of machine gun fire in the distance. It was a relentless pursuit of Bosnian fighters, an ongoing hunt that permeated the air with tension and fear.

The compound swiftly filled to capacity, with people nearly overflowing the space, when the order came from the Dutch captain to close the gates.

A young Bosnian woman was handed a loud hailer, and she translated the words of the Dutch commander. "No more," he shouted, "we can take no more. Please remain calm. You are all under the protection of the United Nations. No harm will come to you. Please be calm."

Some of the panic subsided, but not the shooting from the hills.

Mehmet and his companions hurriedly advanced, their pace quickened by the looming Serb presence on every front. Skirmishes broke out sporadically, with casualties mounting among Mehmet's ranks. Despite the chaos, they tended to their wounded comrades on the move, hastily administering first aid. Traversing the trail, they encountered fallen bodies, both men and women, victims of the ongoing conflict. Among them, Mehmet recognised the face of a young man he knew. He was wearing a blood-splattered T-shirt which said, 'Dutch battalion UN.' It became evident that the Serbs were targeting this route for escape. Mehmet realised they needed to find an alternative route. However, the question remained: which way should they go? He instructed the men to take cover in the bushes and await further instructions.

At the south end of Donji Zelenik the first Serb fighters edged their way into the town. Behind them, surrounded by a protective cloak of fighters, marching with a shooting stick in hand, was General Novak Kustavic, the head of Serb forces in eastern Bosnia. They encountered no resistance. The streets were littered with bodies, and buildings lay in ruins, some still ablaze, giving the town an eerie emptiness. The air was heavy with the scent of death and destruction. Yet, for General Kustavic, there was also the scent of triumph. He saw this as a near-complete victory, a 'liberation' as he termed it. The operation had unfolded smoothly, except for a few minor hitches. The Muslim forces were fleeing, leaving behind a scene of chaos. Now, it was simply a matter of clearing out the remaining resistance. It seemed inevitable that soon the flag of Republika Srpska would fly over Donji Zelenik.

His men carefully searched every building, looking for traps and ambushes. They also kept an eye out for any Muslim fighters still hiding, ready to sacrifice themselves. However, the area was now deserted, with only the dead and the victorious soldiers left behind.

Selma accompanied her father to the northern edge of town, where they reached the gates of the UN compound. The scene before them was one of distress and disorder, with a tumultuous crowd of people expressing their misery and desperation through loud shouts and cries. Despite the chaos, Selma persevered, urging her father forward with determination. He remained silent and passive, clutching onto his small green book, appearing oblivious to the gravity of the situation. Upon reaching the gates, they encountered a formidable line of UN soldiers, clad in thick, light blue uniforms, forming a defensive barrier.

"No more can come in," shouted one of the soldiers firmly. "No more."

"They are with me," said a voice. It was Nasser, an old school friend of Selma's and a UN translator.

"But the captain said no more," the soldier responded.

"I am sure he wouldn't mind them. She is a nurse and can help with the sick, and her father is a respected elder whom people look up to."

The soldier thought for a few seconds and then gestured to the other soldiers to remove the barbed wire barricade.

"Thank you," said Selma.

"No problem," replied Nasser.

"Welcome to the madhouse. Let's see how much crazier things can get."

Darko Zubic swiftly navigated through the dense trees, his target clearly ahead: a group of Muslim fighters attempting to evade capture. Positioned strategically ahead, another contingent of his men lay in wait, herding the fleeing fighters towards a carefully planned trap. As the Muslims retaliated with gunfire, they swiftly adopted a low, rapid escape. In response, the Serbs unleashed a barrage of bullets from both flanks, swiftly decimating the fleeing group. In mere moments, around twenty Muslim fighters lay strewn across the ground, the majority succumbing to fatal wounds. Some remained, their agonised moans echoing amidst the chaos, their capacity to resist shattered, and their will to fight destroyed.

Zubic walked up to one of the wounded and stared down at him.

"Can you see him?" he asked. "Can you see him now?"

"Who?" said the wounded man.

"Your God Balija, that's who. Your fucking Allah."

The man was coughing up blood and was in obvious pain.

"All I can see is a piece of shit," stuttered the man.

"Then let me help you see him," smiled Zubic. He fired a single bullet into the man's head.

"No prisoners," he shouted out. "Send them to their God, never to return to Donji Zelenik."

90

Near a tunnel in Croat-held territory west of Sarajevo, three helicopters were cranked up, their rotor blades spinning as three lines of men formed to board. These were Russian-made Mi-8 helicopters, idle for months due to the threat of Serb missiles. Yet, faced with the urgent need to rescue thousands fleeing from Donji Zelenik, the risk had to be taken.

Leading the rescue operation was Hassan Mesic, his once-dark beard now speckled with grey and fatigue evident in the dark circles under his eyes. Nights of unrest plagued by the fear of attacks and danger to his loved ones had taken their toll. His objective was clear: establish a safe passage as close to the town as possible and evacuate as many people as he could, including his own family. With a team of 60 men from the Black Swans special forces, Hassan was determined to make this mission a success, a mission that held personal significance as it involved the safety of his brother, sister, and father. Among the men stood Grant, ready to play his part in this crucial operation.

"What's that?" asked Hassan, making his voice heard above the sound of the whirring rota blades. He pointed to an AK47 clutched in Grant's hand.

"I thought journalists don't carry weapons or get involved?" shouted Hassan.

"Today, I am not a journalist," he shouted back. "Today I am a fighter," and he boarded the chopper."

The Mi8s lifted off one by one, each taking a different course towards their destination: a landing zone east of the village of Kladanj, serving as the gateway to eastern Bosnia and Donji Zelenik. Their drop zone lay within Serb-held territory, necessitating a nerve-racking flight of twenty-five minutes over enemy-controlled terrain. Packed tightly with men and ammunition, each aircraft faced the constant threat of a single missile, ending their journey abruptly. Yet, flying at low altitudes and employing evasive manoeuvres, they made themselves elusive targets, thwarting the enemy's attempts to take a clear shot. It was another white-knuckle experience for Grant but he didn't mind. His singular focus was on reaching Donji Zelenik and reuniting with Selma. Today was not about impartiality; it was about survival, by any means necessary. As apprehension gripped his mind and body, he confronted a new reality: he was no longer a journalist but a fighter. This transformation contradicted everything he had previously believed and advocated. His father used to tell him that 'the pen is mightier than the sword', but it felt irrelevant in the face of the present danger.

He glanced out the window and spotted the red smoke from a flare marking the landing zone. The helicopters approached from various directions one after another, each arriving safely. Swiftly, soldiers and supplies were unloaded.

Hassan was greeted by a fighter who led him to a nearby house where a group of men awaited in the kitchen. An old wooden table was in the centre of the room. On it lay a large map. Red arrows pointed towards Donji Zelenik, outnumbering the blue ones.

"This is the latest intel we have," said a senior fighter. "All radio contact was lost some time ago, but we are gathering information from our forward lookouts. Some are very close. The red arrows are the Serb forces, the blue are ours, and these are the areas we know for sure from where our people are trying to escape. But the information is scant. The situation is confusing and is constantly changing. All we know for sure is that the Serbs have almost overrun the town, and they are focusing on finding everyone who is escaping. People are congregating around the UN base but Serbs are heading that way. It's unclear what the UN is doing or will do."

"I don't think we can rely on the UN any longer," said Hassan.

He pondered over the map for a few minutes and pointed to an area in green.

"So the closest point where we can reach them is this wooded area. OK, we don't have much time. That is at least five miles away, and with this terrain, it will take two to three hours to reach there. I want three groups. I will take the main one through the west path and we will be the spearhead of the rescue. Two other groups will approach, one from the north, the other from the south, and these will provide diversionary attacks and take the Serbs away from us. It sounds very simple, and it is, but it is dangerous. But remember this: if we hesitate, more of our people will die. We have to be fast and strong. We leave in five minutes, carry only ammunition and, water, and basic food. We can eat when this is all over."

91

Mehmet's strategy of hit-and-run was proving effective. He struck the Serbs forcefully, swiftly vanishing into the dense foliage, constantly shifting position. This relentless approach forced the Serbs to retreat, creating openings in their lines through which civilians, predominantly men, could flee to safety.

A megaphone was heard in the distance. A voice shouted out, "Come down. You will be safe. Nothing will happen to you. Come, we have food and drink. There is nothing to worry about."

One of Mehmet's men climbed a tree to gain a better vantage point. Peering through binoculars, he spotted a group of civilian men descending a hill, their hands raised in surrender, one of them signalling with a white cloth tied to a branch. Turning his gaze, he observed a cluster of Serb fighters clad in camouflage attire, numbering around fifteen or twenty, positioned along the road. As the civilians approached, the Serbs motioned for them to lie prone on the ground, to which they complied without hesitation. Although obstructed from view by foliage, the observer heard the unmistakable sound of gunfire, three or four bursts from a machine gun. Soon after, he witnessed the Serb group advancing down the road, one member wielding a megaphone while another carried the white flag, their demeanour seemingly light-hearted, they seemed to be laughing.

He descended the tree, looked at Mehmet, and then shook his head. Anger contorted his face.

"Follow me," he said and began running through the woods, sprinting as fast as he could. Twenty men trailed behind, struggling to keep pace, while Mehmet and two others surged ahead. His singular focus being retribution. Within five minutes, they caught up with the Serb group below. One by one Mehmet's men joined him.

"Catch your breath. Ibrahim, you need to go ahead. Take something white and you are going to pretend to surrender. We will make our way down to the road. You five will cross the road and come up behind the Serbs, and we will move in from the side. When you hear the first shot open up. Don't leave any of the fuckers alive."

They quietly advanced towards the Serbs. Ibrahim led the way, observing as Mehmet and the others took their positions.

The Serb loudhailer was sounding out to the hills. "It is safe. Come down. No one will hurt you. We have food."

The young Muslim took a deep breath and shouted out, "I am coming down. Don't shoot." As he walked down, he waved the white cloth.

The Serbs stood ready.

The sudden barrage of shots struck them forcefully, catching many off guard. Within seconds most of them were cut down from the side and behind. Those that could turned to return fire. Ibrahim dropped the white cloth and took the AK47 from behind his back. He pumped an entire magazine into the four remaining Serbs standing.

"No wounded left," shouted Mehmet, and each living Serb was finished off with a single bullet. It wasn't a coup de grace. It was a cold-blooded killing. It was an eye for an eye.

He gestured to his men to come.

"Grab what ammo and weapons you can and destroy that fucking megaphone. That will no longer be used as a tool of death. Let's go." And with that, they disappeared back into the woods.

92

As General Kustavic and fifty heavily armed soldiers neared the UN compound in Potachari, chaos intensified. The people there were overwhelmed with fear and apprehension.

Kustavic waved his arms in a calming gesture and then took a megaphone.

"Do not be scared," he said. "We mean you no harm. We want only what is ours and only the ones who committed crimes will face punishment. There is nothing to fear."

The commotion gradually calmed down. The crowd began to hush, seeking reassurance. The general's words hinted at a promise of safety, instilling hope among them.

Kustavic continued, "My men will arrange transport for you to be taken to a safe place for food and medical care. Please follow their instructions."

He pushed his way through the crowd towards the entrance to the UN compound. Muslims were shouting, 'Hvala,' (thank you) to the general as he walked by as if he was some kind of saviour. Some even touched his arm in a benevolent gesture. His bodyguards pushed them aside.

As he approached the entrance, he encountered a row of anxious UN soldiers, each holding their weapons poised. At the forefront stood the general, accompanied by his heavily armed men, all similarly prepared with their weapons.

"This is a UN compound and a place of safety. You cannot enter without permission," said the young Dutch officer.

Kustavic smiled. “I don’t want to come in,” the general replied. “But I will if I have too. Now, ask your commanding officer to come and speak to me if you will.”

Van Gost observed the scene from the upper window of the factory building. He had just spent twenty minutes on the phone with UN headquarters, seeking guidance on what actions to take and what support the UN would provide. However, there was no firm response and no clear direction. Having completed two tours of duty with the UN, the Dutch officer wasn’t surprised. He understood that navigating UN bureaucracy often meant delays and language barriers, with tasks often bogged down in paperwork. Essentially, he gathered that he was expected to do what he could to restore peace. Yet, with only thirty peacekeepers under his command facing thousands of battle-hardened Serb troops, he recognised that restoring calm was not something within his zone of control.

He walked down to the gates. Kustavic saluted the young captain who returned the gesture.

“Morning captain, how are you today?”

“I’ve had better mornings,” came the reply. “Can I ask you why you have broken the ceasefire and what your intentions are?”

“Actually, Captain, it was the Muslims who broke the ceasefire, and we are merely regaining a Serb town which was stolen from us at the cost of many Serb lives. We intend to repatriate these people to a place of safety so they can re-join their own communities.”

“That sounds like ethnic cleansing,” said Van Gost.

The general’s face hardened. “No, it is repatriation. And I need your assistance. Please ask all these people to kindly vacate the compound and come with us.”

"I'm afraid I can't do that, General. These people are under the protection of the United Nations. They will stay here until the UN can afford them safe travel."

Kustavic grinned. His engineers had accessed UN communications and intercepted Van Gost's contact with the UN in New York. He understood there was no resolution, no guidance, and no directives to safeguard these Muslims with the limited resources available, which were practically non-existent. He realised the Dutch battalion in Potachari was in a boat without a paddle, heading towards the waterfall. In simpler terms, they were utterly powerless.

"Captain, I hope you understand the situation clearly. But if you do not hand these people over, then my men will come into the compound and take these people out. You may call this place the property of the United Nations, but let me tell you that this is the sovereign territory of Republika Srpska, and we will not stand by and let a foreign force or Muslim fundamentalists prevent us from retaking what is rightfully ours. I will give you ten minutes to consider this, or you will face the consequences."

Van Gost remained silent, his expression revealing the plight of a man devoid of authority or strategy. He was well aware that in the face of any significant crisis, he lacked the necessary resources – be it manpower, weaponry, or official sanction – to effectively respond. The absence of clear guidance from New York only emphasised his solitary position. At this juncture, he found himself solely responsible. While he felt a duty of care towards the Bosnians, he also recognised his obligation to safeguard his own men. He couldn't bear the thought of facing Dutch families to explain the loss of their sons due to his misjudgements. Today, there were no easy decisions; he understood that well.

"Wait a little longer," he said. It came out as a request, not a demand.

Kustavic nodded in agreement. Van Gost went back into the compound and instructed three of his men to go with those who spoke English to record the names of everyone seeking shelter.

When completed, he went to the Serb commander and held three large pieces of paper in his hand.

"General, I have a list of the names of all people who are in this compound and are alive. This is now an official UN document. We will check later to see that these people are all alive and safe and, as you promised, repatriated."

Kustavic grinned and nodded, signalling to his men to get ready. Van Gost instructed that the compound should be cleared, leaving only the UN personnel.

The air filled with cries from the elderly and women as they grasped the unfolding situation.

"Please, no," someone begged Van Gost. He looked away, partly through shame, partly through a sense of helplessness.

The UN soldiers gently nudged those who were hesitant to move from the back. Nasser, the translator, earnestly urged Van Gost to reconsider, with Selma joining in.

"Don't do this," she begged. "The Serbs wouldn't dare to attack a UN base. The consequences would be disastrous for them. They are not that stupid. Stand up to them. They understand force. There are no guarantees they will keep their promises."

"I have a list of the names," he said, waving it high in the air. It felt a little like Neville Chamberlain. The British Prime Minister, waving a piece of paper after having met Hitler in Germany in 1938 and saying, 'Peace in our time.'

"I have proof," explained Van Gost, waving the papers. "The Serbs would never dare harm these people."

There was a look of disgust on Selma's face. "You don't know the Serbs at all, do you?" she replied. "Of all the things they have done in this war, do you really think they are now going to start respecting human rights? You are more stupid than I thought."

Nasser grabbed the UN commander's hand and pleaded with him for his father to be able to stay. "He is old and sick," he said. "He's not a fighter; he is a poor, broken man. Please let him stay."

Van Gost's face was expressionless. "I'm sorry, it is out of my control, and he will have to go. He is not working for the UN. You can stay; you are an official translator of the UN, and you are under our protection."

"I thought we were all under your protection." Van Gost looked away, deflecting Nasser's look of disgust.

Father and son hugged and cried, but Haris's father implored him to remain.

"You can do more from here," he said. "It is better that at least one of us is safe." With that, he turned and walked away. Haris was overcome with emotion. Tears welled in his eyes.

Selma realised the hopelessness of the situation. There seemed to be no way to sway the captain's decision. No words could persuade him to reconsider, nor any sense of shame to alter his resolve. With a shake of her head and a stern look directed at the imposing figure in uniform, she gently took her father's arm and began to lead him towards the barrier.

Outside a line of buses had pulled up. A Serb soldier shouted, "Women and children to the left, men to the right."

"No," she said. "My father comes with me."

A soldier grabbed her roughly by the arm and pulled it from her father. "Listen, you bitch, if you want you and your father to stay alive, you will do what we say. Now get in line and watch your mouth."

Two lines were formed, with men on the right and women and children on the left. Yousef Mesic seemed unaware of what was happening, simply walking with his Koran, reciting as he went. Selma doubted if he even recognised her.

Fahrudin and Samir came up to Selma, "Don't worry, we will look after him," Samir said. "He will be OK with us."

Three tall Serb fighters stood in between the lines while others searched the procession of people. The tallest man pointed to boys in the line of women and children. "Him," he said and "Him."

Two boys were pulled out and thrown into the line with men.

"But he is only fourteen," said a woman. "He is only a child. Please let him go with me."

"Hey, lady, a lot of your children have been playing with dangerous toys. You should have told them not to."

As Selma was passing the three men, a shout went out. "Stop. Not her."

She turned and looked at another tall fighter. It was Darko Zubic.

"Hi Selma, long time no see. Remember me? How are you? No bus for an old school friend like you. Come and join me in my car. I've been wanting to have a chat with you for some time. We have much to talk about."

Before she could utter a word, two strong soldiers clad in blue camouflage uniforms swiftly seized her. She kicked and screamed. It was to no avail. She knew it was pointless to resist. But she did anyway. Her bag dropped in the struggle. The contents flew out. It was a futile show of resistance. Van Gost and a handful of UN soldiers watched as she was bundled into Zubic's black

Mercedes. He said nothing and then turned and walked back to his office. The Mercedes drove off. Selma's possessions lay beside the road, a book, a hair brush makeup, a mirror and Buzz Lightyear.

93

The going was tough, the snow had largely melted but the thaw had created muddy paths, thick in some places, which slowed the going. But Hassan and each man knew the urgency of the situation. Bosnia was known for its mountains and rolling hills and it's wild bears. It was also a favourite hunting ground for Josip Tito. There was a different kind of hunting happening now. Serbs, tracking down and killing Bosnians. Hassan wondered how many more would die before they could reach safety.

Grant struggled with the challenging terrain, unaccustomed to its physical demands. The pathways were slippery, and the weight of his AK47 and spare magazines, totalling four and a half kilos, burdened him. He felt a mixture of relief and worry for not bringing his company-issued body armour, realising it would have added an extra twelve kilos, too much for him to bear. Nonetheless, he had his Kevlar helmet for some protection. Yet, his thoughts were not on himself, but on Selma and the urgent mission to save her and countless others. With every step he looked at the filming possibilities he would normally have taken. Great images of lines of heavily armed fighters. It was what TV news frontline action was all about. He was into what they called in the business, the Bang Bang Zone. Where you see outgoing firing, but not the death and destruction it creates when incoming. You couldn't put people off their evening dinner by showing the gore and reality of conflict.

Grant was determined to refrain from complaining inwardly or expressing any weakness. Instead, he focused on maintaining pace with the others, and not show that he was a weak, ineffective TV voyeur as he had once been called by a combatant.

Hassan raised his arm signalling the fighters to stop. In unison they knelt. There was a sound of moving bushes and breaking branches. Each man ensured the assault rifle safety catch was switched off. A fighter next to Grant obliged with the journalist's gun. "Maybe better," he said and smiled, a short smile.

Now was the time not to think as a journalist but as a fighter. It was a mental adjustment he felt difficult to make. Grant silently castigated himself. 'Stay alert and prepared,' he commanded inwardly.

The breaking bushes sound stopped, and a shout raised. "Burek," it said. It was the name of the Bosnian staple breakfast pastry and the codeword for the mission.

A man hurried forward and spoke quietly to Hassan. Hassan quickly directed men to both sides, informing them that fighters were approaching and to be prepared.

The noise began softly, like leaves rustling in the wind, then grew louder as branches snapped underfoot and twigs crackled. Hassan and his comrades stood poised, weapons in hand. There was a palatable sense of nervousness.

From amidst the bushes stepped a woman, carrying a bundle on her back and accompanied by two young children clinging to her skirt. Behind her trailed five other civilians – two women and three men – followed by the imposing figure of Hagija. Thirty more people followed, including five armed fighters.

They were the first group of escapees to break free. Relief washed over everyone as the two groups united. They embraced and exchanged handshakes.

Hagija and Hassan embraced.

"Can you give me a debrief? Asked Hassan.

"It's bad," said Hagija. "I think the Serbs are killing or capturing all of our fighters. Some have been taken away. They are dividing women and children, and the UN has handed them over to the Serbs."

"Bastards," commented Hassan. "How the fuck could they do that? They are supposed to be fucking well protecting us. Fuckers."

"Look," continued Hagija. "Your little brother is hitting them hard and causing them confusion. Now, with your men, we can get more people out and create a corridor for more to escape. It can work. It's only half an hour to the town."

Hassan organised his forces into three predetermined groups. Hagija accompanied him, while the other two groups headed north and south, respectively. They were instructed to communicate solely via walkie-talkie at precisely 1:05 p.m., within thirty-five minutes.

"Sretan put," (good luck) Hassan said, and each group headed off.

94

Mehmet's guerrilla-style hit-and-run tactics continued to pose problems for the Serbs. They diverted attention and allowed more people to escape through the thin Serb cordon. But it was at a cost. He lost half of his force, either dead or wounded. He knew that time and bodies were running out. As well as that ammunition stocks were getting low. Each attack was aimed not only at neutralising the enemy but also at replenishing his dwindling ammunition stocks.

He needed to ensure that every attack was effective, aiming to both inflict damage and draw the fighters away from the main Bosnian escape routes towards the western part of the town. This required targeting the Serbs in their most fortified positions, mainly to the north and east. Suddenly, one of his men sprinted back along a narrow path typically traversed by goat herders.

"I found it," he said excitedly. "It's here." He unravelled a map of Donji Zelenik and the surrounding hills. "Just here." He pointed to a hill top to the east of the town.

"Are you sure?" Mehmet asked. "Absolutely. I saw him. Kustavic was there. This is definitely his forward command post. There were maybe fifty or sixty men around the tents, and I saw two large aerials. This is definitely from where that Bastard is directing his men. If we destroy that, we can create enough confusion to give us more time."

Mehmet pondered deeply. There was no time to take a longer route around the hills from his current position in the west. He would need to stealthily sneak through the town during daylight, hoping not to be spotted. Then, they would have to position themselves without detection and confront a formidable, well-armed force. With only twenty-five able-bodied men remaining, the task seemed daunting. However, Mehmet also recognised the opportunity for a daring attack. The Serbs would never anticipate an assault passing through the town. Despite the odds, surprise could be on their side if they succeeded. It was a big if. Many lives depended on that if and it was clear to the young Bosnian, the former engineer and peace lover, that there was no choice. They had to do it. It was little short of a suicide mission. He reasoned though that it was better to commit suicide than be murdered.

He shook the hands of each of the wounded comrades that he was leaving behind.

"Sretan put," he said, (good luck.) "Allah Immanet," and then he led his men into the bushes and down towards the edge of town.

Another Serb megaphone had been deployed, broadcasting familiar assurances of safety and promising fair treatment for all.

"We'll get those fuckers on the way back," said Mehmet.

They paused at a familiar bush-covered hill, a spot from his childhood hide-and-seek games. From there, he gazed towards the southern part of town, spotting the mosque and the orthodox church across the road, which was divided into two lanes for a one-way traffic system. In the middle was what was once the Konzum grocery shop. All the windows had been blown out and there was a huge gaping hole where the door used to be. It looked as if it, and half the wall, had been blown away by an artillery or tank round.

A truck rumbled down the road as Mehmet peered through his binoculars. He spotted Serb soldiers in the back, but otherwise, the street seemed eerily deserted, with only a few scattered bodies. Mehmet deduced that the Serbs had completed a thorough search of the buildings and had now progressed to the capturing phase of their operation. Sensing an opportunity, he briefed his comrades on the plan: they would advance one by one to the Konzum shop in the centre, then wait for a clear moment to dash across the road towards the orthodox church. With careful coordination, each man made their sprint across the open patch of road, covering for the one behind them. Mehmet took his turn as the third to go.

Mehmet suddenly stopped at the crossing, startled by a loud engine noise emanating from the direction of the mayor's office. It was a Serb tank, a T-72, rumbling down the road; its presence impossible to ignore. As it appeared, the Bosnians could hear the Serbs singing. A small group of eight or nine individuals sat atop the tank, casually drinking from a bottle.

"Let's hit them," said one of the Bosnians to Mehmet. He shook his head strongly.

“First things first. Command post then celebrating chetniks.”

The tank vanished, and the crossing proceeded. Shots still echoed from the hills to the west, while the east remained quiet.

They made their way up past the orthodox church and the mosque. The minaret had been cut in two during the bombardments and half the dome roof of the mosque had caved in. In contrast, it looked as if the Orthodox church had remained unscathed.

The group climbed the hill and entered the bushes. They broke into a semi-run and then a brisk walk. Following the guide, they arrived at the spot he had visited two hours earlier, nestled among a cluster of trees with a view of a small hill. At the sheltered side of the hill, away from the town, stood three sizable green tents and two communication antennas, just as the guide had described. Positioned by the largest tent were two armed guards. Adjacent to the tents sat a black Mitsubishi four-wheel drive vehicle, which Mehmet recognised as Kustavic’s car.

On the left side of the main communications tent, there seemed to be a kitchen bustling with activity as food was being prepared. Steam rose into the air, carrying the enticing aroma of cooking food. A group of men sat at trestle tables, enjoying their meal, while a few others stood in line, likely waiting to be served. The act of fighting seemed to sharpen their appetites. Mehmet estimated there were around fifty fighters in total.

He devised a strategy to strike at three locations. His troops were split into three teams, each assigned specific attack points. Leading a group of five, he aimed for the main tent, while the remaining two groups, consisting of ten men each, targeted the food and ammunition stores, respectively. The orders were straightforward: eliminate the Serbs and gather any usable weapons and ammunition. The assault was set to commence in fifteen minutes. Watches were synchronised.

"Sretan put and Allah Ihmanet," Mehmet said "Alahu Akbar. They are killing us for being Muslims; let us show them how Muslims fight, and if it is to be, then we die fighting."

The air filled with pumped fists and embraces as they gathered. Many were not soldiers before, but mechanics, engineers, bakers, and farmers. Now, they were confronted with the greatest challenge of their lives. After the pumped up acts for motivation subsided, a sombre atmosphere settled, like a chill mist on a winter morning. Having witnessed death and suffering since the war began, each man pondered if today would be his last. With resolve, they assumed their positions.

General Kustavic sat at the operations table inside the communications tent. Spread out in front of him was a map showing Donji Zelenik and its surroundings, marked with blue and red arrows representing Serb and Muslim forces, respectively. The blue arrows outnumbered the red ones, indicating Serb dominance. A self-satisfied expression of victory graced his face.

Next to the map sat a plate of meat Burek, a small cup of Turkish coffee, and a glass of Rakia. General Kustavic enjoyed his meal heartily that day. Everything had unfolded as planned, and the UN force had surrendered completely. This left Kustavic with the freedom to pursue his desires, which primarily involved inflicting suffering upon the Muslims who had killed his people.

A young officer approached the table and saluted. Kustavic nodded, indicating for him to speak.

"I have the latest figures, my general. We have taken forty thousand Muslims prisoner. The majority are women and children."

Kustavic replied, "What about Mesic and Hagija and the rest of his fighters?"

"So far, we have figures that at least five hundred Muslim fighters have been killed, but no sign of Mesic or Hagija, sir."

Kustavic was not happy. "I am also getting reports of hit-and-run attacks which are causing us problems. This must be Mesic. Why have we not neutralised him? Why is he killing Serbs now? Why can't you do your fucking job?"

The man stuttered, "I'm, I'm sorry, sir, but this is a big area, and the terrain is difficult. The hills slow the hunt, and there is thick undergrowth which provides the Balija with cover. We are doing all we can, but we need a lot of men to supervise the prisoners and the women and children."

"How many fighters have been captured?" he asked.

"It is difficult to say, General. Most of the men are wearing civilian clothes and they were not armed."

Kustavic jumped to his feet. "They are all fucking Balija fighters," he shouted. "Don't be fooled by their clothes. These are the same people who came into our villages, killed our families, stole our food and destroyed our homes. These are not fucking civilians. We are not the fucking Red Cross, lieutenant. We are the defenders of Republika Srpska. Make sure you understand that. Men and boys are to be treated the same as Balija fighters. These are your orders."

He handed him a piece of paper. On it were a series of locations and a number. It represented the number of prisoners to be taken to each place. In bold print was printed there words. MOVEMENT ONLY DURING DARKNESS.

Kustavic returned to the map. "We need two more companies to be here." He pointed to a hilly section to the west of Donji Zelenik. "This is where they will send reinforcements from Tuzla. We need to be ready. Dismissed."

The young officer saluted, turned on his heels, and departed. Kustavic returned to the map, his burek, and his coffee. He lifted the cup to his lips just as the first volley of shots pierced the tent. The radio officer fell first, a fatal headshot ending his life instantly. The general swiftly dropped to the floor. Two other fighters outside collapsed. Rushing outside, chaos and confusion awaited him. He endeavoured to rally his men, finding most either lying down or kneeling, attempting to discern the source of the attacks. Then, hand grenades were hurled in.

"Grenade," came a shout. Then, a scream.

The Serb general's demeanour lacked smugness now. The flawless plan hadn't accounted for this. The boldness of the attack both surprised and impressed him. He rose to his feet, realising the main thrust of the attack came from over the eastern hill.

"Follow me," he shouted, trying to rally his men. Five or six men rose swiftly and dashed, firing haphazardly into the shrubbery where their unseen adversaries lurked. Suddenly, gunfire erupted from the north, felling two Serbs with bullet wounds. Almost simultaneously, an onslaught from the south took down two more, among them the general. The lone survivor attempted to retreat, only to be swiftly struck down by a barrage of bullets from Mehmet's gun as he emerged from the bushes.

He approached Kustavic's location and stood beside him, peering down. Kustavic was clutching his stomach, blood seeping through his hands.

"It's not looking good, General," Mehmet said in a sarcastic tone. "I bet this wasn't in your fucking murdering plan, was it? No section stating the mighty Serb superior forces would succumb to lowlife Balija fighters. No, that would be unthinkable. Tut, tut, tut. A bit of a fuck up, really, wouldn't you say?"

Mehmet strongly nudged Kustavic's hands away from the stomach wound with the barrel of his AK47. The blood began to flow more rapidly.

"Oh no, that's not good. I think, General, you are a gonner. My God decided that I would live, and yours decided that you are fucking history. What about that? Well, you fucker, you will not kill any more innocent Muslims. Your days of inflicting misery on innocent people are over."

He pulled a gun out of his pocket. It was the Second World War German Luger pistol.

"Recognise this, General? It was a sort of gift from a relative of yours, General Petrovic. I think he was your uncle, a man who also brought misery to innocent people. Not anymore. And nor will you."

One of his men shouted, "Serbs are starting to come, we need to go."

"OK, finish off all the Serb wounded." He turned to Kustavic.

"Bye, General, enjoy your journey into fucking hell." He fired four shots at close range into the Serb. It was the shape of an orthodox crucifix. The final shot, the coup de grace was in the forehead between the eyes.

Mehmet smiled. "Let's go," and they disappeared into the bushes. They had lost three men killed and four wounded. But the confusion their attack caused would help slow the Serb mopping up operation.... he hoped.

95

Zubic's Mercedes navigated the large craters and potholes in the street flanked by destroyed buildings and burned out cars. There were two bodies lying on the pavement. Selma could see they were women, old women. She thought she recognised one as a former neighbour. Their heads were covered in scarves and there were pools of blood next to the corpses. She sat on the back seat between two soldiers. Zubic was in the front passenger seat. He turned to look at her.

"Friends of yours?" he asked with a sarcastic tone. "No fun being old, eh?"

She remembered Zubic as a nasty little boy, overweight and without many friends. She never liked him or the few boys who associated with him. If ever there was a personification of evil then it was Zubic. Menacing, ugly, violent and inhumane. He was all of these and more. Selma weighed up the situation. She knew escape was almost impossible. But her resolve strengthened. She told herself that she would not go quietly, no matter what. If she was to die then she would take some with her, anyway she could.

The car pulled up. Selma recognised her house.

"Home sweet home," smirked Zubic. The house resembled the traditional chalet-style homes often seen in the villages and towns of eastern Bosnia, characterised by its high-pitched roof and steep sides. Outside, stacks of cut logs were neatly arranged along the walls, ready to fuel fires during the cold winters. In the front garden, there was a disused well, while to the right of the house stood some bare apple trees, one of which had an old, decaying swing hanging from it. At the back of the house were cherry trees, from which her father would annually harvest cherries for making slivavic.

"I always liked this house," said the burly Serb in mock affection. "I was never invited in, of course. I never made it to the A list, did I? How about you inviting me in now, dear Selma."

The two soldiers on either side pulled her out of the car forcefully, overwhelming her with their strength, making it impossible for her to resist.

"You don't need an invitation," she replied.

"Oh, but I do, Selma. I do. Now, invite me in." It was an order. It was menacing.

She remained silent. Zubic slapped her hard across the face. "Now invite me in, you bitch," he repeated.

The force of the blow nearly sent her stumbling. Tears welled in her eyes, accompanied by the stark realisation that Zubic took pleasure in his control.

"Won't you come in," she said almost in a whisper.

"Sorry, can't hear you. What did you say? A little louder if you don't mind."

"Won't you come in," she said, raising her voice a little.

"Hear that, boys, I am being invited into the Mesic house, finally, after all these years, after all those snubs and insults. Well, I don't mind if I do." His voice was bouncy and jovial. He was clearly enjoying every moment.

The front door hung off its hinges, torn away. Shattered windows revealed the havoc wreaked inside, where chaos reigned. Outside, scars of conflict marred the building's facade, remnants of shell fragments leaving their mark.

Carefully avoiding the debris, Selma followed Zubic into the living room, a scene of devastation. Furniture lay broken, memories shattered. Amongst the wreckage, a photo frame lay face down on the floor. Retrieving it gently, Selma found a splintered image of happier times, capturing her family's smiles, her father's included. It was a glimpse back to a time when peace prevailed, before the shadow of war fell upon them all. Seeing her father's joyful expression stirred mixed emotions within her – a reminder of what they had lost, of the toll war had taken on them. A solitary footprint marred the photo, a stark symbol of the intrusion of conflict into their lives.

"Do you remember when we were at school Selma? I asked you out once to go and have an ice cream. It took a lot of guts for an eleven-year-old to ask a girl out. I saved my pocket money for just that occasion. And you know what you said, do you? You said you would think about it and would let me know. You know what? I am still waiting for you to let me know, you bitch. Then there were the added insults that I and a couple of others were NEVER invited to your birthday parties. But you know what, I used to stand and watch your parties from across the road, behind that big tree."

Zubic paced back and forth, resembling a restless animal awaiting its meal. His face flushed red, struggling to contain his emotions as anger brewed within him. Selma observed his growing agitation.

"Do you know how that made me feel? How being an outcast from your privileged group of friends affected my confidence? No, how could you? You were too busy enjoying yourself and being superior. Using your beauty to get what you want. But look where your beauty has got you now. In a bombed-out, damaged house, in a town that is without Muslims and your privileged group. This is now my town, a Serb town, and you are the people who won't be coming to the party."

Selma sensed that whatever was unfolding wouldn't end well. A feeling of impending doom intensified, yet alongside it, she felt herself becoming stronger. However, deep down, she understood that whatever she had to lose was likely already gone.

"I never invited you because you were a fucking little creep who no one liked. You were violent and selfish and altogether a horrible person. Why would I invite someone like that? You were the worst part of being in our class and I can see now that you are in your element. A big, powerful, fat, bully who can do what he wants because of force. You don't scare me. Your kind will never win in the end.

Evil has a limited shelf life. And whatever god you follow will punish you one day."

The subsequent slap hit her even harder, causing her to tumble to the floor. Blood gushed from her mouth as she struggled to regain her footing. Desperately, she lunged towards the imposing figure of the big Serbian. With a swift motion, her nails scratched deep lines across his face before his associates intervened, pulling her away. In retaliation, Zubic wiped his bloodied fingers across her lips, forcing them into her mouth. Summoning all her strength, she bit down fiercely, causing him to cry out in agony as two of his fingers were cut. Clutching his injured hand, he wrapped it hastily in a handkerchief, his face contorting with fury. Another blow to her stomach left her gasping for air, her body doubling over in pain. Then, a vicious kick connected squarely with her jaw, rendering her unconscious on the ground.

"Take her upstairs," he ordered his men. "I'm not finished with Selma Mesic, the Balija bitch."

96

They spotted bodies strewn across the track up ahead, seemingly two men and a woman. Hassan signalled for the men to halt and motioned for some to veer left while others went right. Proceeding cautiously, they approached the scene. Grant Singleton trailed behind, recalling the advice to follow the footsteps of the man ahead whenever possible. Memories of a previous encounter with mines flooded his mind, back in Sri Lanka where Tamil Tiger mines aimed to impede the military's advances. Mines were sinister devices, inflicting grievous injuries—

limbs torn apart, legs shattered, sometimes causing blindness. Their purpose wasn't solely to kill, but to incapacitate.

Grant followed Hassan up to the bodies.

"They've been shot," explained Hassan.

Nearby lay a small holdall, a carrier bag, and a suitcase. These possessions symbolised everything they could salvage from a world turned upside down, a world that, for them, had come to an abrupt end. With no time to spare, Hassan urged the men onward. The sight of lifeless bodies and the escalating gunfire indicated they were getting closer.

Suddenly, a deafening explosion resonated to their right, albeit at a distance. Grant recognised it as the blast of a tank or artillery shell. He pondered why soldiers would unleash such weaponry on fleeing civilians who posed no immediate threat. It reminded him that warfare, particularly in the twentieth century, showed little regard for chivalry or honour.

They were startled by a cry resembling that of a child. Hassan signalled for the group to stop once more, and they paused, listening intently. The cries ceased, indicating the source was nearby. Unsure if they were in danger, Hassan proceeded cautiously, instructing some of his men to flank the area where the sounds originated. As they navigated through the bushes, they discovered a gathering of around thirty people, one of whom held an old-fashioned hunting rifle. The others carried a few meagre possessions. They had no arms. These were not fighters. When they saw Hassan at first they thought they'd been discovered by the Serbs and fear racked their bodies.

Hassan greeted them with, 'Allah Immanet.' The collective sigh of relief was palpable. They almost cried out loud with happiness.

"Shush," Hassan ordered. "We must be quiet."

The man with the gun came up to the tall Bosnian. "Hello Hassan, I'm Fikret, remember me?"

"Yes, yes, of course I do. It's good to see you still alive."

"That's down to God and a lot of luck," he replied. "The Serbs are picking us off one by one. They don't care if it is a combatant or a civilian. They've been enticing people to surrender with promises they'll be safe. But they are being taken away. I was one of the last to leave the UN compound. The Dutch commander was complying with the Serbs and handing over our people. We decided to take our chances through the woods. But they are using tank and artillery shells."

"Have you seen my brother Mehmet?" he asked.

"Not for a while. He was attacking the Serbs all over. He ordered me and a few others to try and escape with civilians. The last time I saw him, he said he was going to cut the snake's head off. I don't know what happened, but all of a sudden, groups of Serbs left their positions on this side and went back to the road. Maybe Mehmet was successful."

"Well, two of my men will lead you back towards Tuzla. More units are coming to help in the rescue operation. We are securing an escape route. So you have to move quickly."

"What about my father and Selma?" Hassan asked.

"Your father was taken by the Serbs. He was put into a truck. I don't know where it went. Selma was taken by Darko."

"Darko Zubic?" asked Hassan.

Fikret nodded. "In his car, a black Mercedes."

"Did you see where they were heading?"

"It was through town southwards. That's all I know. Sorry."

The civilians headed up the hill, through the bushes in the direction of safety.

As soon as they disappeared two shots rang out. Everyone hit the ground. Hassan felt a stinging in his left arm and dropped his rifle. He saw the blood before he saw the Serb who advanced quickly. He raised his Kalashnikov and a solitary shot rang out. It was not from the Serb. Grant stood, the AK47 still raised against his shoulder.

The sudden realisation that he had taken a life made him feel sick. But it was a momentary feeling. He had saved Hassan and probably himself as well. This Serb, he knew, was no humanitarian. He was part of a group that was picking off civilians. Grant's conscience cleared easily, the feeling in the stomach would take longer.

"You see, Hassan, I am not a journalist today." Hassan smiled. "No, you are not. You are a fighter."

The medic swiftly tended to his arm. The bullet had passed cleanly through, causing no major damage, leaving behind a clear entry and exit wound. While it would be painful, he could still fight.

"Thank you, my friend. The power of the media. I'm glad you brought the gun rather than the camera. I owe you a drink when this is all over. But first there is work to do, much work."

"We need to find your brother and sister," Grant said. "But who is Darko Zubic?"

"Not a nice chap, as you English would say. Not nice at all."

97

Mehmet seized the RPG, his gaze fixed on the tank's barrel protruding from the town's post and telecommunications building. No clear shot lay ahead. Their only option: an attack from behind. Identifying a hillock near the clinic – once a kindergarten, now a makeshift hospital for Donji Zelenik's daily struggles – Mehmet knew it was the prime vantage point. With two men in tow, he directed the others to the western woods, advising caution to preserve their dwindling force.

The three dashed from building to building, weaving through the chaos. Serbs lurked all around, yet the tank remained elusive. They navigated an alley and circled behind what once served as the mayor's office, now a heap of ruins.

Entering the clinic, which was once a bustling school, through a rear window, they encountered a scene of disarray. Bloodied bandages and scattered medical supplies littered the floor, while packs of syringes lay forgotten in a corner. Urgently, they made their way towards the front of a classroom. Mehmet cautiously nudged open the door to the makeshift operating room, which couldn't open. Squeezing through, he confronted a heart-wrenching sight: the lifeless form of his comrade, Nedret, with half his head blown off. Despite the shock, Mehmet composed himself swiftly. On the operating table lay a fallen soldier, identified by his camouflage trousers. A single bullet hole visible on the forehead marked his demise. The IV drip lay abandoned on the floor, and a male nursing assistant slumped lifelessly against the far wall, joining the silent ranks of the fallen.

This wasn't the moment for hesitation. Mehmet understood he needed to act swiftly. He cautiously made his way to the front of the kindergarten, scanning through the broken window. A loud boom echoed as the tank fired once more.

The quickness of the explosion indicated the targets were nearby, nestled in the hills. With a clear sight of the tank's rear, Mehmet loaded the shell into the barrel and swiftly disarmed it by removing the white tag. He adjusted the small metal sight and gauged the distance. An RPG's accuracy extended to about a hundred and fifty metres. Judging he was within seventy metres, he knew speed was crucial to evade detection. However, rushing too much risked missing the shot, inviting a whole world of problems.

He and his team looked around cautiously for any nearby Serbs. After confirming the area was clear with nods and thumbs-ups, Mehmet rose to his feet. He carefully aimed just below the turret, targeting the spot where the extra shell rounds were stacked.

"Now for the fireworks," he whispered and took a deep breath, partly to help steady his aim but also to save his eardrums from the pressure created by firing. Burst eardrums caused by excessive pressure were not uncommon when using an RPG.

He softly pressed the trigger, his body recoiled from the pressure and moments later, the impact struck. A precise strike. The tank and its additional shells erupted in a massive explosion, sending a towering blaze into the air. A soldier, caught in the flames, emerged from the turret, then collapsed to the ground. His agonising screams echoed loudly. Nearby Serbs hurried to offer aid. Mehmet and his fellow soldiers unleashed a continuous barrage of rapid gunfire. Four of the enemy were struck. It proved effective. But their location was now exposed.

"Let's get out of here," shouted Mehmet. They hurried back the way they came, sprinting with all their might. Suddenly, Serb soldiers emerged from various directions, pursuing them relentlessly. Closing in from two sides, they trapped the three men near the mayor's office.

“Shit,” said one of them. “We are almost surrounded.”

Mehmet looked around and decided they had no choice but to fight their way out.

“We’ll go via the junior school,” he said, “and then cross the stream by the bakery. It will be a steep climb, but it will slow the Chetniks.”

They left by the rear door, Mehmet first, followed by the other two. A spray of bullets hit the wall.

“Keep going,” ordered Mehmet, and they raced across to the school. A hail of fire was laid down by the pursuing Serbs.

“Where’s Malik?” asked Mehmet. They glanced back. The young fighter had been injured. He lay near the doorway, gesturing for them to move forward. With determination, he dragged himself back inside to provide covering fire for his comrades. It was a bad stomach wound. They knew it was a hopeless situation for him. Knowing he was beyond help was hard to bear. But war brought choices, difficult choices. Life and death choices. For a few minutes Malik, resigned to his fate, laid down enough covering fire to allow them to escape. The Serbs closed in on the bakery. The young Bosnian managed to wound two pursuers before his life was extinguished in a spray of bullets.

Mehment and the other fighter raced from building to building using whatever they could for cover, but they were being swamped. Serbs were coming from every direction. The noose was tightening.

He discovered a piece of bread lying on the floor. Sharing half with his companion, he understood this meal might be their final one before the impending confrontation. Both men inspected their magazines, each left with only one. With 64 bullets between them, they recognised the importance of each shot, they had to make them count.

They readied for the attack they knew was coming when prolonged bursts of rapid fire erupted from behind and to the side of them. Mehmet saw Bosnian fighters attacking the Serbs. Three men were firing RPGs at the enemy and succeeded in pushing them back. But it wouldn't be for long. They knew that. It was purely to delay enough to enable a getaway.

A voice sounded from the back of the bakery. "Hi Bro, how are you doing?" It was Hassan. The relief was profound. Mehmet hugged his older brother. "What took you?" he smiled. Before Hassan could respond, a crack of single shot rang out. Hassan collapsed onto the floor, his body wracked with pain. Two hundred metres away, on a small hillock shrouded by bushes, lay a Serb sniper, concealed in green webbing adorned with small branches and leaves. In this deadly game, once the sound of a bullet or shell explosion reached your ears, it was already too late; it had either narrowly missed or found its target. Mehmet, Grant, and the other Bosnian fighters reacted swiftly, hitting the ground to evade the imminent danger. The younger Mesic, his instincts kicking in, knelt low, dragging his injured brother away from the door and window, out of the sniper's line of sight. Hassan was still alive but blood was pouring from his chest. Grant produced a battle front dressing, courtesy of ATV, and handed it to Mehmet. He located the wound, blood streaming through his hands, and then searched at the back of his brother to find the exit wound if there was one. There was. He tore the shirt away and pressed the dressing into the wound staunching the flow of blood. Then he took another and placed it under the back where the exit point was. All the time shots peppered the building, fragments of wall and concrete were breaking with impacts. The shooting was coming from all sides as the Serbs closed in. Hassan's men returned fire. Men with the RPGs unleashed more rockets in a desperate bid to repel the advancing enemy.

"We are down to our last few rockets," shouted one of the fighters. "We need to move. We are sitting ducks here."

They were, but there was no way Mehmet was going to leave his big brother here, no matter what the danger.

"Out the back, there is a picket fence. Break a section off the size of my brother and bring it. Quickly." They had no stretcher, only improvisation.

"Cover the front door," Mehmet shouted.

Grant stood almost mesmerised by what was happening.

"You," Mehmet shouted again. Grant realised he was talking to him, and he moved to the front door.

"Keep low," Mehmet ordered. "And lay down some covering fire."

Grant attempted to fire a burst of bullets, but to his dismay, nothing happened when he pulled the trigger; the gun had jammed. A nearby fighter leaned over and took the weapon, swiftly clearing the barrel.

"Now try," he said with a faint smile.

Grant felt a twinge of embarrassment, but the adrenaline coursing through his veins left no room for anything but survival instinct. He hurried to the door and unleashed a burst of rapid fire. The other fighter did the same. Suddenly, one of the RPG men stood up near Grant and fired a round into a building no more than eighty metres away. Almost instantly, a return RPG round slammed into the back wall, sending dust and smoke billowing through the ruined structure.

The journalist's ears went numb, feeling as if one of his eardrums had burst from the pressure, and his head began to spin. He attempted to stand but lost his balance. As he looked around, he spotted the Bosnian who had fired the RPG lying on the floor. He remained motionless, with part of his head missing and a sizable pool of blood forming amidst the debris and dust.

Grant attempted to intervene, but an arm seized him and forcibly pulled him back. Startled, he turned to see a fighter shouting at him, though his ears were still ringing from the RPG impact, making it difficult to hear. Gradually, as his senses began to return, he discerned the words being shouted by the fighter.

"He's dead. We can do nothing. We have to go."

To Grant, this world felt surreal, one he typically observed from a safe distance or arrived later to cover the aftermath. But now he found himself thrust into the heart of this nightmare, witnessing and experiencing the full horror and brutality of war. Fear began to give way to anger. He forcefully loaded another magazine into his gun and cautiously peered out from the side of the window, spotting Serbs in motion. Without hesitation, he unleashed a prolonged burst of gunfire. A scream pierced the air, but Grant couldn't discern whether his shots had found their mark. It didn't matter. What mattered was that a Serb had been hit. With each bullet fired and each casualty inflicted, the war became increasingly personal to him.

Hassan attempted to whisper something to Mehmet, but before he could, he fell unconscious. The large Bosnian was carefully manoeuvred out of the back door on his makeshift stretcher. Other fighters provided cover fire to buy time for the evacuation of casualties. Their goal was to reach the treeline at the rear, the only realistic chance for escape.

Mehmet and Grant suddenly recalled Selma's presence, realising they couldn't leave her behind. They knew they had to reach her as soon as possible.

Another, smaller group of fighters emerged from the bushes, and Mehmet immediately recognised them as part of Hagija's group.

"Mehmet, good to see you."

"Where's Hagija?"

"He's securing a route from the rear of the UN base."

"Any idea where my sister has been taken?"

"We think that maybe he has taken her to the south part of town, maybe to a house. Maybe yours."

Mehmet's expression betrayed his initial anger, swiftly followed by concern upon hearing the news. He was all too aware of Zubic's twisted and violent nature. He understood that whatever schemes this misfit and troublemaker concocted would undoubtedly lead to something bad.

"He took her in a black Mercedes with three of his men."

There was only one main road in Donji Zelenik, making it highly likely that Zubic was taking her southwards, perhaps towards their home. 'There was nowhere else to take her,' he thought. Now was not the time to examine why. Now was the time to act and act quickly.

"How long ago was she taken?" he asked.

"About 20 minutes."

Time was running out, and the Serbs were tightening their grip. If he was going to take action, it had to be now. He scolded himself for even considering 'if.' He knew exactly what needed to be done. Ordering the remaining men to proceed with Hassan, he selected three individuals for the task ahead.

"You come with me. We will catch up with the others when we get Selma.

"Hey, journalist, you go with them."

Singleton's voice was defiant. "No, I am going with you. Today I am NOT a journalist; I am a Bosnian fighter. So jebece (fuck you)."

Mehmet almost smiled. "You must really like my sister. OK your choice, let's go."

They made their way around the back of the house, where two remaining fighters laid down a blanket of fire, supplemented by the last of the RPG rockets. Their aim was to force the Serbs to keep their heads down for a few crucial minutes, buying enough time to reach the house. The life of his sister depended on it.

98

The truck came to an abrupt halt, and they sat there in silence, the passing moments stretching out for what seemed an age. Fahrudin and Samir found themselves seated next to each other, gripped by fear. Through holes in the tarpaulin cover at the back of the truck, slivers of light pierced the darkness within.

It was crowded with Bosnians, some seated on benches along the sides while others huddled on the floor in the centre. The twins recognised some faces, but not all. They had been confined there for most of the night, enduring an eerie quiet. Donji Zelenik had been inundated by thousands of displaced people, forced to flee their homes in what the world termed 'ethnic cleansing.' Yet that phrase failed to capture the full extent of the desperation and psychological trauma experienced by those affected.

Fahrudin and Samir drew closer together, their already pale complexions now almost translucent. They had served as radio operators, non-combatants, unsuited for warfare. They represented the majority: weak and harmless individuals who nonetheless sought to contribute to the battle for survival. Both had paid a heavy price; their faces bore the marks of beatings, battered and swollen. They had been subjected to violence for merely acting as the mouthpiece for what Serb fighters labelled as the Islamic fundamentalists in Donji Zelenik. It hadn't taken many blows before they confessed to being extremists, supposedly part of an Islamic revolution aimed at expelling all Serbs from Bosnia. Both realised that bravery was futile.

Yousef Mesic sat beside them, a picture of calmness and acceptance. Not once did he express anger, sorrow, or even resignation. He neither pleaded nor posed questions. Whatever their fate, Yousef had long ago surrendered to it. In his hands rested the small Quran, which he continuously read, silently mouthing the words. Occasionally, he paused, his eyes scanning the page as if he were either revisiting a passage or searching for a specific phrase or prayer.

Several of the men could be heard groaning in pain, predominantly young men whom the Serbs deemed to be fighters. Their beatings were particularly savage.

One man cried out for water, while another expressed an urgent need to urinate. A few were suffering from bullet wounds or shrapnel injuries.

The rear flap was pulled back slightly, revealing the face of a man wearing something that all Bosnian Muslims recognised with disdain: the woollen Chetnik hat adorned with the badge of the four Cs, symbolising the Serb nation.

"Shut up fuckers," the man shouted. "We have no water. I keep telling you that."

"I need to take a piss," pleaded one man.

The request went unanswered. The Serb guard vanished, and the flap closed, shrouding the truck once more in semi-darkness. Then, it was pulled back again, revealing the Serb guard who hurled a pot inside.

"Here you are, an ensuite toilet," and he laughed a deep, cruel laugh. Embarrassment quickly fades when survival becomes your sole concern, especially when you're on your knees. The young man grabbed the pot, unzipped his fly, and began urinating into it. The pot, made of aluminium and small in size, made it difficult for him to avoid splashing those around him, despite his efforts. However, not a single word of complaint or anger was uttered by anyone present. Their sense of embarrassment had disintegrated long ago.

Suddenly, the flap opened wider once more, allowing daylight to flood into the back of the truck, nearly blinding the captives. They squinted against the brightness. This time, a different Serb entered, neither wearing a Chetnik hat nor a uniform. He glanced around, scanning each man until his gaze settled on one in particular.

"Yousef?" he said. "Yousef, it's me."

It was Milan Zubic. He was once the neighbour of the Mesic elder, his fishing companion, and his best friend. They had shared moments playing tavli and brewing slivavic together. However, Milan vanished when the conflict began.

Yousef's eyes didn't divert from the Koran. He continued reading.

"Yousef, you can come with me. I have permission. Come, my friend, everything will be OK."

The old man halted his reading, lifting his head to gaze directly at Milan. There were no words or discernible emotion on his face, but the intensity of his stare pierced deeper than any wound, struck harder than any blow, and left Milan reeling in devastation. He had never before felt such a profound sense of embarrassment. It was as though he had been brought to his knees, both physically and emotionally, for the first time. Embarrassment tightened its grip on him like a stranglehold, morphing into excruciating shame.

Milan's expression bordered on a plea as he looked at his old friend, searching for a glimmer of recognition. Unspoken but deeply felt, he also sought some form of forgiveness, a chance to be absolved of neglecting his closest companion. Yousef's gaze remained fixed on him, unyielding. He uttered no words. To Milan, the silence felt interminable. Securing permission to take Yousef required extensive negotiation and came at a considerable financial expense. Bribery, still thrived in the former Yugoslavia, even amidst the turmoil of war.

"You can come with me see I have a signed permission. Everything will be OK." There was an emotional edge to his voice, as if he was on the verge of crying.

Yousef remained silent. Then, with what appeared to be one final, profound gaze, a look that Milan sensed he would carry to his grave, Yousef Mesic turned his eyes back to his Koran and resumed murmuring his silent verses.

The Serb appeared distraught as he weakly released the flap, allowing the truck to return to its semi-dark state. Milan resigned himself to a life without Yousef Mesic.

99

When Selma regained consciousness, she attempted to sit up, realising she was lying on a large bed, her parents' bed, which she recognised. Across from her hung a watercolour painting of the Stari Most, the Old Bridge in Mostar, built by order of Sultan Suleiman in the sixteenth century as a symbol of friendship. Selma understood that here there was no longer any semblance of friendship. As she tried to move, a sharp pain shot through her side, indicating that her ribs were either broken or badly bruised. She felt dried blood on the side of her head, recalling how Zubic had treated her like a human football. Her stomach also ached, and she discovered that one of her hands was handcuffed to the headboard.

There was a knock on the door.

"Can I come in?" It was Darko with a mock, jovial, almost polite voice.

"Oh, thank you so much. And how are we, ready for whatever lies ahead in this brave new world? Look what I found?" He held up a photo of Josip Tito, the former dictator of Yugoslavia, the half Slovenian, half-Croat figure who ruled the country with an iron fist for over forty years. Tito's brand of communism differed from the stark version promoted by Russia, but it was equally intolerant of dissent, opposition, or freedom of thought.

"So your family were Tito's people," Zubic continued, "supporters of the man who suppressed the Serb people and stopped what was rightfully ours, Greater Serbia. He was a criminal and should have been punished…as his people, Tito's people, are now getting what they deserve. He got it so wrong. He thought suppression could prevent legitimate rights and could heal the wrongs of the past. Wrong again. Totally fucking wrong."

He smashed his hand through the glass and threw the photo to the floor. For good measure, he stamped on it in a last act of contempt.

"But you know what, in death, he has given us what he deprived us of in life: freedom. We now have our freedom, and our destiny will be fulfilled."

He gave a big, radiant smile.

"You are fucking crazy," said Selma. The words were piercing and uncompromising. "You have destroyed lives and villages and this country for what, for Greater fucking Serbia? How will you be great? What have you to offer society, the world, apart from violence and ideas stuck in the past? Where is the modern thinking that a country needs? Your medieval approach will never succeed. You think by spilling blood it will give you standing and what you want. This is the twentieth century. The time of cavemen has passed. We had a good life. It was going to get even better until people like you decided differently. You should be ashamed of what you have done. You are disgusting."

The slap struck harder and with greater force than before. Despite her efforts to remain silent, Selma couldn't help but emit a cry of pain, almost a scream. Tears streamed down her face, mingling with the lines of drying blood.

Outside, at the back of the house, Selma's cry pierced the air, alerting Mehmet, Grant, and the three fighters who were stealthily approaching from an overlooking hill. Their attention was drawn to the black Mercedes parked nearby. Selma's twin struggled to contain the rising fury within him as he realised the scream originated from an upstairs bedroom. He feared the worst. In hushed tones, he directed his men to flank the house from the right and left, instructing Grant to remain by his side. As they surveyed the scene, they noticed two Serb soldiers lounging in the front garden, smoking and drinking from a plastic bottle, likely filled with alcohol. Mehmet understood that approaching the house undetected would be challenging. A diversion was needed, but what? Grant, however, spotted a potential solution.

"I could try," he said. "They wouldn't suspect a journalist of being a fighter. They would take me, of course, but then you could get the jump on them. What do you think?"

With time being a luxury they couldn't afford and limited realistic options available, Mehmet knew they needed to act swiftly. While utilising Singleton wasn't the optimal choice, Mehmet believed it could serve as a distraction long enough to overpower the Serbs.

He nodded. "OK, it's worth a try, but you need to approach from a distance so they can see you clearly and in good time otherwise, they might start blasting away before they ask questions. Leave your gun here."

Grant cautiously manoeuvred around the neighbouring houses to the north, carefully navigating through a garden to reach the road. As he straightened up and proceeded towards the Mesic House, his heart raced and his breathing became erratic. It was quite possibly the most perilous undertaking he had ever attempted. His hand trembled slightly.

As Selma recovered from the blow, she wiped blood from her face. Zubic grabbed her by the hair.

"Enough of the foreplay bitch. Now I am going to fuck you, and then I am going to wring your pretty little neck. You will finally learn your arrogance has consequences."

He started to tear at her clothes. She frantically resisted. He hit her again and again. Still, she held out.

Suddenly, there was a shout from outside. Zubic heard the word "Stop." He hurried to the front of the house and spotted the solitary figure of Singleton advancing. From the side, Mehmet and two fighters were also closing in. Gunfire erupted, and the two Serbs dropped to the ground. Grant followed suit as bullets flew seemingly in every direction. Zubic retrieved a grenade from his pocket and hurled it at Mehmet, but he anticipated the attack.

"Move," he shouted and dived over a pile of timber. His men were not so fortunate; their reactions were sluggish. The grenade detonated mere feet away, sending shrapnel tearing into their bodies. Both sustained stomach wounds, their conditions appearing dire. As the third Bosnian fighter rushed to render aid, he failed to notice the last Serb fighter peering from the kitchen window. With a single shot, the Serb cut him down, ending his life instantly. Mehmet, reacting swiftly, darted towards the back of the house, bursting through the door and making a beeline for the kitchen. Catching sight of the burly Serb just as he was exiting, Mehmet launched himself at the man, and they grappled fiercely on the floor. Despite being outweighed and overpowered, Mehmet's unwavering determination enabled him to gain the upper hand. He drew his Kalashnikov bayonet and pushed it slowly into his enemy's stomach. His struggle stopped, the strength ebbed from his body. He wasn't dead but his death wasn't far away. The young Bosnian left him and raced up the stairs, his Luger pistol at the ready.

Upon reaching the top, he paused, taking a sharp breath and straining his ears for any hint of Zubic's whereabouts. Only silence greeted him. After a tense minute, he cautiously ascended the final steps, scanning the hallway vigilantly. Despite his thorough search, there was no sign of Zubic. Every floorboard creaked beneath his weight, and he constantly glanced over his shoulder. Approaching the bedroom, he hesitated briefly before kicking the door open and barging inside, only to find it empty, save for Selma lying handcuffed to the bed.

"He's gone," she said. "Thank God. And thank God you are here, brother."

He moved forward to release her.

"No, I'm not, you motherfucker, I am still here. And that's a big problem for you."

Zubic approached from behind. He pressed his AK47 against Mehmet's back. "On your knees," he ordered and jabbed the barrel of the rifle into his back to reinforce the command.

Mehmet sunk slowly to his knees.

Selma witnessed the hatred blazing in the Serb's eyes. No laws could restrain him now. In Donji Zelenik, humanity seemed non-existent, devoid of common decency. A man had regressed to his most primal and debased state. In the absence of external controls, only one's conscience dictated actions, and it was evident to Selma that Darko Zubic lacked anything resembling a conscience. She sensed what was about to unfold.

She began to plead, "Please, Darko, let my brother go. I'll give you what you want. Just let him go. He can't hurt you. You are in control. Show some mercy. I'll go with you. I will be good, very good."

"Sis, don't promise this bastard anything," Mehmet cut her off.

The stock of the AK47 hit him hard on the back of the head, not enough to knock him out but enough to stop him talking.

"What you don't understand is that I am a compassionate man," Darko explained. "I don't like to see suffering and will do anything to avoid it."

He squeezed the trigger, and a single bullet tore through the back of Mehmet's head, exiting through the front and piercing the bedroom wall just above Selma's head. A gory spray of blood and brain matter splattered onto the bed and Selma's legs.

For a fleeting moment, she layfrozen, gripped by shock, as if ensnared in a stranglehold. Then, a primal scream erupted from her, followed by uncontrollable sobs as the harsh reality of the situation crashed upon her. The image of her brother's execution, his lifeless form slumped on the ground, the abrupt and irreversible loss of a cherished loved one, overwhelmed her senses. Her screams intensified, reverberating through the room, mingling with her tears. Amidst the tumult of emotions, she directed her anguished outcry towards Zubic.

"You fucking murdering bastard, I'll kill you. I will cut you to pieces, and I will send you to hell for what you have done."

"Oh, I don't think so. You will meet your maker before I see mine. And when I die, it will be in Greater Serbia. But actually, I find you a little boring. I don't need a Balija bitch when there are better Serb women around. I don't actually need you for anything anymore. But thank you for the invite to your house. It has been, hmm, a refreshing experience."

He raised the barrel of his AK47 and pointed it at his hostage.

"What do you say in your world? Ah yes Allahu Akbar."

The crack of the gun echoed around the room. Selma had closed her eyes, ready for the execution.

She heard a sudden bang, then a heavy thump. Opening her eyes, she saw Grant Singleton standing in the doorway, holding a Kalashnikov. In front of him, at the foot of the bed, lay Zubic's slumped body.

"I'm glad that this was one time you didn't miss a deadline," she said with a half-smile. But it was tempered by the killing of her brother. "Help me get free," she said.

Grant remained partially stunned by his actions. Taking a man's life in such a cold-blooded manner weighed heavily on him. Regardless of the man's identity or deeds, the act of ending a human life proved hard for Grant to come to terms with.

He couldn't find the key for the handcuff, so he broke the wooden headboard to free Selma. After a brief hug with the journalist, Selma walked over to her brother's body. Turning him over, she noticed blood still oozing from the bullet wound. Mehmet's eyes remained open. With care, she closed them and kissed his forehead before standing up.

"We need to go now," she said pragmatically as she wiped away the tears. She knew they were still in danger. Serbs were all around, and she feared that some would be alerted by the firing and explosions. A metre from Mehmet was the body of Zubic. As she walked by, she shouted, "Motherfucker," and kicked the prone body hard.

Zubic let out a groan. He was still alive, barely. He was lying face down. Selma pulled his coat until Zubic rolled onto his back.

"You are going to meet your maker first, you piece of shit."

She picked up the Luger pistol lying next to Mehmet's body.

"This is for my brother, my father, my mother and my people," She said. "Allahu Akbar."

She fired one shot at the Serb's forehead. He died instantly. Blood started pouring from the back of his head. His eyes looked empty, filled with what Grant thought was fear, the fear of someone who knew they were going to die.

She turned to Grant and said matter-of-factly, "OK, we can go now." Without looking back, she walked out of the room.

The journalist surveyed the grim scene before him—bodies strewn about, destruction everywhere, and an AK47 clutched in his hands. It felt like a scene ripped from someone else's life, not his own. Yet harsh reality reminded him it was indeed his. Facing the truth, he couldn't ignore the unsettling realisation of how someone, especially Selma, could carry on seemingly unaffected by grief. With time, he was grasping the complexity of understanding war. It wasn't as simple as crafting a short news segment. The scars left by conflict weren't just physical; the deepest wounds were often those of the mind. He acknowledged that, after witnessing such cruelty and inhumanity, no one could emerge unchanged. Himself included.

100

The twins had lost track of time. When they lined up at the trucks by the UN base, their watches and personal items were confiscated. It felt like ages ago. As the canvas flap of the Tata truck was pulled back, they glimpsed the first light of day. They had sat cramped, without food or water, all night. Sleep was nearly impossible, but when it came, each man leaned on the next for support. Only one man remained awake throughout the night. Yousef Mesic clung to the Quran, lost in his devotion. He didn't speak or acknowledge his one-time friend Milan Zubic when he approached. Yousef was in a different world, consumed by his faith, seemingly unaware of his surroundings and the distress of those around him.

"OK, everyone out," shouted the guard, pulling the flap more open, "breakfast time."

Fahrudin and Samir guided Yousef to the back of the truck, assisting him as he clambered over the tailgate and onto the damp earth below. Recent rain had left the ground muddy, causing his feet to become stuck. Despite this, a faint smile appeared on his face as he gazed upward. The sound of birds singing in the nearby trees added to the moment's tranquilly.

"Move along," shouted the guard. He wore the insignia of the First Zvornik Infantry Brigade. The brothers knew of this brigade. They'd heard members interject their radio messages with threats. They remembered the continued promises of, 'You all will die.' They were lost, uncertain of their location, but certain it was not a safe place to be. After enduring hours of a start-and-stop journey, they found themselves in unfamiliar countryside. The terrain bore no resemblance to any place they knew. They had been taken deep into Serb territory, deep within Republika Srpska.

They were ordered to march in single file. The guard led the way. All along the track were Serb soldiers. Some shouted insults. "Balija bastards, Muslim animals."

"No Caliphate here, you fuckers. This is free Christian Serb territory and always will be."

The Twins felt increasingly anxious. They could sense the hatred in the faces around them, and they were overwhelmed by the anger emanating from the uniformed men as they passed by.

Yousef followed the commands without protest. While he couldn't quite make out the words, he sensed their urgency from the tone alone. Holding the Quran in his hands provided solace and direction amidst the chaos. Amidst the turmoil, he envisioned his wife, Sarah, in the garden, her gentle smile and soothing voice offering him comfort. He was captivated by her beauty and flooded with memories of tranquil fields of corn and the gentle caress of summer breezes. For a fleeting moment, it felt as though his youth had returned, with its carefree innocence untouched by the harshness of life. He had believed those days, along with Sarah, were lost to him forever. Yet here they were, both resurrected in his mind and heart, restoring his sense of strength and solace.

Suddenly, the man ahead halted, his head shaking as if in sadness, and he heard the soft sound of someone crying, much like a child's sobs. Sarah's presence gave him courage. Yousef paused his reading and placed his hand on the man's shoulder, giving it a reassuring squeeze. Although no words were exchanged, the gesture conveyed kindness and determination, bringing comfort to the man. His tears gradually ceased, and he cleared his throat before resuming their journey. Yousef returned his gaze to the Quran, feeling the presence of God alongside him as well as Sarah's supportive spirit.

They walked into a field and saw a large pit ahead. Behind it, there was a big mound of newly dug soil. The realisation hit them like the first rays of the morning sunlight. Suddenly, one prisoner broke from the line and sprinted towards some bushes near the cornfield. Two shots were fired rapidly. The man dropped to the ground and lay still. His suffering had come to an end.

Samir, the weaker of the twins, began to cry. He knew, like everyone else, what was about to happen. A soldier nudged him forward with the butt of his rifle, urging him towards the edge of the pit. Some men begged for mercy, while others remained silent. Meanwhile, Yousef continued reading. About twenty Serb soldiers stood a short distance away, They ordered their captives to look at the ground not at them. Yousef positioned himself between Samir and Fahrudin, tucking his book into his pocket and clasping their hands. Despite the grim situation, he took in the scent of the countryside, felt the breeze, and listened to the birds. In his mind's eye, he could see Sarah, feeling a sense of solace as if he were also in the presence of God. Even in the darkest moments, Yousef held on to hope. He had found his--***** peace.

101

Selma was one of the few who knew the tracks of their escape route. She led the men carefully through the hills away from Donji Zelenik. In her hand was an AK47, in her belt the luger her brother had used to kill general Demetris Petranovic, commander of the Balsac military academy and which she used to finish off Darko Zubic. She had taken over the mantle of responsibility and leadership her brothers had taken on. Hassan was on a stretcher carried by four men. He was in pain but his condition was stable. Selma knew he would survive. He was a fighter. She had no time to dwell on what had happened to Mehmet nor where her father was. The task now was to get back to Tuzla as safely as possible. She led a handful of men, twenty three in number, seven of them including Hassan were wounded. All of them apart from Hassan could walk. But it made progress slow. Stops were frequent to allow the wounded to catch their breath but also to listen out for Serbs who were hunting them down. As they ventured further, the pursuit dwindled. The rugged, overgrown terrain proved a challenge for the Serbs, who now found themselves facing determined Bosnians fighting for survival. Slowly, they ended the pursuit and bands of Serb hunters returned to the safety of Donji Zelenik, comfortable in the spoils of victory.

After trudging for around three hours, Selma and the group finally met up with the Bosnian forces from Tuzla. There were embraces and greetings, but no one smiled. The day had brought a heavy toll in lives lost, and the full extent of the tragedy was yet to be known.

Another two hours passed before they reached the somewhat safer UN-monitored positions, ten kilometres away from Tuzla. Grant was aiding one of the wounded when he heard the voice of the UN general, Gaston Leconte.

"How are you, Mon ami?" he said when he saw Grant.

He handed the wounded fighter over to a medic, then turned to the general. He felt the urge to express his frustration, to call out the general's optimism about peace as unrealistic, and to acknowledge feeling deceived by the Serbs. However, he refrained from doing so.

"Bosnia has had better days, General, better days."

Leconte wasn't foolish. He understood the futility of making excuses to overlook injustices and evade the truth.

"I know, my friend, that words at this time mean nothing, but we, the UN, the International community, the politicians and the aid organisations, can see clearly what has happened, and I am sure that only good will come out of this. This day may change the entire course of the war."

Grant looked at him long and hard and shook his head slowly. "Tell that to the families of all those who died today, General. Tell them their loved ones didn't die in vain. I don't know what their reaction would be. I know it wouldn't be good."

He walked on to an aid tent operated by the UNHCR, the United Nations High Commissioner for Refugees. In front of it was the figure of Harry Bentley the owner of a booming voice and a long grey beard. It gave him the aura of a biblical character.

"They will burn in hell for this," he shouted to Grant. "They will burn in hell."

"I've got the matches," said Grant. He was about to speak when there was another voice.

"Hey bro, miss me?" It was Mo, Mohammed Farouk Bin Tahed, standing there on crutches, his left leg strapped up and a flask in his hand.

"I think you need this, mate. It's Egypt's finest." It was vodka but tasted like nectar. Grant hugged his cameraman and then took a big swig from the bottle.

"You are right, nectar. What are you doing here? You should be recuperating?"

"Man, I could only take so many smoked salmon and cucumber sandwiches in that private hospital. I needed a fix. Here I am, not quite ready to go, but...."

They shared another laugh and embraced once more. Grant hadn't laughed in a while, so it felt refreshing. He had missed this feeling. Yet he couldn't shake off the memories of what had occurred and what he had witnessed and what he had done. His expression turned solemn for a brief moment. Mo noticed and extended the bottle once more.

"Don't worry, man, I'm here now. We'll be back to normal in no time." Only they both understood that things could never return to how they were. The mind was like a vast cave with countless tunnels, and for a war correspondent, returning wasn't always simple, especially one who had killed. But that was a matter for another time.

His attention was taken by a booming voice coming from a bunch of civilians who had escaped Donji Zelenik. It belonged to Amelia Degusta. The 'when we', Mungo DeBoer, stood by her side filming the distraught and impoverished displaced civilians who had escaped the Serbs.

"Anyone here lost more than four members of your family?" She boomed without a hint of embarrassment. "OK, three, anyone lost three members of their family, or mother or father."

"Ask them again she urged her translator."

The translator muttered, "Jebece," (fuck you) and walked away.

Grant stepped forward, locking eyes with her intensely. His expression tightened, and he unleashed a sudden burst of anger.

"Why don't you fuck off back to where you came from and do an intensive course in compassion. That is if anyone would take you. You are a fucking disgrace to humanity. This is not about getting the highest level of suffering; everyone has fucking suffered here. Every single person. They will tell you their story. They want the world to know. But show some common fucking decency because every story is fucking important."

She looked at him, stunned. "What is your fucking problem, asshole? Go fuck yourself," and walked off into the crowd of new arrivals.

"Piece of work," commented Mo. "But a famous piece of work, though she has never had any idea about where she is or what is happening but, doesn't seem to hold her back. She's a fucking top-notch female war correspondent." He screwed up his face.

"Total BS. But hey, come on. We need a real drink."

102

The woman wore a crisp white apron over her dark blue dress and white sneakers. She pushed the trolley to the table and set down two plates of warm croissants and pain au chocolat, a plate of Krispy Kreme donuts, a jug of freshly squeezed orange juice, and two pots of coffee with cream. Silently, she turned and departed.

"Hmm, my favourite," said Edward Manners, picking up the glazed jelly Krispy Kreme. "Over 500 calories, but what the fuck? It's worth it. So good."

He stuffed half into his mouth and then wiped his lips with a napkin.

It was the top floor of the Pentagon briefing room, and Manners had been called to an emergency meeting.

"So what's cooking?" he asked, stuffing the remaining half of the doughnut into his mouth. He posed the question despite being aware of the answer. His contacts in Bosnia had provided him with valuable information, particularly regarding Donji Zelenik.

The five four-star generals refrained from joining in the doughnut eating. Some avoided it due to concerns about their weight, while others believed it wasn't the right moment to disregard the intelligence they had received.

The Marine general addressed the meeting and Manners in particular. "Our satellite surveillance has picked up many sites where Bosnian prisoners have been held after the fall of Donji Zelenik."

He pressed a remote, and a scene unfolded on the large screen before them. It displayed three big trucks and a row of men stretching from the back of the trucks to a field with a mound of earth.

"We can't get consecutive images from our satellite technology, but this is the scene this morning, Bosnia time." He clicked his remote, and a picture appeared. This time, there were no trucks, no line of men and no mound of earth.

Manners was known for being brash and loud, often coming across as a bully. None of the generals had much fondness for him, but their close collaboration with the CIA required them to interact with individuals like him.

"And so?" Manners asked, filling his second glass of orange juice, which he had downed in one. "What do we deduce from this?"

"It's pretty obvious," explained the Air Force general. "There have been what we think are mass executions. There are sites like this all over Serb-controlled Bosnia. We estimate that at least five thousand men have been taken to these sites, and we believe they have been executed. There is no other explanation for it. We have no other images of these Bosnians being taken to buildings or prisons, no shots of lines of men outside of the times yesterday. I think there has been a huge massacre here, which is unprecedented in modern times."

"And so?" repeated Manners. "What do you expect us to do if, indeed, your assessment is correct? Go and invade Serb territory, run the risk of Serbia coming back into the fray and then the Russians coming in to help Serbia? No, that ain't gonna happen, gentlemen. As I have said before, this is not our war. This is a piss poor bunch of ex-Commies arguing over beaches and tourism revenue and centuries-old fallouts. They are all as bad as one another. Do you really expect us to sacrifice American lives to sort their shit out? No, of course not. Of course, what is happening ain't pretty, but there is nothing we or the Europeans, and it's on their patch, are prepared to do or are going to do."

He closed his file firmly shut.

"The orders from on high are that we say nothing but sit tight and see what develops. This remains top secret, under the highest classification and goes nowhere else without the strict orders of the president. In the meantime, there are more pressing matters."

He passed around five folders.

"There is strong intel that our old friend Saddam Hussein is allowing anti-American terrorist groups to set up in Iraq and that there is credible evidence that the Iraqi Intelligence Services are planning to assassinate the President and the Emir of Kuwait. That is where I suggest you, gentlemen focus your attention. Bosnia is not on the front burner for the USA. Anyone for another doughnut?"

103

Grant Singleton had set aside his AK47, but his journalistic onslaught proved just as lethal. Instead of stepping back, he remained entrenched in Sarajevo. His sights were fixed on the UN, scrutinising the failures that led to the fall of Donji Zelenik. And wherever he went, others followed. Despite his superiors' attempts to coax him into a break for mental and physical recuperation, complete with the offer of a psychologist in London and a lavish trip to Hawaii or a similarly exotic locale, Grant refused. The war raged on, and so did his personal battle. It appeared that every media outlet worldwide was lambasting the UN for its perceived ineptitude and alleged cowardice. Journalists were asking the same question: where are they, where are the men and boys who were taken by the Serbs? There was growing indignation but few answers. The UN and the international community gave a collective 'hmm' when asked to find explanations.

Grant presented a series of critical reports highlighting the errors made in Donji Zelenik, pointing out the shortcomings of UN protection and the lack of response after the Serbs violated the ceasefire. He questioned why the Dutch UN unit surrendered without resistance. The UN commander's list of individuals was never produced, and the Dutch soldiers were promptly withdrawn to the Netherlands. There was no significant pressure on the Serbs, no ultimatums or threats. Their bold plan seemed to have succeeded as they challenged the international community, which then backed down.

Selma had retreated into herself. Firstly, her mother had been killed, followed by Mehmet. Her father was missing, presumed dead, and Hassan was recuperating from his injuries. She proved hard to comfort. Her emotions had fluctuated from guilt for not being able to save her father to anger and a desire to retaliate in some manner. The protective wall she had built around her after witnessing the death of Mehmet came crashing down.

Grant spent as much time with her as he could, but his journalist 'attacks' meant eighteen-hour days, countless 'lives' and reports. It was a weapon, and he meant to use it.

Reports slowly emerged, detailing the atrocities committed by the Serbs. Resourceful journalists ventured into Serb-controlled territories, uncovering sites of executions and mass graves. As they pieced together this grim puzzle, the enormity of the tragedy became increasingly apparent. Despite the UN's hesitation and avoidance of crucial questions, global public pressure compelled governments to investigate and confront the issue. This scrutiny led to the revelation of the largest mass killings since World War II. The list of victims compiled by the Bosnian government dwarfed Van Gost's initial tally, quickly surpassing five thousand names and growing daily. The ongoing denials from the Serbs began to be met with scepticism and ridicule. Grant observed a growing consensus for some form of international action, which offered him a glimmer of hope. However, his experience in Bosnia taught him that justice and war seldom coexisted. Words were one thing, action was another. In a region devoid of strategic importance or economic interests for the global powers, the pursuit of justice seemed nothing more than a distant aspiration.

He climbed the stairs to the tenth floor of the Holiday Inn. Pausing, he listened intently. The sound of rapid gunfire echoed, just like the first time he heard it. It felt like a long time had passed, but it had only been less than a year. Strangely, he found comfort in knowing that the Mad Machine gunner was still there.

Walking through the door of number 1004 amidst the crimson glow of a Maglite torch, Grant encountered a familiar group of fellow journalists: Bunty from the BBC, Ron O'Sullivan with his doomsday outlook, Burt from Reuters, known for his knack for dismantling reputations, Tanya, the force of nature, Harriet, the seasoned CTN camerawoman whose face bore the marks of countless battles, Chuck Brown, and Mo, who waved from the corner with a crutch in hand. A joint had already been lit, and a bottle was making its rounds among them. Grant noticed two more joints waiting to be ignited. Amidst the distant explosions and tracer fire streaking across the night sky, Grant couldn't shake the feeling of belonging that washed over him in this unconventional setting, a feeling he never quite experienced back in London among his so-called 'normal' friends with their typical jobs, weekends, and parties. To him, that life was so fucking normal it felt like a slow death. Here he was alive. Strange, he thought, alive amongst the death. Try explaining that to one of the normal brigade, he mused.

And then it dawned on him, "Where's Bourdain?" he asked, looking around. Pascal Bourdain, AKA Spit the Frog, could always be relied upon to join the tenth-floor night-time relaxation classes. Grant was surprised.

"Ah yes, Spit-don't-waste-your-bullets-on-me-because-I-am-immortal, well he got shot in the arm on sniper alley, quite bad, almost had to be amputated," explained Bert.

"Yes," continued Tanya. "Apparently, he's now so aware of his own mortality that he even walks down the Champs-Élysées wearing body armour." There was a collective joint guffawing and screams of laughter.

"I heard Kevlar Y fronts are being worn," added Bunty.

The situation wasn't amusing, and everyone was aware of that. Deep down, they were relieved that he was alive; nobody wished for a colleague's demise, regardless of their quirks. Spit, despite his flaws, was more than just a joke; he had his own unique personality. However, the sharp edge of dark humour spared no one, leaving Spit defenceless in his absence.

Grant took a big swig from the bottle.

"A toast, Spit the Frog and immortality, may that hope never die." It was a terrible pun, but it brought more raucous laughter.

"Spit the Immortal," spluttered the drunken rabble, followed by a swift sliva, which was then followed by a deep, penetrating gasp. Slivavic only became smooth and palatable after about the seventh glass, which was when most people moved beyond caring.

Grant struggled for breath and tensed his mouth and throat.

"What the fuck, I reckon that contravenes the UN's Human Rights Convention. It's fucking beautiful," and he took another gulp. He swiftly took a deep puff from the shared joint, feeling the tension in his body ebb away. Gradually, the anxiety and stress started to fade, leaving him feeling more relaxed. It was a simple way to unwind, and it worked wonders for him.

When the laughter subsided, Chuck became more serious. "Man, you've been through it. Are you gonna give us details or are we gonna have to wait for the book."

Grant smiled. "No immediate plans to write a book, too much to dissect and to understand and come to terms with. It's going to take time, maybe a long time. There are things I would want to tell, and there are others that I wouldn't because whatever you write or say is ammunition to one side or another. No balance any more. No way for someone to look at the good and the bad. With our friends, we accept the bad because they are our friends. It's the hypocrisy of life, of us all. I'm not sure I want to add to that."

The group nodded in agreement, a shared sentiment evident as they reflected on their observations and the implications conveyed by their reports and images. The overriding question that was always there was, 'Did it make the slightest difference? Was it worth the risk? Did it do the victims justice, and did it help in any way?'

"So, a fucking holiday to Hawaii, I hear," smiled Brown. "But have they mentioned the shrink yet?"

"They have, which is another reason I am not too keen to head back to London just yet. I'd sooner work on my demons here."

"Well, they will be giving you treatment for PTSD thing, that's for sure. It's all the current rage. Post-Traumatic Stress Disorder. A shrink talked to me last time I was back in the States. What the fuck. She needed counselling after talking to me."

"Yeah, I think I've had that for a long time," said Bunty. "It was when I was in the fifth form, and we were playing cricket against a rival school, and I dropped a catch at silly mid-on, and we went on to lose the match. Everyone blamed me, and I was never selected again. I don't think I ever recovered. So I reckon that's why I am here."

"Silly mid what? Fuck, you English are fucked up. PTSD from cricket. Now I have heard everything. I reckon some of the hack packs in Sarajevo are saying they have it. Maybe from a foreign editor shouting at them and not being able to get smoked salmon sandwiches on room service. You Brits need to be like the Irish and drink more."

"And you need to be more like us and pass the bottle around," said Tanya. "That way, we can keep the PTSD at bay."

A moment of silence fell over the group, a common occurrence. Memories and reflections would often sneak into their minds, triggered by images or experiences. These recollections often touched on darker aspects of life. Yet, they would return to the present, usually with a joke, often dark, or a dismissive comment about a journalist they disliked.

Burt threw one out. "My Foreign editor asked what I was doing today, and I said nothing. He said you were doing nothing yesterday, and I said yes, but I hadn't finished."

They all broke out into excessive laughter, partly because it was a funny joke but mainly because the drugs and alcohol were lowering the humour threshold.

"I'm not sure I want to keep covering war and desperation," sighed Grant. "It's like my reservoir of suffering is continually overflowing, and I'm starting to drown in inhumanity. Besides Selma has agreed to come to London with me and try and pick up the pieces of her life. For the first time, I feel I'd like to settle. I have never had this feeling before."

He glanced at Tanya, aware of his words. She smiled and sipped her drink. They both knew their connection was fleeting, a product of wartime chaos. Tanya accepted that Grant had found a deeper bond with Selma, without resentment. She, too, longed for a meaningful relationship of her own. In the chaos of frontline journalism, relationships often suffer as casualties of war.

He smiled back. "But that's a plan. It depends a lot on her father and what has happened to him, whether he is still alive or, as it seems if he is one of the thousands killed by the Serbs. Anyway, she will need to leave Bosnia, but I'm sure Bosnia will never leave her.

As the last of the sliva was devoured, there was a communal groan.

"Nearly time for bed," said Bunty.

"But not yet," replied Mo and from his bag, he took out a bottle of Egyptian Blue Nile vodka. "I was saving this for a special occasion."

He passed it round, and the hacks filled the cups and glasses.

"Habibi, I hear what you are saying. We can only take so much of hell; there has got to be heaven somewhere, and each of us needs to find it. So, I propose a toast. Life and heaven and the pursuit of peace and happiness."

Each repeated in a slur-like chorus, "peace and happiness," and they all downed the shots in one. Compared to the sliva, it was as smooth as silk.

Mo refilled everyone's glasses and signalled for patience with a gesture. Delving into his bag, he retrieved a toy and passed it to Grant, a second Buzz Lightyear. This action carried a clear message of purpose.

"Because we lost the other," he said. "I know we all need peace and tranquillity, but I'd just like to say one word for you to consider during your pursuit of peace….. Afghanistan."

They gazed into each other's eyes. Grant felt conflicting emotions towards this man, love mingled with a hint of dislike. His playful manner sometimes veered towards slyness.

"To infinity and beyond," shouted Mo in a toast.

"To infinity and beyond," repeated the group apart from Grant.

He hesitated. He looked long and hard around the room. Then he raised his glass.

"To Infinity and Beyond, life beyond fucking infinity."

104

Grant stepped out of the hotel, facing the Serb sniper positions for the first time. The ceasefire appeared to hold, signalled by the peaceful sounds of birds chirping and the distant clang of a tram moving along its tracks, a rare occurrence after a year of dormancy. The international community, particularly the UN, exerted enough pressure on the Serbs following the massacres near Donji Zelenik. While the exact death toll remained unknown, the guns had finally fallen silent on this spring day. Today, there would be no more lives lost to senseless violence.

Selma emerged from the door, holding a single medium-sized bag containing the essence of her existence. Grant had used all his powers to persuade her to leave Sarajevo, if only temporarily. She sought to release her grief and anger, longing for the chance to lead a semblance of a normal life, if such a thing existed.

A car arrived, driven by her brother Hassan. He stepped out, his shoulder and chest still heavily bandaged, moving slowly with the support of a cane, bearing the lingering pain. However, he greeted her with a smile, content knowing his sister would be safe and in the company of someone she cared for.

They hugged. He shook Grant's hand.

"You need to look after her, my friend," he said.

"I seem to remember you saying that it would be me who needed looking after," he replied. They both laughed.

A young boy walked up to Grant. It was Igor. He held out his hand. "Chocolada," he said.

Grant glimpsed the youngster outside the underground car park for the first time, which had become his makeshift home during wartime. Igor's search for a bar of chocolate seemed as enduring as the siege of Sarajevo, yet it remained unfulfilled.

"Samo malo," said Grant smiling (just a minute.) "Mo, hand me that bag."

He rummaged through the bag and pulled out a hefty 850-gramme bar of Cadbury's extra-large Dairy Milk chocolate. It had been sent to Sarajevo via special delivery by ATV.

The boy's face lit up, but it was covered in almost disbelief. "Chocolada," he said with open mouth. "Chocolada," he accepted the bar like it was some sort of religious relic. He began to walk away and then turned.

"Hvala," he said, "Hvala ti puno," (Thanks a lot), and he beamed the biggest, broadest smile Grant could remember seeing in Bosnia. The boy turned again, his pace shifting from a walk to a run. They could hear his enthusiastic shouts of 'chocolada' reverberating for several minutes as he vanished into the back streets of Sarajevo.

Everyone laughed.

"It's good to hear laughter," said Hassan. "I am not sure when I last heard a child's laugh like that and seen such happiness. I have missed it. And I will miss my sister too. But hey, I have always wanted to see London."

"Maybe that can happen sooner than later," said Grant. "Maybe this ceasefire will lead to the end of the war. Maybe sense will prevail."

"Maybe," replied Hassan. "But you know, in the Balkans, sense lives in fifty-year cycles. And at the end of each cycle, we return to the bad old ways of killing and destruction. It seems to be in our DNA. But we also know to enjoy what you have while you've got it. Nothing lasts forever."

They said their goodbyes.

They headed towards the airport in silence. Selma battled with her inner demons, while Grant grappled with a sense of unease, pondering whether the ceasefire was born of genuine desire or merely external pressure. He questioned whether the cycle of death and destruction had truly reached its end or if more turmoil lay ahead.

THE END

ABOUT THE AUTHOR

Tony Birtley is a multi-award-winning Television journalist who has spent four decades covering some of the world's most dangerous and prominent wars including Lebanon, Afghanistan, Chechnya, Sri Lanka, Libya, Kosovo, Myanmar and Bosnia. It was here that he covered the conflict from 1992 for four years. His reports from the besieged town of Srebrenica helped make the enclave a safe haven for two years until it was overrun by Serb forces and led to 8,000 Muslim men and youths being killed in one of the biggest mass killings since the Second World War. Birtley was wounded three times, the last time seriously. He has worked for some of the world's major news organisations including ABC News in the US, CNN, ITN, Channel 4 News, the BBC and Aljazeera English. He has had spells as Middle East and Asia correspondent and counts a number of world exclusives to his name. In the course of reporting he has been beaten up, arrested and taken hostage. For the book he has drawn heavily from his own personal experiences as well as those of others to try and give a comprehensive picture of the causes and effects of the war in the heart of Europe. He describes it as a highly emotional journey. He is married with four children.

Printed in Dunstable, United Kingdom

78870652R00292